Praise fo

"Like all writers of original
we have missed something which was plainly to be seen in the real world . . . She is a master of peculiar perception and an incomparable storyteller . . . a writer of the highest class."

— V. S. Pritchett

"Carson McCullers never rewrote the front pages to brand them novels. Although she was concerned about the barbarism of racism in her native South, her short stories and novels were allegorical, yet crystalline. She dignified the individual, especially life's losers . . . She reflected the lonely heart with a golden hand."

— *New York Times*

"I have found in her works such intensity and nobility of spirit as we have not had in our prose writing since Herman Melville."

— Tennessee Williams

"Enormously talented . . . Miss McCullers [has] powers of observation and recollection quite beyond the ordinary, and an unusual gift for translating remembered sensation into language."

— Diana Trilling

"The most impressive aspect of [her work] is the astonishing humanity that enables a white writer, for the first time in Southern fiction, to handle Negro characters with as much ease and justice as those of her own race. This cannot be accounted for stylistically or politically; it seems to stem from an attitude toward life which enables Miss McCullers to rise above the pressures of her environment and embrace white and black humanity in one sweep of apprehension and tenderness."

— Richard Wright

"Her art was great, somber, and above all extremely mature."

— Elizabeth Bowen

"Her genius for prose remains one of the few satisfying achievements of our second-rate culture."

— Gore Vidal

Books by Carson McCullers

The Heart Is a Lonely Hunter, *a novel*

Reflections in a Golden Eye, *a novel*

The Member of the Wedding, *a novel*

The Ballad of the Sad Café, *a novella and stories*

The Member of the Wedding, *a play*

The Square Root of Wonderful, *a play*

Clock Without Hands, *a novel*

Sweet as a Pickle and Clean as a Pig, *poems for children*

The Mortgaged Heart, *stories, essays, and poems*

Collected Stories of Carson McCullers

Illumination and Night Glare, *a memoir*

Carson McCullers

Collected Stories

INCLUDING

The Member of the Wedding

AND

The Ballad of the Sad Café

INTRODUCTION BY

Virginia Spencer Carr

A MARINER BOOK
HOUGHTON MIFFLIN COMPANY
Boston • New York

First Mariner Books edition 1998

For information about permission to reprint
selections from this book, write to Permissions,
Houghton Mifflin Company, 215 Park Avenue South,
New York, New York 10003.

LIBRARY OF CONGRESS CATALOGING-IN-
PUBLICATION DATA IS AVAILABLE.
ISBN 0-395-92505-3

Printed in the United States of America

QUM 10 9 8 7 6

Contents

Introduction

Carson McCullers left behind an impressive literary legacy when she died at the age of fifty in 1967: five novels, two plays, twenty short stories, some two dozen nonfiction pieces, a book of children's verse, and a handful of distinguished poems. Her most acclaimed fiction appeared in the 1940s. McCullers was taken for a *Wunderkind* when she published *The Heart Is a Lonely Hunter* (1940) at twenty-three. Set in a small Southern mill town resembling Columbus, Georgia, where she was born Lula Carson Smith on February 19, 1917, the novel reflects the author's milieu and is her most autobiographical tale.

Reviews of McCullers's subsequent books were mixed. *Reflections in a Golden Eye* (1941), set on an army post not unlike Fort Benning on the outskirts of her hometown, disappointed readers and reviewers alike, who thought the characters bizarre, morbid, grotesque. Some recognized the novel as a beautifully sculpted, albeit chilling, *tour de force*. In the preface to a paperback reissue in 1950, Tennessee Williams called it a pure and powerful work "conceived in that Sense of the Awful which is the desperate black root of nearly all significant modern art."

McCullers herself was partial to her novella *The Ballad of the Sad Café* (1943), which most critics consider — along with *The Member of the Wedding* (1946) — her best work. The stage version of *The Member of the Wedding* starred Julie Harris and Ethel Waters and launched young Brandon de Wilde's dramatic career. It swept most of the theater awards in 1950, had a long run on Broadway, and, along with the sale of its movie rights, made the playwright financially independent. It also broadened and enhanced her critical reputation and whetted her desire to write again for the theater. Seven years later *The Square Root of Wonderful* was produced on Broadway with Anne Baxter in the lead role of Mollie Lovejoy. The play was soundly drubbed by the critics and closed after a forty-five-day run.

In 1951 an omnibus edition of McCullers's novels and selected short stories provoked new attention and acclaim by serious critics, but *Clock Without Hands* (1961) was alternately praised and damned by reviewers who had waited fifteen years for her fifth novel. The book climbed to sixth place on the best-seller list, which carried it for five months and boosted McCullers's popularity among lay readers, but not her critical reputation. Meanwhile, her health had become so impaired during the last ten years of her life (she suffered three paralyzing strokes before she was thirty and was repeatedly hospitalized for surgery and death-threatening illnesses) that those who knew her well marveled that she was able to complete another major work.

Yet the frail author kept on writing daily, for life itself depended upon her ability to spin out tales in manuscript as well as in her head. "I wouldn't want to live if I couldn't write," she told a friend during her last trip to Georgia, and to Edith Sitwell she said that writing was a "search for God."

McCullers's fictional characters were her close friends (at times her demons) and more real to her than most of the reality that surrounded her. Her cousin Virginia Storey, who saw her intermittently throughout her life, said that "Carson loved to take the truth between her teeth and run with it, a habit she never got over."

Despite her absence from the South for almost twenty-five years, McCullers continued to draw heavily from her roots there. In 1949 when a friend expressed surprise upon hearing that she was going back to Georgia for a visit — convinced that her life there had been a source of no little distress — McCullers answered glibly: "I must go home periodically to renew my sense of horror." Ironically, the South of her imagination and memory was always truer than that conjured up by any visit, and merely arriving at the old train depot was enough to make her yearn for a quick retreat. To McCullers as she was growing up, as well as to Mick Kelly in *The Heart Is a Lonely*

Hunter and Frankie Addams in *The Member of the Wedding*, snow, Alaska, and such fictional place names as Winter Hill were symbols of escape from a hated environment.

Whereas all of McCullers's novels are set in the South, at least half of the short stories are not, although her characters are often transplanted Southerners for whom their homeland remains a memory of pain and anguish. Unlike many of the characters in her novels, those in her short stories behave quite normally. They have none of the physical grotesqueries that mark her longer works. Another significant difference is the way McCullers transformed reality into fiction in her short tales. Readers who know something of her girlhood in Georgia recognize easily the autobiographical elements in such characters as Mick and Frankie, while the self-portraits in her short fiction are more cleverly disguised.

In some of the short stories McCullers made her autobiographical characters young boys or men. Once out of the South and enjoying considerable fame as the young author of *The Heart Is a Lonely Hunter*, McCullers readily acknowledged her sexual ambivalence. To poet Louis Untermeyer she said in 1940, "By the time I was six I was sure that I was born a man." McCullers often fell in love with women, but such infatuations seldom led to physical relationships. Although she adored such men as composer David Diamond, her cousin Jordan Massee, her Charleston friends Edwin Peacock and John Zeigler, psychiatrists Rowland F. Fullilove and Sidney Isenberg, playwright Tennessee Williams, and director John Huston, probably the only man she knew intimately was Reeves McCullers, whom she married twice. In three of the short stories — "Instant of the Hour After," "Who Has Seen the Wind?" and "A Domestic Dilemma" — her husband appears full cloth.

The most prevalent theme in McCullers's short fiction is that of rejection or unrequited love. The title character in "Sucker," written soon after her graduation from high school, was rejected by his adolescent cousin Pete, whom he idolized. Pete, in love with Maybelle, discovered belatedly what became McCullers's basic tenet: "If a person admires you a lot you despise him and don't care — and it is the person who doesn't notice you that you are apt to admire."

Another tale of unrequited love is "Poldi," which McCullers wrote at nineteen while studying with Sylvia Chatfield Bates, her creative writing teacher at New York University. Although the unattractive, overweight cellist Poldi appears to be the main character, it is the hapless lover Hans with whom the reader sympathizes. "Sucker" and "Poldi" are early examples of McCullers's pervading thesis of love, expressed poignantly six years later by the balladeer / narrator of *The Ballad of the Sad Café* to help explain Miss Amelia's outrageous love for the little hunchback Cousin Lymon:

> A most mediocre person can be the object of a love which is wild, extravagant, and beautiful as the poison lilies of the swamp. A good man may be the stimulus for a love both violent and debased, or a jabbering madman may bring about in the soul of someone a tender and simple idyll. Therefore, the value and quality of any love is determined solely by the lover himself.
>
> It is for this reason that most of us would rather love than be loved. . . . The lover craves any possible relation with the beloved, even if this experience can cause him only pain.

"Wunderkind," her first published story, expresses rejection of a different sort. Here the main character is the young pianist Frances, who teeters between adolescence and maturity in an unsuccessful struggle to play with the passion, sensitivity, and technique she had once shown when taken for a *Wunderkind*. The pupil's painfully acquired self-knowledge leads to her stumbling flight from the master's studio, to which she knows she will never return. Frances's abject sense of loss is obviously her teacher's also, but in their confusion and hurt neither will admit it.

"Wunderkind" is a subtle mirror image of McCullers's emotional and physical break at seventeen with her piano teacher Mary Tucker, with whom she worked assiduously for four years. McCullers aspired to become a concert pianist until her teacher informed her that the lessons would have to stop because of her husband's military transfer. The distressed pupil's means of handling the dark pronouncement was to declare that she had already decided to give up her musical career and become a writer instead.

McCullers and her piano teacher were estranged for fifteen years. Finally, Mrs. Tucker wrote to congratulate her upon the dramatic success of *The Member of the Wedding* and to admit her own great hurt and disappointment over their break. McCullers explained that the tale could never have been written had it not been for Mrs. Tucker and her family, whom she would always love. They were her "we of me," just as in *The Member of the Wedding* Frankie believes that she has discovered her new identity by falling in love with her brother and his bride: "They are the we of me," insists Frankie, who is certain that the "three of them would go into the world" and always be together. Instead, she is dragged screaming from the honeymoon car.

Another tale of rejection written for her creative writing class at NYU is "Breath from the Sky," a story in which a fragile young woman named Constance is about to be sent away to a sanatorium in Georgia for what appears to be advanced tuberculosis. The author herself suffered from rheumatic fever — misdiagnosed as tuberculosis — and at fifteen was sent to Alto, Georgia (called Mountain Heights in the tale), to recuperate. Constance's unspoken fear is that she will never return and that her siblings (McCullers named the sister Mick, who evolved into the more obviously autobiographical Mick in *The Heart Is a Lonely Hunter*) will continue their unfettered lives as though she had never existed. Implicit is that Constance's mother's apparent indifference is but her way of dealing with the tragedy. The reader may surmise by the end of the tale that "Breath from the Sky" is the mother's story as well, and McCullers's friends and relatives in Georgia were quick to recognize Constance's mother as the author's own.

It is noteworthy that the children in McCullers's fiction lack strong emotional ties with their mothers. As her brother Lamar Smith saw it, "Sister did not want to strip herself that bare and reveal her utter dependency upon our mother. She was too vulnerable. She was our mother's favorite child, and somehow my sister Rita and I understood. We were convinced that Sister was a genius, and that our mother was too for helping it flower." Consequently, McCullers's fictional mothers — if they are mentioned at all — either die in childbirth, as does Frankie's in *The Member of the Wedding*; are too preoccupied in helping to support the family when the father cannot, as is Mick's in *The Heart Is a Lonely Hunter*; attempt suicide, as does Hugh's in "The Haunted Boy"; or drink too much, as does Emily Meadows in "A Domestic Dilemma." On the other hand, most of the fathers in McCullers's fiction are treated sympathetically. Like Mick and Frankie's fathers, they suffer because they fail to communicate with their daughters, who are vaguely aware and discomfited by a sense of loss but cannot breach it.

In "The Haunted Boy," another story of wounded adolescence and rejection set in Georgia, Hugh is haunted by the fear that he will return from school one day and discover his mother lying in a pool of blood on the bathroom floor, just as he had before when she failed in a suicide attempt that sent her to the state mental hospital. The boy's hostility, resentment, and guilt suffered "for the mother he loved the best in the world" make him turn to his friend John for succor, but John is aloof to his needs. Hugh recognizes now that he hates John, for "you hate people you have to need so badly." The "haunted" boy's admission reflects the ambivalence of McCullers's own feelings toward her mother, on whom she had become increasingly dependent after her husband's suicide in 1953. "The Haunted Boy" was published five months after her mother's death (1955) and is but another version of McCullers's thesis of love.

"Correspondence" — McCullers's only story in the epistolary form — is still another conversion of life into art. The tale consists of four letters from Henky Evans, a naive girl who pours out her adolescent heart to a Brazilian pen pal who never answers. Finally, she tells him that she cannot waste any more of her "valuable time" writing to him, but wants to know why he "put his name on the pen pal list" if he did not intend to fulfill his part of the agreement. In actuality, McCullers interrupted her work on *The Ballad of the Sad Café* to write this story, prompted by her husband's failure to answer her letters while she was at an artists' colony. Her realization at last that he had gone off secretly with *their* best friend — that she had been excluded from their "we of me" — was a decisive factor in their divorce.

The concept of the "immense complexity of love" — a phrase from her short story "A Domestic Dilemma" — surfaces repeatedly in McCullers's various writings, especially in her domestic tales that reflect many aspects of her life with Reeves McCullers. The earliest story of domestic discord, "Instant of the Hour After," written at nineteen, depicts a wretched evening in the life of a young wife and husband whose marriage is disintegrating because of his inability to control his drinking. Although the wife loves her husband, she is put off by his torrent of meaningless words and sarcasm when he is drunk; she wonders vaguely what life might have been like had she married Phillip, their close friend. Phillip has already left the apartment when the story opens, for his chess game was aborted by his host's having passed out. McCullers was not married when she wrote this story, but she and Reeves were already living together in New York while he worked sporadically on a novel, having illusions of becoming a successful writer himself.

They were married in 1937, a few months after McCullers presented "Instant of the Hour After" to Sylvia Chatfield Bates for a critique. The unpleasant husband in the story is a ringer for Reeves, who was already well on his way to alcoholism at twenty-three. They were divorced in 1941, then remarried in 1945 upon his return home from the war, an injured and decorated company commander in the U.S. Army Rangers. Reeves was forced to retire with a medical disability although his wounds (to the wrist and hand) were not disabling. Without his own personal cause or a job, he soon became hopelessly alcoholic. Countless embittered separations and reconciliations marked their troubled second marriage, which ended with Reeves's suicide in Paris.

"Instant of the Hour After" is McCullers's only story in which both the husband and wife drink heavily. The young wife sees herself trapped with her husband in a bottle, "skeetering angrily up and down the cold blank glass like minute monkeys" until they collapse, exhausted, "looking like fleshy specimens in a laboratory. With nothing said between them." Despite her teacher's encouragement that she revise the tale, McCullers apparently found the material too close to home to attempt to rework it.

Twenty years after she wrote "Instant of the Hour After" — three years after Reeves's suicide — McCullers treated a similar domestic crisis in "Who Has Seen the Wind?" Whereas the husband in "Instant of the Hour After" was twenty, the alcoholic husband — a failed writer — in the later tale was forty (Reeves's age when he died). The most convincing line in the story is the husband's warning, to an eager young man who has published one story in seven years, that a "small, one-story talent" is the "most treacherous thing that God can give." On the verge of insanity, the husband threatens to kill his wife, then disappears into a blinding snowstorm and "the unmarked way ahead." Before Reeves killed himself he had tried repeatedly to convince his wife to commit suicide with him.

McCullers, who had tried to write "Who Has Seen the Wind?" as a play before turning it into the long story that was eventually published, attempted repeatedly to rework it for the theater. Finally, after three years and considerable revision of both plot and characterization, the tale became the play *The Square Root of Wonderful*, in which the protagonist has divorced the man to whom she was married twice, a failed writer of one successful novel.

A third tale in which marital harmony is set on edge by alcohol is "A Domestic Dilemma," its tone being reminiscent of "The Instant of the Hour After." This time it is the sherry-tippling housewife Emily Meadows who precipitates the conflict. Emily drinks furtively and cannot be trusted with the safe rearing of their two young children. Her husband, Martin, assumes some responsibility for the dilemma, for he has uprooted his wife from the South and moved her to an unnamed suburban town on the Hudson River (obviously Nyack, New York). Homesick and unable to adjust to the "stricter, lonelier mores of the North," Emily stays to herself, reads magazines and murder mysteries, and finds her interior life "insufficient without the artifice of alcohol." When Martin finds her drunk upstairs in the bedroom and their children unsupervised, he dreads the decisions he must make. Finally, after a drunken scene in front of the children, he puts his wife to bed, tenderly bathes the children, and settles them for the night. Returning to the bedroom, he watches his sleeping wife "for the last time," and suddenly all thoughts of "blame and blemish abate" as "sorrow parallel[s] desire in the immense complexity of love."

"Court in the West Eighties," "The Orphanage," "Like That," "The Aliens," "Untitled Piece" (apprentice tales published posthumously), and such other fine stories as "The Jockey," "Madame Zilensky and the King of Finland," "A Tree · A Rock · A Cloud," "Art and Mr. Mahoney," and "The Sojourner" — indeed, every story in this collection combines notable autobiographical elements of characterization and setting with artistic integrity. McCullers was well into the writing of "Illuminations and Night Glare," a long, unpublished memoir, when she suffered a massive brain hemorrhage and died on September 29, 1967, after forty-five days in an irreversible coma. She was buried beside her mother on a hill overlooking the Hudson River in Nyack, New York. America had lost its lonely hunter.

Virginia Spencer Carr
Georgia State University, Atlanta
January 1987

Collected Stories

Sucker

It was always like I had a room to myself. Sucker slept in my bed with me but that didn't interfere with anything. The room was mine and I used it as I wanted to. Once I remember sawing a trap door in the floor. Last year when I was a sophomore in high school I tacked on my wall some pictures of girls from magazines and one of them was just in her underwear. My mother never bothered me because she had the younger kids to look after. And Sucker thought anything I did was always swell.

Whenever I would bring any of my friends back to my room all I had to do was just glance once at Sucker and he would get up from whatever he was busy with and maybe half smile at me, and leave without saying a word. He never brought kids back there. He's twelve, four years younger than I am, and he always knew without me even telling him that I didn't want kids that age meddling with my things.

Half the time I used to forget that Sucker isn't my brother. He's my first cousin but practically ever since I remember he's been in our family. You see his folks were killed in a wreck when he was a baby. To me and my kid sisters he was like our brother.

Sucker used to always remember and believe every word I said. That's how he got his nick-name. Once a couple of years ago I told him that if he'd jump off our garage with an umbrella it would act as a parachute and he wouldn't fall hard. He did it and busted his knee. That's just one instance. And the funny thing was that no matter how many times he got fooled he would still believe me. Not that he was dumb in other ways — it was just the way he acted with me. He would look at everything I did and quietly take it in.

There is one thing I have learned, but it makes me feel guilty and is hard to figure out. If a person admires you a lot you despise him and don't care — and it is the person who doesn't notice you that you are apt to admire. This is not easy to realize. Maybelle Watts, this senior at school, acted like she was the Queen of Sheba and even humiliated me. Yet at this same time I would have done anything in the world to get her attentions. All I could think about day and night was Maybelle until I was nearly crazy. When Sucker was a little kid and on up until the time he was twelve I guess I treated him as bad as Maybelle did me.

Now that Sucker has changed so much it is a little hard to remember him as he used to be. I never imagined anything would suddenly happen that would make us both very different. I never knew that in order to get what has happened straight in my mind I would want to think back on him as he used to be and compare and try to get things settled. If I could have seen ahead maybe I would have acted different.

I never noticed him much or thought about him and when you consider how long we have had the same room together it is funny the few things I remember. He used to talk to himself a lot when he'd think he was alone — all about him fighting gangsters and being on ranches and that sort of kids' stuff. He'd get in the bathroom and stay as long as an hour and sometimes his voice would go up high and excited and you could hear him all over the house. Usually, though, he was very quiet. He didn't have many boys in the neighborhood to buddy with and his face had the look of a kid who is watching a game and waiting to be asked to play. He didn't mind wearing the sweaters and coats that I outgrew, even if the sleeves did flop down too big and make his wrists look as thin and white as a little girl's. That is how I remember him — getting a little bigger every year but still being the same. That was Sucker up until a few months ago when all this trouble began.

Maybelle was somehow mixed up in what happened so I guess I ought to start with her. Until I knew her I hadn't given much time to girls. Last fall she sat next to me in General Science class and that was when I first began to notice her. Her hair is the brightest yellow I ever saw and occasionally she will wear it set into curls with some sort of gluey stuff. Her fingernails are pointed and manicured and painted a shiny red. All during class I used to watch Maybelle, nearly all the time except when I thought she was going to look my way or when the teacher called on me. I couldn't keep my eyes off her hands, for one thing. They are very little and white except for that red stuff, and when she would turn the pages of her book she always licked her thumb and held out her little finger and turned very slowly. It is impossible to describe Maybelle. All the boys are crazy about her but she didn't even notice me. For one thing she's almost two years older than I am. Between periods I used to try and pass very close to her in the halls but she would hardly ever smile at me. All I could do was sit and look at her in class — and sometimes it was like the whole room could hear my heart beating and I wanted to holler or light out and run for Hell.

At night, in bed, I would imagine about Maybelle. Often this would keep me from sleeping until as late as one or two o'clock. Sometimes Sucker would wake up and ask me why I couldn't get settled and I'd tell him to hush his mouth. I suppose I was mean to him lots of times. I guess I wanted to ignore somebody like Maybelle did me. You could always tell by Sucker's face when his feelings were hurt. I don't remember all the ugly remarks I must have made because even when I was saying them my mind was on Maybelle.

That went on for nearly three months and then somehow she began to change. In the halls she would speak to me and every morning she copied my homework. At lunch time once I danced with her in the gym. One afternoon I got up nerve and went around to her house with a carton of cigarettes. I knew she smoked in the girls' basement and sometimes outside of school — and I didn't want to take her candy because I think that's been run into the ground. She was very nice and it seemed to me everything was going to change.

It was that night when this trouble really started. I had come into my room late and Sucker was already asleep. I felt too happy and keyed up to get in a comfortable position and I was awake thinking about Maybelle a long time. Then I dreamed about her and it seemed I kissed her. It was a surprise to wake up and see the dark. I lay still and a little while passed before I could come to and understand where I was. The house was quiet and it was a very dark night.

Sucker's voice was a shock to me. "Pete? . . ."

I didn't answer anything or even move.

"You do like me as much as if I was your own brother, don't you, Pete?"

I couldn't get over the surprise of everything and it was like this was the real dream instead of the other.

"You have liked me all the time like I was your own brother, haven't you?"

"Sure," I said.

Then I got up for a few minutes. It was cold and I was glad to come back to bed. Sucker hung on to my back. He felt little and warm and I could feel his warm breathing on my shoulder.

"No matter what you did I always knew you liked me."

I was wide awake and my mind seemed mixed up in a strange way. There was this happiness about Maybelle and all that — but at the same time something about Sucker and his voice when he said these things made me take notice. Anyway I guess you understand people better when you are happy than when something is worrying you. It was like I had never really thought about Sucker until then. I felt I had always been mean to him. One night a few weeks before I had heard him crying in the dark. He said he had lost a boy's beebee gun and was scared to let anybody know. He wanted me to tell him what to do. I was sleepy and tried to make him hush and when he wouldn't I kicked at him. That was just one of the things I remembered. It seemed to me he had always been a lonesome kid. I felt bad.

There is something about a dark cold night that makes you feel close to someone you're sleeping with. When you talk together it is like you are the only people awake in the town.

"You're a swell kid, Sucker," I said.

It seemed to me suddenly that I did like him more than anybody else I knew — more than any other boy, more than my sisters, more in a certain way even than Maybelle. I felt good all over and it was like when they play sad music in the movies. I wanted to show Sucker how much I really thought of him and make up for the way I had always treated him.

We talked for a good while that night. His voice was fast and it was like he had been saving up these things to tell me for a long time. He mentioned that he was going to try to build a canoe and that the kids down the block wouldn't let him in on their football team and I don't know what all. I talked some too and it was a good feeling to think of him taking in everything I said so seriously. I even spoke of Maybelle a little, only I made out like it was her who had been running after me all this time. He asked questions about high school and so forth. His voice was excited and he kept on talking fast like he could never get the words out in time. When I went to sleep he was still talking and I could still feel his breathing on my shoulder, warm and close.

During the next couple of weeks I saw a lot of Maybelle. She acted as though she really cared for me a little. Half the time I felt so good I hardly knew what to do with myself.

But I didn't forget about Sucker. There were a lot of old things in my bureau drawer I'd been saving — boxing gloves and Tom Swift books and second rate fishing tackle. All this I turned over to him. We had some more talks together and it was really like I was knowing him for the first time. When there was a long cut on his cheek I knew he had been monkeying around with this new first razor set of mine, but I didn't say anything. His face seemed different now. He used to look timid and sort of like he was afraid of a whack over the head. That expression was gone. His face, with those wide-open eyes and his ears sticking out and his mouth never quite shut, had the look of a person who is surprised and expecting something swell.

Once I started to point him out to Maybelle and tell her he was my kid brother. It was an afternoon when a murder mystery was on at the movie. I had earned a dollar working for my Dad and I gave Sucker a quarter to go and get candy and so forth. With the rest I took Maybelle. We were sitting near the back and I saw Sucker come in. He began to stare at the screen the minute he stepped past the ticket man and he stumbled down the aisle without noticing where he was going. I started to punch Maybelle but couldn't quite make up my mind. Sucker looked a little silly — walking like a drunk with his eyes glued to the movie. He was wiping his reading glasses on his shirt tail and his knickers flopped down. He went on until he got to the first few rows where the kids usually sit. I never did punch Maybelle. But I got to thinking it was good to have both of them at the movie with the money I earned.

I guess things went on like this for about a month or six weeks. I felt so good I couldn't settle down to study or put my mind on anything. I wanted to be friendly with everybody. There were times when I just had to talk to some person. And usually that would be Sucker. He felt as good as I did. Once he said: "Pete, I am gladder that you are like my brother than anything else in the world."

Then something happened between Maybelle and me. I never have figured out just what it was. Girls like her are hard to understand. She began to act different toward me. At first I wouldn't let myself believe this and tried to think it was just my imagination. She didn't act glad to see me anymore. Often she went out riding with this fellow on the football team who owns this yellow roadster. The car was the color of her hair and after school she would ride off with him, laughing and looking into his face. I couldn't think of anything to do about it and she was on my mind all day and night. When I did get a chance to go out with her she was snippy and didn't seem to notice me. This made me feel like something was the matter — I would worry about my shoes clopping too loud on the floor or the fly of my pants, or the bumps on my chin. Sometimes when Maybelle was around, a devil would get into me and I'd hold my face stiff and call grown men by their last names without the Mister and say rough things. In the night I would wonder what made me do all this until I was too tired for sleep.

At first I was so worried I just forgot about Sucker. Then later he began to get on my nerves. He was always hanging around until I would get back from high school, always looking like he had something to say to me or wanted me to tell him. He made me a magazine rack in his Manual Training class and one week he saved his lunch money and bought me three packs of cigarettes. He couldn't seem to take it in that I had things on my mind and didn't want to fool with him. Every afternoon it would be the same — him in my room with this waiting expression on his face. Then I wouldn't say anything or I'd maybe answer him rough-like and he would finally go on out.

I can't divide that time up and say this happened one day and that the next. For one thing I was so mixed up the weeks just slid along into each other and I felt like Hell and didn't care. Nothing definite was said or done. Maybelle still rode around with this fellow in his yellow roadster and sometimes she would smile at me and sometimes not. Every afternoon I went from one place to another where I thought she would be. Either she would act almost nice and I would begin thinking how things would finally clear up and she would care for me — or else she'd behave so that if she hadn't been a girl I'd have wanted to grab her by that white little neck and choke her. The more ashamed I felt for making a fool of myself the more I ran after her.

Sucker kept getting on my nerves more and more. He would look at me as though he sort of blamed me for something, but at the same time knew that it wouldn't last long. He was growing fast and for some reason began to stutter when he talked. Sometimes he had nightmares or would throw up his breakfast. Mom got him a bottle of cod liver oil.

Then the finish came between Maybelle and me. I met her going to the drug store and asked for a date. When she said no I remarked something sarcastic. She told me she was sick and tired of my being around and that she had never cared a rap about me. She said all that. I just stood there and didn't answer anything. I walked home very slowly.

For several afternoons I stayed in my room by myself. I didn't want to go anywhere or talk to anyone. When Sucker would come in and look at me sort of funny I'd yell at him to get out. I didn't want to think of Maybelle and I sat at my desk reading *Popular Mechanics* or whittling at a toothbrush rack I was making. It seemed to me I was putting that girl out of my mind pretty well.

But you can't help what happens to you at night. That is what made things how they are now.

You see a few nights after Maybelle said those words to me I dreamed about her again. It was like that first time and I was squeezing Sucker's arm so tight I woke him up. He reached for my hand.

"Pete, what's the matter with you?"

All of a sudden I felt so mad my throat choked — at myself and the dream and Maybelle and Sucker and every single person I knew. I remembered all the times Maybelle had humiliated me and everything bad that had ever happened. It seemed to me for a second that nobody would ever like me but a sap like Sucker.

"Why is it we aren't buddies like we were before? Why — ?"

"Shut your damn trap!" I threw off the cover and got up and turned on the light. He sat in the middle of the bed, his eyes blinking and scared.

There was something in me and I couldn't help myself. I don't think anybody ever gets that mad but once. Words came without me knowing what they would be. It was only afterward that I could remember each thing I said and see it all in a clear way.

"Why aren't we buddies? Because you're the dumbest slob I ever saw! Nobody cares anything about you! And just because I felt sorry for you sometimes and tried to act decent don't think I give a damn about a dumb-bunny like you!"

If I'd talked loud or hit him it wouldn't have been so bad. But my voice was slow and like I was very calm. Sucker's mouth was part way open and he looked as though he'd knocked his funny bone. His face was white and sweat came out on his forehead. He wiped it away with the back of his hand and for a minute his arm stayed raised that way as though he was holding something away from him.

"Don't you know a single thing? Haven't you ever been around at all? Why don't you get a girl friend instead of me? What kind of a sissy do you want to grow up to be anyway?"

I didn't know what was coming next. I couldn't help myself or think.

Sucker didn't move. He had on one of my pajama jackets and his neck stuck out skinny and small. His hair was damp on his forehead.

"Why do you always hang around me? Don't you know when you're not wanted?"

Afterward I could remember the change in Sucker's face. Slowly that blank look went away and he closed his mouth. His eyes got narrow and his fists shut. There had never been such a look on him before. It was like every second he was getting older. There was a hard look to his eyes you don't see usually in a kid. A drop of sweat rolled down his chin and he didn't notice. He just sat there with those eyes on me and he didn't speak and his face was hard and didn't move.

"No you don't know when you're not wanted. You're too dumb. Just like your name — a dumb Sucker."

It was like something had busted inside me. I turned off the light and sat down in the chair by the window. My legs were shaking and I was so tired I could have bawled. The room was cold and dark. I sat there for a long time and smoked a squashed cigarette I had saved. Outside the yard was black and quiet. After a while I heard Sucker lie down.

I wasn't mad any more, only tired. It seemed awful to me that I had talked like that to a kid only twelve. I couldn't take it all in. I told myself I would go over to him and try to make it up. But I just sat there in the cold until a long time had passed. I planned how I could straighten it out in the morning. Then, trying not to squeak the springs, I got back in bed.

Sucker was gone when I woke up the next day. And later when I wanted to apologize as I had planned he looked at me in this new hard way so that I couldn't say a word.

All of that was two or three months ago. Since then Sucker has grown faster than any boy I ever saw. He's almost as tall as I am and his bones have gotten heavier and bigger. He won't wear any of my old clothes any more and has bought his first pair of long pants — with some leather suspenders to hold them up. Those are just the changes that are easy to see and put into words.

Our room isn't mine at all any more. He's gotten up this gang of kids and they have a club. When they aren't digging trenches in some vacant lot and fighting they are always in my room. On the door there is some foolishness written in Mercurochrome saying "Woe to the Outsider who Enters" and signed with crossed bones and their secret initials. They have rigged up a radio and every afternoon it blares out music. Once as I was coming in I heard a boy telling something in a loud voice about what he saw in the back of his big brother's automobile. I could guess what I didn't hear. *That's what her and my brother do. It's the truth — parked in the car.* For a minute Sucker looked surprised and his face was almost like it used to be. Then he got hard and tough again. "Sure, dumbbell. We know all that." They didn't notice me. Sucker began telling them how in two years he was planning to be a trapper in Alaska.

But most of the time Sucker stays by himself. It is worse when we are alone together in the room. He sprawls across the bed in those long corduroy pants with the suspenders and just stares at me with that hard, half-sneering look. I fiddle around my desk and can't get settled because of those eyes of his. And the thing is I just have to study because I've gotten three bad cards this term already. If I flunk English I can't graduate next year. I don't want to be a bum and I just have to get my mind on it. I don't care a flip for Maybelle or any particular girl any more and it's only this thing between Sucker and me that is the trouble now. We never speak except when we have to before the family. I don't even want to call him Sucker any more and unless I forget I call him by his real name, Richard. At night I can't study with him in the room and I have to hang around the drug store, smoking and doing nothing, with the fellows who loaf there.

More than anything I want to be easy in my mind again. And I miss the way Sucker and I were for a while in a funny, sad way that before this I never would have believed. But everything is so different that there seems to be nothing I can do to get it right. I've sometimes thought if we could have it out in a big fight that would help. But I can't fight him because he's four years younger. And another thing — sometimes this look in his eyes makes me almost believe that if Sucker could he would kill me.

Court in the West Eighties

It was not until spring that I began to think about the man who lived in the room directly opposite to mine. All during the winter months the court between us was dark and there was a feeling of privacy about the four walls of little rooms that looked out on each other. Sounds were muffled and far away as they always seem when it is cold and windows everywhere are shut. Often it would snow and, looking out, I could see only the quiet white flakes sifting down against the gray walls, the snow-edged bottles of milk and covered crocks of food put out on the window sills, and perhaps a light coming out on the dimness in a thin line from behind closed curtains. During all this time I can remember seeing only a few incomplete glimpses of this man living across from me — his red hair through the frosty window glass, his hand reaching out on the sill to bring in his food, a flash of his calm drowsy face as he looked out on the court. I paid no more attention to him than I did to any of the other dozen or so people in that building. I did not see anything unusual about him and had no idea that I would come to think of him as I did.

There was enough to keep me busy last winter without looking at things outside my window. This was my first year at university, the first time I had been in New York. Also there was the necessity of trying to get and keep a part time job in the mornings. I have often thought that when you are an eighteen year old girl, and can't fix it so you look any older than your age, it is harder to get work than at any other time. Maybe I would say the same thing, though, if I were forty. Anyway those months seem to me now about the toughest time I've had so far. There was work (or job-hunting) in the morning, school all afternoon, study and reading at night — together with the newness and strangeness of this place. There was a queer sort of hungriness, for food and for other things too, that I could not get rid of. I was too busy to make any friends down at school and I had never been so much alone.

Late at night I would sit by the window and read. A friend of mine back home would sometimes send me three or four dollars to get certain books in secondhand book stores here that he can't get in the library. He would write for all sorts of things — books like "A Critique of Pure Reason," or "Tertium Organum," and authors like Marx and Strachey and George Soule. He has to stay back home now and help out his family because his Dad is unemployed. He has a job as a garage mechanic. He could get some sort of office work, but a mechanic's wages are better and, lying under an automobile with his back to the ground, he has a chance to think things out and make plans. Before mailing him the books I would study them myself, and although we had talked about many of the things in them in simpler words there would sometimes be a line or two that would make a dozen things I'd half known definite and sure.

Often such sentences as these would make me restless and I'd stare out the window a long time. It seems strange now to think of me standing there alone and this man asleep in his room on the other side and me not knowing anything about him and caring less. The court would be dark for the night, with the snow on the roof of the first floor down below, like a soundless pit that would never awaken.

Then gradually the spring began to come. I cannot understand why I was so unconscious of the way in which things began to change, of the milder air and the sun that began to grow stronger and light up the court and all the rooms around it. The thin, sooty-gray patches of snow disappeared and the sky was bright azure at noon. I noticed that I could wear my sweater instead of my coat, that sounds from outside were beginning to get so clear that they bothered me when reading, that every morning the sun was bright on the wall of the opposite building. But I was busy with the job I had and school and the restlessness that these books I read in my spare time made me feel. It was not until one morning when I found the heat in our building turned off and stood looking out through the open window that I realized the great change that had come about. Oddly enough, too, it was then when I saw the man with the red hair plainly for the first time.

He was standing just as I was, his hands on the window sill, looking out. The early sun shone straight in his face and I was surprised at his nearness to me and at the clarity with which I could see him. His hair, bright in the sunlight, came up from his forehead red and coarse as a sponge. I saw that his mouth was blunt at the corners, his shoulders straight and muscular under his blue pajama jacket. His eyelids drooped slightly and for some reason this gave him a look of wisdom and deliberateness. As I watched him he went inside a moment and returned with a couple of potted plants and set them on the window sill in the sun. The distance between us was so little that I could plainly see his neat blunt hands as they fondled the plants, carefully touching the roots and the soil. He was humming three notes over and over — a little pattern that was more an expression of well-being than a tune. Something about the man made me feel that I could stand there watching him all morning. After a while he looked up once more at the sky, took a deep breath and went inside again.

The warmer it got the more things changed. All of us around the court began to pin back our curtains to let the air into our small rooms and move our beds close to the windows. When you can see people sleep and dress and eat you get to feel that you understand them — even if you don't know their names. Besides the man with the red hair there were others whom I began to notice now and then.

There was the cellist whose room was at a right angle with mine and the young couple living above her. Because I was at my window so much I could not help but see nearly everything that happened to them. I knew the young couple were going to have a baby soon and that, although she didn't look so well, they were very happy. I knew about the cellist's ups and downs too.

At night when I wasn't reading I would write to this friend of mine back home or type out things that happened to come into my head on the typewriter he got me when I left for New York. (He knew I would have to type out assignments at school.) The things I'd put down weren't of any importance — just thoughts that it did me good to try to get out of my mind. There would be a lot of x marks on the paper and maybe a few sentences such as: *fascism and war cannot exist for long because they are death and death is the only evil in the world,* or *it is not right that the boy next to me in Economics should have had to wear newspapers under his sweater all winter because he didn't have any overcoat,* or *what are the things that I know and can always believe?* While I would sit writing like this I would often see the man across from me and it would be as if he were somehow bound up in what I was thinking — as if he knew, maybe, the answers to the things that bothered me. He seemed so calm and sure. When the trouble we began to have in the court started I could not help but feel he was the one person able to straighten it out.

The cellist's practicing annoyed everybody, especially the girl living directly above her who was pregnant. The girl was very nervous and seemed to be having a hard time. Her face was meager above her swollen body, her little hands delicate as a sparrow's claws. The way she had her hair skinned back tightly to her head made her look like a child. Sometimes when the practicing was particularly loud she would lean down toward the cellist's room with an exasperated expression and look as though she might call out to her to stop awhile. Her husband seemed as young as she did and you could tell they were happy. Their bed was close to the window and they would often sit on it Turkish fashion, facing each other, talking and laughing. Once they were sitting that way eating some oranges and throwing the peels out the window. The wind blew a bit of a peel into the cellist's room and she screamed up to them to quit littering everyone else with their trash. The young man laughed, loud so the cellist could hear him, and the girl laid down her half finished orange and wouldn't eat anymore.

The man with the red hair was there the evening that happened. He heard the cellist and looked a long time at her and at the young couple. He had been sitting as he often did, at the chair by the window — in his pajamas, relaxed and doing nothing at all. (After he came in from work he rarely went out again.) There was something contented and kind about his face and it seemed to me he wanted to stop the tension between the rooms. He just looked, and did not even get up from his chair, but that is the feeling I had. It makes me restless to hear people scream at each other and that night I felt tired and jittery for some reason. I put the Marx book I was reading down on the table and just looked at this man and imagined about him.

I think the cellist moved in about the first of May, because during the winter I don't remember hearing her practice. The sun streamed in on her room in the late afternoon, showing up a collection of what looked to be photographs tacked on the wall. She went out often and sometimes she had a certain man in to see her. Late in the day she would sit facing the court with her cello, her knees spread wide apart to straddle the instrument, her skirts pulled up to the thighs so as not to strain the seams. Her music was raw toned and lazily played. She seemed to go into a sort of coma when she worked and her face took on a cowish look. Nearly always she had stockings drying in the window (I could see them so plainly that I could tell she sometimes only washed the feet to save wear and trouble) and some mornings there was a gimcrack tied on to the cord of the window shade.

I felt that this man across from me understood the cellist and everyone else on the court as well. I had a feeling that nothing would surprise him and that he understood more than most people. Maybe it was the secretive droop of his eyelids. I'm not sure what it was. I just knew that it was good to watch him and think about him. At night he would come in with a paper sack and carefully take his food out and eat it. Later he would put on his pajamas and do exercises in his room and after that he'd usually just sit, doing nothing, until almost midnight. He was an exquisite housekeeper, his window sill was never cluttered up. He would tend his plants every morning, the sun shining on his healthily pale face. Often he carefully watered them with a rubber bulb that looked like an ear syringe. I could never guess for sure just what his job in the day time was.

About the end of May there was another change in the court. The young man whose wife was pregnant began to quit going regularly to work. You could tell by their faces he had lost his job. In the morning he would stay at home later than usual, would pour out her milk from the quart bottle they still kept on the window sill and see that she drank the whole amount before it had time to sour. Sometimes at night after everyone else was asleep you could hear the murmuring sound of his talking. Out of a late silence he would say *listen here* so loud that it was enough to wake all of us, and then his voice would drop and he would start a low, urgent monologue to his wife. She almost never said anything. Her face seemed to get smaller and sometimes she would sit on the bed for hours with her little mouth half open like a dreaming child's.

The university term ended but I stayed on in the city because I had this five hour job and wanted to attend summer school. Not going to classes I saw even fewer people than before and stayed closer to home. I had plenty of time to realize what it meant when the young man started coming in with a pint of milk instead of a quart, when finally one day the bottle he brought home was only one of the half pint size.

It is hard to tell how you feel when you watch someone go hungry. You see their room was not more than a few yards from mine and I couldn't quit thinking about them. At first I wouldn't believe what I saw. This is not a tenement house far down on the East side, I would tell myself. We are living in a fairly good, fairly average part of town — in the West eighties. True our court is small, our rooms just big enough for a bed, a dresser and a table, and we are almost as close as tenement people. But from the street these buildings look fine; in both entrances there is a little lobby with something like marble on the floor, an elevator to save us walking up our six or eight or ten flights of stairs. From the street these buildings look almost rich and it is not possible that inside someone could starve. I would say: because their milk is cut down to a fourth of what they used to get and because I don't see him eating (giving her the sandwich he goes out to get each evening at dinner time) that is not a sign they are hungry. Because she just sits like that all day, not taking any interest in anything except the window sills where some of us keep our fruit that is because she is going to have the baby very soon now and is a little unnatural. Because he walks up and down the room and yells at her sometimes, his throat sounding choked up, that is just the ugliness in him.

After reasoning with myself like this I would always look across at the man with the red hair. It is not easy to explain about this faith I had in him. I don't know what I could have expected him to do, but the feeling was there just the same. I quit reading when I came home and would often just sit watching him for hours. Our eyes would meet and then one of us would look away. You see all of us in the court saw each other sleep and dress and live out our hours away from work, but none of us ever spoke. We were near enough to throw our food into each others' windows, near enough so that a single machine gun could have killed us all together in a flash. And still we acted as strangers.

After a while the young couple didn't have any sort of milk bottle on their window sill and the man would stay home all day, his eyes looped with brown circles and his mouth a sharp straight line. You could hear him talking in bed every night — beginning with his loud *listen here*. Out of all the court the cellist was the only one who didn't show in some little gesture that she felt the strain.

Her room was directly below theirs so she probably had never seen their faces. She practiced less than usual now and went out more. This friend of hers that I mentioned was in her place almost every night. He was dapper like a little cat — small, with a round oily face and large almond shaped eyes. Sometimes the whole court would hear them quarreling and after a while he would usually go out. One night she brought home one of those balloon-men they sell along Broadway — a long balloon for the body and a round small one for the head, painted with a grinning mouth. It was a brilliant green, the crepe paper legs were pink and the big cardboard feet black. She fastened the thing to the cord of the shade where it dangled, turning slowly and shambling its paper legs whenever a breeze came.

By the end of June I felt I could not have stayed in the court much longer. If it had not been for the man with red hair I would have moved. I would have moved before the night when everything came finally to a show down. I couldn't study, couldn't keep my mind on anything.

There was one hot night I well remember. The cellist and her friend had their light turned on and so did the young couple. The man across from me sat looking out on the court in his pajamas. He had a bottle by his chair and would draw it up to his mouth occasionally. His feet were propped on the window sill and I could see his bare crooked toes. When he had drunk a good deal he began talking to himself. I couldn't hear the words, they were merged together into one low rising and falling sound. I had a feeling, though, that he might be talking about the people in the court because he would gaze around at all the windows between swallows. It was a queer feeling — like what he was saying might straighten things out for all of us if we could only catch the words. But no matter how hard I listened I couldn't understand any of it. I just looked at his strong throat and at his calm face that even when he was tight did not lose its expression of hidden wisdom. Nothing happened. I never knew what he was saying. There was just that feeling that if his voice had been only a little less low I would have learned so very much.

It was a week later when this thing happened that brought it all to a finish. It must have been about two o'clock one night when I was waked up by a strange sound. It was dark and all the lights were out. The noise seemed to come from the court and as I listened to it I could hardly keep myself from trembling. It was not loud (I don't sleep very well or otherwise it wouldn't have waked me) but there was something animal-like about it — high and breathless, between a moan and an exclamation. It occurred to me that I had heard such a sound sometime in my life before, but it went too far back for me to remember.

I went to the window and from there it seemed to be coming from the cellist's room. All the lights were off and it was warm and black and moonless. I was standing there looking out and trying to imagine what was wrong when a shout came from the young couple's apartment that as long as I live I will never be able to forget. It was the young man and between the words there was a choking sound.

"Shut up! You bitch down there shut up! I can't stand —"

Of course I knew then what the sound had been. He left off in the middle of the sentence and the court was quiet as death. There were no *shhh*s such as usually follow a noise in the night here. A few lights were turned on, but that was all. I stood at the window feeling sick and not able to stop trembling. I looked across at the red headed man's room and in a few minutes he turned on his light. Sleepy eyed, he gazed all around the court. *Do something do something,* I wanted to call over to him. In a moment he sat down with a pipe in his chair by the window and switched off his light. Even after everybody else seemed to be sleeping again there was still the smell of his tobacco in the hot dark air.

After that night things began to get like they are now. The young couple moved and their room remained vacant. Neither the man with the red hair nor I stayed inside as much as before. I never saw the cellist's dapper looking friend again and she would practice fiercely, jabbing her bow across the strings. Early in the mornings when she would get the brassiere and stockings she had hung out to dry she would snatch them inside and turn her back to the window. The balloon-man still dangled from her shade cord, turning slowly in the air, grinning and brilliant green.

And now yesterday the man with the red hair left for good, too.

Poldi

When Hans was only a block from the hotel a chill rain began to fall, draining the color from the lights that were just being turned on along Broadway. He fastened his pale eyes on the sign reading COLTON ARMS, tucked a sheet of music under his overcoat, and hurried on. By the time he stepped inside the dingily marbled lobby his breath was coming in sharp pants and the sheet of music was crumpled.

Vaguely he smiled at a face before him. "Third floor — this time."

You could always tell how the elevator boy felt about the permanent people of the hotel. When those for whom he had the most respect stepped out on their floors he always held the door open for an extra moment in an attitude of unctuousness. Hans had to jump furtively so that the sliding door would not nip his heels.

Poldi —

He stood hesitantly in the dim corridor. From the end came the sound of a cello — playing a series of descending phrases that tumbled over each other helter skelter like a handful of marbles dropped downstairs. Stepping down to the room with the music he stood for a moment just outside the door. A wobbly lettered notice was pinned there by a thumbtack.

Poldi Klein
Please Do Not Disturb While Practicing

The first time he had seen that, he recalled, there had been an E before the ING of practicing.

The heat seemed to be very low; the folds of his coat smelled wet

It is late summer, the time people usually move. I watched him pack up all the things he had and tried not to think of never seeing him again. I thought about school starting soon and about a list of books I would make out to read. I watched him like a complete stranger. He seemed happier than he had been in a long time, humming a little tune as he packed, fondling his plants for a while before taking them in from the sill. Just before leaving he stood at the window looking out on the court for the last time. His calm face did not squint in the glare, but his eyelids drooped until they were almost shut and the sun made a haze of light around his bright hair that was almost like a sort of halo.

Tonight I have thought a long time about this man. Once I started to write my friend back home who has the mechanic's job about him, but I changed my mind. The thing is this — it would be too hard explaining to anybody else, even this friend, just how it was. You see when it comes right down to it there are so many things about him I don't know — his name, his job, even what nationality he is. He never did do anything, and I don't even know just exactly what I expected him to do. About the young couple I don't guess he could have helped it any more than I could. When I think back over the times I have watched him I can't remember a thing unusual that he ever did. When describing him nothing stands out except his hair. Altogether he might seem just like a million other men. But no matter how peculiar it sounds I still have this feeling that there is something in him that could change a lot of situations and straighten them out. And there is one point in a thing like this — as long as I feel this way, in a sense it is true.

and let out little whiffs of coldness. Crouching over the half warm radiator that stood by the end window did not relieve him.

Poldi — I've waited for a long time. And many times I've walked outside until you're through and thought about the words I wish to say to you. Gott! How pretty — like a poem or a little song by Schumann. Start like that. Poldi —

His hand crept along the rusty metal. Warm, she always was. And if he held her it would be so that he would want to bite his tongue in two.

Hans, you know the others have meant nothing to me. Joseph, Nikolay, Harry — all the fellows I've known. And this Kurt *only three times she couldn't* that I've talked about this last week — Poof! They all are nothing.

It came to him that his hands were crushing the music. Glancing down he saw that the brutally colored back sheet was wet and faded, but that the notation inside was undamaged. Cheap stuff. Oh well —

He walked up and down the hall, rubbing his pimply forehead. The cello whirred upward in an unclear arpeggio. That concert — the Castelnuovo-Tedesco — How long was she going to keep on practicing? Once he paused and stretched out his hand toward the door knob. No, that time he had gone in and she had looked — and looked and told him —

The music rocked lushly back and forth in his mind. His fingers jerked as he tried to transcribe the orchestral score to the piano. She would be leaning forward now, her hands gliding over the finger-board.

The sallow light from the window left most of the corridor dim. With a sudden impulse he knelt down and focussed his eye to the keyhole.

Only the wall and the corner; she must be by the window. Just the wall with its string of staring photographs — Casals, Piatigorsky, the fellow she liked best back home, Heifetz — and a couple of valentines and Christmas cards tucked in between. Nearby was the picture called Dawn of the barefooted woman holding up a rose with the dingy pink paper party hat she had gotten last New Year cocked over it.

The music swelled to a crescendo and ended with a few quick strokes. Ach! The last one a quarter tone off. Poldi —

He stood up quickly and, before the practicing should continue, knocked on the door.

"Who is it?"

"Me — H-Hans."

"All right. You can come in."

She sat in the fading light of the court window, her legs sprawled broadly to clench her cello. Expectantly she raised her eyebrows and let her bow droop to the floor.

His eyes fastened on the trickles of rain on the window glass. "I — I just came in to show you the new popular song we're playing tonight. The one you suggested."

She tugged at her skirt that had slid up above her stocking rolls and the gesture drew his gaze. The calves of her legs bulged out and there was a short run in one stocking. The pimples on his forehead deepened in color and he stared furtively at the rain again.

"Did you hear me practicing outside?"

"Yes."

"Listen, Hans, did it sound spiritual — did it sing and lift you to a higher plane?"

Her face was flushed and a drop of perspiration dribbled down the little gully between her breasts before disappearing under the neck of her frock. "Ye-es."

"I think so. I believe my playing has deepened much in the last month." Her shoulders shrugged expansively. "Life does that to me — it happens every time something like this comes up. Not that it's ever been like this before. It's only after you've suffered that you can play."

"That's what they claim."

She stared at him for a moment as though seeking a stronger confirmation, then curved her lips down petulantly. "That wolf, Hans, is driving me crazy. You know that Fauré thing — in E — well it takes in that note over and over and nearly drives me to drink. I get to dreading that E — it stands out something awful."

"You could have it shifted?"

"Well — but the next thing I take up would probably be in that key. No, that won't do any good. Besides, it costs something and I'd have to let them have my cello for a few days and what should I use? Just what, I ask you?"

When he made money she could get — "I don't notice it so much."

"It's a darn shame, I think. People who play like Hell can have good cellos and I can't even have a decent one. It's not right for me to put up with a wolf like that. It damages my playing — anybody can tell you that. How should I get any tone from that cheese box?"

A phrase from a sonata he was learning weaved itself in and out of his mind. "Poldi — " What was it now? *I love you love you.*

"And for what do I bother anyway — this lousy job we have?" With a dramatic gesture she got up and balanced her instrument in the corner of the room. When she switched on the lamp the bright circle of light made shadows follow the curves of her body.

"Listen, Hans, I'm so restless till I could scream."

The rain splashed on the window. He rubbed his forehead and watched her walk up and down the room. All at once she caught sight of the run in her stockings and, with a hiss of displeasure, spat on the end of her finger and bent over to transfer the wetness to the bottom of the run.

"Nobody has such a time with stockings as cellists. And for what? A room in a hotel and five dollars for playing trash three hours every night in the week. A pair of stockings twice every month I have to buy. And if at night I just rinse out the feet the tops run just the same."

She snatched down a pair of stockings that hung side by side with a brassiere in the window and, after peeling off the old ones, began to pull them on. Her legs were white and traced with dark hairs. There were blue veins near the knees. "Excuse me — you don't mind, do you? You seem to me like my little brother back home. And we'll get fired if I start wearing things like that down to play."

He stood at the window and looked at the rain blurred wall of the next building. Just opposite him was a milk bottle and a jar of mayonnaise on a window ledge. Below, someone had hung some clothes out to dry and forgotten to take them in; they flapped dismally in the wind and rain. A little brother — Jesus!

"And dresses," she went on impatiently. "All the time getting split at the seams because of having to stretch your knees out. But at that it's better than it used to be. Did you know me when everybody was wearing those short skirts — and I had such a time being modest when I played and still keeping with the style? Did you know me then?"

"No," Hans answered. "Two years ago the dresses were about like they are now."

"Yes, it was two years ago we first met, wasn't it?"

"You were with Harry after the con—"

"Listen, Hans." She leaned forward and looked at him urgently. She was so close that her perfume came sharp to his nostrils. "I've just been about crazy all day. It's about him, you know."

"Wh-Who?"

"You understand well enough—him—Kurt! How, Hans, he loves me, don't you think so?"

"Well—but Poldi—how many times have you seen him? You hardly know each other." He turned away from her at the Levins' when she was praising his work and—

"Oh, what does it matter if I've only been with him three times. I should worry. But the look in his eyes and the way he spoke about my playing. Such a soul he has. It comes out in his music. Have you ever heard the Beethoven funeral march sonata played so well as he did it that night?"

"It was good—"

"He told Mrs. Levin my playing had so much temperament."

He could not look at her; his grey eyes kept their focus on the rain.

"So gemütlich he is. Ein Edel Mensch! But what can I do? Huh, Hans?"

"I don't know."

"Quit looking so pouty. What would you do?"

He tried to smile. "Have—have you heard from him—he telephoned you or written?"

"No—but I'm sure it's just his delicateness. He wouldn't want me to feel offended or turn him down."

"Isn't he engaged to marry Mrs. Levin's daughter next spring?"

"Yes. But it's a mistake. What would he want with a cow like her?"

"But Poldi—"

She smoothed down the back of her hair, holding her arms above her head so that her broad breasts stood out tautly and the muscles of her underarms flexed beneath the thin silk of her dress. "At his concert, you know, I had a feeling he was playing just to me. He looked straight at me every time he bowed. That's the reason he didn't answer my letter—he's so afraid he'll hurt someone and then he can always tell me what he means in his music."

The adams-apple jutting from Hans' thin neck moved up and down as he swallowed. "You wrote to him?"

"I had to. An artist cannot subdue the greatest of the things that come to her."

"What did you say?"

"I told him how much I love him — that was ten days ago — a week after I saw him first at the Levins'."

"And you heard nothing?"

"No. But can't you see how he feels? I knew it would be that way so day before yesterday I wrote another note telling him not to worry — that I would always be the same."

Hans vaguely traced his hairline with his slender fingers. "But Poldi — there have been so many others — just since I've known you." He got up and put his finger on the photograph next to Casals'.

The face smiled at him. The lips were thick and topped by a dark moustache. On the neck there was a little round spot. Two years ago she had pointed it out to him so many times, telling him that the hicky where his violin rested used always to be so angry-red. And how she used to stroke it with her finger. How she had called it Fiddler's Ill Luck — and how between them it had gotten down to simply his Zilluck. For several moments he stared at that vague splotch on the picture, wondering if it had been photographed or was simply the smudge from the number of times she had pointed it out to him.

The eyes stared at him sharp seeing and dark. Hans' knees felt weak; he sat down again.

"Tell me, Hans, he loves — don't you think so? You think really that he loves me but is only waiting until he feels it's best to reply — you think so?"

A thin haze seemed to cover everything in the room. "Yes," he said slowly.

Her expression changed. "Hans!"

He leaned forward, trembling.

"You — you look so queer. Your nose is wiggling and your lips shake like you are ready to cry. What —"

Poldi —

A sudden laugh broke into her question. "You look like a peculiar little cat my Papa used to have."

Quickly he moved toward the window so that his face was turned away from her. The rain still slithered down the glass, silvery, half opaque. The lights of the next building were on; they shone softly through the grey twilight. Ach! Hans bit his lips. In one of the windows it looked like — like a woman — Poldi in the arms of a big man with dark hair. And on the window sill looking in, beside the bottle of milk and the mayonnaise jar, was a little yellow cat out in the rain. Slowly Hans' bony knuckles rubbed his eyelids.

Breath from the Sky

Her peaked, young face stared for a time, unsatisfied, at the softer blue of the sky that fringed the horizon. Then with a quiver of her open mouth she rested her head again on the pillow, tilted the panama hat over her eyes, and lay motionless in the canvas striped chair. Chequered shade patterns jerked over the blanket covering her thin body. Bee drones sounded from the spirea bushes that sprayed out their white blossoms nearby.

Constance dozed for a moment. She awoke to the smothering smell of hot straw — and Miss Whelan's voice.

"Come on now. Here's your milk."

Out of her sleepy haze a question came that she had not intended to ask, that she had not even been consciously thinking about: "Where's Mother?"

Miss Whelan held the glistening bottle in her plump hands. As she poured the milk it frothed white in the sunlight and crystal frost wreathed the glass.

"Where — ?" Constance repeated, letting the word slide out with her shallow release of breath.

"Out somewhere with the other kids. Mick was raising a fuss about bathing suits this morning. I guess they went to town to buy those."

Such a loud voice. Loud enough to shatter the fragile sprays of the spirea so that the thousands of tiny blossoms would float down, down, down in a magic kaleidoscope of whiteness. Silent whiteness. Leaving only the stark, prickly twigs for her to see.

"I bet your mother will be surprised when she finds where you are this morning."

"No," whispered Constance, without knowing the reason for the denial.

"I should think she would be. Your first day out and all. I know *I* didn't think the doctor would let you talk him into coming out. Especially after the time you had last night."

She stared at the nurse's face, at her white clad bulging body, at her hands serenely folded over her stomach. And then at her face again — so pink and fat that why — why wasn't the weight and the bright color uncomfortable — why didn't it sometimes droop down tiredly toward her chest — ?

Hatred made her lips tremble and her breath come more shallowly, quickly.

In a moment she said: "If I can go three hundred miles away next week — all the way to Mountain Heights — I guess it won't hurt to sit in my own side yard for a little while."

Miss Whelan moved a pudgy hand to brush back the girl's hair from her face. "Now, now," she said placidly. "The air up there'll do the trick. Don't be impatient. After pleurisy — you just have to take it easy and be careful."

Constance's teeth clamped rigidly. Don't let me cry, she thought. Don't, please, let her look at me ever again when I cry. Don't ever let her look at me or touch me again. Don't, please — Ever again.

When the nurse had moved off fatly across the lawn and gone back into the house, she forgot about crying. She watched a high breeze make the leaves of the oaks across the street flutter with a silver sheen in the sun. She let the glass of milk rest on her chest, bending her head slightly to sip now and then.

Out again. Under the blue sky. After breathing the yellow walls of her room for so many weeks in stingy hot breaths. After watching the heavy footboard of her bed, feeling it crush down on her chest. Blue sky. Cool blueness that could be sucked in until she was drenched in its color. She stared upward until a hot wetness welled in her eyes.

As soon as the car sounded from far off down the street she recognized the chugging of the engine and turned her head toward the strip of road visible from where she lay. The automobile seemed to tilt precariously as it swung into the driveway and jerked to a noisy stop. The glass of one of the rear windows had been cracked and plastered with dingy adhesive tape. Above this hung the head of a police dog, tongue palpitating, head cocked.

Mick jumped out first with the dog. "Looka there, Mother," she called in a lusty child's voice that rose up almost to a shriek. "She's *out.*"

Mrs. Lane stepped to the grass and looked at her daughter with a hollow, strained face. She drew deeply at her cigarette that she held in her nervous fingers, blew out airy grey ribbons of smoke that twisted in the sunshine.

"Well —" Constance prompted flatly.

"Hello, stranger," Mrs. Lane said with a brittle gaiety. "Who let you out?"

Mick clung to the straining dog. "See, Mother! King's trying to get to her. He hasn't forgotten Constance. See. He knows her good as anybody — don't you, boyoboyoboy —"

"Not so loud, Mick. Go lock that dog in the garage."

Lagging behind her mother and Mick was Howard — a sheepish expression on his pimply, fourteen year old face. "Hello, Sister," he mumbled after a gangling moment. "How do you feel?"

To look at the three of them, standing there in the shade from the oaks, somehow made her more tired than she had felt since she came out. Especially Mick — trying to straddle King with her muscular little legs, clinging to his flexed body that looked ready any moment to spring out at her.

"See, Mother! King —"

Mrs. Lane jerked one shoulder nervously. "Mick — Howard take that animal away this instant — now mind me — and lock him up somewhere." Her slender hands gestured without purpose. "This instant."

The children looked at Constance with sidelong gazes and moved off across the lawn toward the front porch.

"Well —" said Mrs. Lane when they were gone. "Did you just pick up and walk out?"

"The doctor said I could — finally — and he and Miss Whelan got that old rolling chair out from under the house and — helped me."

The words, so many of them at once, tired her. And when she gave a gentle gasp to catch her breath, the coughing started again. She leaned over the side of the chair, Kleenex in hand, and coughed until the stunted blade of grass on which she had fastened her stare had, like the cracks in the floor beside her bed, sunk ineffaceably into her memory. When she had finished she stuffed the Kleenex into a cardboard box beside the chair and looked at her mother — standing by the spirea bush, back turned, vacantly singeing the blossoms with the tip of her cigarette.

Constance stared from her mother to the blue sky. She felt that she must say something. "I wish I had a cigarette," she pronounced slowly, timing the syllables to her shallow breath.

Mrs. Lane turned. Her mouth, twitching slightly at the corners, stretched out in a too bright smile. "Now *that* would be pretty!" She dropped the cigarette to the grass and ground it out with the toe of her shoe. "I think maybe I'll cut them out for a while myself. My mouth feels all sore and furry — like a mangy little cat."

Constance laughed weakly. Each laugh was a huge burden that helped to sober her.

"Mother —"

"Yes."

"The doctor wanted to see you this morning. He wants you to call him."

Mrs. Lane broke off a sprig of the spirea blossoms and crushed it in her fingers. "I'll go in now and talk to him. Where's that Miss Whelan? Does she just set you out on the lawn by yourself when I'm gone — at the mercy of dogs and —"

"Hush, Mother. She's in the house. It's her afternoon off, you know, today."

"Is it? Well, it isn't afternoon."

The whisper slid out easily with her breath. "Mother —"

"Yes, Constance."

"Are — are you coming back out?" She looked away as she said it — looked at the sky that was a burning, fevered blue.

"If you want me to — I'll be out."

She watched her mother cross the lawn and turn into the gravel path that led to the front door. Her steps were as jerky as those of a little glass puppet. Each bony ankle stiffly pushing past the other, the thin bony arms rigidly swinging, the delicate neck held to one side.

She looked from the milk to the sky and back again. "Mother," her lips said, but the sound came out only in a tired exhalation.

The milk was hardly started. Two creamy stains drooped from the rim side by side. Four times, then, she had drunk. Twice on the bright cleanliness, twice with a shiver and eyes shut. Constance turned the glass half an inch and let her lips sink down on an unstained part. The milk crept cool and drowsy down her throat.

When Mrs. Lane returned she wore her white string garden gloves and carried rusty, clinking shears.

"Did you phone Doctor Reece?"

The woman's mouth moved infinitesimally at the corners as though she had just swallowed. "Yes."

"Well —"

"He thinks it best — not to put off going too long. This waiting around — The sooner you get settled the better it'll be."

"When, then?" She felt her pulse quiver at her finger tips like a bee on a flower — vibrate against the cool glass.

"How does the day after tomorrow strike you?"

She felt her breath shorten to hot, smothered gasps. She nodded.

From the house came the sound of Mick's and Howard's voices. They seemed to be arguing about the belts of their bathing suits. Mick's words merged into a scream. And then the sounds hushed.

That was why she was almost crying. She thought about water, looking down into great jade swirls of it, feeling the coolness of it on her hot limbs, splashing through it with long, effortless strokes. Cool water — the color of the sky.

"Oh, I do feel so dirty —"

Mrs. Lane held the shears poised. Her eyebrows quivered upward over the white sprays of blossoms she held. "Dirty?"

"Yes — yes. I haven't been in a bathtub for — for three months. I'm sick of being just sponged — stingily —"

Her mother crouched over to pick up a scrap of a candy wrapper from the grass, looked at it stupidly for a moment, and let it drop to the grass again.

"I want to go swimming — feel all the cool water. It isn't fair — isn't fair that I can't."

"Hush," said Mrs. Lane with testy sibilance. "Hush, Constance. You don't have to worry over nonsense."

"And my hair —" She lifted her hand to the oily knot that bumped out from the nape of her neck. "Not washed with water in — months — nasty awful hair that's going to run me wild. I can stand all the pleurisy and drains and t.b. but —"

Mrs. Lane was holding the flowers so tightly that they curled limply into each other as though ashamed. "Hush," she repeated hollowly. "This isn't necessary."

The sky burned brightly — blue jet flames. Choking and murderous to air.

"Maybe if it were just cut off short —"

The garden shears snipped shut slowly. "Here — if you want me to — I guess I could clip it. Do you really want it short?"

She turned her head to one side and feebly lifted one hand to tug at the bronze hairpins. "Yes — real short. Cut it all off."

Dank brown, the heavy hair hung several inches below the pillow. Hesitantly Mrs. Lane bent over and grasped a handful of it. The blades, blinding bright in the sun, began to shear through it slowly.

Mick appeared suddenly from behind the spirea bushes. Naked, except for her swimming trunks, her plump little chest gleamed silky white in the sun. Just above her round child's stomach were scolloped two soft lines of plumpness. "Mother! Are you giving *her* a haircut?"

Mrs. Lane held the dissevered hair gingerly, staring at it for a moment with her strained face. "Nice job," she said brightly. "No little fuzzes around your neck, I hope."

"No," said Constance, looking at her little sister.

The child held out an open hand. "Give it to me, Mother. I can stuff it into the cutest little pillow for King. I can —"

"Don't dare let her touch the filthy stuff," said Constance between her teeth. Her hand fingered the stiff, loose fringes around her neck, then sank tiredly to pluck at the grass.

Mrs. Lane crouched over and, moving the white flowers from the newspaper where she had laid them, wrapped up the hair and left the bundle lying on the ground behind the invalid's chair.

"I'll take it when I go in —"

The bees droned on in the hot stillness. The shade had grown blacker, and the little shadows that had fluttered by the side of the oak trees were still. Constance pushed the blanket down to her knees. "Have you told Papa about my going so soon?"

"Yes, I telephoned him."

"To Mountain Heights?" asked Mick, balancing herself on one bare leg and then the other.

"Yes, Mick."

"Mother, isn't that where you went to see Unca Charlie?"

"Yes."

"Is that where he sent us the cactus candy from — a long time ago?"

Lines, fine and grey as the web of a spider, cut through the pale skin around Mrs. Lane's mouth and between her eyes. "No, Mick. Mountain Heights is just the other side of Atlanta. That was Arizona."

"It was funny tasting," said Mick.

Mrs. Lane began cutting the flowers again with hurried snips. "I — I think I hear that dog of yours howling somewhere. Go tend to him — go — run along, Mick."

"You don't hear King, Mother. Howard's teaching him to shake hands out on the back porch. Please don't make me go." She laid her hands on her soft mound of stomach. "Look! You haven't said anything about my bathing suit. Aren't I nice in it, Constance?"

The sick girl looked at the flexed, eager muscles of the child before her, and then gazed back at the sky. Two words shaped themselves soundlessly on her lips.

"Gee! I wanna hurry up and get in. Did you know they're making people walk through a kind of ditch thing so you won't get sore toes this year — And they've got a new chute-ty-chute."

"Mind me this instant, Mick, and go on in the house."

The child looked at her mother and started off across the lawn. As she reached the path that led to the door she paused and, shading her eyes, looked back at them. "Can we go soon?" she asked, subdued.

"Yes, get your towels and be ready."

For several minutes the mother and daughter said nothing. Mrs. Lane moved jerkily from the spirea bushes to the fever-bright flowers that bordered the driveway, snipping hastily at the blooms, the dark shadow at her feet dogging her with noonday squatness. Constance watched her with eyes half closed against the glare, with her bony hands against the bubbling, thumping dynamo that was her chest. Finally she shaped the words on her lips and let them emerge. "Am I going up there by myself?"

"Of course, my dear. We'll just put you on a bicycle and give you a shove —"

She mashed a string of phlegm with her tongue so that she would not have to spit, and thought about repeating the question.

There were no more blooms ready for cutting. The woman looked sidewise at her daughter from over the flowers in her arm, her blue veined hand shifting its grasp on the stems. "Listen, Constance — The garden club's having some sort of a to-do today. They're all having lunch at the club — and then going to somebody's rock garden. As long as I'm taking the children over I thought I — you don't mind if I go, do you?"

"No," said Constance after a moment.

"Miss Whelan promised to stay on. Tomorrow maybe —"

She was still thinking about the question that she must repeat, but the words clung to her throat like gummy pellets of mucus and she felt that if she tried to expel them she would cry. She said instead, with no special reason: "Lovely —"

"Aren't they? Especially the spirea — so graceful and white."

"I didn't even know they'd started blooming until I got out."

"Didn't you? I brought you some in a vase last week."

"In a vase —" Constance murmured.

"At night, though. That's the time to look at them. Last night I stood by the window — and the moonlight was on them. You know how white flowers are in the moonlight —"

Suddenly she raised her bright eyes to those of her mother. "I heard you," she said half accusingly. "In the hall — tipping up and down. Late. In the living room. And I thought I heard the front door open and close. And when I was coughing once I looked at the window and I thought I saw a white dress up and down the grass like a ghost — like a —"

"Hush!" said her mother in a voice as jagged as splintered glass. "Hush. Talking is exhausting."

It was time for the question — as though her throat were swollen with its matured syllables. "Am I going by myself to Mountain Heights, or with Miss Whelan, or —"

"I'm going with you. I'll take you up on the train. And stay a few days until you're settled."

Her mother stood against the sun, stopping some of the glare so that she could look into her eyes. They were the color of the sky in the cool morning. They were looking at her now with a strange stillness — a hollow restfulness. Blue as the sky before the sun had burned it to its gaseous brilliance. She stared with trembling, open lips, listening to the sound her breath made. "Mother —"

The end of the word was smothered by the first cough. She leaned over the side of the chair, feeling them beat at her chest like great blows risen from some unknown part inside her. They came, one after another with equal force. And when the last toneless one had wrenched itself clear she was so tired that she hung with unresisting limpness on the chair arm, wondering if the strength to raise her dizzy head would ever again be hers.

In the gasping minute that followed, the eyes that were still before her stretched to the vastness of the sky. She looked, and breathed, and struggled up to look again.

Mrs. Lane had turned away. But in a moment her voice rang out bitterly bright. "Goodbye, pet — I'll run along now. Miss Whelan'll be out in a minute and you'd better go right in. So long —"

As she crossed the lawn Constance thought she saw a delicate shudder shake her shoulders — a movement as perceptible as that of a crystal glass that had been thumped too soundly.

Miss Whelan stood placidly in her line of vision as they left. She only had a glimpse of Howard's and Mick's half naked bodies and the towels they flapped lustily at each other's rears. Of King thrusting his panting head above the broken window glass with its dingy tape. But she heard the overfed roar of the engine, the frantic stripping of the gears as the car backed from the driveway. And even after the last sound of the motor had trailed into silence, it was as though she could still see her mother's strained white face bent over the wheel —

"What's the matter?" asked Miss Whelan calmly. "Your side's not hurting you again, I hope."

She turned her head twice on the pillow.

"There now. Once you're in again you'll be all right."

Her hands, limp and colorless as tallow, sank over the hot wetness that streamed down her cheeks. And she swam without breath in a wide, ungiving blueness like the sky's.

The Orphanage

How the Home came to be associated with the sinister bottle belongs to the fluid logic of childhood, for at the beginning of this episode I must have been not more than seven. But the Home, as a dwelling for the orphans in our town, might have in its mysterious ugliness been partly to blame. It was a large, gabled house, painted in a blackish green, and set back in a rake-printed front yard that was absolutely bare except for two magnolia trees. The yard was surrounded by a wrought iron fence, and the orphans were seldom to be seen there when you stopped on the sidewalk to gaze inside. The back yard, on the other hand, was for a long time a secret place to me; the Home was on a corner, and a high board fence concealed what went on inside, but when you passed there would be the sound of unseen voices and sometimes a noise like that of clanging metal. This secrecy and the mysterious noises made me very much afraid. I would often pass the Home with my Grandmother, on the way home from the main street of town, and now, in memory, it seems that we always walked by in twilight wintertime. The sounds behind the board fence seemed tinged with menace in the fading light, and the iron picket gate in front was to the touch of a finger bitter cold. The gloom of the grassless yard and even the gleams of yellow light from the narrow windows seemed somehow in keeping with the dreadful knowledge that came to me about this time.

My initiator was a little girl named Hattie, who must have been about nine or ten. I don't remember her last name, but there are some other facts about this Hattie that are unforgettable. For one thing, she told me that George Washington was her uncle. Another time she explained to me what made colored people colored. If a girl, said Hattie, kissed a boy she turned into a colored person, and when she was married her children were colored, too. Only brothers were excepted from this law. Hattie was a small child for her age, with snaggled front teeth, and greasy blond hair held back by a jeweled barrette. I was forbidden to play with her, perhaps because my Grandmother or parents sensed an unwholesome element in the relation; if this supposition is true they were quite right. I had once kissed Tit, who was my best friend but only a second cousin, so that day by day I was slowly turning into a colored person. It was summer, and day by day I was turning darker. Perhaps I had some notion that Hattie, having once revealed this fearful transformation, might somehow have the power to stop it. In the dual bondage of guilt and fear, I followed her around the neighborhood, and often she demanded nickels and dimes.

The memories of childhood have a strange shuttling quality, and areas of darkness ring the spaces of light. The memories of childhood are like clear candles in an acre of night, illuminating fixed scenes from the surrounding darkness. I don't remember where Hattie lived, but one passageway, one room, have an uncanny clarity. Nor do I know how I happened to go to this room, but anyway I was there with Hattie and my cousin, Tit. It was late afternoon, the room was not quite dark. Hattie was wearing an Indian dress, with a headband of bright red feathers, and she had asked if we knew where babies come from. The Indian feathers in her band looked, for some reason, scary to me.

"They grow in the insides of ladies," Tit said.

"If you swear you will never tell a living soul then I will show you something."

We must have sworn, though I remember a reluctance, and a dread of further revelations. Hattie climbed up on a chair and brought down something from a closet shelf. It was a bottle, with something queer and red inside.

"Do you know what this is?" she asked.

The thing inside the bottle resembled nothing I had ever seen before. It was Tit who asked: "What is it?"

Hattie waited and her face beneath the band of feathers wore a crafty expression. After some moments of suspense, she said:

"It's a dead pickled baby."

The room was very quiet. Tit and I exchanged a sidelong look of horror. I could not look again at the bottle, but Tit was gazing at it with fascinated dread.

"Whose?" he asked finally in a low voice.

"See the little old red head with the mouth. And the little teensy red legs squelched up under it. My brother brought it home when he was learning to be a drug store man."

Tit reached out a finger and touched the bottle, then put his hands behind his back. He asked again, this time in a whisper: "Whose? Whose baby?"

"It is an orphan," Hattie said.

I remember the light whispering sound of our footsteps as we tiptoed from the room, and that the passageway was dark and at the end there was a curtain. That, thank goodness, is my final recollection of this Hattie. But the pickled orphan haunted me for some time; I dreamed once that the Thing had got out of the jar and was scuttling around the Orphans' Home and I was locked in there and It was scuttling after me — Did I believe that in that gloomy, gabled house there were shelves with rows of these eerie bottles? Probably yes — and no. For the child knows two layers of reality — that of the world, which is accepted like an immense collusion of all adults — and the unacknowledged, hidden secret, the profound. In any case, I kept close to my Grandmother when in the late afternoon we passed by the Home on our way from town. At that time I knew none of the orphans, as they went to the Third Street School.

It was a few years later that two occurrences came about that brought me in a direct relation with the Home. Meanwhile, I looked on myself as a big girl, and had passed the place a thousand times, walking alone, or on skates, or bicycle. The terror had diminished to a sort of special fascination. I always stared at the Home in passing, and sometimes I would see the orphans, walking with Sunday slowness on their way to Sunday school and church, grouped in marching formation with the two biggest orphans leading and the two smallest orphans at the end. I was about eleven when changes occurred that drew me in closer as a spectator, and opened an unexpected area of romance. First, my Grandmother was made a member of the Board of the Orphans' Home. That was in the autumn. Then at the beginning of the spring term the orphans were transferred to the Seventeenth Street School, where I was going, and three of the orphans were in the room with me in the sixth grade. The transfer was made because of a change in the boundary line of the school districts. My Grandmother was elected to the Board because she enjoyed Boards, Committees, and the meetings of associations, and a former member of the Board had died at about that time.

My Grandmother visited the Home about once a month, and on her second visit I went with her. It was the best time of the week, a Friday afternoon, spacious with the sense of coming holiday. The afternoon was cold, and the late sunlight made fiery reflections on the windowpanes. Inside, the Home was quite different from the way I had imagined it. The wide hall was bare, and the rooms were uncurtained, rugless, and scantily furnished. Heat came from stoves in the dining room and in the general room that was next to the front parlor. Mrs. Wesley, the matron of the Home, was a large woman, rather hard of hearing, and she kept her mouth slightly ajar when anyone of importance spoke. She always seemed to be short of breath, and she spoke through her nose in a placid voice. My Grandmother had brought some clothes (Mrs. Wesley called them garments) donated by the various churches and they shut themselves in the cold parlor to talk. I was entrusted to a girl of my own age, named Susie, and we went out immediately to the board fenced back yard.

That first visit was awkward. Girls of all ages were playing different games. There was in the yard a joggling board, and an acting bar, and a hopscotch game was marked on the ground. Confusion made me see the yard full of children as an unassorted whole. One little girl came up to me and asked me what was my father. And, as I was slow in answering she said: "My father was a walker on the railroad." Then she ran to the acting bar and swung by her knees — her hair hung straight down from her red face and she wore brown cotton bloomers.

Instant of the Hour After

Light as shadows her hands fondled his head and then came placidly to rest; the tips of her fingers hovered on his temples, throbbed to the warm slow beat inside his body, and her palms cupped his hard skull.

"Re*ver*berating va-cuity," he mumbled so that the syllables lolloped ponderously into each other.

She looked down at his lax, sound body that stretched the length of the couch. One foot — the sock wrinkled around the ankle — hung limp over the edge. And as she watched his sensitive hand left his side and crept up drunkenly to his mouth — to touch his lips that had remained pursed out and loose after his words. "Immense hollowness —" he mouthed behind his feeling fingers.

"Enough out of you tonight — my darling," she said. "The show's over and the monkey's dead."

They had turned off the heat an hour before and the apartment was beginning to chill. She looked at the clock, the hands of which pointed to one. Not much heat anyway at that hour, she thought. No draughts, though; opalescent ribbons of smoke lay motionless close to the ceiling. Speculatively her glance shifted to the whiskey bottle and the confused chessmen on the card table. To a book that lay face downward on the floor — and a lettuce leaf lying forlornly in the corner since Marshall had lost it while waving his sandwich. To the dead little butts of cigarettes and the charred matches scattered.

"Here cover up," she said absently, unfolding a blanket at the foot of the couch. "You're so susceptible to draughts."

His eyes opened and stared stolidly up at her — blue-green, the color of the sweater he wore. One of them was shot through at the corner with fragile fibers of pink, giving him somehow the guileless expression of an Easter bunny. So much younger than twenty, he always looked — With his head thrown back on her knees so that his neck was arched above his rolled collar and tender seeming with the soft outline of the cords and cartilages. With his dark hair springing from the pallor of his face.

"Vacant majesty —"

As he spoke his eyelids drooped until the eyes beneath had been narrowed to a slit that seemed to sneer at her. And she knew with a sudden start that he was not as drunk as he pretended to be.

"You needn't hold forth any longer," she said. "Phillip's gone home and there's just me."

"It's in the na-a-ature of things — that such a viewpoint — view —"

"He's gone home," she repeated. "You talked him out." She had a fleet picture of Phillip bending to pick up the cigarette butts — his agile, blond little body and his calm eyes — "He washed up the dishes we messed and even wanted to sweep the floor, but I made him leave it."

"He's a —" started Marshall.

"Seeing *you* — and how tired I was — he even offered to pull out the couch and get you to bed."

"A cute procedure —" he mouthed.

"I made him run along." She remembered for a moment his face as she shut the door between them, the sound of his footsteps going down stairs, and the feeling — half of pity for loneliness, half of warmth — that she always felt when she listened to the sounds of others going out into the night away from them.

"To listen to him — one would think his reading were rigidly narrowed to — to G. K. Chesterton and George Moore," he said, giving a drunken lilt to the words. "Who won at chess — me or him?"

"You," she said. "But you did your best work before you got so drunk."

"Drunk —" he murmured, moving his long body laxly, changing the position of his head. "God! your knees are bony. Bo-ony!"

"But I thought sure you'd give him the game when you made that idiotic move with your queen's pawn." She thought of their fingers hovering over the carved precision of their pieces, brows frowned, the glow of the light on the bottle beside them.

His eyes were closed again and his hand had crumpled down on his chest. "Lousy simile —" he mumbled. "Granted about the mountain. Joyce climbed laboriously — O-O-OK — but when he reached the top — top reached —"

"You can't stand this drinking, darling —" Her hands moved over the soft angle of his chin and rested there.

"He wouldn't say the world was *fla-at*. All along that's what they said. Besides the villagers could walk around — around with their jackasses and see that for themselves. With their asses."

"Hush," she said. "You've talked about that long enough. You get on one subject and go on and on ad infinitum. And don't land anywhere."

"A crater —" he breathed huskily. "And at least after the immensity of his climb he could have expected — some lovely leaps of Hell fire — some —"

Her hand clenched on his chin and shook it. "Shut up," she said. "I heard you when you improvised on that so brilliantly before Phillip left. You were obscene. And I'd almost forgotten."

A smile crept out across his face and his blue fringed eyes looked up at her. "Obscene —? Why should you put yourself in place of those symbols — sym —"

"If it were with anyone but Phillip that you talk like that I'd — I'd leave you."

"Immense va-cuity," he said, closing his eyes again. "Dead hollowness. Hollowness, I say. With maybe in the ashes at the bottom a —"

"Shut up."

"A squirming, fatbellied cretin."

It came to her that she must have drunk more than she realized, for the objects in the room seemed to take on a strange look of suffering. The butts of the cigarettes looked overmouthed and limp. The rug, almost brand new, seemed trampled and choked in design by the ashes. Even the last of the whiskey lay pale and quiet in the bottle. "Does it relieve you any?" she asked with slow calm. "I hope that times like this —"

She felt his body stiffen and, like an aggravating child, he interrupted her words with a sudden burst of unmelodic humming.

She eased her thighs from beneath his head and stood up. The room seemed to have grown smaller, messier, ranker with smoke and spilled whiskey. Bright lines of white weaved before her eyes. "Get up," she said dully. "I've got to pull out this darn couch and make it up."

He folded his hands on his stomach and lay solid, unstirring.

"You are detestable," she said, opening the door of the closet and taking down the sheets and blankets that lay folded on the shelves.

When she stood above him once more, waiting for him to rise, she felt a moment of pain for the drained pallor of his face. For the shades of darkness that had crept down halfway to his cheekbones, for the pulse that always fluttered in his neck when he was drunk or fatigued.

"Oh Marshall, it's bestial for us to get all shot like this. Even if you don't have to work tomorrow — there are years — fifty of them maybe — ahead." But the words had a false ring and she could only think of tomorrow.

He struggled to sit up on the edge of the couch and when he had reached that position his head dropped down to rest in his hands. "Yes, Pollyanna," he mumbled. "Yes, my dear croaking Pol — Pol. Twenty is a lovely lovely age Blessed God."

His fingers that weaved through his hair and closed into weak fists filled her with a sudden, sharp love. Roughly she snatched at the corners of the blanket and drew them around his shoulders. "Up now. We can't fool around like this all night."

"Hollowness —" he said wearily, without closing his sagging jaw.

"Has it made you sick?"

Holding the blanket close he pulled himself to his feet and lumbered toward the card table. "Can't a person even *think* without being called obscene or sick or drunk. No. No understanding of thought. Of deep deep thought in blackness. Of rich morasses. Morrasses. With their asses."

The sheet billowed down through the air and the round swirls collapsed into wrinkles. Quickly she tucked in the corners and smoothed the blankets on top. When she turned around she saw that he sat hunched over the chessmen — ponderously trying to balance a pawn on a turreted castle. The red checked blanket hung from his shoulders and trailed behind the chair.

She thought of something clever. "You look," she said, "like a brooding king in a bad-house." She sat on the couch that had become a bed and laughed.

With an angry gesture he embrangled his hands in the chessmen so that several pieces clattered to the floor. "That's right," he said. "Laugh your silly head off. That's the way it's always been done."

The laughs shook her body as though every fiber of her muscles had lost its resistance. When she had finished the room was very still.

After a moment he pushed the blanket away from him so that it crumpled in a heap behind the chair. "He's blind," he said softly. "Almost blind."

"Watch out, there's probably a draught — Who's blind?"

"Joyce," he said.

She felt weak after her laughter and the room stood out before her with painful smallness and clarity. "That's the trouble with you, Marshall," she said. "When you get like this you go on and on so that you wear a person out."

He looked at her sullenly. "I must say you're pretty when you're drunk," he said.

"I don't get drunk — couldn't if I wanted to," she said, feeling a pain beginning to bear down behind her eyes.

"How 'bout that night when we —"

"I've told you," she said stiffly between her teeth, "I wasn't drunk. I was ill. And you would make me go out and —"

"It's all the same," he interrupted. "You were a thing of beauty hanging on to that table. It's all the same. A sick woman — a drunk woman — ugh."

Nervelessly she watched his eyelids droop down until they had hidden all the goodness in his eyes.

"And a pregnant woman," he said. "Yeah. It'll be some sweet hour like this when you come to simper your sweet sneakret into my ear. Another cute little Marshall. Ain't we fine — look what we can do. Oh, God, what dreariness."

"I loathe you," she said, watching her hands (that were surely not a part of her?) begin to tremble. "This drunk brawling in the middle of the night —"

As he smiled his mouth seemed to her to take on the same pink, slitted look that his eyes had. "You love it," he whispered soberly. "What would you do if once a week I didn't get soused. So that — glutinously — you can paw over me. And Marshall darling this and Marshall that. So you can run your greedy little fingers all over my face — Oh yes. You love me best when I suffer. You — you —"

As he lurched across the room she thought she saw that his shoulders were shaking.

"Here Mama," he taunted. "Why don't you offer to come help me point." As he slammed the door to the bathroom some vacant coathangers that had been hung on the doorknob clashed at each other with tinny sibilance.

"I'm leaving you —" she called hollowly when the noise from the coathangers had died down. But the words had no meaning to her. Limp, she sat on the bed and looked at the wilted lettuce leaf across the room. The lampshade had been knocked atilt so that it clung dangerously to the bulb — so that it made a hurtful passage of brightness across the grey disordered room.

"Leaving you," she repeated to herself — still thinking about the late-at-night squalor around them.

She remembered the sound of Phillip's footsteps as he had descended. Nightlike and hollow. She thought of the dark outside and the cold naked trees of early spring. She wanted to picture herself leaving the apartment at that hour. With Phillip maybe. But as she tried to see his face, his small calm little body, the outlines were vague and there was no expression there. She could only recall the way his hands had poked at the sugar-grained bottom of a glass with the dishcloth — as they had done when he helped her with the dishes that night. And as she thought of following the empty sounds of the footsteps they grew softer, softer — until there was only black silence left.

With a shiver she got up from the couch and moved toward the whiskey bottle on the table. The parts of her body felt like tiresome appendages; only the pain behind her eyes seemed her own. She hesitated, holding the neck of the bottle. That — or one of the Alka-Seltzers in the top bureau drawer. But the thought of the pale tablet writhing to the top of the glass, consumed by its own effervescence — seemed sharply depressing. Besides, there was just enough for one more drink. Hastily she poured, noting again how the glittering convexity of the bottle always cheated her.

It made a sharp little path of warmness down into her stomach but the rest of her body remained chill. "Oh damn," she whispered — thinking of picking up that lettuce leaf in the morning, of the cold outside, listening for any sound from Marshall in the bathroom. "Oh damn. I can never get drunk like that."

And as she stared at the empty bottle she had one of those grotesque little imaginings that were apt to come to her at that hour. She saw herself and Marshall — in the whiskey bottle. Revolting in their smallness and perfection. Skeetering angrily up and down the cold blank glass like minute monkeys. For a moment with noses flattened and stares of longing. And then after their frenzies she saw them lying in the bottom — white and exhausted — looking like fleshy specimens in a laboratory. With nothing said between them.

She was sick with the sound of the bottle as it crashed through the orange peels and paper wads in the waste basket and clanked against the tin at the bottom.

"Ah —" said Marshall, opening the door and carefully placing his foot across the threshold. "Ah — the purest enjoyment left to man. At the last sweet point — pissing."

She leaned against the frame of the closet door — pressing her cheek against the cold angle of the wood. "See if you can get undressed."

"Ah —" he repeated, sitting down on the couch that she had made. His hands left his trouser flaps and began to fumble with his belt. "All but the belt — Can't sleep with a belt buckle. Like your knees. Bo-ony."

She thought that he would lose his balance trying to jerk out the belt all at once — (once before, she remembered, that had happened). Instead he slid the leather out slowly, strap by strap, and when he was through he placed it neatly under the bed. Then he looked up at her. The lines around his mouth were drawn down — making grey threads in the pallor of his face. His eyes looked widely up at her and for a moment she thought that he would cry. "Listen —" he said slowly, clearly.

She heard only the labored sound of his swallowing.

"Listen —" he repeated. And his white face sank into his hands.

Slowly, with a rhythm not of drunkenness, his body swayed from side to side. His blue sweatered shoulders were shaking. "Lord God," he said quietly. "How I — suffer."

She found the strength to drag herself from the doorway, to straighten the lampshade, and switch off the light. In the darkness an arc of blue rocked before her eyes — to the movement of his swaying body. And from the bed came the sound of his shoes being dropped to the floor, the creaking of the springs as he rolled over toward the wall.

She lay down in the darkness and pulled up the blankets — suddenly heavy and chill feeling to her fingers. As she covered his shoulders she noticed that the springs still sputtered beneath them, and that his body was quivering. "Marshall —" she whispered. "Are you cold?"

"Those chills. One of those damn chills."

Vaguely she thought of the missing top to the hot water bottle and the empty coffee sack in the kitchen. "Damn —" she repeated vacantly.

His knees urged close to hers in the darkness and she felt his body contract to a shivering little ball. Tiredly she reached out for his head and drew it to her. Her fingers soothed the little hollow at the top of his neck, crept up the stiff shaved part to the soft hair at the top, moved on to his temples where again she could feel the beating there.

"Listen —" he repeated, turning his head upward so that she could sense his breath on her throat.

"Yes Marshall."

His hands flexed into fists that beat tensely behind her shoulders. Then he lay so still that for a moment she felt a strange fear.

"It's this —" he said in a voice drained of all tone. "My love for you, darling. At times it seems that — in some instant like this — it will destroy me."

Then she felt his hands relax to cling weakly to her back, felt the chill that had been brooding in him all the evening make his body jerk with great shudders. "Yes," she breathed, pressing his hard skull to the hollow between her breasts. "Yes —" she said as soon as words and the creaking of the springs and the rank smell of smoke in the darkness had drawn back from the place where, for the moment, all things had receded.

Like That

Even if Sis is five years older than me and eighteen we used always to be closer and have more fun together than most sisters. It was about the same with us and our brother Dan, too. In the summer we'd all go swimming together. At nights in the wintertime maybe we'd sit around the fire in the living room and play three-handed bridge or Michigan, with everybody putting up a nickel or a dime to the winner. The three of us could have more fun by ourselves than any family I know. That's the way it always was before this.

Not that Sis was playing down to me, either. She's smart as she can be and has read more books than anybody I ever knew — even school teachers. But in High School she never did like to priss up flirty and ride around in cars with girls and pick up the boys and park at the drugstore and all that sort of thing. When she wasn't reading she'd just like to play around with me and Dan. She wasn't too grown up to fuss over a chocolate bar in the refrigerator or to stay awake most of Christmas Eve night either, say, with excitement. In some ways it was like I was heaps older than her. Even when Tuck started coming around last summer I'd sometimes have to tell her she shouldn't wear ankle socks because they might go down town or she ought to pluck out her eyebrows above her nose like the other girls do.

In one more year, next June, Tuck'll be graduated from college. He's a lanky boy with an eager look to his face. At college he's so smart he has a free scholarship. He started coming to see Sis the last summer before this one, riding in his family's car when he could get it, wearing crispy white linen suits. He came a lot last year but this summer he came even more often — before he left he was coming around for Sis every night. Tuck's O.K.

It began getting different between Sis and me a while back, I guess, although I didn't notice it at the time. It was only after a certain night this summer that I had the idea that things maybe were bound to end like they are now.

It was late when I woke up that night. When I opened my eyes I thought for a minute it must be about dawn and I was scared when I saw Sis wasn't on her side of the bed. But it was only the moonlight that shone cool looking and white outside the window and made the oak leaves hanging down over the front yard pitch black and separate seeming. It was around the first of September, but I didn't feel hot looking at the moonlight. I pulled the sheet over me and let my eyes roam around the black shapes of the furniture in our room.

I'd waked up lots of times in the night this summer. You see Sis and I have always had this room together and when she would come in and turn on the light to find her nightgown or something it woke me. I liked it. In the summer when school was out I didn't have to get up early in the morning. We would lie and talk sometimes for a good while. I'd like to hear about the places she and Tuck had been or to laugh over different things. Lots of times before that night she had talked to me privately about Tuck just like I was her age — asking me if I thought she should have said this or that when he called and giving me a hug, maybe, after. Sis was really crazy about Tuck. Once she said to me: "He's so lovely — I never in the world thought I'd know anyone like him — "

We would talk about our brother too. Dan's seventeen years old and was planning to take the co-op course at Tech in the fall. Dan had gotten older by this summer. One night he came in at four o'clock and he'd been drinking. Dad sure had it in for him the next week. So he hiked out to the country and camped with some boys for a few days. He used to talk to me and Sis about diesel motors and going away to South America and all that, but by this summer he was quiet and not saying much to anybody in the family. Dan's real tall and thin as a rail. He has bumps on his face now and is clumsy and not very good looking. At nights sometimes I know he wanders all around by himself, maybe going out beyond the city limits sign into the pine woods.

Thinking about such things I lay in bed wondering what time it was and when Sis would be in. That night after Sis and Dan had left I had gone down to the corner with some of the kids in the neighborhood to chunk rocks at the street light and try to kill a bat up there. At first I had the shivers and imagined it was a smallish bat like the kind in Dracula. When I saw it looked just like a moth I didn't care if they killed it or not. I was just sitting there on the curb drawing with a stick on the dusty street when Sis and Tuck rode by slowly in his car. She was sitting over very close to him. They weren't talking or smiling — just riding slowly down the street, sitting close, looking ahead. When they passed and I saw who it was I hollered to them. "Hey, Sis!" I yelled.

The car just went on slowly and nobody hollered back. I just stood there in the middle of the street feeling sort of silly with all the other kids standing around.

That hateful little old Bubber from down on the other block came up to me. "That your sister?" he asked.

I said yes.

"She sure was sitting up close to her beau," he said.

I was mad all over like I get sometimes. I hauled off and chunked all the rocks in my hand right at him. He's three years younger than me and it wasn't nice, but I couldn't stand him in the first place and he thought he was being so cute about Sis. He started holding his neck and bellering and I walked off and left them and went home and got ready to go to bed.

When I woke up I finally began to think of that too and old Bubber Davis was still in my mind when I heard the sound of a car coming up the block. Our room faces the street with only a short front yard between. You can see and hear everything from the sidewalk and the street. The car was creeping down in front of our walk and the light went slow and white along the walls of the room. It stopped on Sis's writing desk, showed up the books there plainly and half a pack of chewing gum. Then the room was dark and there was only the moonlight outside.

The door of the car didn't open but I could hear them talking.

Him, that is. His voice was low and I couldn't catch any words but it was like he was explaining something over and over again. I never heard Sis say a word.

I was still awake when I heard the car door open. I heard her say, "Don't come out." And then the door slammed and there was the sound of her heels clopping up the walk, fast and light like she was running.

Mama met Sis in the hall outside our room. She had heard the front door close. She always listens out for Sis and Dan and never goes to sleep when they're still out. I sometimes wonder how she can just lie there in the dark for hours without going to sleep.

"It's one-thirty, Marian," she said. "You ought to get in before this."

Sis didn't say anything.

"Did you have a nice time?"

That's the way Mama is. I could imagine her standing there with her nightgown blowing out fat around her and her dead white legs and the blue veins showing, looking all messed up. Mama's nicer when she's dressed to go out.

"Yes, we had a grand time," Sis said. Her voice was funny — sort of like a piano in the gym at school, high and sharp on your ear. Funny.

Mama was asking more questions. Where did they go? Did they see anybody they knew? All that sort of stuff. That's the way she is.

"Goodnight," said Sis in that out of tune voice.

She opened the door of our room real quick and closed it. I started to let her know I was awake but changed my mind. Her breathing was quick and loud in the dark and she did not move at all. After a few minutes she felt in the closet for her nightgown and got in the bed. I could hear her crying.

"Did you and Tuck have a fuss?" I asked.

"No," she answered. Then she seemed to change her mind. "Yeah, it was a fuss."

There's one thing that gives me the creeps sure enough — and that's to hear somebody cry. "I wouldn't let it bother me. You'll be making up tomorrow."

The moon was coming in the window and I could see her moving her jaw from one side to the other and staring up at the ceiling. I watched her for a long time. The moonlight was cool looking and there was a wettish wind coming cool from the window. I moved over like I sometimes do to snug up with her, thinking maybe that would stop her from moving her jaw like that and crying.

She was trembling all over. When I got close to her she jumped like I'd pinched her and pushed me over quick and kicked my legs over. "Don't," she said. "Don't."

Maybe Sis had suddenly gone batty, I was thinking. She was crying in a slower and sharper way. I was a little scared and I got up to go to the bathroom a minute. While I was in there I looked out the window, down toward the corner where the street light is. I saw something then that I knew Sis would want to know about.

"You know what?" I asked when I was back in the bed.

She was lying over close to the edge as she could get, stiff. She didn't answer.

"Tuck's car is parked down by the street light. Just drawn up to the curb. I could tell because of the box and the two tires on the back. I could see it from the bathroom window."

She didn't even move.

"He must be just sitting out there. What ails you and him?"

She didn't say anything at all.

"I couldn't see him but he's probably just sitting there in the car under the street light. Just sitting there."

It was like she didn't care or had known it all along. She was as far over the edge of the bed as she could get, her legs stretched out stiff and her hands holding tight to the edge and her face on one arm.

She used always to sleep all sprawled over on my side so I'd have to push at her when it was hot and sometimes turn on the light and draw the line down the middle and show her how she really was on my side. I wouldn't have to draw any line that night, I was thinking. I felt bad. I looked out at the moonlight a long time before I could get to sleep again.

The next day was Sunday and Mama and Dad went in the morning to church because it was the anniversary of the day my aunt died. Sis said she didn't feel well and stayed in bed. Dan was out and I was there by myself so naturally I went into our room where Sis was. Her face was white as the pillow and there were circles under her eyes. There was a muscle jumping on one side of her jaw like she was chewing. She hadn't combed her hair and it flopped over the pillow, glinty red and messy and pretty. She was reading with a book held up close to her face. Her eyes didn't move when I came in. I don't think they even moved across the page.

It was roasting hot that morning. The sun made everything blazing outside so that it hurt your eyes to look. Our room was so hot that you could almost touch the air with your finger. But Sis had the sheet pulled up clear to her shoulders.

"Is Tuck coming today?" I asked. I was trying to say something that would make her look more cheerful.

"Gosh! Can't a person have *any* peace in this house?"

She never did used to say mean things like that out of a clear sky. Mean things, maybe, but not grouchy ones.

"Sure," I said. "Nobody's going to notice you."

I sat down and pretended to read. When footsteps passed on the street Sis would hold onto the book tighter and I knew she was listening hard as she could. I can tell between footsteps easy. I can even tell without looking if the person who passes is colored or not. Colored people mostly make a slurry sound between the steps. When the steps would pass Sis would loosen the hold on the book and bite at her mouth. It was the same way with passing cars.

I felt sorry for Sis. I decided then and there that I never would let any fuss with any boy make me feel or look like that. But I wanted Sis and me to get back like we'd always been. Sunday mornings are bad enough without having any other trouble.

"We fuss lots less than most sisters do," I said. "And when we do it's all over quick, isn't it?"

She mumbled and kept staring at the same spot on the book.

"That's one good thing," I said.

She was moving her head slightly from side to side — over and over again, with her face not changing. "We never do have any real long fusses like Bubber Davis's two sisters have —"

"No." She answered like she wasn't thinking about what I'd said.

"Not one real one like that since I can remember."

In a minute she looked up the first time. "I remember one," she said suddenly.

"When?"

Her eyes looked green in the blackness under them and like they were nailing themselves into what they saw. "You had to stay in every afternoon for a week. It was a long time ago."

All of a sudden I remembered. I'd forgotten it for a long time. I hadn't wanted to remember. When she said that it came back to me all complete.

It was really a long time ago — when Sis was about thirteen. If I remember right I was mean and even more hardboiled than I am now. My aunt who I'd liked better than all my other aunts put together had had a dead baby and she had died. After the funeral Mama had told Sis and me about it. Always the things I've learned new and didn't like have made me mad — mad clean through and scared.

That wasn't what Sis was talking about, though. It was a few mornings after that when Sis started with what every big girl has each month, and of course I found out and was scared to death. Mama then explained to me about it and what she had to wear. I felt then like I'd felt about my aunt, only ten times worse. I felt different toward Sis, too, and was so mad I wanted to pitch into people and hit.

I never will forget it. Sis was standing in our room before the dresser mirror. When I remembered her face it was white like Sis's there on the pillow and with the circles under her eyes and the glinty hair to her shoulders — it was only younger.

I was sitting on the bed, biting hard at my knee. "It shows," I said. "It does too!"

She had on a sweater and a blue pleated skirt and she was so skinny all over that it did show a little.

"Anybody can tell. Right off the bat. Just to look at you anybody can tell."

Her face was white in the mirror and did not move.

"It looks terrible. I wouldn't ever ever be like that. It shows and everything."

She started crying then and told Mother and said she wasn't going back to school and such. She cried a long time. That's how ugly and hardboiled I used to be and am still sometimes. That's why I had to stay in the house every afternoon for a week a long time ago . . .

Tuck came by in his car that Sunday morning before dinner time. Sis got up and dressed in a hurry and didn't even put on any lipstick.

She said they were going out to dinner. Nearly every Sunday all of us in the family stay together all day, so that was a little funny. They didn't get home until almost dark. The rest of us were sitting on the front porch drinking ice tea because of the heat when the car drove up again. After they got out of the car Dad, who had been in a very good mood all day, insisted Tuck stay for a glass of tea.

Tuck sat on the swing with Sis and he didn't lean back and his heels didn't rest on the floor — as though he was all ready to get up again. He kept changing the glass from one hand to the other and starting new conversations. He and Sis didn't look at each other except on the sly, and then it wasn't at all like they were crazy about each other. It was a funny look. Almost like they were afraid of something. Tuck left soon.

"Come sit by your Dad a minute, Puss," Dad said. Puss is a nickname he calls Sis when he feels in a specially good mood. He still likes to pet us.

She went and sat on the arm of his chair. She sat stiff like Tuck had, holding herself off a little so Dad's arm hardly went around her waist. Dad smoked his cigar and looked out on the front yard and the trees that were beginning to melt into the early dark.

"How's my big girl getting along these days?" Dad still likes to hug us up when he feels good and treat us, even Sis, like kids.

"O.K.," she said. She twisted a little bit like she wanted to get up and didn't know how to without hurting his feelings.

"You and Tuck have had a nice time together this summer, haven't you, Puss?"

"Yeah," she said. She had begun to see-saw her lower jaw again. I wanted to say something but couldn't think of anything.

Dad said: "He ought to be getting back to Tech about now, oughtn't he? When's he leaving?"

"Less than a week," she said. She got up so quick that she knocked Dad's cigar out of his fingers. She didn't even pick it up but flounced on through the front door. I could hear her half running to our room and the sound the door made when she shut it. I knew she was going to cry.

It was hotter than ever. The lawn was beginning to grow dark and the locusts were droning out so shrill and steady that you wouldn't notice them unless you thought to. The sky was bluish grey and the trees in the vacant lot across the street were dark. I kept on sitting on the front porch with Mama and Papa and hearing their low talk without listening to the words. I wanted to go in our room with Sis but I was afraid to. I wanted to ask her what was really the matter. Was hers and Tuck's fuss so bad as that or was it that she was so crazy about him that she was sad because he was leaving? For a minute I didn't think it was either one of those things. I wanted to know but I was scared to ask. I just sat there with the grown people. I never have been so lonesome as I was that night. If ever I think about being sad I just remember how it was then — sitting there looking at the long bluish shadows across the lawn and feeling like I was the only child left in the family and that Sis and Dan were dead or gone for good.

It's October now and the sun shines bright and a little cool and the sky is the color of my turquoise ring. Dan's gone to Tech. So has Tuck gone. It's not at all like it was last fall, though. I come in from High School (I go there now) and Sis maybe is just sitting by the window reading or writing to Tuck or just looking out. Sis is thinner and sometimes to me she looks in the face like a grown person. Or like, in a way, something has suddenly hurt her hard. We don't do any of the things we used to. It's good weather for fudge or for doing so many things. But no she just sits around or goes for long walks in the chilly late afternoon by herself. Sometimes she'll smile in a way that really gripes — like I was such a kid and all. Sometimes I want to cry or to hit her.

But I'm hardboiled as the next person. I can get along by myself if Sis or anybody else wants to. I'm glad I'm thirteen and still wear socks and can do what I please. I don't want to be any older if I'd get like Sis has. But I wouldn't. I wouldn't like any boy in the world as much as she does Tuck. I'd never let any boy or any thing make me act like she does. I'm not going to waste my time and try to make Sis be like she used to be. I get lonesome — sure — but I don't care. I know there's no way I can make myself stay thirteen all my life, but I know I'd never let anything really change me at all — no matter what it is.

I skate and ride my bike and go to the school football games every Friday. But when one afternoon the kids all got quiet in the gym basement and then started telling certain things — about being married and all — I got up quick so I wouldn't hear and went up and played basketball. And when some of the kids said they were going to start wearing lipstick and stockings I said I wouldn't for a hundred dollars.

You see I'd never be like Sis is now. I wouldn't. Anybody could know that if they knew me. I just wouldn't, that's all. I don't want to grow up — if it's like that.

Wunderkind

She came into the living room, her music satchel plopping against her winter-stockinged legs and her other arm weighted down with schoolbooks, and stood for a moment listening to the sounds from the studio. A soft procession of piano chords and the tuning of a violin. Then Mister Bilderbach called out to her in his chunky, guttural tones:

"That you, Bienchen?"

As she jerked off her mittens she saw that her fingers were twitching to the motions of the fugue she had practiced that morning. "Yes," she answered. "It's me."

"I," the voice corrected. "Just a moment."

She could hear Mister Lafkowitz talking — his words spun out in a silky, unintelligible hum. A voice almost like a woman's, she thought, compared to Mister Bilderbach's. Restlessness scattered her attention. She fumbled with her geometry book and *Le Voyage de Monsieur Perrichon* before putting them on the table. She sat down on the sofa and began to take her music from the satchel. Again she saw her hands — the quivering tendons that stretched down from her knuckles, the sore finger tip cupped with curled, dingy tape. The sight sharpened the fear that had begun to torment her for the past few months.

Noiselessly she mumbled a few phrases of encouragement to herself. A good lesson — a good lesson — like it used to be — Her lips closed as she heard the stolid sound of Mister Bilderbach's footsteps across the floor of the studio and the creaking of the door as it slid open.

For a moment she had the peculiar feeling that during most of the fifteen years of her life she had been looking at the face and shoulders that jutted from behind the door, in a silence disturbed only by the muted, blank plucking of a violin string. Mister Bilderbach. Her teacher, Mister Bilderbach. The quick eyes behind the horn-rimmed glasses; the light, thin hair and the narrow face beneath; the lips full and loose shut and the lower one pink and shining from the bites of his teeth; the forked veins in his temples throbbing plainly enough to be observed across the room.

"Aren't you a little early?" he asked, glancing at the clock on the mantelpiece that had pointed to five minutes of twelve for a month. "Josef's in here. We're running over a little sonatina by someone he knows."

"Good," she said, trying to smile. "I'll listen." She could see her fingers sinking powerless into a blur of piano keys. She felt tired — felt that if he looked at her much longer her hands might tremble.

He stood uncertain, halfway in the room. Sharply his teeth pushed down on his bright, swollen lip. "Hungry, Bienchen?" he asked. "There's some apple cake Anna made, and milk."

"I'll wait till afterward," she said. "Thanks."

"After you finish with a very fine lesson — eh?" His smile seemed to crumble at the corners.

There was a sound from behind him in the studio and Mister Lafkowitz pushed at the other panel of the door and stood beside him.

"Frances?" he said, smiling. "And how is the work coming now?"

Without meaning to, Mister Lafkowitz always made her feel clumsy and overgrown. He was such a small man himself, with a weary look when he was not holding his violin. His eyebrows curved high above his sallow, Jewish face as though asking a question, but the lids of his eyes drowsed languorous and indifferent. Today he seemed distracted. She watched him come into the room for no apparent purpose, holding his pearl-tipped bow in his still fingers, slowly gliding the white horsehair through a chalky piece of rosin. His eyes were sharp bright slits today and the linen handkerchief that flowed down from his collar darkened the shadows beneath them.

"I gather you're doing a lot now," smiled Mister Lafkowitz, although she had not yet answered the question.

She looked at Mister Bilderbach. He turned away. His heavy shoulders pushed the door open wide so that the late afternoon sun came through the window of the studio and shafted yellow over the dusty living room. Behind her teacher she could see the squat long piano, the window, and the bust of Brahms.

"No," she said to Mister Lafkowitz, "I'm doing terribly." Her thin fingers flipped at the pages of her music. "I don't know what's the matter," she said, looking at Mister Bilderbach's stooped muscular back that stood tense and listening.

Mister Lafkowitz smiled. "There are times, I suppose, when one —"

A harsh chord sounded from the piano. "Don't you think we'd better get on with this?" asked Mister Bilderbach.

"Immediately," said Mister Lafkowitz, giving the bow one more scrape before starting toward the door. She could see him pick up his violin from the top of the piano. He caught her eye and lowered the instrument. "You've seen the picture of Heime?"

Her fingers curled tight over the sharp corner of the satchel. "What picture?"

"One of Heime in the *Musical Courier* there on the table. Inside the top cover."

The sonatina began. Discordant yet somehow simple. Empty but with a sharp-cut style of its own. She reached for the magazine and opened it.

There Heime was — in the left-hand corner. Holding his violin with his fingers hooked down over the strings for a pizzicato. With his dark serge knickers strapped neatly beneath his knees, a sweater and rolled collar. It was a bad picture. Although it was snapped in profile his eyes were cut around toward the photographer and his finger looked as though it would pluck the wrong string. He seemed suffering to turn around toward the picture-taking apparatus. He was thinner — his stomach did not poke out now — but he hadn't changed much in six months.

Heime Israelsky, talented young violinist, snapped while at work in his teacher's studio on Riverside Drive. Young Master Israelsky, who will soon celebrate his fifteenth birthday, has been invited to play the Beethoven Concerto with —

That morning, after she had practiced from six until eight, her dad had made her sit down at the table with the family for breakfast. She hated breakfast; it gave her a sick feeling afterward. She would rather wait and get four chocolate bars with her twenty cents lunch money and munch them during school — bringing up little morsels from her pocket under cover of her handkerchief, stopping dead when the silver paper rattled. But this morning her dad had put a fried egg on her plate and she had known that if it burst — so that the slimy yellow oozed over the white — she would cry. And that had happened. The same feeling was upon her now. Gingerly she laid the magazine back on the table and closed her eyes.

The music in the studio seemed to be urging violently and clumsily for something that was not to be had. After a moment her thoughts drew back from Heime and the concerto and the picture — and hovered around the lesson once more. She slid over on the sofa until she could see plainly into the studio — the two of them playing, peering at the notations on the piano, lustfully drawing out all that was there.

She could not forget the memory of Mister Bilderbach's face as he had stared at her a moment ago. Her hands, still twitching unconsciously to the motions of the fugue, closed over her bony knees. Tired, she was. And with a circling, sinking away feeling like the one that often came to her just before she dropped off to sleep on the nights when she had over-practiced. Like those weary half-dreams that buzzed and carried her out into their own whirling space.

A *Wunderkind* — a *Wunderkind* — a *Wunderkind*. The syllables would come out rolling in the deep German way, roar against her ears and then fall to a murmur. Along with the faces circling, swelling out in distortion, diminishing to pale blobs — Mister Bilderbach, Mrs. Bilderbach, Heime, Mister Lafkowitz. Around and around in a circle revolving to the guttural *Wunderkind*. Mister Bilderbach looming large in the middle of the circle, his face urging — with the others around him.

Phrases of music seesawing crazily. Notes she had been practicing falling over each other like a handful of marbles dropped downstairs. Bach, Debussy, Prokofieff, Brahms — timed grotesquely to the far off throb of her tired body and the buzzing circle.

Sometimes — when she had not worked more than three hours or had stayed out from high school — the dreams were not so confused. The music soared clearly in her mind and quick, precise little memories would come back — clear as the sissy "Age of Innocence" picture Heime had given her after their joint concert was over.

A *Wunderkind* — a *Wunderkind*. That was what Mister Bilderbach had called her when, at twelve, she first came to him. Older pupils had repeated the word.

Not that he had ever said the word to her. "Bienchen —" (She had a plain American name but he never used it except when her mistakes were enormous.) "Bienchen," he would say, "I know it must be terrible. Carrying around all the time a head that thick. Poor Bienchen —"

Mister Bilderbach's father had been a Dutch violinist. His mother was from Prague. He had been born in this country and had spent his youth in Germany. So many times she wished she had not been born and brought up in just Cincinnati. How do you say *cheese* in German? Mister Bilderbach, what is Dutch for *I don't understand you?*

The first day she came to the studio. After she played the whole Second Hungarian Rhapsody from memory. The room graying with twilight. His face as he leaned over the piano.

"Now we begin all over," he said that first day. "It — playing music — is more than cleverness. If a twelve-year-old girl's fingers cover so many keys to a second — that means nothing."

He tapped his broad chest and his forehead with his stubby hand. "Here and here. You are old enough to understand that." He lighted a cigarette and gently blew the first exhalation above her head. "And work — work — work —. We will start now with these Bach Inventions and these little Schumann pieces." His hands moved again — this time to jerk the cord of the lamp behind her and point to the music. "I will show you how I wish this practiced. Listen carefully now."

She had been at the piano for almost three hours and was very tired. His deep voice sounded as though it had been straying inside her for a long time. She wanted to reach out and touch his muscle-flexed finger that pointed out the phrases, wanted to feel the gleaming gold band ring and the strong hairy back of his hand.

She had lessons Tuesday after school and on Saturday afternoons. Often she stayed, when the Saturday lesson was finished, for dinner, and then spent the night and took the streetcar home the next morning. Mrs. Bilderbach liked her in her calm, almost dumb way. She was much different from her husband. She was quiet and fat and slow. When she wasn't in the kitchen, cooking the rich dishes that both of them loved, she seemed to spend all her time in their bed upstairs, reading magazines or just looking with a half-smile at nothing. When they had married in Germany she had been a *lieder* singer. She didn't sing any more (she said it was her throat). When he would call her in from the kitchen to listen to a pupil she would always smile and say that it was *gut,* very *gut.*

When Frances was thirteen it came to her one day that the Bilderbachs had no children. It seemed strange. Once she had been back in the kitchen with Mrs. Bilderbach when he had come striding in from the studio, tense with anger at some pupil who had annoyed him. His wife stood stirring the thick soup until his hand groped out and rested on her shoulder. Then she turned — stood placid — while he folded his arms about her and buried his sharp face in the white, nerveless flesh of her neck. They stood that way without moving. And then his face jerked back suddenly, the anger diminished to a quiet inexpressiveness, and he had returned to the studio.

After she had started with Mister Bilderbach and didn't have time to see anything of the people at high school, Heime had been the only friend of her own age. He was Mister Lafkowitz's pupil and would come with him to Mister Bilderbach's on evenings when she would be there. They would listen to their teachers' playing. And often they themselves went over chamber music together — Mozart sonatas or Bloch.

A *Wunderkind* — a *Wunderkind.*

Heime was a *Wunderkind.* He and she, then.

Heime had been playing the violin since he was four. He didn't have to go to school; Mister Lafkowitz's brother, who was crippled, used to teach him geometry and European history and French verbs in the afternoon. When he was thirteen he had as fine a technique as any violinist in Cincinnati — everyone said so. But playing the violin must be easier than the piano. She knew it must be.

Heime always seemed to smell of corduroy pants and the food he had eaten and rosin. Half the time, too, his hands were dirty around the knuckles and the cuffs of his shirts peeped out dingily from the sleeves of his sweater. She always watched his hands when he played — thin only at the joints with the hard little blobs of flesh bulging over the short-cut nails and the babyish-looking crease that showed so plainly in his bowing wrist.

In the dreams, as when she was awake, she could remember the concert only in a blur. She had not known it was unsuccessful for her until months after. True, the papers had praised Heime more than her. But he was much shorter than she. When they stood together on the stage he came only to her shoulders. And that made a difference with people, she knew. Also, there was the matter of the sonata they played together. The Bloch.

"No, no — I don't think that would be appropriate," Mister Bilderbach had said when the Bloch was suggested to end the programme. "Now that John Powell thing — the Sonate Virginianesque."

She hadn't understood then; she wanted it to be the Bloch as much as Mister Lafkowitz and Heime.

Mister Bilderbach had given in. Later, after the reviews had said she lacked the temperament for that type of music, after they called her playing thin and lacking in feeling, she felt cheated.

"That oie oie stuff," said Mister Bilderbach, crackling the newspapers at her. "Not for you, Bienchen. Leave all that to the Heimes and vitses and skys."

A *Wunderkind*. No matter what the papers said, that was what he had called her.

Why was it Heime had done so much better at the concert than she? At school sometimes, when she was supposed to be watching someone do a geometry problem on the blackboard, the question would twist knife-like inside her. She would worry about it in bed, and even sometimes when she was supposed to be concentrating at the piano. It wasn't just the Bloch and her not being Jewish — not entirely. It wasn't that Heime didn't have to go to school and had begun his training so early, either. It was —?

Once she thought she knew.

"Play the Fantasia and Fugue," Mister Bilderbach had demanded one evening a year ago — after he and Mister Lafkowitz had finished reading some music together.

The Bach, as she played, seemed to her well done. From the tail of her eye she could see the calm, pleased expression on Mister Bilderbach's face, see his hands rise climactically from the chair arms and then sink down loose and satisfied when the high points of the phrases had been passed successfully. She stood up from the piano when it was over, swallowing to loosen the bands that the music seemed to have drawn around her throat and chest. But —

"Frances —" Mister Lafkowitz had said then, suddenly, looking at her with his thin mouth curved and his eyes almost covered by their delicate lids. "Do you know how many children Bach had?"

She turned to him, puzzled. "A good many. Twenty some odd."

"Well then —" The corners of his smile etched themselves gently in his pale face. "He could not have been so cold — then."

Mister Bilderbach was not pleased; his guttural effulgence of German words had *Kind* in it somewhere. Mister Lafkowitz raised his eyebrows. She had caught the point easily enough, but she felt no deception in keeping her face blank and immature because that was the way Mister Bilderbach wanted her to look.

Yet such things had nothing to do with it. Nothing very much, at least, for she would grow older. Mister Bilderbach understood that, and even Mister Lafkowitz had not meant just what he said.

In the dreams Mister Bilderbach's face loomed out and contracted in the center of the whirling circle. The lip surging softly, the veins in his temples insisting.

But sometimes, before she slept, there were such clear memories; as when she pulled a hole in the heel of her stocking down, so that her shoe would hide it. "Bienchen, Bienchen!" And bringing Mrs. Bilderbach's work basket in and showing her how it should be darned and not gathered together in a lumpy heap.

And the time she graduated from Junior High.

"What you wear?" asked Mrs. Bilderbach the Sunday morning at breakfast when she told them about how they had practiced to march into the auditorium.

"An evening dress my cousin had last year."

"Ah — Bienchen!" he said, circling his warm coffee cup with his heavy hands, looking up at her with wrinkles around his laughing eyes. "I bet I know what Bienchen wants —"

He insisted. He would not believe her when she explained that she honestly didn't care at all.

"Like this, Anna," he said, pushing his napkin across the table and mincing to the other side of the room, swishing his hips, rolling up his eyes behind his horn-rimmed glasses.

The next Saturday afternoon, after her lessons, he took her to the department stores downtown. His thick fingers smoothed over the filmy nets and crackling taffetas that the saleswomen unwound from their bolts. He held colors to her face, cocking his head to one side, and selected pink. Shoes, he remembered too. He liked best some white kid pumps. They seemed a little like old ladies' shoes to her and the Red Cross label in the instep had a charity look. But it really didn't matter at all. When Mrs. Bilderbach began to cut out the dress and fit it to her with pins, he interrupted his lessons to stand by and suggest ruffles around the hips and neck and a fancy rosette on the shoulder. The music was coming along nicely then. Dresses and commencement and such made no difference.

Nothing mattered much except playing the music as it must be played, bringing out the thing that must be in her, practicing, practicing, playing so that Mister Bilderbach's face lost some of its urging look. Putting the thing into her music that Myra Hess had, and Yehudi Menuhin — even Heime!

What had begun to happen to her four months ago? The notes began springing out with a glib, dead intonation. Adolescence, she thought. Some kids played with promise — and worked and worked until, like her, the least little thing would start them crying, and worn out with trying to get the thing across — the longing thing they felt — something queer began to happen — But not she! She was like Heime. She had to be. She —

Once it was there for sure. And you didn't lose things like that. A *Wunderkind*. . . . A *Wunderkind*. . . . Of her he said it, rolling the words in the sure, deep German way. And in the dreams even deeper, more certain than ever. With his face looming out at her, and the longing phrases of music mixed in with the zooming, circling round, round, round — A *Wunderkind*. A *Wunderkind*. . . .

This afternoon Mister Bilderbach did not show Mister Lafkowitz to the front door, as he usually did. He stayed at the piano, softly pressing a solitary note. Listening, Frances watched the violinist wind his scarf about his pale throat.

"A good picture of Heime," she said, picking up her music. "I got a letter from him a couple of months ago — telling about hearing Schnabel and Huberman and about Carnegie Hall and things to eat at the Russian Tea Room."

To put off going into the studio a moment longer she waited until Mister Lafkowitz was ready to leave and then stood behind him as he opened the door. The frosty cold outside cut into the room. It was growing late and the air was seeped with the pale yellow of winter twilight. When the door swung to on its hinges, the house seemed darker and more silent than ever before she had known it to be.

As she went into the studio Mister Bilderbach got up from the piano and silently watched her settle herself at the keyboard.

"Well, Bienchen," he said, "this afternoon we are going to begin all over. Start from scratch. Forget the last few months."

He looked as though he were trying to act a part in a movie. His solid body swayed from toe to heel, he rubbed his hands together, and even smiled in a satisfied, movie way. Then suddenly he thrust this manner brusquely aside. His heavy shoulders slouched and he began to run through the stack of music she had brought in. "The Bach — no, not yet," he murmured. "The Beethoven? Yes. The Variation Sonata. Opus 26."

The keys of the piano hemmed her in — stiff and white and dead-seeming.

"Wait a minute," he said. He stood in the curve of the piano, elbows propped, and looked at her. "Today I expect something from you. Now this sonata — it's the first Beethoven sonata you ever worked on. Every note is under control — technically — you have nothing to cope with but the music. Only music now. That's all you think about."

He rustled through the pages of her volume until he found the place. Then he pulled his teaching chair halfway across the room, turned it around and seated himself, straddling the back with his legs.

For some reason, she knew, this position of his usually had a good effect on her performance. But today she felt that she would notice him from the corner of her eye and be disturbed. His back was stiffly tilted, his legs looked tense. The heavy volume before him seemed to balance dangerously on the chair back. "Now we begin," he said with a peremptory dart of his eyes in her direction.

Her hands rounded over the keys and then sank down. The first notes were too loud, the other phrases followed dryly.

Arrestingly his hand rose up from the score. "Wait! Think a minute what you're playing. How is this beginning marked?"

"*An-andante.*"

"All right. Don't drag it into an *adagio* then. And play deeply into the keys. Don't snatch it off shallowly that way. A graceful, deep-toned *andante* —"

She tried again. Her hands seemed separate from the music that was in her.

"Listen," he interrupted. "Which of these variations dominates the whole?"

"The dirge," she answered.

"Then prepare for that. This is an *andante* — but it's not salon stuff as you just played it. Start out softly, *piano,* and make it swell out just before the arpeggio. Make it warm and dramatic. And down here — where it's marked *dolce* make the counter melody sing out. You know all that. We've gone over all that side of it before. Now play it. Feel it as Beethoven wrote it down. Feel that tragedy and restraint."

She could not stop looking at his hands. They seemed to rest tentatively on the music, ready to fly up as a stop signal as soon as she would begin, the gleaming flash of his ring calling her to halt. "Mister Bilderbach — maybe if I — if you let me play on through the first variation without stopping I could do better."

"I won't interrupt," he said.

Her pale face leaned over too close to the keys. She played through the first part, and, obeying a nod from him, began the second. There were no flaws that jarred on her, but the phrases shaped from her fingers before she had put into them the meaning that she felt.

When she had finished he looked up from the music and began to speak with dull bluntness: "I hardly heard those harmonic fillings in the right hand. And incidentally, this part was supposed to take on intensity, develop the foreshadowings that were supposed to be inherent in the first part. Go on with the next one, though."

She wanted to start it with subdued viciousness and progress to a feeling of deep, swollen sorrow. Her mind told her that. But her hands seemed to gum in the keys like limp macaroni and she could not imagine the music as it should be.

When the last note had stopped vibrating, he closed the book and deliberately got up from the chair. He was moving his lower jaw from side to side — and between his open lips she could glimpse the pink healthy lane to his throat and his strong, smoke-yellowed teeth. He laid the Beethoven gingerly on top of the rest of her music and propped his elbows on the smooth, black piano top once more. "No," he said simply, looking at her.

Her mouth began to quiver. "I can't help it. I —"

Suddenly he strained his lips into a smile. "Listen, Bienchen," he began in a new, forced voice. "You still play the Harmonious Blacksmith, don't you? I told you not to drop it from your repertoire."

"Yes," she said. "I practice it now and then."

His voice was the one he used for children. "It was among the first things we worked on together — remember. So strongly you used to play it — like a real blacksmith's daughter. You see, Bienchen, I know you so well — as if you were my own girl. I know what you have — I've heard you play so many things beautifully. You used to —"

He stopped in confusion and inhaled from his pulpy stub of cigarette. The smoke drowsed out from his pink lips and clung in a gray mist around the lank hair and childish forehead.

"Make it happy and simple," he said, switching on the lamp behind her and stepping back from the piano.

For a moment he stood just inside the bright circle the light made. Then impulsively he squatted down to the floor. "Vigorous," he said.

She could not stop looking at him, sitting on one heel with the other foot resting squarely before him for balance, the muscles of his strong thighs straining under the cloth of his trousers, his back straight, his elbows staunchly propped on his knees. "Simply now," he repeated with a gesture of his fleshy hands. "Think of the blacksmith — working out in the sunshine all day. Working easily and undisturbed."

She could not look down at the piano. The light brightened the hairs on the backs of his outspread hands, made the lenses of his glasses glitter.

"All of it," he urged. "Now!"

She felt that the marrows of her bones were hollow and there was no blood left in her. Her heart that had been springing against her chest all afternoon felt suddenly dead. She saw it gray and limp and shriveled at the edges like an oyster.

His face seemed to throb out in space before her, come closer with the lurching motion in the veins of his temples. In retreat, she looked down at the piano. Her lips shook like jelly and a surge of noiseless tears made the white keys blur in a watery line. "I can't," she whispered. "I don't know why, but I just can't — can't any more."

His tense body slackened and, holding his hand to his side, he pulled himself up. She clutched her music and hurried past him.

Her coat. The mittens and galoshes. The schoolbooks and the satchel he had given her on her birthday. All from the silent room that was hers. Quickly — before he would have to speak.

As she passed through the vestibule she could not help but see his hands — held out from his body that leaned against the studio door, relaxed and purposeless. The door shut to firmly. Dragging her books and satchel she stumbled down the stone steps, turned in the wrong direction, and hurried down the street that had become confused with noise and bicycles and the games of other children.

The Aliens

In August of the year 1935 a Jew sat alone on one of the rear seats of a bus headed south. It was late afternoon and the Jew had been travelling since five o'clock in the morning. That is to say he had left New York at daybreak and except for a number of necessary brief stops he had been waiting patiently on his rear seat for the time when he would reach his destination. Behind him was the great city — that marvel of immensity and intricate design. And the Jew, who had set out at such an early hour on this journey, carried in him a last memory of a city strangely hollow and unreal. As the sun was rising he had walked alone in the unpeopled streets. As far ahead as he could see there were the skyscrapers, pastel mauve and yellow in color, clear and sharp as stalactites against the sky. He had listened to the sound of his own quiet footsteps and for the first time in that city he had heard on the streets the clear articulation of a single human voice. But even then there was the feeling of the multitude, some subtle warning of the raucous fury of the hours soon to come, the turmoil, the constant struggles around closing subway doors, the vast roaring of the city day. Such then was his last impression of the place he had left behind him. And now before him was the South.

The Jew, a man of about fifty years of age, was a patient traveller. He was of middle height and only slightly under average weight. As the afternoon was hot he had removed his black coat and hung it carefully on the back of his seat. He wore a blue striped shirt and gray checked trousers. And of these rather threadbare trousers he was careful to the point of anxiousness, lifting the cloth at the knee each time he crossed his legs, flicking with his handkerchief the dust that seeped in the open window. Although there was no passenger beside him he kept himself well within the limits of his portion of the seat. On the rack above him there was a cardboard lunch box and a dictionary.

The Jew was an observant person — and already with some care he had scanned each fellow passenger. Especially he had noticed the two Negroes who, although they had boarded the bus at widely separate points, had been talking and laughing together on the back seat all the afternoon. Also he watched with interest the passing landscape. He had a quiet face — this Jew — with a high, white forehead, dark eyes behind horn rimmed spectacles, and a rather strained, pale mouth. And for a patient traveller, a man of such composure, he had one annoying habit. He smoked constantly and as he smoked he quietly worried the end of his cigarette with his thumb and forefinger, rubbing and pulling out shreds of tobacco so that often the cigarette was so ragged that he was obliged to nip off the end before putting it to his lips again. His hands were slightly calloused at the fingertips and developed to a state of delicate muscular perfection; they were a pianist's hands.

At seven o'clock the long summer twilight had just begun. After a day of glare and heat the sky was now tempered to a restful greenish blue. The bus wound along a dusty unpaved road, flanked by deep fields of cotton. It was here that a halt was made to pick up a new passenger — a young man carrying a brand new cheap tin suitcase. After a moment of awkward hesitation the young man sat down beside the Jew.

"Good evenin', sir."

The Jew smiled — for the young man had a sunburned pleasant face — and replied to this greeting in a voice that was soft and slightly accented. For a while these were the only words that were said between them. The Jew looked out of the window and the young man watched him shyly from the corner of his eye. Then the Jew took down his lunch box from the rack above his head and prepared to eat his evening meal. In the box there was a sandwich made with rye bread and two lemon tarts. "Will you have some?" he asked politely.

The young man blushed. "Why, much obliged. You see, when I come in I had to wash and I didn't get a chance to eat my supper." His sunburned hand hovered hesitantly over the two tarts until he chose the one that was stickier and a little crushed around the edges. He had a warm musical voice — with the vowels long drawn and the final consonants unsounded.

They ate in silence with the slow enjoyment of those who know the worth of food. Then when his tart was finished the Jew moistened his fingertips with his mouth and wiped them with his handkerchief. The young man watched and gravely copied him. Dark was coming. Already the pine trees in the distance were blurred and there were flickering lights in the lonely little houses set back in the fields along the way. The Jew had been looking intently out the window and at last he turned to the young man and asked with a nod of his head toward the fields outside: "What is that?"

The young man strained his eyes and saw above the trees in the distance the outline of a smokestack. "Can't tell from here," he said. "It might be a gin or even a sawmill."

"I mean out there all around — growing."

The young man was puzzled. "I can't see what it is you're talkin' about."

"The plants with the white flowers."

"Why man!" said the southerner slowly. "That's *cotton.*"

"Cotton," repeated the Jew. "Of course. I should have known."

There was a long pause in which the young man looked at the Jew with anxiety and fascination. Several times he wet his lips as though about to speak. After some deliberation he smiled genially to the Jew and nodded his head with elaborate reassurance. And then (God knows from what experience in what small-town Greek café) he leaned over so that his face was only a few inches from the Jew's and said with a labored accent: *"You Greek fallow?"*

The Jew, bewildered, shook his head.

But the young man nodded and smiled even more insistently. He repeated his question in a very loud voice. "I say *you Greek fallow?"*

The Jew drew back into his corner. "I can hear O.K. I just do not understand that idiom."

The summer twilight faded. The bus had left the dusty road and was travelling now on a paved but winding highway. The sky was a deep somber blue and the moon was white. The fields of cotton (belonging perhaps to some huge plantation) were behind them and now on either side of the road the land was fallow and uncultivated. Trees on the horizon made a dark black fringe against the blue of the sky. The atmosphere had a dusky lavender tone and perspective was curiously difficult, so that objects which were far appeared near and things close at hand seemed distant. Silence had settled in the bus. There was only the vibrant throb of the motor, so constant that by now it was scarcely realized.

The sunburned young man sighed. And the Jew glanced quickly into his face. The southerner smiled and asked the Jew in a soft voice: "Where is your home, sir?"

To this question the Jew had no immediate answer. He pulled out shreds of tobacco from the end of his cigarette until it was too mangled for further use and then stamped out the stub on the floor. "I mean to make my home in the town where I am going — Lafayetteville."

This answer, careful and oblique, was the best that the Jew could give. For it must be understood at once that this was no ordinary traveller. He was no denizen of the great city he had left behind him. The time of his journey would not be measured by hours, but by years — not by hundreds of miles, but by thousands. And even such measurements as these would be in only one sense accurate. The journey of this fugitive — for the Jew had fled from his home in Munich two years before — more nearly resembled a state of mind than a period of travelling computable by maps and timetables. Behind him was an abyss of anxious wandering, suspense, of terror and of hope. But of this he could not speak with a stranger.

"I'm only going a hundred and eight miles away," said the young man. "But this is the furtherest I've ever been away from home."

The Jew raised his eyebrows with polite surprise.

"I'm going to visit with my sister who's only been wedded about a year. I think a mighty lot of this sister and now she's —" He hesitated and seemed to be rummaging in his mind for some choice and delicate expression. "She's with young." His blue eyes fastened doubtfully on the Jew as though uncertain that a man who had never before seen cotton would understand this other fundament of nature.

The Jew nodded and bit his lower lip with restrained amusement.

"Her time is just about here and her husband is cooking his tobacco. So I thought maybe I would come in handy."

"I hope she will have an easy time," the Jew said.

Here there was an interruption. By now it was quite dark and the driver of the bus pulled to the side of the road and turned on the lights inside. The sudden brightness awoke a child who had been sleeping and she began to fret. The Negroes on the back seat, for a long time silent, resumed their languorous dialogue. An old man on the front seat who spoke with the hollow insistence of the deaf began to joke with his companion.

"Are your folks already at this town where you going?" the young man asked the Jew.

"My family?" The Jew took off his spectacles, breathed on the lenses, and polished them on the sleeve of his shirt. "No, they will join me there when I have settled myself — my wife and my two daughters."

The young man leaned forward so that his elbows rested on his knees and his chin was cupped in his palms. Beneath the electric light his face was round and rosy and warm. Beads of perspiration glistened on his short upper lip. His blue eyes had a sleepy look and there was something childish about the way the soft brown bangs of his hair lay damp on his forehead. "I mean to get married sometime soon," he said. "I been picking around for a long time amongst the girls. And now I got them finally narrowed down to three."

"Three?"

"Yeah — all fine good looking girls. And that's another reason why I thought it fit to go off on this trip just now. You see when I come back I can look at them fresh and maybe make up my mind which one I want to ask."

The Jew laughed — a smooth hearty laugh that changed him completely. All trace of strain left his face, his head was thrown back, and his hands clasped tight. And although the joke was at his own expense, the southerner laughed with him. Then the Jew's laughter ended as abruptly as it had begun, finished with a great intake and release of breath that trailed off in a groan. The Jew closed his eyes for a moment and seemed to be according this morsel of fun a place in some inward repertoire of the ridiculous.

The two travellers had eaten together and had laughed together. By now they were no longer strangers. The Jew settled himself more comfortably in his seat, took a tooth-pick from his vest pocket and made use of it unobtrusively, half hiding his mouth with his hand. The young man removed his tie and unbuttoned his collar to the point where brown curling hairs showed on his chest. But it was evident that the southerner was not so much at ease as was the Jew. Something perplexed him. He seemed to be trying to frame some question that was painful and difficult to ask. He rubbed the damp bangs on his forehead and rounded his mouth as though about to whistle. At last he said: "You *are* a foreign man?"

"Yes."

"You come from abroad?"

The Jew inclined his head and waited. But the young man seemed unable to go further. And while the Jew waited for him either to speak or to be silent the bus stopped to take on a Negro woman who had signaled from the roadside. The sight of this new passenger disturbed the Jew. The Negro was of indeterminate age and, had she not been clothed in a filthy garment that served as a dress, even her sex would have been difficult at first glance to define. She was deformed — although not in any one specific limb; the body as a whole was stunted, warped and undeveloped. She wore a dilapidated felt hat, a torn black skirt and a blouse that had been roughly fashioned from a meal sack. At one corner of her mouth there was an ugly open sore and beneath her lower lip she carried a wad of snuff. The whites of her eyes were not white at all, but of a muddy yellow color veined with red. Her face as a whole had a roving, hungry, vacant look. As she walked down the aisle of the bus to take her place on the back seat the Jew turned questioningly to the young man and asked in a quiet, taut voice: "What is the matter with her?"

The young man was puzzled. "Who? You mean the nigger?"

"Sh —" the Jew cautioned, for they were on the next to the last seat and the Negro was just behind them.

But already the southerner had turned in his seat and was staring behind him with such frankness that the Jew winced. "Why there's nothing the matter with her," he said when he had completed this scrutiny. "Not that I can see."

The Jew bit his lip with embarrassment. His brows were drawn and his eyes were troubled. He sighed and looked out of the window although, because of the light in the bus and the darkness outside, there was little to be seen. He did not notice that the young man was trying to catch his eye and that several times he moved his lips as though about to speak. Then finally the young man's question was spoken. "Was you ever in Paris, France?"

The Jew said yes.

"That's one place I always wanted to go. I know this man was over there in the war and somehow all my life I wanted to go to

Paris, France. But understand —" The young man stopped and looked earnestly into the Jew's face. "Understand it's not the wimming." (For, due either to the influence of the Jew's careful syllables or to some spurious attempt at elegance the young man actually pronounced the word "wimming.") "It's not because of the French girls you hear about."

"The buildings — the boulevards?"

"No," said the young man with a puzzled shake of his head. "It's not any of those things. That's how come I can't understand it. Because when I think about Paris just one thing is in my mind." He closed his eyes thoughtfully. "I always see this little narrow street with tall houses on both sides. It's dark and it's cold and raining. And nobody is in sight except this French fellow standing on the corner with his cap pulled down over his eyes." The young man looked anxiously into the Jew's face. "Now how come I would have this homesick feeling for something like that? Why — do you reckon?"

The Jew shook his head. "Maybe too much sun," he said finally.

Soon after this the young man reached his destination — a little crossroads village that appeared to be deserted. The southerner took his time about leaving the bus. He pulled down his tin suitcase from the rack and shook hands with the Jew. "Goodbye, Mister —" The fact that he did not know the name seemed to come as a sudden surprise to him. "Kerr," said the Jew. "Felix Kerr." Then the young man was gone. At the same stop the Negro woman — that derelict of humanity the sight of whom had so disturbed the Jew — left the bus also. And the Jew was alone again.

He opened his lunch box and ate the sandwich made with rye bread. Afterward he smoked a few cigarettes. For a time he sat with his face close to the window screen and tried to gather some impression of the landscape outside. Since nightfall clouds had gathered in the sky and there were no stars. Now and then he saw the dark outline of a building, vague stretches of land, or a clump of trees close to the roadside. At last he turned away.

Inside the bus the passengers had settled down for the night. A few were sleeping. He looked about him with a certain rather jaded curiosity. Once he smiled to himself, a thin smile that sharpened the corners of his mouth. But then, even before the last trace of this smile had faded, a sudden change came over him. He had been watching the deaf old man in overalls on the front seat and some small observation seemed suddenly to cause in him intense emotion. Over his face came a swift grimace of pain. Then he sat with his head bowed, his thumb pressed to his right temple and his fingers massaging his forehead.

For this Jew was grieving. Although he was careful of his checked threadbare trousers, although he had eaten with enjoyment and had laughed, although he hopefully awaited this new strange home that lay ahead of him — in spite of these things there was a long dark sorrow in his heart. He did not grieve for Ada, his good wife to whom he had been faithful for twenty-seven years, or for his little daughter, Grissel, who was a charming child. These two — God be willing — would join him here as soon as he could prepare for them. Neither was this grief concerned with his anxiety for his friends, nor with the loss of his home, his security, and his content. The Jew sorrowed for his elder daughter, Karen, whose whereabouts and state of welfare were unknown to him.

And grief such as this is not a constant thing, demanding in measure, taking its toll in fixed proportion. Rather (for the Jew was a musician) such grief is like a subordinate but urgent theme in an orchestral work — an endless motive asserting itself with all possible variations of rhythm and tonal coloring and melodic structure, now suggested nervously in flying-spiccato passage from the strings, again emerging in the pastoral melancholy of the English horn, or sounding at times in a strident but truncated version down deep among the brasses. And this theme, although for the most part subtly concealed, affects by its sheer insistence the music as a whole far more than the apparent major melodies. And also there are times in this orchestral work when this motive which has been restrained so long will at a signal volcanically usurp all other musical ideas, commanding the full orchestra to recapitulate with fury all that hitherto had been insinuated. But with grief there is a difference here. For it is no fixed summons, such as the signal from the conductor's hand, that activates a dormant sorrow. It is the uncalculated and the indirect. So that the Jew could speak of his daughter with composure and without a quiver could pronounce her name. But when on the bus he saw a deaf man bend his head to one side to hear some bit of conversation the Jew was at the mercy of his grief. For his daughter had the habit of listening with her face turned slightly away and of looking up with one quick glance only when the speaker was done. And this old man's casual gesture was the summons that released in him the grief so long restrained — so that the Jew winced and bowed his head.

For a long time the Jew sat tense in his seat and rubbed his forehead. Then at eleven o'clock the bus made a scheduled stop. By turns the passengers hastily visited a cramped, stale urinal. Later in a café they gulped down drinks and ordered food that could be carried away and eaten with the hands. He had a beer and on his return to the bus prepared for sleep. He took from his pocket a fresh, unfolded handkerchief and, settling himself in his corner with his head resting in the crotch made by the side of the bus and the rounded back of his seat, he placed the handkerchief over his eyes to guard them from the light. He rested quietly with his legs crossed and his hands clasped loosely in his lap. By midnight he was sleeping.

Steadily, in darkness, the bus travelled southward. Sometime in the middle of the night the dense summer clouds dispersed and the sky was clear and starry. They were travelling down the long coastal plain that lies to the east of the Appalachian hills. The road wound through melancholy fields of cotton, and tobacco, through long and lonesome stretches of pine woods. The white moonlight made dreary silhouettes of the tenant shacks close by the roadside. Now and then they went through dark, sleeping towns and sometimes the bus stopped to take on or leave off some traveller. The Jew slept the heavy sleep of those who are mortally tired. Once the jolting of the bus caused his head to fall forward on his chest but this did not disturb his slumber. Then just before daylight, the bus reached a town somewhat larger than most of those through which they had been passing. The bus stopped and the driver laid his hand on the Jew's shoulder to awaken him. For at last his journey was ended.

Untitled Piece

The young man at the table of the station lunch room knew neither the name nor the location of the town where he was, and he had no knowledge of the hour more exact than that it was some time between midnight and morning. He realized that he must already be in the south, but that there were many more hours journeying before he would reach home. For a long time he had sat at the table over a half finished bottle of beer, relaxed to a gangling position — with his thighs fallen loose apart and with one foot stepping on the other ankle. His hair needed cutting and hung down softly ragged over his forehead and his expression as he stared down at the table was absorbed, but mobile and quick to change with his shifting thoughts. The face was lean and suggestive of restlessness and a certain innocent, naked questioning. On the floor beside the boy were two suitcases and a packing box, each tagged neatly with a card on which was typewritten his name — Andrew Leander, and an address in one of the larger towns in Georgia.

He had come into the place in a drunken turmoil, caused partly by the swallows of corn a man on the bus had offered him, mostly by a surge of expectancy that had come to him during the last few hours of travelling. And that feeling was not unaccountable. Three years before, when he was seventeen years old, the boy had left home in an inner quandary of violence, a gawky wanderer going with fear into the unknown, expecting never to come back. And now after these three years he was returning.

Sitting at the table in the lunch room of that little nameless town, Andrew had become more calm. All during the time of his absence he had put away thoughts of his home town and his family — of his Dad and his sisters, Sara and Mick, and of the colored girl Vitalis, who worked for them. But as he sat with his beer (so completely a stranger, that it was as though he were magically suspended from the very earth) the memories of all of them at home revolved inside him with the clarity of a reel of films — sometimes precise and patterned, again in a chaos of disorder.

And there was one little episode that kept recurring again and again in his mind, although until that night he had not thought of it in years. It was about the time he and his sister made a glider in the back yard, and perhaps he kept remembering it because the things he had felt at that time were so much like the expectancy this journey now brought.

At that time they had all been kids and at the age when all the new things they learned about on the radio and in books and at the movies could set them wild with eagerness. He had been thirteen, Sara a year younger, and little Mick (she didn't count in things like this) was still in kindergarten. He and Sara had read about gliders in a science magazine in the school library and immediately they began to build one in their back yard. (They began to build it one afternoon in the middle of the week and by Saturday they had worked so hard that it was almost finished.) The article had not given any exact directions for making the glider; they had had to go by the way they imagined it should be and to use whatever materials they could find. Vitalis would not give them a sheet to cover the wings and so they had to cut up his canvas camping tent to use instead. For the frame they used some bamboo sticks and some light wood they snitched from the carpenters who were building a garage up on the next block. When it was finished the glider was not very big, and seemed very different from the ones they had seen in the movies — but he and Sara kept telling each other than it was just as good and that there was nothing to keep their ship from flight.

That Saturday was a time that none of them would ever forget. The sky was a deep, blazing blue, the color of gas flames, and at times there was a thick and sultry breeze. All morning he and Sara stayed out in the hot sun of the back yard working. Her face was strained and pale with excitement and her full, almost sullen lips were red and dry as though from a fever. She kept running back and forth to get things she thought they might need, her thin legs overgrown and clumsy, her damp hair streaming out behind her shoulders. Little Mick hung around the back steps, watching. It seemed to him then that they were as different as any sisters could be. Mick sat quietly, her hands on her fat little knees, not saying much but gazing at everything they did with a wondering look to her face and with her little mouth softly open. Even Vitalis was out there with them most of the time. She didn't know whether to believe in it or not. She was a nervous, light colored girl and there was something about the glider that excited her as much as it did the rest of them — and that scared her too. As she watched them her fingers kept fooling with her red earrings or picking at her swollen quivering lips.

They all felt that there was something wild about the day. It was like they were shut off from all other people in the world and nothing mattered except the four of them planning and working out in the quiet, sun-baked yard. It was as though they had never wanted anything except this glider and its flight from the earth up toward the hot blue sky.

It was the launching that gave them the most worry. He kept saying to Sara: "We ought to have a car to hitch it to because that's the way the real flyers get them up. Or else one of those elastic ropes like they described in the magazine."

But beside their garage was a tall pine tree, with the limbs growing high and stretching out almost as far as the house. From one of these branches hung a swing and it was from this that they intended to make their start. He and Sara took out the board seat and put in its place a larger plank. And it was from the start that the swing would give them that they would be launched.

Vitalis felt like she ought to be responsible and she was afraid. "I been having this here queer feeling all day."

There was a hot slow breeze and from the top of the pine came a gentle soughing. She held up her hands to feel the wind and stood for a moment looking at the sky — intent as some savage rapt in prayer.

"You all think just because your mother ain't living that you don't have to mind nobody. Why don't you wait till your Daddy come home and ask him? I been having this here feeling all day that something bad ghy happen from that thing."

"Hush," said Sara.

"I know it ain't no real airplane even if it do have them big wings made out of a old torn up tent. And I know you just as human as I is. And your head just as easy to bust."

But no matter what she said Vitalis believed in the glider as much as any of them. When she was in the kitchen they could see her come to the window every few minutes and stare out at them, her broad nose pressed to the glass, her dark face quivering.

By the time they were finished the sun was almost down. The sky had blanched to a pale jade color and the breeze that had been blowing most of the day seemed cooler and stronger to them. The yard was very quiet and neither he nor Sara said anything or looked at each other as they tensely balanced the glider on the swing. They had already argued about who would be the one to go up first and he had won. They called Vitalis out from the house and told her to help Sara give the final push and when she did not want to they said they would call Chandler West or some other kid in the neighborhood so she might as well be the one. Little Mick got up from the steps where she had been looking at them all day long and watched him step carefully up into the swing and squat down on the frame of the glider, gripping the wood with the rubber soles of his sneakers.

"Do you think you'll go as far as Atlanta or Cleveland?" she asked. Cleveland was the place where their cousin lived and that was how she knew the name.

It seemed to him as he crouched in there trying to keep his balance that already he was leaving the ground. He could feel his heart beating almost in his throat and his hands were shaking.

Vitalis said: "And even if this slow little wind do carry you up in the air, what you ghy do then? Is you just ghy fly around up there all night like you is an angel?"

"Will you be back in time for supper, Drew?" Mick asked.

Sara looked like she didn't hear anything that was said. There were drops of sweat on her forehead and he could hear her breath coming quick and shallow. She and Vitalis each took a rope of the swing and pulled with all their strength. Even little Mick helped them balance the glider. It seemed like it took them hours to hoist him up as far as their head while he waited, crouched tensely, with his jaw stiff and his eyes half closed. During that moment he thought of himself soaring up and up into the cool blue sky and the joy of it was such as he never felt before.

Then came the part that afterward was the hardest to understand. As soon as the glider left the swing it crashed and he fell so hard that for a long time his stomach moved round and round in dizzy turns and he felt like someone was standing on his chest so that he could not breathe. But for some reason that did not matter at all. He got up from the ground and it was as though he would not let himself believe what had happened. He had not fallen on the glider and it was not hurt except for a little tear in the wing. He undid his belt buckle and tried to take a deep breath. He and Sara did not talk but kept themselves busy getting ready for the next take-off. And the queer thing was that they both knew that this second trial would be just like the first and that their glider would not fly. In a part of them they knew this but there was something that would not let them think about it — the wanting and the excitement that would not let them be quiet or stop to reason.

Vitalis was different and her voice went up high and sing-song. "Here Andrew done almost bust hisself wide open and still you all ghy keep on with this thing. Time you all is near bout twenty-five and old as I is you'll learn some sense."

Even Mick began to talk. She was always a quiet kid and hadn't said more than ten words all the time she had been hanging around. That was the way she always was. She just looked with her little mouth half open and seemed to wonder about and take in everything you did or said without trying to answer. "When I'm twelve years old and a big girl I'm going to fly and I'm not going to fall. You just wait and see."

"Quit your talking like that," Vitalis said. She did not want to watch them so she went into the house. Now and then they could see her dark face peering out at them from the kitchen window. He had to launch Sara by himself.

When she got into the glider it was almost dark. She crashed even worse than he did but she did not act like she was hurt and at first he did not notice the bump over her eye and the long bloody smear on her knee where the skin had scraped off. The glider was not even damaged much this time and it was like they were really wild as Vitalis made them out to be. "Just one more time I'm going to try," Sara said. "It keeps sticking to the seat and when I fix that it's just got to go up." She ran into the house, stepping light on the leg she had hurt, and came back with a hunk of butter on a piece of waxed bread wrapper to grease the swing. Vitalis's high singing voice called out to them from the kitchen but no one answered.

After the third time it was all over. He let Sara go because he was too heavy for her to launch. Their glider was smashed so you wouldn't know what it was and he had to help Sara get up from the ground this tme. Her eye was swollen and she looked sick. She stood with her weight on one foot and when she pulled up her skirt to show him a big bruise on her thigh, her leg was trembling so that she almost lost her balance. Everything was over and he felt dead and empty inside.

It was almost dark and they stood there for a while just looking at each other. Mick still sat on the steps, watching them with a scared look and not saying anything. Their faces were white in the half-darkness and the smells of supper from the kitchen were strong in the hot still air. It was very quiet and again it seemed that lonely feeling came to him like they were the only people in the world.

Finally, Sara said: "I don't care. I'm glad anyway even if it didn't work. I'd rather for it to be like it is now than not to have tried to build it. I don't care."

He broke off a piece of the pine bark and looked at Vitalis moving around in the soft yellow light of the kitchen.

"It ought to have worked though. It ought to have flown. I just can't see why it didn't."

In the dark sky there was a white star shining. Very slowly they walked across the yard toward their back steps and they were glad that their faces were half secret in the darkness. Quietly they went into the house and after that Vitalis was the only one who ever spoke of what had happened on that day.

The young man finished his beer on the table and motioned to the sleepy waiter to bring him another. All at once he decided not to take the next bus, but to stay in this strange town until morning. He half closed his eyes to shut out the crude light, the few weary travellers waiting at the tables, the dirty checked cloth before him.

It seemed to him that no one had ever felt just as he did. The past, the seventeen years of his life when he was at home, was before him like a dark and complex arabesque. But it was not a pattern to be comprehended at a glance, being more like a musical work that unfolds contrapuntally voice by voice and cannot be understood until after the time that it takes to reproduce it. It took shape in a vague design, less composed of events than of emotions. The last three years in New York did not enter into this pattern at all and were no more than a dark background to reflect for the moment the clarity of what had passed before. And through all this, in counterpart to the interwoven feelings, there was music in his mind.

Music had always meant a lot to him and Sara. Long ago, before Mick was even born and when their mother was still living, they would blow together on combs wrapped in toilet paper. Later there were harps from the ten cent store and the sad wordless songs that colored people sang. Then Sara began to take music lessons and although she didn't like either her teacher or the pieces she was given, she stuck to her practicing pretty well. She liked to pick out the jazz songs she heard or just to sit at the piano, playing aimless notes that weren't music at all.

He was about twelve when the family got a radio and after that things began to change. They began to dial to symphony orchestras and programmes that were very different from the ones they had listened to before. In a way this music was strange to them and again it was like something they had been waiting for all of their lives. Then their Dad gave them a portable Victrola one Christmas and some Italian opera records. Over and over they would wind up their Victrola and finally they wore the records out — there began to be scratching noises in the music and the singers sounded like they were holding their noses. The next year they got some Wagner and Beethoven.

All of that was before the time when Sara tried to run away from home. Because they lived in the same house and were together so much he was slow to notice the way she was changing. Of course she was growing very fast and couldn't wear a dress two months before her wrists would be showing and the skirt would be shorter than her bony knees — but that wasn't what it was. She reminded him of someone who had been sleepily stumbling through a dark room when a light was turned on. Often there was a lost, dazed look about her face that was hard to understand.

She would throw herself into first one thing and then another. For a while there were movies. She went to the show every Saturday with him and Chandler West and the rest of the kids, but when it was over and they had seen everything through she wouldn't come out with them but would stay on in the movie until almost dark. She always started looking at the picture as soon as she passed the ticket man and would stumble down the aisle without ever looking at the seats until she had almost reached the screen — then she would sit on about the third row with her neck bent back and her mouth not quite closed. Even after she had seen everything through twice she would keep turning back to look as she walked out of the show so that she would bump into people and was almost like somebody drunk. On week days she would save all but a dime of her lunch money and buy movie magazines. She had the pictures of Clive Brook and four or five other stars tacked up on the wall of her room and when she would go to the drug store to buy the magazines she would get a chocolate milk and look through all they had, then buy the ones with the most in them about the stars she liked. Movies were all she cared about for about three months. Then all of a sudden that was over and she didn't even go to the show anymore on Saturdays.

Then there was the Girl Scout Camp she and the girls she knew were going on, out at a lake about twenty miles from town. That was all she talked about the month beforehand. She would priss around in front of the mirror in the khaki shorts and boy's shirts they were supposed to have, her hair slicked back close to her head, thinking it was grand to try to act like a boy. But after she had been on the camp just four days he came in one afternoon and found her playing the Victrola. She had made one of the counsellors bring her home and she looked all done in. She said all they did was swim and run races and shoot bows and arrows. And there weren't any mattresses on the cots and at night there were mosquitoes and she had growing pains in her legs and couldn't sleep. "I just ran and ran and then lay awake in the dark all night," she kept saying. "That's all there was to it." He laughed at her, but when she started crying — not in the way kids like Mick bawled but slowly and unsobbing — it was almost like he was part of her and crying, too. For a long time they sat on the floor together, playing their records. They were always a lot closer than most brothers and sisters.

Music to them was something like the glider should have been. But it wasn't sudden like that and it didn't let them down. Maybe it was like whiskey was to their Dad. They knew it was something that would stay with them always.

Sara played the piano more and more after she got to high school. She didn't like it there any more than he did and sometimes she would even worry him into writing excuses for her and signing their Dad's name. The first term she got seven bad cards. Their Dad never knew what to do about Sara and whenever she did something wrong he would just clear his throat and look at her in an embarrassed way like he didn't know how to say what was in his mind. Sara looked like pictures of their mother and he loved her a lot — but it was in a funny sort of timid way. He didn't fuss at all about the bad cards. She was just twelve and that was young to be in high school anyway.

There is a time when everybody wants to run away — no matter how well they get along with their family. They feel they have to leave because of something they have done, or something they want to do, or maybe they don't know why it is they run away. Maybe it is a kind of slow hunger that makes them feel like they have to get out and go in search of something. He ran away from home once when he was eleven. A girl on the next block took her money out of the school savings bank and got a bus to Hollywood because the actress she had a crush on answered one of her letters and said that if she was ever in California to drop in and see her and swim in her swimming pool. Her folks couldn't get in touch with her for ten days and then her mother went out to Hollywood to bring her back. She had swum in the actress's pool and was trying to get a job in the movies. She was not sorry to come back home. Even Chandler West who was always slow and dumb tried to run away. Although Chandler had lived across the street from them all their lives there was something about him no one could ever understand. Even as little kids he and Sara felt that. It happened after Chandler had failed all his subjects at school, most of them for the second time. He said afterward that he wanted to build a hut up in the Canadian woods and live there by himself as a trapper. He was too dumb to hitch hike and he just kept walking toward the north until finally he was arrested for sleeping in a ditch and sent home. His mother had almost gone crazy and while he was gone her eyes were wild and like an animal's. You would think that Chandler was the only person that she had ever loved. And maybe it was from her that he was running away, too.

So there was nothing very peculiar about what Sara did — that is unless you were a grown person like their Dad who just didn't understand things like that. There wasn't any real reason for her wanting to leave. It was just the way she had begun to feel in the last year. Maybe music had something to do with it. Or it might have been because she had grown so much and just didn't know what to do with herself.

It happened on her thirteenth birthday and it was Monday morning. Vitalis had the breakfast table fixed nice with flowers and a new table cloth. Sara didn't seem any different that morning from any other time. But suddenly as she was eating her grits she saw a kinky hair on her plate and she burst out crying. Vitalis's feelings were hurt because she had tried to have breakfast so nice that morning. Sara grabbed her school books and went out the door. She said she wasn't mad with anybody about anything but that she was leaving home for good. He knew she was just talking and would just stay away until school was out. If it hadn't been for Vitalis their Dad would never have known about it. Sara went up the street running and when she came to the vacant lot at the corner she threw all her school books in the high grass there. When he went to pick them up there were papers scattered everywhere in the wind—homework and funny things she had drawn in her tablet.

Vitalis phoned their Dad who had already gone to work and he came home in the automobile. He was very worried and serious. He kept pulling his lower lip tight against his teeth and clearing his throat. All three of them got in the automobile to go find her. The rest would have been funny if you hadn't been mixed up in it. They found her after about half an hour — walking down the road between high school and downtown. But when their Dad blew the horn she wouldn't get in the car, or even look around at them. She just kept going with her head in the air and her pleated skirt switching above her skinny knees. Their Dad had never been so nervous and mad. He couldn't get out and chase a girl down the street and so he had to just creep the car along behind her and blow the horn. They passed kids going to school who stared and giggled and it was awful. He was madder with Sara than their Dad. If they had had a closed car he would have leaned back and hid his face. But it was a Model T Ford and there wasn't anything to do but shuffle his feet and try to look like he didn't care.

After a while she gave up and got in the car. Their Dad didn't know what to say and all of them were stiff and quiet. Sara was shamed and sad. She tried to cover it up by humming to herself in a don't-care way. They got out quietly at the high school. But that wasn't the end.

The next month Uncle Jim, who was kin to them on their mother's side, came down from Detroit on the way to spend his vacation in Florida. Aunt Esther, his wife, was with him. She was a Jew and played the violin. Both of them had always liked Sara a lot — and in their Christmas boxes her present was always better than his or Mick's. They didn't have any children and there was something about them that was different from most married people. The first night they sat up very late with their Dad and maybe he told them all about Sara. Anyway, before they left, their Dad asked Sara how she would like to go to school a year in Detroit and live with them. Right away she said that she would like it — she had never been farther away from home than Atlanta and she wanted to sleep on a train and live in a strange place and see snow in the winter time.

It happened so quickly that he could not get it into his head. He had not thought about the time when any of them would ever be away for long. He knew their Dad felt Sara was growing to the age where maybe she needed somebody who was at home more than he was. And the climate might do her good in Detroit and they didn't have many kinfolks. Before they were even born Uncle Jim had lived at their house a year — when he was still young and before he left for the north. But still he could not understand their Dad's letting her go. She left in a week — because the school term had only been going a month and they didn't want to waste more time. It was so sudden that it didn't give him time to think. She was to be gone ten months and that seemed almost as long as forever. He did not know that it would be almost twice that time before he would again see her. He felt dazed and it was like a dream when they said goodbye.

That winter the house was a lonesome place. Mick was too little to think about anything but eating and sleeping and drawing on colored paper at kindergarten. When he would come in from school all the rooms seemed quiet and more than empty. Only in the kitchen was it any different and there Vitalis was always cooking and singing to herself and it was warm and full of good smells and life. If he did not go out he would usually hang around there and watch her and they would talk while she fixed him something to eat. She knew about the lonesome feeling and was good to him.

Most afternoons he was out with Chandler West and the rest of the gang of boys who were sophomores at high school. They had a club and a scrub football team. The vacant lot on the corner of the block was sold and the buyer began to build a house. When the carpenters and bricklayers left in the late afternoon the gang would climb up on the roof or run through the naked incompleted rooms. It was strange the way he felt about this house. Every afternoon he would take off his shoes and socks so he wouldn't slip and climb to the sharp pointed top of the roof. Then he would stand there, holding his hands out for balance and look around at all that lay below him or at the pale twilight sky. From underneath the boys would be scuffling together and calling out to each other — their voices were changing and the empty rooms made long drawn echoes, so that the sounds seemed not human and unrelated to words.

Standing there alone on the roof he always felt he had to shout out — but he did not know what it was he wanted to say. It seemed like if he could put this thing into words he would no longer be a boy with big rough bare feet and hands that hung down clumsy from the outgrown sleeves of his lumberjack. He would be a great man, a kind of God, and what he called out would make things that bothered him and all other people plain and simple. His voice would be great and like music and men and women would come out of their houses and listen to him and because they knew that what he said was true they would all be like one person and would understand everything in the world. But no matter how big this feeling was he could never put any of it into words. He would balance there choked and ready to burst and if his voice had not been squeaky and changing he would have tried to yell out the music of one of their Wagner records. He could do nothing. And when the rest of the gang would come out from the house and look up at him he felt a sudden panic, as though his corduroy pants had dropped from him. To cover up his nakedness he would yell something silly like *Friends Romans Countrymen* or *Shake-Spear Kick Him In The Rear* and then he would climb down feeling empty and shamed and more lonesome than anybody else in the world.

On Saturday mornings he worked down at his Dad's store. This was a long narrow jeweller's shop in the middle of one of the main business blocks downtown. Down the length of the place was a bright glass showcase with the sections displaying stones and silver. His Dad's watchmaking bench was in the very front of the shop, looking out on the front window and the street. Day after day he would sit there over his work — a large man, more than six feet tall, and with hands that at first looked too big for their delicate work. But after you watched his Dad awhile that first feeling changed. People who noticed his hands always wanted to stare at them — they were fat and seemed without bones or muscles and the skin, darkened with acids, was smooth as old silk. His hands did not seem to belong to the rest of him, to his bent broad back and his strained muscular neck. When he worked at a hard job his whole face would show it. The eye that wore his jeweller's glass would stare down round and intent and distorted while the other was squinted almost shut. His whole big face looked crooked and his mouth gaped open with strain. Although when he was not busy he liked to stare out at the heads and shoulders of the people passing on the street, he never glanced at them while he was at work.

At the store his Dad usually gave him odd jobs such as that of polishing silverware or running errands. Sometimes he cleaned watch springs with a brush soaked in gasoline. Occasionally if there were several customers in the place and the salesgirl was busy he would awkwardly stand behind the counter and try to make a sale. But most of the time there was nothing much for him to do except hang around. He hated staying at the store on Saturdays because he could always think of so many other things he wanted to do. There were long stretches when the store would be very quiet — with only the droning ticks of the watches or the echoing sounds of a clock striking.

On the days when Harry Minowitz was there this was different. Harry took in the extra work of two or three jewellers in the town and his Dad let him use the bench at the back of the store in exchange for certain jobs. There was nothing that Harry didn't know about even the finest of watch mechanics and because of this (and for other reasons too) he had the nickname of "The Wizard." His Dad didn't like Jews because there were a couple in town who were slick as grease and bad on other jewellers' business. So it was funny the way he depended on Harry.

Harry was small and pale and he always seemed tired. His nose was large for his peaked face and next to his eyes it was the first thing you noticed. Perhaps that was because he had the habit of slowly rubbing it with his thumb and second finger when he was thinking, gently feeling the hump in it and pressing down the tip. When he was in doubt about a question put to him he would not shrug or shake his head — but slowly turn his slender hands palm upward and suck in his hollow cheeks. Usually a cigarette drooped from his mouth and his thin lips seemed too relaxed to hold it. His dark eyes had a way of staring sharply at a person, then the lids would suddenly droop down as though he understood everything and was still bored. At the same time there was a certain jauntiness about him. His clothes were dapper and he wore a stiff derby hat at an angle on the back of his head. Nothing could ever surprise Harry, but in his own quiet way he could always laugh at everything, even himself. He had come to the town ten years before and he lived alone in a small room on one of the overcrowded streets down by the river. Though he seemed to know half the people in the town by their names and faces he had few friends and was a solitary man.

During the winter after Sara left when Andrew worked at the store every Saturday he liked to watch Harry and think about him. There was a time when he would rather have been noticed and admired by him than any other person. He had never tried to ape his Dad like some boys did. But there was something sure and nonchalant about Harry that seemed wonderful to him. He had lived in cities like Los Angeles and New York and he knew languages and people that were strange to men like his Dad. He wanted to be good friends with Harry but he didn't know how to go about it. When they were together something made him talk loud and hold his face stiff and call grown men by their last names without the Mister. Then he would be embarrassed, stumble over his big feet and get in everybody's way. He felt that Harry saw through all of this and was laughing. This made him mad. There were times when if Minowitz hadn't been so old he would have picked a fight with him and tried to bash his ears in. But although Harry looked like he might be any age he knew that he must be around thirty — and a nearly six foot tall boy of fourteen coudn't fight with a smaller man who was that much older.

Then one morning Harry brought "the dolls" to the store. That was the name somebody gave to the set of chessmen he had worked on for ten years. At first it was a surprise to realize that even Harry could be a crank about something — he had known that he liked chess and owned a fine set of pieces, but that was all. He learned that Harry would go anywhere to find a partner who could give him a good game. And next to playing he liked to just fondle and work with these little doll-like men. They had been carved years ago by a friend of his father — out of ebony and some light hard wood. Some of the pieces had shrunken little Chinese faces and all of the parts were curious and beautiful. For years Harry had worked in his spare time to inlay this set with chased gold.

It was these chessmen that made them friends. When Harry saw how interested he was he began to tell him about the work and also to explain the moves in a chess game. Within a few weeks he learned how to play a fair game for a beginner. And after that he and Harry would play together often on Saturdays in the back of the store. He got so that even at night when he couldn't sleep he would think about chess. He hadn't thought that he could ever like a game so much.

Sometimes Harry would have him up to his place for an evening. The room he lived in was very neat and bare. They would sit silently over a little card table, going through the game without a word. As Harry played his face was as pale and frozen looking as one of his little carved pieces — only his sharp black eyebrows moved and his fingers as he slowly rubbed his nose. The first few times he left as soon as the games were over because he was afraid Harry might get tired of him if he stayed longer and think he was just a boring kid. But before he knew it all that was changed and they would talk sometimes until late at night. There were times when he would feel almost like a drunk man and try to put into words all the things he had kept stored up for a long time. He would talk and talk until he was breathless and his cheeks burned — about the things he wanted to do and see and make up his mind about. Harry listened with his head cocked to one side and his unsurprised silence made what he wanted to say come faster and even more clearly than he had thought it.

Harry was always quiet, but the things he did mention suggested more than he ever said. He had a younger brother named Baruch who was a pianist studying in New York. The way he would speak of his brother showed that he cared more about him than he did anyone else. Andrew tried to imagine Baruch — and in his mind he was bigger and surer and knew more than any of the kids in his gang. Often when he thought of this boy there was a sad longing feeling because they didn't know each other. Harry had other brothers — one who had a cigarette shop in Cincinnati, and another who was a piano tuner. You could tell he was close to all his family. But this Baruch was his favorite.

Sometimes when he would hurry down the dark streets on the way home he would feel a peculiar quiver of fear inside him. He didn't know why. It was like he had given all he had to a stranger who might cheat him. He wanted to run run run through the dark streets without stopping. Once when this happened he stopped on a corner and leaned against the lamp post and began to try to remember exactly what he had said. A panic came over him because it seemed that the thing he had tried to tell was too naked. He didn't know why this was so. The words jangled in his head and mocked him.

"Don't you ever hate being yourself? I mean like the times when you wake up suddenly and say I am I and you feel smothered. It's like everything you do and think about is at loose ends and nothing fits together. There ought to be a time when you see everything like you're looking through a periscope. A kind of a — colossal periscope where nothing is left out and everything in the world fits in with every other thing. And no matter what happens after that it won't — won't stick out like a sore thumb and make you lose your balance. That's one reason I like chess because it's sort of that way. And music — I mean good music. Most jazz and theme songs in the movies are like something a kid like Mick would draw on a piece of tablet paper — maybe a sort of shaky line all erased and messy. But the other music is sometimes like a great fine design and for a minute it makes you that way too. But about that sort of periscope — there's really no such thing. And maybe that's what everybody wants and they just don't know it. They try one thing after another but that want is never really gone. Never."

And when he had finished talking Harry's face was still pale and frozen, like one of his wizened chess kings. He had nodded his head and that was all. Andrew hated him. But even so he knew that the next week he would go back.

That year he often went out roaming through the town. Not only did he get to know all the streets in the suburb where he lived, and those of the main blocks downtown, and the Negro sections — but he began to be familiar, also, with that part of town called South Highlands. This was the place where the most important business of the town, the three cotton factories, was situated. For a mile up the river there was nothing but these mills and the glutted little streets of shacks where the workers lived. This huge section seemed almost entirely separate from the rest of the town and when Andrew first began to go there he felt almost as though he were a hundred miles from home. Some afternoons he would walk up and down the steep foul sidestreets for hours. He just walked without speaking to anybody with his hands in his pockets, and the more he saw the more there was this feeling that he would have to keep walking on and on through those streets until his mind was settled. He saw things there that scared him in an entirely new way — new, because it was not for himself he was afraid and he couldn't even put the reason into thought. But the fear kept on in him and sometimes it seemed it would almost choke him. Always people sitting on their front steps or standing in doorways would stare at him — and most of the faces were a pale yellow and had no expression except that of watching without any special interest. The streets were always full of kids in overalls. Once he saw a boy as old as he was piss on his own front steps when there were girls around. Another time a half grown fellow tried to trip him up and they had to fight. He had never been much of a fighter but in a scrap he always used his fists and butted with his head. But this boy was different. He fought like a cat and scratched and bit and kept snarling under his breath. The funny thing was that the fight was almost over and he felt himself on the ground and being choked when the fellow suddenly got limp like an old sack and in a minute more he gave up. Then when they were on their feet and just looking at each other he, the boy, did a crazy thing. He spat at him and slunk down to the ground and lay there on his back. The spit landed on his shoe and was thick like he had been saving it up a long time. But he looked down at him lying there on the ground and he felt sick and didn't even think about making him fight again. It was a cold day but the boy didn't have on anything but a pair of overalls and his chest was nothing but bones and his stomach stuck way out. He felt sick like he had hit a baby or a girl or somebody that should have been fighting on his side. The hoarse wailing whistles that marked the change in the mill shifts called out to him.

But even after that there was something in him that made him still walk the streets of South Highlands. He was looking for something but he didn't know what it was.

In the Negro sections he felt none of this dim fear. Those parts of the town were a sort of home to him — especially the little street called Sherman's Quarter where Vitalis lived. This street was on the edge of the City Limits and was only a few blocks from his own house. Most of the colored people there did yard work or cooked for white people or took in washing. Behind the Quarter were the long miles of fields and pine woods where he would go on camping trips. As a kid he knew the names of everybody living anywhere near. When he would go camping he used to borrow a certain skinny little hound from an old man at the end of the Quarter and if he brought back a possum or a fish sometimes they would cook it and eat together. He knew the backs of those houses like his own yard — the black washpots, the barrel hoops, the plum bushes, the privies, the old automobile body without wheels that had set for years behind one of the houses. He knew the Quarter on Sunday mornings when the women would comb and plait their children's hair in the sun on the front steps, when the grown girls would walk up and down in their trailing bright silk dresses, and the men would watch and softly whistle blues songs. And after supper time he knew it too. Then the light from the oil lamps would flicker from the houses and throw out long shadows. And there was the smell of smoke and fish and corn. And somebody was always dancing or playing the harp.

But there was one time when the Quarter was strange to him, and that was late at night. Several times on his way home late from hunting or when he was just restless, he had walked through the street at that time. The doors were all closed to the moonlight and the houses looked shrunk and had the look of shanties that have been empty a long time. At the same time there was that silence that never comes to a deserted place — and can only be sensed where there are many people sleeping. But as he would listen to this utter quietness he would always gradually become aware of a sound, and it was this that made the Quarter strange to him in the late night. The sound was never the same and it seemed always to come from a different place. Once it was like a girl laughing — softly laughing on and on. Again it was the low moan of a man in the darkness. The sound was like music except that it had no shape — it made him pause to hear and quiver as would a song. And when he would go home to bed the sound would still be inside him; he would twist in the darkness and his hard brown limbs would chafe each other because he could find no rest.

He never told Harry Minowitz about any of his walks. He could not imagine trying to tell anyone about that sound, least of all Harry, because it was a secret thing.

And he never talked to Harry about Vitalis.

When after school he would go back to the kitchen to Vitalis there were three words he always said. It was like answering *present* at the school roll-call. He would put down his books and stand in the doorway a moment and say: "I'm so hungry." The little sentence never changed and often he would not realize he had even spoken. Sometimes when he had just finished all the food he could eat and was still sitting there in the chair before the stove, restless but somehow not wanting to leave, he would mechanically mouth those three words. Just watching Vitalis brought them to his mind.

"You eats more than any lanky boy I ever seen," she would say. "What the matter with you? I believe you just eats cause you want to do something and you don't know what else to do."

But she always had food for him. Maybe pot liquor and cornbread or biscuit and syrup. Sometimes she even made candy just for him or cut off a piece of the steak they were going to have for supper.

Watching Vitalis was almost as good as eating and his eyes would follow her around. She was not coal black like some colored girls and her hair was always neatly plaited and shining with oil. Early every morning Sylvester, her boy-friend, walked to work with her and she usually wore a fancy red satin dress and earrings and high heeled green shoes. Then when she got in the house she would take off her shoes and wiggle her toes a while before putting on the bedroom slippers she wore to work in. She always hung her satin dress on the back porch and changed to a gingham one she kept at the house. She had the walk of colored people who have carried baskets of clothes on their heads. Vitalis was good and there wasn't anybody else like her.

Their talks together were warm and idle. What she didn't understand didn't gnaw on her and bother her. Sometimes he would blurt out things to her — and in a way it was like talking to himself. Her answers were always comfortable. They would make him feel like a kid again and he would laugh. One day he told her a little about Harry.

"I seen him down to your Daddy's store many a time. He a puny little white man, ain't he? You know this here is a funny thing —

nearly bout all little puny peoples is biggety. The littler they is the larger they thinks they is. Just watch the way they rares up they heads when they walk. Great big mens — like Sylvester and like you ghy be — they ain't that way at all. When they be about six foots tall they liable to act soft and shamed like chilluns. Once I knowed a little biggety dwarf man name Hunch. I wish you could have seed the way on a Sunday he would commence to walk around. He carried a great big umbrella and he would priss down them streets by hisself like he was God —"

Then there was a morning when he came into the kitchen after playing a new Beethoven record he had gotten. The music had been in his head half the night and he had waked up early so as to play it awhile before school time. When he came into the kitchen Vitalis was changing her shoes. "Honey," she said. "You ought to been here a minute ago. I come in the kitchen and you was playing that there gramophone in your room. Sound like band music folks march by. Then I done looked down at the floor and you know what I seen? A whole fambly of little mices the size of your finger, setting up on their hind legs and dancing. That the truth. Them rats really does like such music."

Maybe it was for words like this that he was always going in to Vitalis and saying, "I'm so hungry." It wasn't only for warmed up food and coffee she would give him.

Sometimes they would talk about Sara. All the eighteen months that she was away she hardly ever wrote. And then the letter would just be about Aunt Esther and her music lessons and what they were going to have for dinner that night. He knew she was changed. And he had a feeling she was in trouble or something important was happening to her. But it got so that Sara was very vague to him — and it was terrible but when he tried to remember her face he couldn't see it clearly. She got to be almost like their dead mother to him.

So it was Harry Minowitz and Vitalis who were nearest to him during that time. Vitalis and Harry. When he tried to think of them together he would have to laugh. It was like putting red with lavender — or a Bach fugue with a sad nigger whistling. Everything he knew seemed that way. Nothing fitted.

Sara came back but that didn't change things much. They weren't close like they had been before. Their Dad had thought it was time for her to come home but she didn't seem glad to be back with her own family. And all the next year she would often get very quiet and just stare ahead like she was homesick. They didn't go with the same crowd of boys and girls anymore and often they didn't even wait for each other to walk to school in the mornings. Sara had learned a lot of music in Detroit and her piano playing was different and very careful. He could tell that she had loved their Aunt Esther a lot but for some reason she didn't talk about her much.

The trouble was that he saw Sara in a hazy way at that time. That was the way everything looked to him then. Crazy and upsidedown. And he was getting to be a man and he did not know what was going to come. And always he was hungry and always he felt that something was just about to happen. And that happening he felt would be terrible and would destroy him. But he would not mold that prescience into thought. Even the time — the two long years after Sara returned — seemed to have passed through his body and not his mind. It was just long months of either floundering or quiet vacantness. And when he thought back over it there was little that he could realize.

He was getting to be a man and he was seventeen years old.

It was then that the thing happened that he had expected without knowing in his mind. This thing he had never imagined and afterward it seemed to have leapt up out of nowhere — to his mind it seemed that way but there was another part of him where this was not so.

The time was late summer and in a few weeks he was planning to leave for Atlanta to enter Tech. He did not want to go to Tech — but it was cheap because he could take the co-op course and his Dad wanted him to graduate from there and be an engineer. There didn't seem to be anything else that he could do and in a way he was eager to leave home so that he could live in a new place by himself. That late summer afternoon he was walking in the woods behind Sherman's Quarter, thinking of this and of a hundred vague things. Remembering all the other times when he had walked through those woods made him restless and he felt lost and alone.

It was almost sundown when he left the woods and started through the street where Vitalis lived. Although it was Sunday afternoon the houses were very quiet and everyone seemed to be gone. The air was sultry and there was the smell of sun-baked pine straw. On the edges of the little street were trampled weeds and a few early goldenrods.

As he was walking past the houses, his ankles grey with the lazy swirls of dust that his footsteps made and his eyes tired from the sun, he suddenly heard Vitalis speak to him.

"What you doing round this way, Andrew?"

She was sitting on her front steps and seemed to be alone in the empty Quarter. "Nothing," he said. "Just wandering around."

"They having a big funeral down at our church. It the preacher dead this time. Everybody done gone but me. I just now got away from your house. Even Sylvester done gone."

He didn't know what to say but just the sight of her made him mumble, "Gosh I'm so hungry. All this walking around. And thirsty—"

"I'll get you some."

She got up slowly and he noticed for the first time that she was barefooted and her green shoes and stockings were on the porch. She stooped to put them on. "I done taken these off cause ever body done gone except a sick lady in one of them end houses. These here green shoes has always scrunched my toes—and sometimes the ground sure do feel good to my feets."

On the little stoop behind the house he drank the cool water and dashed some of it into his burning face. Again he felt as though he were hearing that strange sound he had heard late at night along this street. When he went back through the house where Vitalis had been waiting for him he felt his body tremble. He did not know why they both paused a moment in the dim little room. It was very quiet and a clock ticked slowly. There was a kewpie doll with a gauze sash on the mantelpiece and the air was close and musty.

"What ails you, Andrew? Why you shaking so? What is it ails you, Honey?"

It wasn't him and it wasn't her. It was the thing in both of them. It was the strange sound he had heard there late at night. It was the dim room and the quietness. And all the afternoons he had spent with her in the kitchen. And all his hunger and the times when he had been alone. After it happened that was what he thought.

Later she went out of the house with him and they stood by a pine tree on the edge of the woods. "Andrew, quit your looking at me like that," she kept saying. "Everthing is all right. Don't you worry none about that."

It was like he was staring at her from the bottom of a well and that was all he could think.

"That ain't nothing real wrong. It ain't the first time with me and you a grown man. Quit your looking at me like that, Andrew."

This had never been in his mind. But it had been there waiting and had crept up and smothered his other thoughts — And this was not the only thing that would do him that way. Always. Always.

"Us didn't mean nothing. Sylvester ain't ghy ever know — or your Daddy. Us haven't arranged this. Us haven't done no real sin."

He had imagined how it would be when he was twenty. And she had a pale face like a flower and that was all he knew of her.

"Peoples can't plan on everthing."

He left her. Harry's chessmen, those precise and shrunken little dolls, neat problems in geometry, music that spun itself out immense and symmetrical. He was lost lost and it seemed to him that the end had surely come. He wanted to put his hands on all that had happened to him in his life, to grasp it to him and shape it whole. He was lost lost. He was alone and naked. And along with the chessmen and the music he suddenly remembered an aerial map of New York that he had seen — with the sharp skyscrapers and the blocks neatly plotted. He wanted to go far away and Atlanta was too near his home. He remembered the map of New York, frozen and delicate it was and he knew that was where he was going. That was all that he knew.

In the restaurant of the town where he had gotten off of the bus Andrew Leander finished the last of his beers. The place was closing and there would not be a bus to Georgia until morning. He could not get Vitalis and Sara and Harry and his Dad from his mind. And there were others besides them. He realized suddenly that he had hardly remembered Chandler. Chandler West who lived across the street — whom he had been with so often and who was at the same time so obscure. And the girl who wore red fingernail polish at high school. And the little rat of a boy named Peeper whom he had once talked with at South Highlands.

He got up from the table and picked up his bags. He was the last one in the restaurant and the waiter was ready to lock up. For a moment he hung around near the door that opened into the dark quiet street.

When he had first sat down at the table everything had seemed for the first time so clear. And now he was more lost than ever. But somehow it didn't matter. He felt strong. In that dark sleepy place he was a stranger — but after three years he was going home. Not just to Georgia but to a nearer home than that. He was drunk and there was power in him to shape things. He thought of all of them at home whom he had loved. And it would not be himself but through all of them that he would find this pattern. He felt drunk and sick for home. He wanted to go out and lift up his voice and search in the night for all that he wanted. He was drunk drunk. He was Andrew Leander.

"Say," he said to the boy who was waiting to lock the door. "Can you give me the name of some place around here where I can get a room for the night?"

The boy gave him some directions and in the surface of his mind he noted them. The street was dark and silent and he stood a moment longer in the open doorway. "Say," he said again. "I got off the bus half drunk. Will you tell me the name of this place?"

The Jockey

The jockey came to the doorway of the dining room, then after a moment stepped to one side and stood motionless, with his back to the wall. The room was crowded, as this was the third day of the season and all the hotels in the town were full. In the dining room bouquets of August roses scattered their petals on the white table linen and from the adjoining bar came a warm, drunken wash of voices. The jockey waited with his back to the wall and scrutinized the room with pinched, crêpy eyes. He examined the room until at last his eyes reached a table in a corner diagonally across from him, at which three men were sitting. As he watched, the jockey raised his chin and tilted his head back to one side, his dwarfed body grew rigid, and his hands stiffened so that the fingers curled inward like gray claws. Tense against the wall of the dining room, he watched and waited in this way.

He was wearing a suit of green Chinese silk that evening, tailored precisely and the size of a costume outfit for a child. The shirt was yellow, the tie striped with pastel colors. He had no hat with him and wore his hair brushed down in a stiff, wet bang on his forehead. His face was drawn, ageless, and gray. There were shadowed hollows at his temples and his mouth was set in a wiry smile. After a time he was aware that he had been seen by one of the three men he had been watching. But the jockey did not nod; he only raised his chin still higher and hooked the thumb of his tense hand in the pocket of his coat.

The three men at the corner table were a trainer, a bookie, and a rich man. The trainer was Sylvester — a large, loosely built fellow with a flushed nose and slow blue eyes. The bookie was Simmons. The rich man was the owner of a horse named Seltzer, which the jockey had ridden that afternoon. The three of them drank whiskey with soda, and a white-coated waiter had just brought on the main course of the dinner.

It was Sylvester who first saw the jockey. He looked away quickly, put down his whiskey glass, and nervously mashed the tip of his red nose with his thumb. "It's Bitsy Barlow," he said. "Standing over there across the room. Just watching us."

"Oh, the jockey," said the rich man. He was facing the wall and he half turned his head to look behind him. "Ask him over."

"God no," Sylvester said.

"He's crazy," Simmons said. The bookie's voice was flat and without inflection. He had the face of a born gambler, carefully adjusted, the expression a permanent deadlock between fear and greed.

"Well, I wouldn't call him that exactly," said Sylvester. "I've known him a long time. He was O.K. until about six months ago. But if he goes on like this, I can't see him lasting another year. I just can't."

"It was what happened in Miami," said Simmons.

"What?" asked the rich man.

Sylvester glanced across the room at the jockey and wet the corner of his mouth with his red, fleshy tongue. "A accident. A kid got hurt on the track. Broke a leg and a hip. He was a particular pal of Bitsy's. A Irish kid. Not a bad rider, either."

"That's a pity," said the rich man.

"Yeah. They were particular friends," Sylvester said. "You would always find him up in Bitsy's hotel room. They would be playing rummy or else lying on the floor reading the sports page together."

"Well, those things happen," said the rich man.

Simmons cut into his beefsteak. He held his fork prongs downward on the plate and carefully piled on mushrooms with the blade of his knife. "He's crazy," he repeated. "He gives me the creeps."

All the tables in the dining room were occupied. There was a party at the banquet table in the center, and green-white August moths had found their way in from the night and fluttered about the clear candle flames. Two girls wearing flannel slacks and blazers walked arm in arm across the room into the bar. From the main street outside came the echoes of holiday hysteria.

"They claim that in August Saratoga is the wealthiest town per capita in the world." Sylvester turned to the rich man. "What do you think?"

"I wouldn't know," said the rich man. "It may very well be so."

Daintily, Simmons wiped his greasy mouth with the tip of his forefinger. "How about Hollywood? And Wall Street—"

"Wait," said Sylvester. "He's decided to come over here."

The jockey had left the wall and was approaching the table in the corner. He walked with a prim strut, swinging out his legs in a half-circle with each step, his heels biting smartly into the red velvet carpet on the floor. On the way over he brushed against the elbow of a fat woman in white satin at the banquet table; he stepped back and bowed with dandified courtesy, his eyes quite closed. When he had crossed the room he drew up a chair and sat at a corner of the table, between Sylvester and the rich man, without a nod of greeting or a change in his set, gray face.

"Had dinner?" Sylvester asked.

"Some people might call it that." The jockey's voice was high, bitter, clear.

Sylvester put his knife and fork down carefully on his plate. The rich man shifted his position, turning sidewise in his chair and crossing his legs. He was dressed in twill riding pants, unpolished boots, and a shabby brown jacket—this was his outfit day and night in the racing season, although he was never seen on a horse. Simmons went on with his dinner.

"Like a pot of seltzer water?" asked Sylvester. "Or something like that?"

The jockey didn't answer. He drew a gold cigarette case from his pocket and snapped it open. Inside were a few cigarettes and a tiny gold penknife. He used the knife to cut a cigarette in half. When he had lighted his smoke he held up his hand to a waiter passing by the table. "Kentucky bourbon, please."

"Now, listen, Kid," said Sylvester.

"Don't Kid me."

"Be reasonable. You know you got to behave reasonable."

The jockey drew up the left corner of his mouth in a stiff jeer. His eyes lowered to the food spread out on the table, but instantly he looked up again. Before the rich man was a fish casserole, baked in a cream sauce and garnished with parsley. Sylvester had ordered eggs Benedict. There was asparagus, fresh buttered corn, and a side dish of wet black olives. A plate of French-fried potatoes was in the corner of the table before the jockey. He didn't look at the food again, but kept his pinched eyes on the centerpiece of full-blown lavender roses. "I don't suppose you remember a certain person by the name of McGuire," he said.

"Now, listen," said Sylvester.

The waiter brought the whiskey, and the jockey sat fondling the glass with his small, strong, callused hands. On his wrist was a gold link bracelet that clinked against the table edge. After turning the glass between his palms, the jockey suddenly drank the whiskey neat in two hard swallows. He set down the glass sharply. "No, I don't suppose your memory is that long and extensive," he said.

"Sure enough, Bitsy," said Sylvester. "What makes you act like this? You hear from the kid today?"

"I received a letter," the jockey said. "The certain person we were speaking about was taken out from the cast on Wednesday. One leg is two inches shorter than the other one. That's all."

Sylvester clucked his tongue and shook his head. "I realize how you feel."

"Do you?" The jockey was looking at the dishes on the table. His gaze passed from the fish casserole to the corn, and finally fixed on the plate of fried potatoes. His face tightened and quickly he looked up again. A rose shattered and he picked up one of the petals, bruised it between his thumb and forefinger, and put it in his mouth.

"Well, those things happen," said the rich man.

The trainer and the bookie had finished eating, but there was food left on the serving dishes before their plates. The rich man dipped his buttery fingers in his water glass and wiped them with his napkin.

"Well," said the jockey. "Doesn't somebody want me to pass them something? Or maybe perhaps you desire to reorder. Another hunk of beefsteak, gentlemen, or —"

"Please," said Sylvester. "Be reasonable. Why don't you go on upstairs?"

"Yes, why don't I?" the jockey said.

His prim voice had risen higher and there was about it the sharp whine of hysteria.

"Why don't I go up to my god-damn room and walk around and

write some letters and go to bed like a good boy? Why don't I just—" He pushed his chair back and got up. "Oh, foo," he said. "Foo to you. I want a drink."

"All I can say is it's your funeral," said Sylvester. "You know what it does to you. You know well enough."

The jockey crossed the dining room and went into the bar. He ordered a Manhattan, and Sylvester watched him stand with his heels pressed tight together, his body hard as a lead soldier's, holding his little finger out from the cocktail glass and sipping the drink slowly.

"He's crazy," said Simmons. "Like I said."

Sylvester turned to the rich man. "If he eats a lamb chop, you can see the shape of it in his stomach a hour afterward. He can't sweat things out of him any more. He's a hundred and twelve and a half. He's gained three pounds since we left Miami."

"A jockey shouldn't drink," said the rich man.

"The food don't satisfy him like it used to and he can't sweat it out. If he eats a lamb chop, you can watch it tooching out in his stomach and it don't go down."

The jockey finished his Manhattan. He swallowed, crushed the cherry in the bottom of the glass with his thumb, then pushed the glass away from him. The two girls in blazers were standing at his left, their faces turned toward each other, and at the other end of the bar two touts had started an argument about which was the highest mountain in the world. Everyone was with somebody else; there was no other person drinking alone that night. The jockey paid with a brand-new fifty-dollar bill and didn't count the change.

He walked back to the dining room and to the table at which the three men were sitting, but he did not sit down. "No, I wouldn't presume to think your memory is that extensive," he said. He was so small that the edge of the table top reached almost to his belt, and when he gripped the corner with his wiry hands he didn't have to stoop. "No, you're too busy gobbling up dinners in dining rooms. You're too—"

"Honestly," begged Sylvester. "You got to behave reasonable."

"Reasonable! Reasonable!" The jockey's gray face quivered, then set in a mean, frozen grin. He shook the table so that the plates rattled, and for a moment it seemed that he would push it over. But suddenly he stopped. His hand reached out toward the plate nearest to him and deliberately he put a few of the French-fried potatoes in his mouth. He chewed slowly, his upper lip raised, then he turned and spat out the pulpy mouthful on the smooth red carpet which covered the floor. "Libertines," he said, and his voice was thin and broken. He rolled the word in his mouth, as though it had a flavor and a substance that gratified him. "You libertines," he said again, and turned and walked with his rigid swagger out of the dining room.

Sylvester shrugged one of his loose, heavy shoulders. The rich man sopped up some water that had been spilled on the tablecloth, and they didn't speak until the waiter came to clear away.

Madame Zilensky and the King of Finland

To Mr. Brook, the head of the music department at Ryder College, was due all the credit for getting Madame Zilensky on the faculty. The college considered itself fortunate; her reputation was impressive, both as a composer and as a pedagogue. Mr. Brook took on himself the responsibility of finding a house for Madame Zilensky, a comfortable place with a garden, which was convenient to the college and next to the apartment house where he himself lived.

No one in Westbridge had known Madame Zilensky before she came. Mr. Brook had seen her pictures in musical journals, and once he had written to her about the authenticity of a certain Buxtehude manuscript. Also, when it was being settled that she was to join the faculty, they had exchanged a few cables and letters on practical affairs. She wrote in a clear, square hand, and the only thing out of the ordinary in these letters was the fact that they contained an occasional reference to objects and persons altogether unknown to Mr. Brook, such as "the yellow cat in Lisbon" or "poor Heinrich." These lapses Mr. Brook put down to the confusion of getting herself and her family out of Europe.

Mr. Brook was a somewhat pastel person; years of Mozart minuets, of explanations about diminished sevenths and minor triads, had given him a watchful vocational patience. For the most part, he kept to himself. He loathed academic fiddle-faddle and committees. Years before, when the music department had decided to gang together and spend the summer in Salzburg, Mr. Brook sneaked out of the arrangement at the last moment and took a solitary trip to Peru. He had a few eccentricities himself and was tolerant of the peculiarities of others; indeed, he rather relished the ridiculous. Often, when confronted with some grave and incongruous situation, he would feel a little inside tickle, which stiffened his long, mild face and sharpened the light in his gray eyes.

Mr. Brook met Madame Zilensky at the Westbridge station a week before the beginning of the fall semester. He recognized her instantly. She was a tall, straight woman with a pale and haggard face. Her eyes were deeply shadowed and she wore her dark, ragged hair pushed back from her forehead. She had large, delicate hands, which were very grubby. About her person as a whole there was something noble and abstract that made Mr. Brook draw back for a moment and stand nervously undoing his cuff links. In spite of her clothes — a long, black skirt and a broken-down old leather jacket — she made an impression of vague elegance. With Madame Zilensky were three children, boys between the ages of ten and six, all blond, blank-eyed, and beautiful. There was one other person, an old woman who turned out later to be the Finnish servant.

This was the group he found at the station. The only luggage they had with them was two immense boxes of manuscripts, the rest of their paraphernalia having been forgotten in the station at Springfield when they changed trains. That is the sort of thing that can happen to anyone. When Mr. Brook got them all into a taxi, he thought the worst difficulties were over, but Madame Zilensky suddenly tried to scramble over his knees and get out of the door.

"My God!" she said. "I left my — how do you say? — my tick-tick-tick —"

"Your watch?" asked Mr. Brook.

"Oh no!" she said vehemently. "You know, my tick-tick-tick," and she waved her forefinger from side to side, pendulum fashion.

"Tick-tick," said Mr. Brook, putting his hands to his forehead and closing his eyes. "Could you possibly mean a metronome?"

"Yes! Yes! I think I must have lost it there where we changed trains."

Mr. Brook managed to quiet her. He even said, with a kind of dazed gallantry, that he would get her another one the next day. But at the time he was bound to admit to himself that there was something curious about this panic over a metronome when there was all the rest of the lost luggage to consider.

The Zilensky ménage moved into the house next door, and on the surface everything was all right. The boys were quiet children. Their names were Sigmund, Boris, and Sammy. They were always together and they followed each other around Indian file, Sigmund usually the first. Among themselves they spoke a desperate-sounding family Esperanto made up of Russian, French, Finnish, German, and English; when other people were around, they were strangely silent. It was not any one thing that the Zilenskys did or said that made Mr. Brook uneasy. There were just little incidents. For example, something about the Zilensky children subconsciously bothered him when they were in a house, and finally he realized that what troubled him was the fact that the Zilensky boys never walked on a rug; they skirted it single file on the bare floor, and if a room was carpeted, they stood in the doorway and did not go inside. Another thing was this: Weeks passed and Madame Zilensky seemed to make no effort to get settled or to furnish the house with anything more than a table and some beds. The front door was left open day and night, and soon the house began to take on a queer, bleak look like that of a place abandoned for years.

The college had every reason to be satisfied with Madame Zilensky. She taught with a fierce insistence. She could become deeply indignant if some Mary Owens or Bernadine Smith would not clean up her Scarlatti trills. She got hold of four pianos for her college studio and set four dazed students to playing Bach fugues together. The racket that came from her end of the department was extraordinary, but Madame Zilensky did not seem to have a nerve in her, and if pure will and effort can get over a musical idea, then Ryder College could not have done better. At night Madame Zilensky worked on her twelfth symphony. She seemed never to sleep; no matter what time of night Mr. Brook happened to look out of his sitting-room window, the light in her studio was always on. No, it was not because of any professional consideration that Mr. Brook became so dubious.

It was in late October when he felt for the first time that something was unmistakably wrong. He had lunched with Madame Zilensky and had enjoyed himself, as she had given him a very detailed account of an African safari she had made in 1928. Later in the afternoon she stopped in at his office and stood rather abstractly in the doorway.

Mr. Brook looked up from his desk and asked, "Is there anything you want?"

"No, thank you," said Madame Zilensky. She had a low, beautiful, sombre voice. "I was only just wondering. You recall the metronome. Do you think perhaps that I might have left it with that French?"

"Who?" asked Mr. Brook.

"Why, that French I was married to," she answered.

"Frenchman," Mr. Brook said mildly. He tried to imagine the husband of Madame Zilensky, but his mind refused. He muttered half to himself, "The father of the children."

"But no," said Madame Zilensky with decision. "The father of Sammy."

Mr. Brook had a swift prescience. His deepest instincts warned him to say nothing further. Still, his respect for order, his conscience, demanded that he ask, "And the father of the other two?"

Madame Zilensky put her hand to the back of her head and ruffled up her short, cropped hair. Her face was dreamy, and for several moments she did not answer. Then she said gently, "Boris is of a Pole who played the piccolo."

"And Sigmund?" he asked. Mr. Brook looked over his orderly desk, with the stack of corrected papers, the three sharpened pencils, the ivory-elephant paperweight. When he glanced up at Madame Zilensky, she was obviously thinking hard. She gazed around at the corners of the room, her brows lowered and her jaw moving from side to side. At last she said, "We were discussing the father of Sigmund?"

"Why, no," said Mr. Brook. "There is no need to do that."

Madame Zilensky answered in a voice both dignified and final. "He was a fellow-countryman."

Mr. Brook really did not care one way or the other. He had no prejudices; people could marry seventeen times and have Chinese children so far as he was concerned. But there was something about this conversation with Madame Zilensky that bothered him. Suddenly he understood. The children didn't look at all like Madame Zilensky, but they looked exactly like each other, and as they all had different fathers, Mr. Brook thought the resemblance astonishing.

But Madame Zilensky had finished with the subject. She zipped up her leather jacket and turned away.

"That is exactly where I left it," she said, with a quick nod. "*Chez* that French."

Affairs in the music department were running smoothly. Mr. Brook did not have any serious embarrassments to deal with, such as the harp teacher last year who had finally eloped with a garage mechanic. There was only this nagging apprehension about Madame Zilensky. He could not make out what was wrong in his relations with her or why his feelings were so mixed. To begin with, she was a great globe-trotter, and her conversations were incongruously seasoned with references to far-fetched places. She would go along for days without opening her mouth, prowling through the corridor with her hands in the pockets of her jacket and her face locked in meditation. Then suddenly she would buttonhole Mr. Brook and launch out on a long, volatile monologue, her eyes reckless and bright and her voice warm with eagerness. She would talk about anything or nothing at all. Yet, without exception, there was something queer, in a slanted sort of way, about every episode she ever mentioned. If she spoke of taking Sammy to the barbershop, the impression she created was just as foreign as if she were telling of an afternoon in Bagdad. Mr. Brook could not make it out.

The truth came to him very suddenly, and the truth made everything perfectly clear, or at least clarified the situation. Mr. Brook had come home early and lighted a fire in the little grate in his sitting room. He felt comfortable and at peace that evening. He sat before the fire in his stocking feet, with a volume of William Blake on the table by his side, and he had poured himself a half-glass of apricot brandy. At ten o'clock he was drowsing cozily before the fire, his mind full of cloudy phrases of Mahler and floating half-thoughts. Then all at once, out of this delicate stupor, four words came to his mind: "The King of Finland." The words seemed familiar, but for the first moment he could not place them. Then all at once he tracked them down. He had been walking across the campus that afternoon when Madame Zilensky stopped him and began some preposterous rigmarole, to which he had only half listened; he was thinking about the stack of canons turned in by his counterpoint class. Now the words, the inflections of her voice, came back to him with insidious exactitude. Madame Zilensky had started off with the following remark: "One day, when I was standing in front of a *pâtisserie,* the King of Finland came by in a sled."

Mr. Brook jerked himself up straight in his chair and put down his glass of brandy. The woman was a pathological liar. Almost every word she uttered outside of class was an untruth. If she worked all night, she would go out of her way to tell you she spent the evening at the cinema. If she ate lunch at the Old Tavern, she would be sure to mention that she had lunched with her children at home. The woman was simply a pathological liar, and that accounted for everything.

Mr. Brook cracked his knuckles and got up from his chair. His first reaction was one of exasperation. That day after day Madame Zilensky would have the gall to sit there in his office and deluge him with her outrageous falsehoods! Mr. Brook was intensely provoked. He walked up and down the room, then he went into his kitchenette and made himself a sardine sandwich.

An hour later, as he sat before the fire, his irritation had changed to a scholarly and thoughtful wonder. What he must do, he told himself, was to regard the whole situation impersonally and look on Madame Zilensky as a doctor looks on a sick patient. Her lies were of the guileless sort. She did not dissimulate with any intention to deceive, and the untruths she told were never used to any possible advantage. That was the maddening thing; there was simply no motive behind it all.

Mr. Brook finished off the rest of the brandy. And slowly, when it was almost midnight, a further understanding came to him. The reason for the lies of Madame Zilensky was painful and plain. All her life long Madame Zilensky had worked — at the piano, teaching, and writing those beautiful and immense twelve symphonies. Day and night she had drudged and struggled and thrown her soul into her work, and there was not much of her left over for anything else. Being human, she suffered from this lack and did what she could to make up for it. If she passed the evening bent over a table in the library and later declared that she had spent that time playing cards, it was as though she had managed to do both those things. Through the lies, she lived vicariously. The lie doubled the little of her existence that was left over from work and augmented the little rag end of her personal life.

Mr. Brook looked into the fire, and the face of Madame Zilensky was in his mind — a severe face, with dark, weary eyes and delicately disciplined mouth. He was conscious of a warmth in his chest, and a feeling of pity, protectiveness, and dreadful understanding. For a while he was in a state of lovely confusion.

Later on he brushed his teeth and got into his pajamas. He must be practical. What did this clear up? That French, the Pole with the piccolo, Bagdad? And the children, Sigmund, Boris, and Sammy — who were they? Were they really her children after all, or had she simply rounded them up from somewhere? Mr. Brook polished his spectacles and put them on the table by his bed. He must come to an immediate understanding with her. Otherwise, there would exist in the department a situation which could become most problematical. It was two o'clock. He glanced out of his window and saw that the light in Madame Zilensky's workroom was still on. Mr. Brook got into bed, made terrible faces in the dark, and tried to plan what he would say next day.

Mr. Brook was in his office by eight o'clock. He sat hunched up behind his desk, ready to trap Madame Zilensky as she passed down the corridor. He did not have to wait long, and as soon as he heard her footsteps he called out her name.

Madame Zilensky stood in the doorway. She looked vague and jaded. "How are you? I had such a fine night's rest," she said.

"Pray be seated, if you please," said Mr. Brook. "I would like a word with you."

Madame Zilensky put aside her portfolio and leaned back wearily in the armchair across from him. "Yes?" she asked.

"Yesterday you spoke to me as I was walking across the campus," he said slowly. "And if I am not mistaken, I believe you said something about a pastry shop and the King of Finland. Is that correct?"

Madame Zilensky turned her head to one side and stared retrospectively at a corner of the window sill.

"Something about a pastry shop," he repeated.

Her tired face brightened. "But of course," she said eagerly. "I told you about the time I was standing in front of this shop and the King of Finland —"

"Madame Zilensky!" Mr. Brook cried. "There *is* no King of Finland."

Madame Zilensky looked absolutely blank. Then, after an instant, she started off again. "I was standing in front of Bjarne's *pâtisserie* when I turned away from the cakes and suddenly saw the King of Finland —"

"Madame Zilensky, I just told you that there is no King of Finland."

"In Helsingfors," she started off again desperately, and again he let her get as far as the King, and then no further.

"Finland is a democracy," he said. "You could not possibly have seen the King of Finland. Therefore, what you have just said is an untruth. A pure untruth."

Never afterward could Mr. Brook forget the face of Madame Zilensky at that moment. In her eyes there was astonishment, dismay, and a sort of cornered horror. She had the look of one who watches his whole interior world split open and disintegrate.

"It is a pity," said Mr. Brook with real sympathy.

But Madame Zilensky pulled herself together. She raised her chin and said coldly, "I am a Finn."

"That I do not question," answered Mr. Brook. On second thought, he did question it a little.

"I was born in Finland and I am a Finnish citizen."

"That may very well be," said Mr. Brook in a rising voice.

"In the war," she continued passionately, "I rode a motorcycle and was a messenger."

"Your patriotism does not enter into it."

"Just because I am getting out the first papers —"

"Madame Zilensky!" said Mr. Brook. His hands grasped the edge of the desk. "That is only an irrelevant issue. The point is that you maintained and testified that you saw — that you saw —" But he could not finish. Her face stopped him. She was deadly pale and there were shadows around her mouth. Her eyes were wide open, doomed, and proud. And Mr. Brook felt suddenly like a murderer. A great commotion of feelings — understanding, remorse, and unreasonable love — made him cover his face with his hands. He could not speak until this agitation in his insides quieted down, and then he said very faintly, "Yes. Of course. The King of Finland. And was he nice?"

An hour later, Mr. Brook sat looking out of the window of his office. The trees along the quiet Westbridge street were almost bare, and the gray buildings of the college had a calm, sad look. As he idly took in the familiar scene, he noticed the Drakes' old Airedale waddling along down the street. It was a thing he had watched a hundred times before, so what was it that struck him as strange? Then he realized with a kind of cold surprise that the old dog was running along backward. Mr. Brook watched the Airedale until he was out of sight, then resumed his work on the canons which had been turned in by the class in counterpoint.

Correspondence

113 Whitehall Street
Darien, Conn.
United States
November 3, 1941

Manoel García,
Calle São José 120,
Rio de Janeiro,
Brazil,
South America

Dear Manoel:

I guess seeing the American address on this letter you already know what it is. Your name was on the list tacked on the blackboard at High School of South American students we could correspond with. I was the one who picked your name.

Maybe I ought to tell you something about myself. I am a girl going on fourteen years of age and this is my first year at High School. It is hard to describe myself exactly. I am tall and my figure is not very good on account of I have grown too rapidly. My eyes are blue and I don't know exactly what color you would call my hair unless it would be a light brown. I like to play baseball and make scientific experiments (like with a chemical set) and read all kinds of books.

All my life I wanted to get to travel but the furtherest I have ever been away from home is Portsmouth, New Hampshire. Lately I have thought a whole lot about South America. Since choosing your name off the list I have thought a whole lot about you also and imagined how you are. I have seen photographs of the harbor in Rio de Janeiro and I can picture you in my mind's eye walking around the beach in the sun. I imagine you with liquid black eyes, brown skin, and black curly hair. I have always been crazy about South Americans although I did not know any of them and I always wanted to travel all over South America and especially to Rio de Janeiro.

As long as we are going to be friends and correspond I think we ought to know serious things about each other right away. Recently I have thought a whole lot about life. I have pondered over a great many things such as why we were put on the earth. I have decided that I do not believe in God. On the other hand I am not an atheist and I think there is some kind of a reason for everything and life is not in vain. When you die I think I believe that something happens to the soul.

I have not decided just exactly what I am going to be and it worries me. Sometimes I think I want to be an arctic explorer and other times I plan on being a newspaper reporter and working in to being a writer. For years I wished to be an actress, especially a tragic actress taking sad roles like Greta Garbo. This summer however when I got up a performance of Camille and I played Camille it was a terrible failure. The show was given in our garage and I can't explain to you what a terrible failure it was. So now I think mostly about newspaper reporting, especially foreign corresponding.

I do not feel exactly like the other Freshmen at High School. I feel like I am different from them. When I have a girl to spend the night with me on Friday night all they want to do is meet people down at the drug store near here and so forth and at night when we lie in the bed if I bring up serious subjects they are likely to go to sleep. They don't care anything much about foreign countries. It is not that I am terribly unpopular or anything like that but I am just not so crazy about the other Freshmen and they are not so crazy about me.

I thought a long time about you, Manoel, before writing this letter. And I have this strong feeling we would get along together. Do you like dogs? I have an airdale named Thomas and he is a one man dog. I feel like I have known you for a very long time and that we could discuss all sorts of things together. My Spanish is not so good naturally as this is my first term on it. But I intend to study diligently so that between us we can make out what we are saying when we meet each other.

I have thought about a lot of things. Would you like to come and spend your summer vacation with me next summer? I think that would be marvelous. Also other plans have been in my mind. Maybe next year after we have a visit together you could stay in my home and go to High School here and I could swap with you and stay in your home and go to South American High School. How does that strike you? I have not yet spoken to my parents about it because I am waiting until I get your opinion on it. I am looking forward exceedingly to hearing from you and find out if I am right about our feeling so much alike about life and other things. You can write to me anything that you want to, as I have said before that I feel I already know you so well. *Adiós* and I send you every possible good wish.

Your affectionate friend,

Henky Evans

P.S. My first name is really Henrietta but the family and people in the neighborhood all call me Henky because Henrietta sounds sort of sissy. I am sending this air mail so that it will get to you quicker. *Adiós* again.

113 Whitehall Street
Darien, Conn.,
U.S.A.
November 25, 1941

Manoel García,
Calle São José 120,
Rio de Janeiro,
Brazil,
South America

Dear Manoel:

Three weeks have gone by and I would have thought that by now there would be a letter from you. But it is entirely possible that communications take much longer than I had figured on, especially on account of the war. I read all the papers and the state of the world prays on my mind. I had not thought I would write to you again until I heard from you but as I said it must take a long time these days for things to reach foreign countries.

Today I am not at school. Yesterday morning when I woke up I was all broken out and swollen and red so that it looked like I had small pox at least. But when the doctor came he said it was hives. I took medicine and since then I have been sick in bed. I have been studying Latin as I am mighty close to flunking it. I will be glad when these hives go away.

There was one thing I forgot in my first letter. I think we ought to exchange pictures. Do you have a photograph of yourself, if so please send it as I want to really be sure if you look like what I think you do. I am enclosing a snapshot. The dog scratching himself in the corner is my dog Thomas and the house in the background is our house. The sun was in my eyes and that is why my face is all screwed up like that.

I was reading a very interesting book the other day about the reincarnation of souls. That means, in case you have not happened to read about it, that you live a lot of lives and are one person in one century and another one later on. It is very interesting. The more I think about it the more I believe it is true. What opinions do you have about it?

One thing I have always found it hard to realize is that about how when it is winter here it is summer below the equator. Of course I know why this is so, but at the same time it always strikes me as peculiar. Of course you are used to it. I have to keep remembering that it is now spring where you are, even if it is November. While the trees are bare here and the furnace is going it is just starting spring in Rio de Janeiro.

Every afternoon I wait for the postman. I have a strong feeling or a kind of a hunch that I will hear from you on this afternoon's mail or tomorrow. Communications must take longer than I had figured on even by air mail.

Affectionately yours,

Henky Evans

113 Whitehall Street
Darien, Conn.,
U.S.A.
December 29, 1941

Manoel García,
Calle São José 120,
Rio de Janeiro,
Brazil,
South America

Dear Manoel García:

I cannot possibly understand why I have not heard from you. Didn't you receive my two letters? Many other people in the class have had letters from South Americans a long time ago. Nearly two months have gone by since I started the correspondence.

Recently it came over me that maybe you have not been able to find anybody who knows English down there and can translate what I wrote. But it seems to me that you would have been able to find somebody and anyway it was understood that the South Americans whose names were on the list were studying English.

Maybe both the letters were lost. I realize how communications can sometimes go astray, especially on account of the war. But even if one letter was lost it seems to me like the other one would have arrived there all right. I just cannot understand it.

But perchance there is some reason I do not know about. Maybe you have been very sick in the hospital or maybe your family moved from your last address. I may hear from you very soon and it will all be straightened out. If there has been some such mistake please do not think that I am mad with you for not hearing sooner. I still sincerely want us to be friends and carry on the correspondence because I have always been so crazy about foreign countries and South America and I felt like I knew you right at the first.

I am all right and I hope you are the same. I won a five pound box of cherry candy in a benefit raffle given to raise money for the needy at Christmas.

As soon as you get this please answer and explain what is wrong, otherwise I just cannot understand what has happened. I beg to remain,

Sincerely yours,

Henrietta Evans

113 Whitehall Street
Darien, Conn.,
U.S.A.
January 20, 1942

Mr. Manoel García,
Calle São José 120,
Rio de Janeiro,
Brazil,
South America

Dear Mr. García:

I have sent you three letters in all good faith and expected you to fulfill your part in the idea of American and South American students corresponding like it was supposed to be. Nearly every other person in the class got letters and some even friendship gifts, even though they were not especially crazy about foreign countries like I was. I expected to hear every day and gave you the benefits of all the doubts. But now I realize what a grave mistake I made.

All I want to know is this. Why would you have your name put on the list if you did not intend to fulfill your part in the agreement? All I want to say is that if I had known then what I know now I most assuredly would have picked out some other South American.

Yrs. truly,

Miss Henrietta Hill Evans

P.S. I cannot waste any more of my valuable time writing to you.

A Tree · A Rock · A Cloud

It was raining that morning, and still very dark. When the boy reached the streetcar café he had almost finished his route and he went in for a cup of coffee. The place was an all-night café owned by a bitter and stingy man called Leo. After the raw, empty street the café seemed friendly and bright: along the counter there were a couple of soldiers, three spinners from the cotton mill, and in a corner a man who sat hunched over with his nose and half his face down in a beer mug. The boy wore a helmet such as aviators wear. When he went into the café he unbuckled the chin strap and raised the right flap up over his pink little ear; often as he drank his coffee someone would speak to him in a friendly way. But this morning Leo did not look into his face and none of the men were talking. He paid and was leaving the café when a voice called out to him:

"Son! Hey Son!"

He turned back and the man in the corner was crooking his finger and nodding to him. He had brought his face out of the beer mug and he seemed suddenly very happy. The man was long and pale, with a big nose and faded orange hair.

"Hey Son!"

The boy went toward him. He was an undersized boy of about twelve, with one shoulder drawn higher than the other because of the weight of the paper sack. His face was shallow, freckled, and his eyes were round child eyes.

"Yeah Mister?"

The man laid one hand on the paper boy's shoulders, then grasped the boy's chin and turned his face slowly from one side to the other. The boy shrank back uneasily.

"Say! What's the big idea?"

The boy's voice was shrill; inside the café it was suddenly very quiet.

The man said slowly: "I love you."

All along the counter the men laughed. The boy, who had scowled and sidled away, did not know what to do. He looked over the counter at Leo, and Leo watched him with a weary, brittle jeer. The boy tried to laugh also. But the man was serious and sad.

"I did not mean to tease you, Son," he said. "Sit down and have a beer with me. There is something I have to explain."

Cautiously, out of the corner of his eye, the paper boy questioned the men along the counter to see what he should do. But they had gone back to their beer or their breakfast and did not notice him. Leo put a cup of coffee on the counter and a little jug of cream.

"He is a minor," Leo said.

The paper boy slid himself up onto the stool. His ear beneath the upturned flap of the helmet was very small and red. The man was nodding at him soberly. "It is important," he said. Then he reached in his hip pocket and brought out something which he held up in the palm of his hand for the boy to see.

"Look very carefully," he said.

The boy stared, but there was nothing to look at very carefully. The man held in his big, grimy palm a photograph. It was the face of a woman, but blurred, so that only the hat and the dress she was wearing stood out clearly.

"See?" the man asked.

The boy nodded and the man placed another picture in his palm. The woman was standing on a beach in a bathing suit. The suit made her stomach very big, and that was the main thing you noticed.

"Got a good look?" He leaned over closer and finally asked: "You ever seen her before?"

The boy sat motionless, staring slantwise at the man. "Not so I know of."

"Very well." The man blew on the photographs and put them back into his pocket. "That was my wife."

"Dead?" the boy asked.

Slowly the man shook his head. He pursed his lips as though about to whistle and answered in a long-drawn way: "Nuuu—" he said. "I will explain."

The beer on the counter before the man was in a large brown mug. He did not pick it up to drink. Instead he bent down and, putting his face over the rim, he rested there for a moment. Then with both hands he tilted the mug and sipped.

"Some night you'll go to sleep with your big nose in a mug and drown," said Leo. "Prominent transient drowns in beer. That would be a cute death."

The paper boy tried to signal to Leo. While the man was not looking he screwed up his face and worked his mouth to question soundlessly: "Drunk?" But Leo only raised his eyebrows and turned away to put some pink strips of bacon on the grill. The man pushed the mug away from him, straightened himself, and folded his loose crooked hands on the counter. His face was sad as he looked at the paper boy. He did not blink, but from time to time the lids closed down with delicate gravity over his pale green eyes. It was nearing dawn and the boy shifted the weight of the paper sack.

"I am talking about love," the man said. "With me it is a science."

The boy half slid down from the stool. But the man raised his forefinger, and there was something about him that held the boy and would not let him go away.

"Twelve years ago I married the woman in the photograph. She was my wife for one year, nine months, three days, and two nights. I loved her. Yes . . ." He tightened his blurred, rambling voice and said again: "I loved her. I thought also that she loved me. I was a railroad engineer. She had all home comforts and luxuries. It never crept into my brain that she was not satisfied. But do you know what happened?"

"Mgneeow!" said Leo.

The man did not take his eyes from the boy's face. "She left me. I came in one night and the house was empty and she was gone. She left me."

"With a fellow?" the boy asked.

Gently the man placed his palm down on the counter. "Why naturally, Son. A woman does not run off like that alone."

The café was quiet, the soft rain black and endless in the street outside. Leo pressed down the frying bacon with the prongs of his long fork. "So you have been chasing the floozie for eleven years. You frazzled old rascal!"

For the first time the man glanced at Leo. "Please don't be vulgar. Besides, I was not speaking to you." He turned back to the boy and said in a trusting and secretive undertone: "Let's not pay any attention to him. O.K.?"

The paper boy nodded doubtfully.

"It was like this," the man continued. "I am a person who feels many things. All my life one thing after another has impressed me. Moonlight. The leg of a pretty girl. One thing after another. But the point is that when I had enjoyed anything there was a peculiar sensation as though it was laying around loose in me. Nothing seemed to finish itself up or fit in with the other things. Women? I had my portion of them. The same. Afterwards laying around loose in me. I was a man who had never loved."

Very slowly he closed his eyelids, and the gesture was like a curtain drawn at the end of a scene in a play. When he spoke again his voice was excited and the words came fast — the lobes of his large, loose ears seemed to tremble.

"Then I met this woman. I was fifty-one years old and she always said she was thirty. I met her at a filling station and we were married within three days. And do you know what it was like? I just can't tell you. All I had ever felt was gathered together around this woman. Nothing lay around loose in me any more but was finished up by her."

The man stopped suddenly and stroked his long nose. His voice sank down to a steady and reproachful undertone: "I'm not explaining this right. What happened was this. There were these beautiful feelings and loose little pleasures inside me. And this woman was something like an assembly line for my soul. I run these little pieces of myself through her and I come out complete. Now do you follow me?"

"What was her name?" the boy asked.

"Oh," he said. "I called her Dodo. But that is immaterial."

"Did you try to make her come back?"

The man did not seem to hear. "Under the circumstances you can imagine how I felt when she left me."

Leo took the bacon from the grill and folded two strips of it between a bun. He had a gray face, with slitted eyes, and a pinched nose saddled by faint blue shadows. One of the mill workers signaled for more coffee and Leo poured it. He did not give refills on coffee free. The spinner ate breakfast there every morning, but the better Leo knew his customers the stingier he treated them. He nibbled his own bun as though he grudged it to himself.

"And you never got hold of her again?"

The boy did not know what to think of the man, and his child's face was uncertain with mingled curiosity and doubt. He was new on the paper route; it was still strange to him to be out in the town in the black, queer early morning.

"Yes," the man said. "I took a number of steps to get her back. I went around trying to locate her. I went to Tulsa where she had folks. And to Mobile. I went to every town she had ever mentioned to me, and I hunted down every man she had formerly been connected with. Tulsa, Atlanta, Chicago, Cheehaw, Memphis.... For the better part of two years I chased around the country trying to lay hold of her."

"But the pair of them had vanished from the face of the earth!" said Leo.

"Don't listen to him," the man said confidentially. "And also just forget those two years. They are not important. What matters is that around the third year a curious thing begun to happen to me."

"What?" the boy asked.

The man leaned down and tilted his mug to take a sip of beer. But as he hovered over the mug his nostrils fluttered slightly; he sniffed the staleness of the beer and did not drink. "Love is a curious thing to begin with. At first I thought only of getting her back. It was a kind of mania. But then as time went on I tried to remember her. But do you know what happened?"

"No," the boy said.

"When I laid myself down on a bed and tried to think about her my mind became a blank. I couldn't see her. I would take out her pictures and look. No good. Nothing doing. A blank. Can you imagine it?"

"Say Mac!" Leo called down the counter. "Can you imagine this bozo's mind a blank!"

Slowly, as though fanning away flies, the man waved his hand. His green eyes were concentrated and fixed on the shallow little face of the paper boy.

"But a sudden piece of glass on a sidewalk. Or a nickel tune in a music box. A shadow on a wall at night. And I would remember. It might happen in a street and I would cry or bang my head against a lamppost. You follow me?"

"A piece of glass . . ." the boy said.

"Anything. I would walk around and I had no power of how and when to remember her. You think you can put up a kind of shield. But remembering don't come to a man face forward — it corners around sideways. I was at the mercy of everything I saw and heard. Suddenly instead of me combing the countryside to find her she begun to chase me around in my very soul. *She* chasing *me,* mind you! And in my soul."

The boy asked finally: "What part of the country were you in then?"

"Ooh," the man groaned. "I was a sick mortal. It was like smallpox. I confess, Son, that I boozed. I fornicated. I committed any sin that suddenly appealed to me. I am loath to confess it but I will do so. When I recall that period it is all curdled in my mind, it was so terrible."

The man leaned his head down and tapped his forehead on the counter. For a few seconds he stayed bowed over in this position, the back of his stringy neck covered with orange furze, his hands with their long warped fingers held palm to palm in an attitude of prayer. Then the man straightened himself; he was smiling and suddenly his face was bright and tremulous and old.

"It was in the fifth year that it happened," he said. "And with it I started my science."

Leo's mouth jerked with a pale, quick grin. "Well none of we boys are getting any younger," he said. Then with sudden anger he balled up a dishcloth he was holding and threw it down hard on the floor. "You draggle-tailed old Romeo!"

"What happened?" the boy asked.

The old man's voice was high and clear: "Peace," he answered.

"Huh?"

"It is hard to explain scientifically, Son," he said. "I guess the logical explanation is that she and I had fleed around from each other for so long that finally we just got tangled up together and lay down and quit. Peace. A queer and beautiful blankness. It was spring in Portland and the rain came every afternoon. All evening I just stayed there on my bed in the dark. And that is how the science come to me."

The windows in the streetcar were pale blue with light. The two soldiers paid for their beers and opened the door — one of the soldiers combed his hair and wiped off his muddy puttees before they went outside. The three mill workers bent silently over their breakfasts. Leo's clock was ticking on the wall.

"It is this. And listen carefully. I meditated on love and reasoned it out. I realized what is wrong with us. Men fall in love for the first time. And what do they fall in love with?"

The boy's soft mouth was partly open and he did not answer.

"A woman," the old man said. "Without science, with nothing to go by, they undertake the most dangerous and sacred experience in God's earth. They fall in love with a woman. Is that correct, Son?"

"Yeah," the boy said faintly.

"They start at the wrong end of love. They begin at the climax. Can you wonder it is so miserable? Do you know how men should love?"

The old man reached over and grasped the boy by the collar of his leather jacket. He gave him a gentle little shake and his green eyes gazed down unblinking and grave.

"Son, do you know how love should be begun?"

The boy sat small and listening and still. Slowly he shook his head. The old man leaned closer and whispered:

"A tree. A rock. A cloud."

It was still raining outside in the street: a mild, gray, endless rain. The mill whistle blew for the six o'clock shift and the three spinners paid and went away. There was no one in the café but Leo, the old man, and the little paper boy.

"The weather was like this in Portland," he said. "At the time my science was begun. I meditated and I started very cautious. I would pick up something from the street and take it home with me. I bought a goldfish and I concentrated on the goldfish and I loved it. I graduated from one thing to another. Day by day I was getting this technique. On the road from Portland to San Diego —"

"Aw shut up!" screamed Leo suddenly. "Shut up! Shut up!"

The old man still held the collar of the boy's jacket; he was trembling and his face was earnest and bright and wild. "For six years now I have gone around by myself and built up my science. And now I am a master, Son. I can love anything. No longer do I have to think about it even. I see a street full of people and a beautiful light comes in me. I watch a bird in the sky. Or I meet a traveler on the road. Everything, Son. And anybody. All stranger and all loved! Do you realize what a science like mine can mean?"

The boy held himself stiffly, his hands curled tight around the counter edge. Finally he asked: "Did you ever really find that lady?"

"What? What say, Son?"

"I mean," the boy asked timidly. "Have you fallen in love with a woman again?"

The old man loosened his grasp on the boy's collar. He turned away and for the first time his green eyes had a vague and scattered look. He lifted the mug from the counter, drank down the yellow beer. His head was shaking slowly from side to side. Then finally he answered: "No, Son. You see that is the last step in my science. I go cautious. And I am not quite ready yet."

"Well!" said Leo. "Well well well!"

The old man stood in the open doorway. "Remember," he said. Framed there in the gray damp light of the early morning he looked shrunken and seedy and frail. But his smile was bright. "Remember I love you," he said with a last nod. And the door closed quietly behind him.

The boy did not speak for a long time. He pulled down the bangs on his forehead and slid his grimy little forefinger around the rim of his empty cup. Then without looking at Leo he finally asked:

"Was he drunk?"

"No," said Leo shortly.

The boy raised his clear voice higher. "Then was he a dope fiend?"

"No."

The boy looked up at Leo, and his flat little face was desperate, his voice urgent and shrill. "Was he crazy? Do you think he was a lunatic?" The paper boy's voice dropped suddenly with doubt. "Leo? Or not?"

But Leo would not answer him. Leo had run a night café for fourteen years, and he held himself to be a critic of craziness. There were the town characters and also the transients who roamed in from the night. He knew the manias of all of them. But he did not want to satisfy the questions of the waiting child. He tightened his pale face and was silent.

So the boy pulled down the right flap of his helmet and as he turned to leave he made the only comment that seemed safe to him, the only remark that could not be laughed down and despised:

"He sure has done a lot of traveling."

Art and Mr. Mahoney

He was a large man, a contractor, and he was the husband of the small, sharp Mrs. Mahoney who was so active in club and cultural affairs. A canny businessman (he owned a brick yard and planing mill), Mr. Mahoney lumbered with tractable amiability in the lead of the artistic Mrs. Mahoney. Mr. Mahoney was well drilled; he was accustomed to speak of "repertory," to listen to lectures and concerts with the proper expression of meek sorrow. He could talk about abstract art, he had even taken part in two of the Little Theatre productions, once as a butler, the other time as a Roman soldier. Mr. Mahoney, diligently trained, so many times admonished — how could he have brought upon them such disgrace?

The pianist that night was José Iturbi, and it was the first concert of the season, a gala night. The Mahoneys had worked very hard during the Three Arts League drive. Mr. Mahoney had sold more than thirty season tickets on his own. To business acquaintances, the men downtown, he spoke of the projected concerts as "a pride to the community" and "a cultural necessity." The Mahoneys had donated the use of their car and had entertained subscribers at a lawn fete — with three white-coated colored boys handing refreshments, and their newly built Tudor house waxed and flowered for the occasion. The Mahoneys' position as sponsors of art and culture was well earned.

The start of the fatal evening gave no hint of what was to come. Mr. Mahoney sang in the shower and dressed himself with detailed care. He had brought an orchid from Duff's Flower Shop. When Ellie came in from her room — they had adjoining separate rooms in the new house — he was brushed and gleaming in his dinner jacket, and Ellie wore the orchid on the shoulder of her blue crepe dress. She was pleased and, patting his arm, she said: "You look so handsome tonight, Terence. Downright distinguished."

Mr. Mahoney's stout body bridled with happiness, and his ruddy face with the forked-veined temples blushed. "You are always beautiful, Ellie. Always so beautiful. Sometimes I don't understand why you married a —"

She stopped him with a kiss.

There was to be a reception after the concert at the Harlows', and of course the Mahoneys were invited. Mrs. Harlow was the "bell cow" in this pasture of the finer things. Oh, how Ellie did despise such country-raised expressions! But Mr. Mahoney had forgotten all the times he had been called down as he gallantly placed Ellie's wrap about her shoulders.

The irony was that, up until the moment of his ignominy, Mr. Mahoney had enjoyed the concert more than any concert that he had ever heard. There was none of that wriggling, tedious Bach. There was some marchy-sounding music and often he was on foot-patting familiarity with the tunes. As he sat there, enjoying the music, he glanced occasionally at Ellie. Her face bore the expression of fixed, inconsolable grief that it always assumed when she listened to classical concert music. Between the numbers she put her hand to her forehead with a distracted air, as though the endurance of such emotion had been too much for her. Mr. Mahoney clapped his pink, plump hands with gusto, glad of a chance to move and respond.

In the intermission the Mahoneys filed sedately down the aisle to the lobby. Mr. Mahoney found himself stuck with old Mrs. Walker.

"I'm looking forward to the Chopin," she said. "I always love minor music, don't you?"

"I guess you enjoy your misery," Mr. Mahoney answered.

Miss Walker, the English teacher, spoke up promptly. "It's Mother's melancholy Celtic soul. She's of Irish descent, you know."

Feeling he had somehow made a mistake, Mr. Mahoney said awkwardly, "I like minor music all right."

Tip Mayberry took Mr. Mahoney's arm and spoke to him chummily. "This fellow can certainly rattle the old ivories."

Mr. Mahoney answered with reserve, "He has a very brilliant technique."

"It's still an hour to go," Tip Mayberry complained. "I wish me and you could slip out of here."

Mr. Mahoney moved discreetly away.

Mr. Mahoney loved the atmosphere of Little Theatre plays and concerts — the chiffon and corsages and decorous dinner jackets. He was warm with pride and pleasure as he went sociably about the lobby of the high school auditorium, greeting the ladies, speaking with reverent authority of movements and mazurkas.

It was during the first number after the intermission that the calamity came. It was a long Chopin sonata: the first movement thundering, the second jerking and mercurial. The third movement he followed knowingly with tapping foot — the rigid funeral march with a sad waltzy bit in the middle; the end of the funeral march came with a chorded final crash. The pianist lifted up his hand and even leaned back a little on the piano stool.

Mr. Mahoney clapped. He was so dead sure it was the end that he clapped heartily half a dozen times before he realized, to his horror, that he clapped alone. With swift fiendish energy José Iturbi attacked the piano keys again.

Mr. Mahoney sat stiff with agony. The next moments were the most dreadful in his memory. The red veins in his temples swelled and darkened. He clasped his offending hands between his thighs.

If only Ellie had made some comforting secret sign. But when he dared to glance at Ellie, her face was frozen and she gazed at the stage with desperate attentiveness. After some endless minutes of humiliation, Mr. Mahoney reached his hand timidly toward Ellie's crepe-covered thigh. Mrs. Mahoney moved away from him and crossed her legs.

For almost an hour Mr. Mahoney had to suffer this public shame. Once he caught a glimpse of Tip Mayberry, and an alien evil shafted through his gentle heart. Tip did not know a sonata from the *Slit Belly Blues*. Yet there he sat, smug, unnoticed. Mrs. Mahoney refused to meet her husband's anguished eyes.

They had to go on to the party. He admitted it was the only proper thing to do. They drove there in silence, but when he had parked the car before the Harlow house Mrs. Mahoney said, "I should think that anybody with a grain of sense knows enough not to clap until everybody else is clapping."

It was for him a miserable party. The guests gathered around José Iturbi and were introduced. (They all knew who had clapped except Mr. Iturbi; he was as cordial to Mr. Mahoney as to the others.) Mr. Mahoney stood in the corner behind the concert-grand piano drinking Scotch. Old Mrs. Walker and Miss Walker hovered with the "bell cow" around Mr. Iturbi. Ellie was looking at the titles in the bookcase. She took out a book and even read for a little while with her back to the room. In the corner he was alone through a good many highballs. And it was Tip Mayberry who finally joined him. "I guess after all those tickets you sold you were entitled to an extra clap." He gave Mr. Mahoney a slow wink of covert brotherhood which Mr. Mahoney at that moment was almost willing to admit.

The Sojourner

The twilight border between sleep and waking was a Roman one this morning: splashing fountains and arched, narrow streets, the golden lavish city of blossoms and age-soft stone. Sometimes in this semi-consciousness he sojourned again in Paris, or war German rubble, or Swiss skiing and a snow hotel. Sometimes, also, in a fallow Georgia field at hunting dawn. Rome it was this morning in the yearless region of dreams.

John Ferris awoke in a room in a New York hotel. He had the feeling that something unpleasant was awaiting him — what it was, he did not know. The feeling, submerged by matinal necessities, lingered even after he had dressed and gone downstairs. It was a cloudless autumn day and the pale sunlight sliced between the pastel skyscrapers. Ferris went into the next-door drugstore and sat at the end booth next to the window glass that overlooked the sidewalk. He ordered an American breakfast with scrambled eggs and sausage.

Ferris had come from Paris to his father's funeral which had taken place the week before in his home town in Georgia. The shock of death had made him aware of youth already passed. His hair was receding and the veins in his now naked temples were pulsing and prominent and his body was spare except for an incipient belly bulge. Ferris had loved his father and the bond between them had once been extraordinarily close — but the years had somehow unraveled this filial devotion; the death, expected for a long time, had left him with an unforeseen dismay. He had stayed as long as possible to be near his mother and brothers at home. His plane for Paris was to leave the next morning.

Ferris pulled out his address book to verify a number. He turned the pages with growing attentiveness. Names and addresses from New York, the capitals of Europe, a few faint ones from his home state in the South. Faded, printed names, sprawled drunken ones. Betty Wills: a random love, married now. Charlie Williams: wounded in the Hürtgen Forest, unheard of since. Grand old Williams — did he live or die? Don Walker: a B.T.O. in television, getting rich. Henry Green: hit the skids after the war, in a sanitarium now, they say. Cozie Hall: he had heard that she was dead. Heedless, laughing Cozie — it was strange to think that she too, silly girl, could die. As Ferris closed the address book, he suffered a sense of hazard, transience, almost of fear.

It was then that his body jerked suddenly. He was staring out of the window when there, on the sidewalk, passing by, was his ex-wife. Elizabeth passed quite close to him, walking slowly. He could not understand the wild quiver of his heart, nor the following sense of recklessness and grace that lingered after she was gone.

Quickly Ferris paid his check and rushed out to the sidewalk. Elizabeth stood on the corner waiting to cross Fifth Avenue. He hurried toward her meaning to speak, but the lights changed and she crossed the street before he reached her. Ferris followed. On the other side he could easily have overtaken her, but he found himself lagging unaccountably. Her fair brown hair was plainly rolled, and as he watched her Ferris recalled that once his father had remarked that Elizabeth had a "beautiful carriage." She turned at the next corner and Ferris followed, although by now his intention to overtake her had disappeared. Ferris questioned the bodily disturbance that the sight of Elizabeth aroused in him, the dampness of his hands, the hard heartstrokes.

It was eight years since Ferris had last seen his ex-wife. He knew that long ago she had married again. And there were children. During recent years he had seldom thought of her. But at first, after the divorce, the loss had almost destroyed him. Then after the anodyne of time, he had loved again, and then again. Jeannine, she was now. Certainly his love for his ex-wife was long since past. So why the unhinged body, the shaken mind? He knew only that his clouded heart was oddly dissonant with the sunny, candid autumn day. Ferris wheeled suddenly and, walking with long strides, almost running, hurried back to the hotel.

Ferris poured himself a drink, although it was not yet eleven o'clock. He sprawled out in an armchair like a man exhausted, nursing his glass of bourbon and water. He had a full day ahead of him as he was leaving by plane the next morning for Paris. He checked over his obligations: take luggage to Air France, lunch with his boss, buy shoes and an overcoat. And something — wasn't there something else? Ferris finished his drink and opened the telephone directory.

His decision to call his ex-wife was impulsive. The number was under Bailey, the husband's name, and he called before he had much time for self-debate. He and Elizabeth had exchanged cards at Christmastime, and Ferris had sent a carving set when he received the announcement of her wedding. There was no reason *not* to call. But as he waited, listening to the ring at the other end, misgiving fretted him.

Elizabeth answered; her familiar voice was a fresh shock to him. Twice he had to repeat his name, but when he was identified, she sounded glad. He explained he was only in town for that day. They had a theater engagement, she said — but she wondered if he would come by for an early dinner. Ferris said he would be delighted.

As he went from one engagement to another, he was still bothered at odd moments by the feeling that something necessary was forgotten. Ferris bathed and changed in the late afternoon, often thinking about Jeannine: he would be with her the following night. "Jeannine," he would say, "I happened to run into my ex-wife when I was in New York. Had dinner with her. And her husband, of course. It was strange seeing her after all these years."

Elizabeth lived in the East Fifties, and as Ferris taxied uptown he glimpsed at intersections the lingering sunset, but by the time he reached his destination it was already autumn dark. The place was a building with a marquee and a doorman, and the apartment was on the seventh floor.

"Come in, Mr. Ferris."

Braced for Elizabeth or even the unimagined husband, Ferris was astonished by the freckled red-haired child; he had known of the children, but his mind had failed somehow to acknowledge them. Surprise made him step back awkwardly.

"This is our apartment," the child said politely. "Aren't you Mr. Ferris? I'm Billy. Come in."

In the living room beyond the hall, the husband provided another surprise; he too had not been acknowledged emotionally. Bailey was a lumbering red-haired man with a deliberate manner. He rose and extended a welcoming hand.

"I'm Bill Bailey. Glad to see you. Elizabeth will be in, in a minute. She's finishing dressing."

The last words struck a gliding series of vibrations, memories of the other years. Fair Elizabeth, rosy and naked before her bath. Half-dressed before the mirror of her dressing table, brushing her fine, chestnut hair. Sweet, casual intimacy, the soft-fleshed loveliness indisputably possessed. Ferris shrank from the unbidden memories and compelled himself to meet Bill Bailey's gaze.

"Billy, will you please bring that tray of drinks from the kitchen table?"

The child obeyed promptly, and when he was gone Ferris remarked conversationally, "Fine boy you have there."

"We think so."

Flat silence until the child returned with a tray of glasses and a cocktail shaker of Martinis. With the priming drinks they pumped up conversation: Russia, they spoke of, and the New York rainmaking, and the apartment situation in Manhattan and Paris.

"Mr. Ferris is flying all the way across the ocean tomorrow," Bailey said to the little boy who was perched on the arm of his chair, quiet and well behaved. "I bet you would like to be a stowaway in his suitcase."

Billy pushed back his limp bangs. "I want to fly in an airplane and be a newspaperman like Mr. Ferris." He added with sudden assurance, "That's what I would like to do when I am big."

Bailey said, "I thought you wanted to be a doctor."

"I do!" said Billy. "I would like to be both. I want to be a atom-bomb scientist too."

Elizabeth came in carrying in her arms a baby girl.

"Oh, John!" she said. She settled the baby in the father's lap. "It's grand to see you. I'm awfully glad you could come."

The little girl sat demurely on Bailey's knees. She wore a pale pink crêpe de Chine frock, smocked around the yoke with rose, and a matching silk hair ribbon tying back her pale soft curls. Her skin was summer tanned and her brown eyes flecked with gold and laughing. When she reached up and fingered her father's horn-rimmed glasses, he took them off and let her look through them a moment. "How's my old Candy?"

Elizabeth was very beautiful, more beautiful perhaps than he had ever realized. Her straight clean hair was shining. Her face was softer, glowing and serene. It was a madonna loveliness, dependent on the family ambiance.

"You've hardly changed at all," Elizabeth said, "but it has been a long time."

"Eight years." His hand touched his thinning hair self-consciously while further amenities were exchanged.

Ferris felt himself suddenly a spectator — an interloper among these Baileys. Why had he come? He suffered. His own life seemed so solitary, a fragile column supporting nothing amidst the wreckage of the years. He felt he could not bear much longer to stay in the family room.

He glanced at his watch. "You're going to the theater?"

"It's a shame," Elizabeth said, "but we've had this engagement for more than a month. But surely, John, you'll be staying home one of these days before long. You're not going to be an expatriate, are you?"

"Expatriate," Ferris repeated. "I don't much like the word."

"What's a better word?" she asked.

He thought for a moment. "Sojourner might do."

Ferris glanced again at his watch, and again Elizabeth apologized. "If only we had known ahead of time —"

"I just had this day in town. I came home unexpectedly. You see, Papa died last week."

"Papa Ferris is dead?"

"Yes, at Johns-Hopkins. He had been sick there nearly a year. The funeral was down home in Georgia."

"Oh, I'm so sorry, John. Papa Ferris was always one of my favorite people."

The little boy moved from behind the chair so that he could look into his mother's face. He asked, "Who is dead?"

Ferris was oblivious to apprehension; he was thinking of his father's death. He saw again the outstretched body on the quilted silk within the coffin. The corpse flesh was bizarrely rouged and the familiar hands lay massive and joined above a spread of funeral roses. The memory closed and Ferris awakened to Elizabeth's calm voice.

"Mr. Ferris' father, Billy. A really grand person. Somebody yo didn't know."

"But why did you call him *Papa* Ferris?"

Bailey and Elizabeth exchanged a trapped look. It was Bailey who answered the questioning child. "A long time ago," he said, "your mother and Mr. Ferris were once married. Before you were born — a long time ago."

"Mr. Ferris?"

The little boy stared at Ferris, amazed and unbelieving. And Ferris' eyes, as he returned the gaze, were somehow unbelieving too. Was it indeed true that at one time he had called this stranger, Elizabeth, Little Butterduck during nights of love, that they had lived together, shared perhaps a thousand days and nights and — finally — endured in the misery of sudden solitude the fiber by fiber (jealousy, alcohol and money quarrels) destruction of the fabric of married love.

Bailey said to the children, "It's somebody's suppertime. Come on now."

"But Daddy! Mama and Mr. Ferris — I —"

Billy's everlasting eyes — perplexed and with a glimmer of hostility — reminded Ferris of the gaze of another child. It was the young son of Jeannine — a boy of seven with a shadowed little face and nobby knees whom Ferris avoided and usually forgot.

"Quick march!" Bailey gently turned Billy toward the door. "Say good night now, son."

"Good night, Mr. Ferris." He added resentfully, "I thought I was staying up for the cake."

"You can come in afterward for the cake," Elizabeth said. "Run along now with Daddy for your supper."

Ferris and Elizabeth were alone. The weight of the situation descended on those first moments of silence. Ferris asked permission to pour himself another drink and Elizabeth set the cocktail shaker on the table at his side. He looked at the grand piano and noticed the music on the rack.

"Do you still play as beautifully as you used to?"

"I still enjoy it."

"Please play, Elizabeth."

Elizabeth arose immediately. Her readiness to perform when asked had always been one of her amiabilities; she never hung back, apol-

she approached the piano there was the added read-

th a Bach prelude and fugue. The prelude was as as a prism in a morning room. The first voice of the gue, an announcement pure and solitary, was repeated intermingling with a second voice, and again repeated within an elaborated frame, the multiple music, horizontal and serene, flowed with unhurried majesty. The principal melody was woven with two other voices, embellished with countless ingenuities — now dominant, again submerged, it had the sublimity of a single thing that does not fear surrender to the whole. Toward the end, the density of the material gathered for the last enriched insistence on the dominant first motif and with a chorded final statement the fugue ended. Ferris rested his head on the chair back and closed his eyes. In the following silence a clear, high voice came from the room down the hall.

"Daddy, how *could* Mama and Mr. Ferris —" A door was closed.

The piano began again — what was this music? Unplaced, familiar, the limpid melody had lain a long while dormant in his heart. Now it spoke to him of another time, another place — it was the music Elizabeth used to play. The delicate air summoned a wilderness of memory. Ferris was lost in the riot of past longings, conflicts, ambivalent desires. Strange that the music, catalyst for this tumultuous anarchy, was so serene and clear. The singing melody was broken off by the appearance of the maid.

"Miz Bailey, dinner is out on the table now."

Even after Ferris was seated at the table between his host and hostess, the unfinished music still overcast his mood. He was a little drunk.

"L'improvisation de la vie humaine," he said. "There's nothing that makes you so aware of the improvisation of human existence as a song unfinished. Or an old address book."

"Address book?" repeated Bailey. Then he stopped, noncommittal and polite.

"You're still the same old boy, Johnny," Elizabeth said with a trace of the old tenderness.

It was a Southern dinner that evening, and the dishes were his old favorites. They had fried chicken and corn pudding and rich, glazed candied sweet potatoes. During the meal Elizabeth kept alive a conversation when the silences were overlong. And it came about that Ferris was led to speak of Jeannine.

"I first knew Jeannine last autumn — about this time of the year — in Italy. She's a singer and she had an engagement in Rome. I expect we will be married soon."

The words seemed so true, inevitable, that Ferris did not at first acknowledge to himself the lie. He and Jeannine had never in that year spoken of marriage. And indeed, she was still married — to a White Russian money-changer in Paris from whom she had been separated for five years. But it was too late to correct the lie. Already Elizabeth was saying: "This really makes me glad to know. Congratulations, Johnny."

He tried to make amends with truth. "The Roman autumn is so beautiful. Balmy and blossoming." He added. "Jeannine has a little boy of seven. A curious trilingual little fellow. We go to the Tuileries sometimes."

A lie again. He had taken the boy once to the gardens. The sallow foreign child in shorts that bared his spindly legs had sailed his boat in the concrete pond and ridden the pony. The child had wanted to go in to the puppet show. But there was not time, for Ferris had an engagement at the Scribe Hotel. He had promised they would go to the guignol another afternoon. Only once had he taken Valentin to the Tuileries.

There was a stir. The maid brought in a white-frosted cake with pink candles. The children entered in their night clothes. Ferris still did not understand.

"Happy birthday, John," Elizabeth said. "Blow out the candles."

Ferris recognized his birthday date. The candles blew out lingeringly and there was the smell of burning wax. Ferris was thirty-eight years old. The veins in his temples darkened and pulsed visibly.

"It's time you started for the theater."

Ferris thanked Elizabeth for the birthday dinner and said the appropriate good-byes. The whole family saw him to the door.

A high, thin moon shone above the jagged, dark skyscrapers. The streets were windy, cold. Ferris hurried to Third Avenue and hailed a cab. He gazed at the nocturnal city with the deliberate attentiveness of departure and perhaps farewell. He was alone. He longed for flighttime and the coming journey.

The next day he looked down on the city from the air, burnished in sunlight, toylike, precise. Then America was left behind and there was only the Atlantic and the distant European shore. The ocean was milky pale and placid beneath the clouds. Ferris dozed most of the day. Toward dark he was thinking of Elizabeth and the visit of the previous evening. He thought of Elizabeth among her family with longing, gentle envy and inexplicable regret. He sought the melody, the unfinished air, that had so moved him. The cadence, some unrelated tones, were all that remained; the melody itself evaded him. He had found instead the first voice of the fugue that Elizabeth had played — it came to him, inverted mockingly and in a minor key. Suspended above the ocean the anxieties of transience and solitude no longer troubled him and he thought of his father's death with equanimity. During the dinner hour the plane reached the shore of France.

At midnight Ferris was in a taxi crossing Paris. It was a clouded night and mist wreathed the lights of the Place de la Concorde. The midnight bistros gleamed on the wet pavements. As always after a transocean flight the change of continents was too sudden. New York at morning, this midnight Paris. Ferris glimpsed the disorder of his life: the succession of cities, of transitory loves; and time, the sinister glissando of the years, time always.

"Vite! Vite!" he called in terror. *"Dépêchez-vous."*

Valentin opened the door to him. The little boy wore pajamas and an outgrown red robe. His gray eyes were shadowed and, as Ferris passed into the flat, they flickered momentarily.

"J'attends Maman."

Jeannine was singing in a night club. She would not be home before another hour. Valentin returned to a drawing, squatting with his crayons over the paper on the floor. Ferris looked down at the drawing — it was a banjo player with notes and wavy lines inside a comic-strip balloon.

"We will go again to the Tuileries."

The child looked up and Ferris drew him closer to his knees. The melody, the unfinished music that Elizabeth had played, came to him suddenly. Unsought, the load of memory jettisoned — this time bringing only recognition and sudden joy.

"Monsieur Jean," the child said, "did you see him?"

Confused, Ferris thought only of another child — the freckled, family-loved boy. "See who, Valentin?"

"Your dead papa in Georgia." The child added, "Was he okay?"

Ferris spoke with rapid urgency: "We will go often to the Tuileries. Ride the pony and we will go into the guignol. We will see the puppet show and never be in a hurry any more."

"Monsieur Jean," Valentin said. "The guignol is now closed."

Again, the terror the acknowledgment of wasted years and death. Valentin, responsive and confident, still nestled in his arms. His cheek touched the soft cheek and felt the brush of the delicate eyelashes. With inner desperation he pressed the child close — as though an emotion as protean as his love could dominate the pulse of time.

A Domestic Dilemma

On Thursday Martin Meadows left the office early enough to make the first express bus home. It was the hour when the evening lilac glow was fading in the slushy streets, but by the time the bus had left the Mid-town terminal the bright city night had come. On Thursdays the maid had a half-day off and Martin liked to get home as soon as possible, since for the past year his wife had not been — well. This Thursday he was very tired and, hoping that no regular commuter would single him out for conversation, he fastened his attention to the newspaper until the bus had crossed the George Washington Bridge. Once on 9-W Highway Martin always felt that the trip was halfway done, he breathed deeply, even in cold weather when only ribbons of draught cut through the smoky air of the bus, confident that he was breathing country air. It used to be that at this point he would relax and begin to think with pleasure of his home. But in this last year nearness brought only a sense of tension and he did not anticipate the journey's end. This evening Martin kept his face close to the window and watched the barren fields and lonely lights of passing townships. There was a moon, pale on the dark earth and areas of late, porous snow; to Martin the countryside seemed vast and somehow desolate that evening. He took his hat from the rack and put his folded newspaper in the pocket of his overcoat a few minutes before time to pull the cord.

The cottage was a block from the bus stop, near the river but not directly on the shore; from the living-room window you could look across the street and opposite yard and see the Hudson. The cottage was modern, almost too white and new on the narrow plot of yard.

In summer the grass was soft and bright and Martin carefully tended a flower border and a rose trellis. But during the cold, fallow months the yard was bleak and the cottage seemed naked. Lights were on that evening in all the rooms in the little house and Martin hurried up the front walk. Before the steps he stopped to move a wagon out of the way.

The children were in the living room, so intent on play that the opening of the front door was at first unnoticed. Martin stood looking at his safe, lovely children. They had opened the bottom drawer of the secretary and taken out the Christmas decorations. Andy had managed to plug in the Christmas tree lights and the green and red bulbs glowed with out-of-season festivity on the rug of the living room. At the moment he was trying to trail the bright cord over Marianne's rocking horse. Marianne sat on the floor pulling off an angel's wings. The children wailed a startling welcome. Martin swung the fat little baby girl up to his shoulder and Andy threw himself against his father's legs.

"Daddy, Daddy, Daddy!"

Martin set down the little girl carefully and swung Andy a few times like a pendulum. Then he picked up the Christmas tree cord.

"What's all this stuff doing out? Help me put it back in the drawer. You're not to fool with the light socket. Remember I told you that before. I mean it, Andy."

The six-year-old child nodded and shut the secretary drawer. Martin stroked his fair soft hair and his hand lingered tenderly on the nape of the child's frail neck.

"Had supper yet, Bumpkin?"

"It hurt. The toast was hot."

The baby girl stumbled on the rug and, after the first surprise of the fall, began to cry; Martin picked her up and carried her in his arms back to the kitchen.

"See, Daddy," said Andy. "The toast —"

Emily had laid the children's supper on the uncovered porcelain table. There were two plates with the remains of cream-of-wheat and eggs and silver mugs that had held milk. There was also a platter of cinnamon toast, untouched except for one tooth-marked bite. Martin sniffed the bitten piece and nibbled gingerly. Then he put the toast into the garbage pail.

"Hoo — phui — What on earth!"

Emily had mistaken the tin of cayenne for the cinnamon.

"I like to have burnt up," Andy said. "Drank water and ran outdoors and opened my mouth. Marianne didn't eat none."

"Any," corrected Martin. He stood helpless, looking around the walls of the kitchen. "Well, that's that, I guess," he said finally. "Where is your mother now?"

"She's up in you all's room."

Martin left the children in the kitchen and went up to his wife. Outside the door he waited for a moment to still his anger. He did not knock and once inside the room he closed the door behind him.

Emily sat in the rocking chair by the window of the pleasant room. She had been drinking something from a tumbler and as he entered she put the glass hurriedly on the floor behind the chair. In her attitude there was confusion and guilt which she tried to hide by a show of spurious vivacity.

"Oh, Marty! You home already? The time slipped up on me. I was just going down —" She lurched to him and her kiss was strong with sherry. When he stood unresponsive she stepped back a pace and giggled nervously.

"What's the matter with you? Standing there like a barber pole. Is anything wrong with you?"

"Wrong with *me?*" Martin bent over the rocking chair and picked up the tumbler from the floor. "If you could only realize how sick I am — how bad it is for all of us."

Emily spoke in a false, airy voice that had become too familiar to him. Often at such times she affected a slight English accent, copying perhaps some actress she admired. "I haven't the vaguest idea what you mean. Unless you are referring to the glass I used for a spot of sherry. I had a finger of sherry — maybe two. But what is the crime in that, pray tell me? I'm quite all right. Quite all right."

"So anyone can see."

As she went into the bathroom Emily walked with careful gravity. She turned on the cold water and dashed some on her face with her cupped hands, then patted herself dry with the corner of a bath towel. Her face was delicately featured and young, unblemished.

"I was just going down to make dinner." She tottered and balanced herself by holding to the door frame.

"I'll take care of dinner. You stay up here. I'll bring it up."

"I'll do nothing of the sort. Why, whoever heard of such a thing?"

"Please," Martin said.

"Leave me alone. I'm quite all right. I was just on the way down —"

"Mind what I say."

"Mind your grandmother."

She lurched toward the door, but Martin caught her by the arm. "I don't want the children to see you in this condition. Be reasonable."

"Condition!" Emily jerked her arm. Her voice rose angrily. "Why, because I drink a couple of sherries in the afternoon you're trying to make me out a drunkard. Condition! Why, I don't even touch whiskey. As well you know. *I* don't swill liquor at bars. And that's more than you can say. I don't even have a cocktail at dinnertime. I only sometimes have a glass of sherry. What, I ask you, is the disgrace of that? Condition!"

Martin sought words to calm his wife. "We'll have a quiet supper by ourselves up here. That's a good girl." Emily sat on the side of the bed and he opened the door for a quick departure.

"I'll be back in a jiffy."

As he busied himself with the dinner downstairs he was lost in the familiar question as to how this problem had come upon his home. He himself had always enjoyed a good drink. When they were still living in Alabama they had served long drinks or cocktails as a matter of course. For years they had drunk one or two — possibly three drinks before dinner, and at bedtime a long nightcap. Evenings before holidays they might get a buzz on, might even become a little tight. But alcohol had never seemed a problem to him, only a bothersome expense that with the increase in the family they could scarcely afford. It was only after his company had transferred him to New York that Martin was aware that certainly his wife was drinking too much. She was tippling, he noticed, during the day.

The problem acknowledged, he tried to analyze the source. The change from Alabama to New York had somehow disturbed her; accustomed to the idle warmth of a small Southern town, the matrix of the family and cousinship and childhood friends, she had failed to accommodate herself to the stricter, lonelier mores of the North. The duties of motherhood and housekeeping were onerous to her. Homesick for Paris City, she had made no friends in the suburban town. She read only magazines and murder books. Her interior life was insufficient without the artifice of alcohol.

The revelations of incontinence insidiously undermined his previous conceptions of his wife. There were times of unexplainable malevolence, times when the alcoholic fuse caused an explosion of unseemly anger. He encountered a latent coarseness in Emily, inconsistent with her natural simplicity. She lied about drinking and deceived him with unsuspected stratagems.

Then there was an accident. Coming home from work one evening about a year ago, he was greeted with screams from the children's room. He found Emily holding the baby, wet and naked from her bath. The baby had been dropped, her frail, frail skull striking the table edge, so that a thread of blood was soaking into the gossamer hair. Emily was sobbing and intoxicated. As Martin cradled the hurt child, so infinitely precious at that moment, he had an affrighted vision of the future.

The next day Marianne was all right. Emily vowed that never again would she touch liquor, and for a few weeks she was sober, cold and downcast. Then gradually she began — not whiskey or gin — but quantities of beer, or sherry, or outlandish liqueurs; once he had come across a hatbox of empty crème de menthe bottles. Martin found a dependable maid who managed the household competently. Virgie was also from Alabama and Martin had never dared tell Emily the wage scale customary in New York. Emily's drinking was entirely secret now, done before he reached the house. Usually the effects were almost imperceptible — a looseness of movement or the heavy-lidded eyes. The times of irresponsibilities, such as the cayenne-pepper toast, were rare, and Martin could dismiss his worries when Virgie was at the house. But, nevertheless, anxiety was always latent, a threat of indefined disaster that underlaid his days.

"Marianne!" Martin called, for even the recollection of that time brought the need for reassurance. The baby girl, no longer hurt, but no less precious to her father, came into the kitchen with her brother. Martin went on with the preparations for the meal. He opened a can of soup and put two chops in the frying pan. Then he sat down by the table and took his Marianne on his knees for a pony ride. Andy watched them, his fingers wobbling the tooth that had been loose all that week.

"Andy-the-candyman!" Martin said. "Is that old critter still in your mouth? Come closer, let Daddy have a look."

"I got a string to pull it with." The child brought from his pocket a tangled thread. "Virgie said to tie it to the tooth and tie the other end to the doorknob and shut the door real suddenly."

Martin took out a clean handkerchief and felt the loose tooth carefully. "That tooth is coming out of my Andy's mouth tonight. Otherwise I'm awfully afraid we'll have a tooth tree in the family."

"A what?"

"A tooth tree," Martin said. "You'll bite into something and swallow that tooth. And the tooth will take root in poor Andy's stomach and grow into a tooth tree with sharp little teeth instead of leaves."

"Shoo, Daddy," Andy said. But he held the tooth firmly between his grimy little thumb and forefinger. "There ain't any tree like that. I never seen one."

"There *isn't* any tree like that and I never *saw* one."

Martin tensed suddenly. Emily was coming down the stairs. He listened to the fumbling footsteps, his arm embracing the little boy with dread. When Emily came into the room he saw from her movements and her sullen face that she had again been at the sherry bottle. She began to yank open drawers and set the table.

"Condition!" she said in a furry voice. "You talk to me like that. Don't think I'll forget. I remember every dirty lie you say to me. Don't you think for a minute that I forget."

"Emily!" he begged. "The children —"

"The children — yes! Don't think I don't see through your dirty plots and schemes. Down here trying to turn my own children against me. Don't think I don't see and understand."

"Emily! I beg you — please go upstairs."

"So you can turn my children — my very own children —" Two large tears coursed rapidly down her cheeks. "Trying to turn my little boy, my Andy, against his own mother."

With drunken impulsiveness Emily knelt on the floor before the startled child. Her hands on his shoulders balanced her. "Listen, my Andy — you wouldn't listen to any lies your father tells you? You wouldn't believe what he says? Listen, Andy, what was your father telling you before I came downstairs?" Uncertain, the child sought his father's face. "Tell me. Mama wants to know."

"About the tooth tree."

"What?"

The child repeated the words and she echoed them with unbelieving terror. "The tooth tree!" She swayed and renewed her grasp on the child's shoulder. "I don't know what you're talking about. But listen, Andy, Mama is all right, isn't she?" The tears were spilling down her face and Andy drew back from her, for he was afraid. Grasping the table edge, Emily stood up.

"See! You have turned my child against me."

Marianne began to cry, and Martin took her in his arms.

"That's all right, you can take *your* child. You have always shown partiality from the very first. I don't mind, but at least you can leave me my little boy."

Andy edged close to his father and touched his leg. "Daddy," he wailed.

Martin took the children to the foot of the stairs. "Andy, you take up Marianne and Daddy will follow you in a minute."

"But Mama?" the child asked, whispering.

"Mama will be all right. Don't worry."

Emily was sobbing at the kitchen table, her face buried in the crook of her arm. Martin poured a cup of soup and set it before her. Her rasping sobs unnerved him; the vehemence of her emotion, irrespective of the source, touched in him a strain of tenderness. Unwillingly he laid his hand on her dark hair. "Sit up and drink the soup." Her face as she looked up at him was chastened and imploring. The boy's withdrawal or the touch of Martin's hand had turned the tenor of her mood.

"Ma-Martin," she sobbed. "I'm so ashamed."

"Drink the soup."

Obeying him, she drank between gasping breaths. After a second cup she allowed him to lead her up to their room. She was docile now and more restrained. He laid her nightgown on the bed and was about to leave the room when a fresh round of grief, the alcoholic tumult, came again.

"He turned away. My Andy looked at me and turned away."

Impatience and fatigue hardened his voice, but he spoke warily. "You forget that Andy is still a little child — he can't comprehend the meaning of such scenes."

"Did I make a scene? Oh, Martin, did I make a scene before the children?"

Her horrified face touched and amused him against his will. "Forget it. Put on your nightgown and go to sleep."

"My child turned away from me. Andy looked at his mother and turned away. The children —"

She was caught in the rhythmic sorrow of alcohol. Martin withdrew from the room saying: "For God's sake go to sleep. The children will forget by tomorrow."

As he said this he wondered if it was true. Would the scene glide so easily from memory — or would it root in the unconscious to fester in the after-years? Martin did not know, and the last alternative sickened him. He thought of Emily, foresaw the morning-after humiliation: the shards of memory, the lucidities that glared from the obliterating darkness of shame. She would call the New York office twice — possibly three or four times. Martin anticipated his own embarrassment, wondering if the others at the office could possibly suspect. He felt that his secretary had divined the trouble long ago and that she pitied him. He suffered a moment of rebellion against his fate; he hated his wife.

Once in the children's room he closed the door and felt secure for the first time that evening. Marianne fell down on the floor, picked herself up and calling: "Daddy, watch me," fell again, got up, and continued the falling-calling routine. Andy sat in the child's low chair, wobbling the tooth. Martin ran the water in the tub, washed his own hands in the lavatory, and called the boy into the bathroom.

"Let's have another look at that tooth." Martin sat on the toilet, holding Andy between his knees. The child's mouth gaped and Martin grasped the tooth. A wobble, a quick twist and the nacreous milk tooth was free. Andy's face was for the first moment split between terror, astonishment, and delight. He mouthed a swallow of water and spat into the lavatory.

"Look, Daddy! It's blood. Marianne!"

Martin loved to bathe his children, loved inexpressibly the tender, naked bodies as they stood in the water so exposed. It was not fair of Emily to say that he showed partiality. As Martin soaped the delicate boy-body of his son he felt that further love would be impossible. Yet he admitted the difference in the quality of his emotions for the two children. His love for his daughter was graver, touched with a strain of melancholy, a gentleness that was akin to pain. His pet names for the little boy were the absurdities of daily inspiration — he called the little girl always Marianne, and his voice as he spoke it was a caress. Martin patted dry the fat baby stomach and the sweet little genital fold. The washed child faces were radiant as flower petals, equally loved.

"I'm putting the tooth under my pillow. I'm supposed to get a quarter."

"What for?"

"*You* know, Daddy. Johnny got a quarter for his tooth."

"Who puts the quarter there?" asked Martin. "I used to think the fairies left it in the night. It was a dime in my day, though."

"That's what they say in kindergarten."

"Who does put it there?"

"Your parents," Andy said. "You!"

Martin was pinning the cover on Marianne's bed. His daughter was already asleep. Scarcely breathing, Martin bent over and kissed her forehead, kissed again the tiny hand that lay palm-upward, flung in slumber beside her head.

"Good night, Andy-man."

The answer was only a drowsy murmur. After a minute Martin took out his change and slid a quarter underneath the pillow. He left a night light in the room.

As Martin prowled about the kitchen making a late meal, it occurred to him that the children had not once mentioned their mother or the scene that must have seemed to them incomprehensible. Absorbed in the instant — the tooth, the bath, the quarter — the fluid passage of child-time had borne these weightless episodes like leaves in the swift current of a shallow stream while the adult enigma was beached and forgotten on the shore. Martin thanked the Lord for that.

But his own anger, repressed and lurking, arose again. His youth was being frittered by a drunkard's waste, his very manhood subtly undermined. And the children, once the immunity of incomprehension passed — what would it be like in a year or so? With his elbows on the table he ate his food brutishly, untasting. There was no hiding the truth — soon there would be gossip in the office and in the town; his wife was a dissolute woman. Dissolute. And he and his children were bound to a future of degradation and slow ruin.

Martin pushed away from the table and stalked into the living room. He followed the lines of a book with his eyes but his mind conjured miserable images: he saw his children drowned in the river, his wife a disgrace on the public street. By bedtime the dull, hard anger was like a weight upon his chest and his feet dragged as he climbed the stairs.

The room was dark except for the shafting light from the half-opened bathroom door. Martin undressed quietly. Little by little, mysteriously, there came in him a change. His wife was asleep, her peaceful respiration sounding gently in the room. Her high-heeled shoes with the carelessly dropped stockings made to him a mute appeal. Her underclothes were flung in disorder on the chair. Martin picked up the girdle and the soft, silk brassière and stood for a moment with them in his hands. For the first time that evening he looked at his wife. His eyes rested on the sweet forehead, the arch of the fine brow. The brow had descended to Marianne, and the tilt at the end of the delicate nose. In his son he could trace the high cheekbones and pointed chin. Her body was full-bosomed, slender and undulant. As Martin watched the tranquil slumber of his wife the ghost of the old anger vanished. All thoughts of blame or blemish were distant from him now. Martin put out the bathroom light and raised the window. Careful not to awaken Emily he slid into the bed. By moonlight he watched his wife for the last time. His hand sought the adjacent flesh and sorrow paralleled desire in the immense complexity of love.

The Haunted Boy

Hugh looked for his mother at the corner, but she was not in the yard. Sometimes she would be out fooling with the border of spring flowers — the candytuft, the sweet William, the lobelias (she had taught him the names) — but today the green front lawn with the borders of many-colored flowers was empty under the frail sunshine of the mid-April afternoon. Hugh raced up the sidewalk, and John followed him. They finished the front steps with two bounds, and the door slammed after them.

"Mamma!" Hugh called.

It was then, in the unanswering silence as they stood in the empty, wax-floored hall, that Hugh felt there was something wrong. There was no fire in the grate of the sitting room, and since he was used to the flicker of firelight during the cold months, the room on this first warm day seemed strangely naked and cheerless. Hugh shivered. He was glad John was there. The sun shone on a red piece in the flowered rug. Red-bright, red-dark, red-dead — Hugh sickened with a sudden chill remembrance of "the other time." The red darkened to a dizzy black.

"What's the matter, Brown?" John asked. "You look so white."

Hugh shook himself and put his hand to his forehead. "Nothing. Let's go back to the kitchen."

"I can't stay but just a minute," John said. "I'm obligated to sell those tickets. I have to eat and run."

The kitchen, with the fresh checked towels and clean pans, was now the best room in the house. And on the enameled table there was a lemon pie that she had made. Assured by the everyday kitchen and the pie, Hugh stepped back into the hall and raised his face again to call upstairs.

"Mother! Oh, Mamma!"

Again there was no answer.

"My mother made this pie," he said. Quickly, he found a knife and cut into the pie — to dispel the gathering sense of dread.

"Think you ought to cut it, Brown?"

"Sure thing, Laney."

They called each other by their last names this spring, unless they happened to forget. To Hugh it seemed sporty and grown and somehow grand. Hugh liked John better than any other boy at school. John was two years older than Hugh, and compared to him the other boys seemed like a silly crowd of punks. John was the best student in the sophomore class, brainy but not the least bit a teacher's pet, and he was the best athlete too. Hugh was a freshman and didn't have so many friends that first year of high school — he had somehow cut himself off, because he was so afraid.

"Mamma always has me something nice for after school." Hugh put a big piece of pie on a saucer for John — for Laney.

"This pie is certainly super."

"The crust is made of crunched-up graham crackers instead of regular pie dough," Hugh said, "because pie dough is a lot of trouble. We think this graham-cracker pastry is just as good. Naturally, my mother can make regular pie dough if she wants to."

Hugh could not keep still; he walked up and down the kitchen, eating the pie wedge he carried on the palm of his hand. His brown hair was mussed with nervous rakings, and his gentle gold-brown eyes were haunted with pained perplexity. John, who remained seated at the table, sensed Hugh's uneasiness and wrapped one dangling leg around the other.

"I'm really obligated to sell those Glee Club tickets."

"Don't go. You have the whole afternoon." He was afraid of the empty house. He needed John, he needed someone; most of all he needed to hear his mother's voice and know she was in the house with him. "Maybe Mamma is taking a bath," he said. "I'll holler again."

The answer to his third call too was silence.

"I guess your mother must have gone to the movie or gone shopping or something."

"No," Hugh said. "She would have left a note. She always does when she's gone when I come home from school."

"We haven't looked for a note," John said. "Maybe she left it under the door mat or somewhere in the living room."

Hugh was inconsolable. "No. She would have left it right under this pie. She knows I always run first to the kitchen."

"Maybe she had a phone call or thought of something she suddenly wanted to do."

"She *might* have," he said. "I remember she said to Daddy that one of these days she was going to buy herself some new clothes." This flash of hope did not survive its expression. He pushed his hair back and started from the room. "I guess I'd better go upstairs. I ought to go upstairs while you are here."

He stood with his arm around the newel post; the smell of varnished stairs, the sight of the closed white bathroom door at the top revived again "the other time." He clung to the newel post, and his feet would not move to climb the stairs. The red turned again to whirling, sick dark. Hugh sat down. *Stick your head between your legs,* he ordered, remembering Scout first aid.

"Hugh," John called. "Hugh!"

The dizziness clearing, Hugh accepted a fresh chagrin — Laney was calling him by his ordinary first name; he thought he was a sissy about his mother, unworthy of being called by his last name in the grand, sporty way they used before. The dizziness cleared when he returned to the kitchen.

"Brown," said John, and the chagrin disappeared. "Does this establishment have anything pertaining to a cow? A white, fluid liquid. In French they call it *lait.* Here we call it plain old milk."

The stupidity of shock lightened. "Oh, Laney, I am a dope! Please excuse me. I clean forgot." Hugh fetched the milk from the refrigerator and found two glasses. "I didn't think. My mind was on something else."

"I know," John said. After a moment he asked in a calm voice, looking steadily at Hugh's eyes: "Why are you so worried about your mother? Is she sick, Hugh?"

Hugh knew now that the first name was not a slight; it was because John was talking too serious to be sporty. He liked John better than any friend he had ever had. He felt more natural sitting across the kitchen table from John, somehow safer. As he looked into John's gray, peaceful eyes, the balm of affection soothed the dread.

John asked again, still steadily: "Hugh, is your mother sick?"

Hugh could have answered no other boy. He had talked with no one about his mother, except his father, and even those intimacies had been rare, oblique. They could approach the subject only when they were occupied with something else, doing carpentry work or the two times they hunted in the woods together — or when they were cooking supper or washing dishes.

"She's not exactly sick," he said, "but Daddy and I have been worried about her. At least, we used to be worried for a while."

John asked: "Is it a kind of heart trouble?"

Hugh's voice was strained. "Did you hear about that fight I had with that slob Clem Roberts? I scraped his slob face on the gravel walk and nearly killed him sure enough. He's still got scars or at least he did have a bandage on for two days. I had to stay in school every afternoon for a week. But I nearly killed him. I would have if Mr. Paxton hadn't come along and dragged me off."

"I heard about it."

"You know why I wanted to kill him?"

For a moment John's eyes flickered away.

Hugh tensed himself; his raw boy hands clutched the table edge; he took a deep, hoarse breath. "That slob was telling everybody that my mother was in Milledgeville. He was spreading it around that my mother was crazy."

"The dirty bastard."

Hugh said in a clear, defeated voice, "My mother *was* in Milledgeville. But that doesn't mean that she was crazy," he added quickly. "In that big State hospital, there are buildings for people who are crazy, and there are other buildings, for people who are just sick. Mamma was sick for a while. Daddy and me discussed it and decided that the hospital in Milledgeville was the place where there were the best doctors and she would get the best care. But she was the furtherest from crazy than anybody in the world. You know Mamma, John." He said again, "I ought to go upstairs."

John said: "I have always thought that your mother is one of the nicest ladies in this town."

"You see, Mamma had a peculiar thing happen, and afterward she was blue."

Confession, the first deep-rooted words, opened the festered secrecy of the boy's heart, and he continued more rapidly, urgent and finding unforeseen relief.

"Last year my mother thought she was going to have a little baby. She talked it over with Daddy and me," he said proudly. "We wanted a girl. I was going to choose the name. We were so tickled. I hunted up all my old toys — my electric train and the tracks . . . I was going to name her Crystal — how does the name strike you for a girl? It reminds me of something bright and dainty."

"Was the little baby born dead?"

Even with John, Hugh's ears turned hot; his cold hands touched them. "No, it was what they call a tumor. That's what happened to my mother. They had to operate at the hospital here." He was embarrassed and his voice was very low. "Then she had something called change of life." The words were terrible to Hugh. "And afterward she was blue. Daddy said it was a shock to her nervous system. It's something that happens to ladies; she was just blue and run-down."

Although there was no red, no red in the kitchen anywhere, Hugh was approaching "the other time."

"One day, she just sort of gave up — one day last fall." Hugh's eyes were wide open and glaring: again he climbed the stairs and opened the bathroom door — he put his hand to his eyes to shut out the memory. "She tried to — hurt herself. I found her when I came in from school."

John reached out and carefully stroked Hugh's sweatered arm.

"Don't worry. A lot of people have to go to hospitals because they are run-down and blue. Could happen to anybody."

"We had to put her in the hospital — the best hospital." The recollection of those long, long months was stained with a dull loneliness, as cruel in its lasting unappeasement as "the other time" — how long had it lasted? In the hospital Mamma could walk around and she always had on shoes.

John said carefully: "This pie is certainly super."

"My mother is a super cook. She cooks things like meat pie and salmon loaf — as well as steaks and hot dogs."

"I hate to eat and run," John said.

Hugh was so frightened of being left alone that he felt the alarm in his own loud heart.

"Don't go," he urged. "Let's talk for a little while."

"Talk about what?"

Hugh could not tell him. Not even John Laney. He could tell no one of the empty house and the horror of the time before. "Do you ever cry?" he asked John. "I don't."

"I do sometimes," John admitted.

"I wish I had known you better when Mother was away. Daddy and me used to go hunting nearly every Saturday. We *lived* on quail and dove. I bet you would have liked that." He added in a lower tone, "On Sunday we went to the hospital."

John said: "It's a kind of a delicate proposition selling those tickets. A lot of people don't enjoy the High School Glee Club operettas. Unless they know someone in it personally, they'd rather stay home with a good TV show. A lot of people buy tickets on the basis of being public-spirited."

"We're going to get a television set real soon."

"I couldn't exist without television," John said.

Hugh's voice was apologetic. "Daddy wants to clean up the hospital bills first because as everybody knows sickness is a very expensive proposition. Then we'll get TV."

John lifted his milk glass. "Skoal," he said. "That's a Swedish word you say before you drink. A good-luck word."

"You know so many foreign words and languages."

"Not so many," John said truthfully. "Just 'kaput' and 'adios' and 'skoal' and stuff we learn in French class. That's not much."

"That's *beaucoup*," said Hugh, and he felt witty and pleased with himself.

Suddenly the stored tension burst into physical activity. Hugh grabbed the basketball out on the porch and rushed into the back yard. He dribbled the ball several times and aimed at the goal his father had put up on his last birthday. When he missed he bounced the ball to John, who had come after him. It was good to be outdoors and the relief of natural play brought Hugh the first line of a poem. "My heart is like a basketball." Usually when a poem came to him he would lie sprawled on the living room floor, studying to hunt rhymes, his tongue working on the side of his mouth. His mother would call him Shelley-Poe when she stepped over him, and sometimes she would put her foot lightly on his behind. His mother always liked his poems; today the second line came quickly, like magic. He said it out loud to John: " 'My heart is like a basketball, bouncing with glee down the hall.' How do you like that for the start of a poem?"

"Sounds kind of crazy to me," John said. Then he corrected himself hastily. "I mean it sounds — odd. Odd, I meant."

Hugh realized why John changed the word, and the elation of play and poems left him instantly. He caught the ball and stood with it cradled in his arms. The afternoon was golden and the wisteria vine on the porch was in full, unshattered bloom. The wisteria was like lavender waterfalls. The fresh breeze smelled of sun-warmed flowers. The sunlit sky was blue and cloudless. It was the first warm day of spring.

"I have to shove off," John said.

"No!" Hugh's voice was desperate. "Don't you want another piece of pie? I never heard of anybody eating just one piece of pie."

He steered John into the house and this time he called only out of habit because he always called on coming in. "Mother!" He was cold after the bright, sunny outdoors. He was cold not only because of the weather but because he was so scared.

"My mother has been home a month and every afternoon she's always here when I come home from school. Always, always."

They stood in the kitchen looking at the lemon pie. And to Hugh the cut pie looked somehow — odd. As they stood motionless in the kitchen the silence was creepy and odd too.

"Doesn't this house seem quiet to you?"

"It's because you don't have television. We put on our TV at seven o'clock and it stays on all day and night until we go to bed. Whether anybody's in the living room or not. There're plays and skits and gags going on continually."

"We have a radio, of course, and a vic."

"But that's not the company of a good TV. You won't know when your mother is in the house or not when you get TV."

Hugh didn't answer. Their footsteps sounded hollow in the hall. He felt sick as he stood on the first step with his arm around the newel post. "If you could just come upstairs for a minute —"

John's voice was suddenly impatient and loud. "How many times have I told you I'm obligated to sell those tickets. You have to be public-spirited about things like Glee Clubs."

"Just for a second — I have something important to show you upstairs."

John did not ask what it was and Hugh sought desperately to name something important enough to get John upstairs. He said finally: "I'm assembling a hi-fi machine. You have to know a lot about electronics — my father is helping me."

But even when he spoke he knew John did not for a second believe the lie. Who would buy a hi-fi when they didn't have television? He hated John, as you hate people you have to need so badly. He had to say something more and he straightened his shoulders.

"I just want you to know how much I value your friendship. During these past months I had somehow cut myself off from people."

"That's O.K., Brown. You oughtn't to be so sensitive because your mother was — where she was."

John had his hand on the door and Hugh was trembling. "I thought if you could come up for just a minute —"

John looked at him with anxious, puzzled eyes. Then he asked slowly: "Is there something you are scared of upstairs?"

Hugh wanted to tell him everything. But he could not tell what his mother had done that September afternoon. It was too terrible and — odd. It was like something a *patient* would do, and not like his mother at all. Although his eyes were wild with terror and his body trembled he said: "I'm not scared."

"Well, so long. I'm sorry I have to go — but to be obligated is to be obligated."

John closed the front door, and he was alone in the empty house. Nothing could save him now. Even if a whole crowd of boys were listening to TV in the living room, laughing at funny gags and jokes, it would still not help him. He had to go upstairs and find her. He sought courage from the last thing John had said, and repeated the words aloud: "To be obligated is to be obligated." But the words did not give him any of John's thoughtlessness and courage; they were creepy and strange in the silence.

He turned slowly to go upstairs. His heart was not like a basketball but like a fast, jazz drum, beating faster and faster as he climbed the stairs. His feet dragged as though he waded through knee-deep water and he held on to the banisters. The house looked odd, crazy. As he looked down at the ground-floor table with the vase of fresh spring flowers that too looked somehow peculiar. There was a mirror on the second floor and his own face startled him, so crazy did it seem to him. The initial of his high school sweater was backward and wrong in the reflection and his mouth was open like an asylum idiot. He shut his mouth and he looked better. Still the objects he saw — the table downstairs, the sofa upstairs — looked somehow cracked or jarred because of the dread in him, although they were the familiar things of everyday. He fastened his eyes on the closed door at the right of the stairs and the fast, jazz drum beat faster.

He opened the bathroom door and for a moment the dread that had haunted him all that afternoon made him see again the room as he had seen it "the other time." His mother lay on the floor and there was blood everywhere. His mother lay there dead and there was blood everywhere, on her slashed wrist, and a pool of blood had trickled to the bathtub and lay dammed there. Hugh touched the doorframe and steadied himself. Then the room settled and he realized this was not "the other time." The April sunlight brightened the clean white tiles. There was only bathroom brightness and the sunny window. He went to the bedroom and saw the empty bed with the rose-colored spread. The lady things were on the dresser. The room was as it always looked and nothing had happened . . . nothing had happened and he flung himself on the quilted rose bed and cried from relief and a strained, bleak tiredness that had lasted so long. The sobs jerked his whole body and quieted his jazz, fast heart.

Hugh had not cried all those months. He had not cried at "the other time," when he found his mother alone in that empty house with blood everywhere. He had not cried but he made a Scout mistake. He had first lifted his mother's heavy, bloody body before he tried to bandage her. He had not cried when he called his father. He had not cried those few days when they were deciding what to do. He hadn't even cried when the doctor suggested Milledgeville, or when he and his father took her to the hospital in the car — although his father cried on the way home. He had not cried at the meals they made — steak every night for a whole month so that they felt steak was running out of their eyes, their ears; then they had switched to hot dogs, and ate them until hot dogs ran out of their ears, their eyes.

They got in ruts of food and were messy about the kitchen, so that it was never nice except the Saturday the cleaning woman came. He did not cry those lonesome afternoons after he had the fight with Clem Roberts and felt the other boys were thinking queer things of his mother. He stayed at home in the messy kitchen, eating fig newtons or chocolate bars. Or he went to see a neighbor's television — Miss Richards, an old maid who saw old-maid shows. He had not cried when his father drank too much so that it took his appetite and Hugh had to eat alone. He had not even cried on those long, waiting Sundays when they went to Milledgeville and he twice saw a lady on a porch without any shoes on and talking to herself. A lady who was a patient and who struck at him with a horror he could not name. He did not cry when at first his mother would say: *Don't punish me by making me stay here. Let me go home.* He had not cried at the terrible words that haunted him — "change of life" — "crazy" — "Milledgeville" — he could not cry all during those long months strained with dullness and want and dread.

He still sobbed on the rose bedspread which was soft and cool against his wet cheeks. He was sobbing so loud that he did not hear the front door open, did not even hear his mother call or the footsteps on the stairs. He still sobbed when his mother touched him and burrowed his face hard in the spread. He even stiffened his legs and kicked his feet.

"Why, Loveyboy," his mother said, calling him a long-ago child name. "What's happened?"

He sobbed even louder, although his mother tried to turn his face to her. He wanted her to worry. He did not turn around until she had finally left the bed, and then he looked at her. She had on a different dress — blue silk it looked like in the pale spring light.

"Darling, what's happened?"

The terror of the afternoon was over, but he could not tell it to his mother. He could not tell her what he had feared, or explain the horror of things that were never there at all — but had once been there.

"Why did you do it?"

"The first warm day I just suddenly decided to buy myself some new clothes."

But he was not talking about clothes; he was thinking about "the other time" and the grudge that had started when he saw the blood and horror and felt *why did she do this to me.* He thought of the grudge against the mother he loved the most in the world. All those last, sad months the anger had bounced against the love with guilt between.

"I bought two dresses and two petticoats. How do you like them?"

"I hate them!" Hugh said angrily. "Your slip is showing."

She turned around twice and the petticoat showed terribly. "It's supposed to show, goofy. It's the style."

"I still don't like it."

"I ate a sandwich at the tearoom with two cups of cocoa and then went to Mendel's. There were so many pretty things I couldn't seem to get away. I bought these two dresses and look, Hugh! The shoes!"

His mother went to the bed and switched on the light so he could see. The shoes were flat-heeled and *blue* — with diamond sparkles on the toes. He did not know how to criticize. "They look more like evening shoes than things you wear on the street."

"I have never owned any colored shoes before. I couldn't resist them."

His mother sort of danced over toward the window, making the petticoat twirl under the new dress. Hugh had stopped crying now, but he was still angry.

"I don't like it because it makes you look like you're trying to seem young, and I bet you are forty years old."

His mother stopped dancing and stood still at the window. Her face was suddenly quiet and sad. "I'll be forty-three years old in June."

He had hurt her and suddenly the anger vanished and there was only love. "Mamma, I shouldn't have said that."

"I realized when I was shopping that I hadn't been in a store for more than a year. Imagine!"

Hugh could not stand the sad quietness and the mother he loved so much. He could not stand his love or his mother's prettiness. He wiped the tears on the sleeve of his sweater and got up from the bed. "I have never seen you so pretty, or a dress and slip so pretty." He crouched down before his mother and touched the bright shoes. "The shoes are really super."

"I thought the minute I laid eyes on them that you would like them." She pulled Hugh up and kissed him on the cheek. "Now I've got lipstick on you."

Hugh quoted a witty remark he had heard before as he scrubbed off the lipstick. "It only shows I'm popular."

"Hugh, why were you crying when I came in? Did something at school upset you?"

"It was only that when I came in and found you gone and no note or anything —"

"I forgot all about a note."

"And all afternoon I felt — John Laney came in but he had to go sell Glee Club tickets. All afternoon I felt —"

"What? What was the matter?"

But he could not tell the mother he loved about the terror and the cause. He said at last: "All afternoon I felt — odd."

Afterward when his father came home he called Hugh to come out into the back yard with him. His father had a worried look — as though he spied a valuable tool Hugh had left outside. But there was no tool and the basketball was put back in its place on the back porch.

"Son," his father said, "there's something I want to tell you."

"Yes, sir?"

"Your mother said that you had been crying this afternoon." His father did not wait for him to explain. "I just want us to have a close understanding with each other. Is there anything about school — or girls — or something that puzzles you? Why were you crying?"

Hugh looked back at the afternoon and already it was far away, distant as a peculiar view seen at the wrong end of a telescope.

"I don't know," he said. "I guess maybe I was somehow nervous."

His father put his arm around his shoulder. "Nobody can be nervous before they are sixteen years old. You have a long way to go."

"I know."

"I have never seen your mother look so well. She looks so gay and pretty, better than she's looked in years. Don't you realize that?"

"The slip — the petticoat is supposed to show. It's a new style."

"Soon it will be summer," his father said. "And we'll go on picnics — the three of us." The words brought an instant vision of glare on the yellow creek and the summer-leaved, adventurous woods. His father added: "I came out here to tell you something else."

"Yes, sir?"

"I just want you to know that I realize how fine you were all that bad time. How fine, how damn fine."

His father was using a swear word as if he were talking to a grown man. His father was not a person to hand out compliments — always he was strict with report cards and tools left around. His father never praised him or used grown words or anything. Hugh felt his face grow hot and he touched it with his cold hands.

"I just wanted to tell you that, Son." He shook Hugh by the shoulder. "You'll be taller than your old man in a year or so." Quickly his father went into the house, leaving Hugh to the sweet and unaccustomed aftermath of praise.

Hugh stood in the darkening yard after the sunset colors faded in the west and the wisteria was dark purple. The kitchen light was on and he saw his mother fixing dinner. He knew that something was finished; the terror was far from him now, also the anger that had bounced with love, the dread and guilt. Although he felt he would never cry again — or at least not until he was sixteen — in the brightness of his tears glistened the safe, lighted kitchen, now that he was no longer a haunted boy, now that he was glad somehow, and not afraid.

Who Has Seen the Wind?

All afternoon Ken Harris had been sitting before a blank page of the typewriter. It was winter and snowing. The snow muted traffic and the Village apartment was so quiet that the alarm clock bothered him. He worked in the bedroom as the room with his wife's things calmed him and made him feel less alone. His prelunch drink (or was it an eye opener?) had been dulled by the can of chili con carne he had eaten alone in the kitchen. At four o'clock he put the clock in the clothes hamper, then returned to the typewriter. The paper was still blank and the white page blanched his spirit. Yet there was a time (how long ago?) when a song at the corner, a voice from childhood, and the panorama of memory condensed the past so that the random and actual were transfigured into a novel, a story — there was a time when the empty page summoned and sorted memory and he felt that ghostly mastery of his art. A time, in short, when he was a writer and writing almost every day. Working hard, he carefully broke the backs of sentences, *x*'d out offending phrases and changed repeated words. Now he sat there, hunched and somehow fearful, a blond man in his late thirties, with circles under his oyster blue eyes and a full, pale mouth. It was the scalding wind of his Texas childhood he was thinking about as he gazed out of his window at the New York falling snow. Then suddenly a valve of memory opened and he said the words as he typed them:

Who has seen the wind?
Neither you nor I;
But when the trees bow down their heads
The wind is passing by.

The nursery verse seemed to him so sinister that as he sat thinking about it the sweat of tension dampened his palms. He jerked the page from the typewriter and, tearing it into many pieces, let it fall in the wastepaper basket. He was relieved that he was going to a party at six o'clock, glad to quit the silent apartment, the torn verse, and to walk in the cold but comforting street.

The subway had the dim light of underground and after the smell of snow the air was fetid. Ken noticed a man lying down on a bench, but he did not wonder about the stranger's history as he might have done another time. He watched the swaying front car of the oncoming express and shrank back from the cindery wind. He saw the doors open and close — it was his train — and stared forlornly as the subway ground noisily away. A sadness fretted him as he waited for the next one.

The Rodgers' apartment was in a penthouse far uptown and already the party had begun. There was the wash of mingled voices and the smell of gin and cocktail canapés. As he stood with Esther Rodgers in the entrance of the crowded rooms he said:

"Nowadays when I enter a crowded party I think of that last party of the Duc de Guermantes."

"What?" asked Esther.

"You remember when Proust — the I, the narrator — looked at all the familiar faces and brooded about the alterations of time? Magnificent passage — I read it every year."

Esther looked disturbed. "There's so much noise. Is your wife coming?"

Ken's face quivered a little and he took a Martini the maid was passing. "She'll be along when she leaves her office."

"Marian works so hard — all those manuscripts to read."

"When I find myself at a party like this it's always almost exactly the same. Yet there is the awful difference. As though the key lowered, shifted. The awful difference of years that are passing, the trickery and terror of time, Proust . . ."

But his hostess had gone and he was left standing alone in the crowded party room. He looked at faces he had seen at parties these last thirteen years — yes, they had aged. Esther now was quite fat and her velvet dress was too tight — dissipated, he thought, and whisky-bloated. There was a change — thirteen years ago when he published *The Night of Darkness* Esther would have fairly eaten him up and never left him alone at the fringe of the room. He had been the fair-haired boy, those days. The fair-haired boy of the Bitch Goddess — was the Bitch Goddess success, money, youth? He saw two young Southern writers at the window — and in ten years their capital of youth would be claimed by the Bitch Goddess. It pleased Ken to think of this and he ate a ham doodad that was passed.

Then he saw someone across the room whom he admired. She was Mabel Goodley, the painter and set-designer. Her blond hair was short and shining and her glasses glittered in the light. Mabel had always loved *The Night* and had given a party for him when he got his Guggenheim. More important, she had felt his second book was better than the first one, in spite of the stupidity of the critics. He started toward Mabel but was stopped by John Howards, an editor he used to see sometimes at parties.

"Hi there," Howards said, "what are you writing these days, or is it a fair question?"

This was a remark Ken loathed. There were a number of answers — sometimes he said he was finishing a long novel, other times he said he was deliberately lying fallow. There was no good answer, no matter what he said. His scrotum tightened and he tried desperately to look unconcerned.

"I well remember the stir *The Doorless Room* made in the literary world of those days — a fine book."

Howards was tall and he wore a brown tweed suit. Ken looked up at him aghast, steeling himself against the sudden attack. But the brown eyes were strangely innocent and Ken could not recognize the guile. A woman with tight pearls around her throat said after a painful moment, "But dear, Mr. Harris didn't write *The Doorless Room*."

"Oh," Howards said helplessly.

Ken looked at the woman's pearls and wanted to choke her. "It couldn't matter less."

The editor persisted, trying to make amends. "But your name is Ken Harris. And you're married to the Marian Campbell who is fiction editor at —"

The woman said quickly: "Ken Harris wrote *The Night of Darkness* — a fine book."

Harris noticed that the woman's throat was lovely with the pearls and the black dress. His face lightened until she said: "It was about ten or fifteen years ago, wasn't it?"

"I remember," the editor said. "A fine book. How could I have confused it? How long will it be before we can look forward to a second book?"

"I wrote a second book," Ken said. "It sank without a ripple. It failed." He added defensively, "The critics were more obtuse even than usual. And I'm not the best-seller type."

"Too bad," said the editor. "It's a casualty of the trade sometimes."

"The book was better than *The Night.* Some critics thought it was obscure. They said the same thing of Joyce." He added, with the writer's loyalty to his last creation, "It's a much better book than the first, and I feel I'm still just starting to do my real work."

"That's the spirit," the editor said. "The main thing is to keep plugging away. What are you writing now — if that's a fair question?"

The violence swelled suddenly. "It's none of your business." Ken had not spoken very loudly but the words carried and there was a sudden area of silence in the cocktail room. "None of your Goddam business."

In the quiet room there came the voice of old Mrs. Beckstein, who was deaf and sitting in a corner chair. "Why are you buying so many quilts?"

The spinster daughter, who was with her mother always, guarding her like royalty or some sacred animal, translating between the mother and the world, said firmly, "Mr. Brown was saying . . ."

The babble of the party resumed and Ken went to the drink table, took another Martini and dipped a piece of cauliflower in some sauce. He ate and drank with his back to the noisy room. Then he took a third Martini and threaded his way to Mabel Goodley. He sat on an ottoman beside her, careful of his drink and somewhat formal. "It's been such a tiring day," he said.

"What have you been doing?"

"Sitting on my can."

"A writer I used to know once got sacroiliac trouble from sitting so long. Could that be coming on you?"

"No," he said. "You are the only honest person in this room."

He had tried so many different ways when the blank pages started. He had tried to write in bed, and for a time he had changed to longhand. He had thought of Proust in his cork-lined room and for a month he had used ear-stoppers — but work went no better and the rubber started some fungus ailment. They had moved to Brooklyn Heights, but that did not help. When he learned that Thomas Wolfe had written standing up with his manuscript on the icebox he had even tried that too. But he only kept opening the icebox and eating. . . . He had tried writing drunk — when the ideas and images were marvelous at the time but changed so unhappily when read afterward. He had written early in the morning and dead sober and miserable. He had thought of Thoreau and Walden. He had dreamed of manual labor and an apple farm. If he could just go for long walks on the moors then the light of creation would come again — but where are the moors of New York?

He consoled himself with the writers who had felt they failed and whose fame was established after death. When he was twenty he daydreamed that he would die at thirty and his name would be blazoned after his death. When he was twenty-five and had finished *The Night of Darkness* he daydreamed that he would die famous, a writer's writer, at thirty-five with a body of work accomplished and the Nobel Prize awarded on his deathbed. But now that he was nearly forty with two books — one a success, the other a defended failure — he did not daydream about his death.

"I wonder why I keep on writing," he said. "It's a frustrating life."

He had vaguely expected that Mabel, his friend, might say something about his being a born writer, might even remind him of his duty to his talent, that she might even mention "genius," that magic word which turns hardship and outward failure to somber glory. But Mabel's answer dismayed him. "I guess writing is like the theatre. Once you write or act it gets in your blood."

He despised actors — vain, posey, always unemployed. "I don't think of acting as a creative art, it's just interpretive. Whereas the writer must hew the phantom rock —"

He saw his wife enter from the vestibule. Marian was tall and slim with straight, short black hair, and she was wearing a plain black dress, an office-looking dress without ornament. They had married thirteen years ago, the year *The Night* had come out, and for a long time he had trembled with love. There were times he awaited her with the soaring wonder of the lover and the sweet trembling when at last he saw her. Those were the times when they made love almost every night and often in the early morning. That first year she had even occasionally come home from the office at her lunch hour and they had loved each other naked in the city daylight. At last desire had steadied and love no longer made his body tremble. He was working on a second book and the going was rough. Then he got a Guggenheim and they had gone to Mexico, as the war was on in Europe. His book was abandoned and, although the flush of success was still on him, he was unsatisfied. He wanted to write, to write, to write — but month after month passed and he wrote nothing. Marian said he was drinking too much and marking time and he threw a glass of rum in her face. Then he knelt on the floor and cried. He was for the first time in a foreign country and the time was automatically valuable because it was a foreign country. He would write of the blue of the noon sky, the Mexican shadows, the water-fresh mountain air. But day followed day — always of value because it was a foreign country — and he wrote nothing. He did not even learn Spanish, and it annoyed him when Marian talked to the cook and other Mexicans. (It was easier for a woman to pick up a foreign language and besides she knew French.) And the very cheapness of Mexico made life expensive; he spent money like trick money or stage money and the Guggenheim check was always spent in advance. But he was in a foreign country and sooner or later the Mexican days would be of value to him as a writer. Then a strange thing happened after eight months: with practically no warning Marian took a plane to New York. He had to interrupt his Guggenheim year to follow her. And then she would not live with him — or let him live in her apartment. She said it was like living with twenty Roman emperors rolled into one and she was through. Marian got a job as an assistant fiction editor on a fashion magazine and he lived in a cold-water flat — their marriage had failed and they were separated, although he still tried to follow her around. The Guggenheim people would not renew his fellowship and he soon spent the advance on his new book.

About this time there was a morning he never forgot, although nothing, absolutely nothing, had happened. It was a sunny autumn day with the sky fair and green above the skyscrapers. He had gone to a cafeteria for breakfast and sat in the bright window. People passed quickly on the street, all of them going somewhere. Inside the cafeteria there was a breakfast bustle, the clatter of trays and the noise of many voices. People came in and ate and went away, and everyone seemed assured and certain of destination. They seemed to take for granted a destination that was not merely the routine of jobs and appointments. Although most of the people were alone they seemed somehow a part of each other, a part of the clear autumn city. While he alone seemed separate, an isolate cipher in the pattern of the destined city. His marmalade was glazed by sunlight and he spread it on a piece of toast but did not eat. The coffee had a purplish sheen and there was a faint mark of old lipstick on the rim of the cup. It was an hour of desolation, although nothing at all happened.

Now at the cocktail party, years later, the noise, the assurance and the sense of his own separateness recalled the cafeteria breakfast and this hour was still more desolate because of the sliding passage of time.

"There's Marian," Mabel said. "She looks tired, thinner."

"If the damned Guggenheim had renewed my fellowship I was going to take Marian to Europe for a year," he said. "The damned Guggenheim — they don't give grants to creative writers any more. Just physicists — people like that who are preparing for another war."

The war had come as a relief to Ken. He was glad to abandon the book that was going badly, relieved to turn from his "phantom rock" to the general experience of those days — for surely the war was the great experience of his generation. He was graduated from Officers' Training School and when Marian saw him in his uniform she cried and loved him and there was no further talk of divorce. On his last leave they made love often as they used to do in the first months of marriage. It rained every day in England and once he was invited by a lord to his castle. He crossed on D-Day and his battalion went all the way to Schmitz. In a cellar in a ruined town he saw a cat sniffing the face of a corpse. He was afraid, but it was not the blank terror of the cafeteria or the anxiety of a white page on the typewriter. Something was always happening — he found three Westphalian hams in the chimney of a peasant's house and he broke his arm in an automobile accident. The war was the great experience of his generation, and to a writer every day was automatically of value because it was the war. But when it was over what was there to write about — the calm cat and the corpse, the lord in England, the broken arm?

* * *

In the Village apartment he returned to the book he had left so long. For a time, that year after the war, there was the sense of a writer's gladness when he has written. A time when the voice from childhood, a song on the corner, all fitted. In the strange euphoria of his lonely work the world was synthesized. He was writing of his youth in the windy, gritty Texas city that was his home town. He wrote of the rebellion of youth and the longing for the brilliant cities, the homesickness for a place he'd never seen. While he was writing *One Summer Evening* he was living in an apartment in New York but his inner life was in Texas and the distance was more than space: it was the sad distance between middle age and youth. So when he was writing his book he was split between two realities — his New York daily life and the remembered cadence of his Texas youth. When the book was published and the reviews were careless or unkind, he took it well, he thought, until the days of desolation stretched one into the other and the terror started. He did odd things at this time. Once he locked himself in the bathroom and stood holding a bottle of Lysol in his hand, just standing there holding the Lysol, trembling and terrified. He stood there for half an hour until with a great effort he slowly poured the Lysol in the lavatory. Then he lay on the bed and wept until, toward the end of the afternoon, he went to sleep. Another time he sat in the open window and let a dozen blank pages of paper float down the six stories to the street below. The wind blew the papers as he dropped them one by one, and he felt a strange elation as he watched them float away. It was less the meaninglessness of these actions than the extreme tension accompanying them that made Ken realize he was sick.

Marian suggested he go to a psychiatrist and he said psychiatry had become an avant-garde method of playing with yourself. Then he laughed, but Marian did not laugh and his solitary laughter finished in a chill of fear. In the end Marian went to the psychiatrist and Ken was jealous of them both — of the doctor because he was the arbiter of the unhappy marriage and of her because she was calmer and he was more unhinged. That year he wrote some television scripts, made a couple of thousand dollars and bought Marian a leopard coat.

"Are you doing any more television programs?" Mabel Goodley asked.

"Naw," he said, "I'm trying very hard to get into my next book. You're the only honest person I know. I can talk with you . . ."

Freed by alcohol and secure in friendship (for after all Mabel was one of his favorite people), he began to talk of the book he had tried so long to do: "The dominant theme is the theme of self-betrayal and the central character is a small-town lawyer named Winkle. The setting is laid in Texas — my home town — and most of the scenes take place in the grimy office in the town's courthouse. In the opening of the book Winkle is faced with this situation . . ." Ken unfurled his story passionately, telling of the various characters and the motivations involved. When Marian came up he was still talking and he gestured to her not to interrupt him as he talked on, looking straight into Mabel's spectacled blue eyes. Then suddenly he had the uncanny sensation of a déjà vu. He felt he had told Mabel his book before — in the same place and in the same circumstance. Even the way the curtain moved was the same. Only Mabel's blue eyes brightened with tears behind the glasses, and he was joyful that she was so much moved. "So Winkle then was impelled to divorce —" his voice faltered. "I have the strange feeling I have told you this before . . ."

Mabel waited for a moment and he was silent. "You have, Ken," she said finally. "About six or seven years ago, and at a party very much like this one."

He could not stand the pity in her eyes or the shame that pulsed in his own body. He staggered up and stumbled over his drink.

After the roar in the cocktail room the little terrace was absolutely silent. Except for the wind, which increased the sense of desertion and solitude. To dull his shame Ken said aloud something inconsequential: "Why, what on earth —" and he smiled with weak anguish. But his shame still smoldered and he put his cold hand to his hot, throbbing forehead. It was no longer snowing, but the wind lifted flurries of snow on the white terrace. The length of the terrace was about six footsteps and Ken walked very slowly, watching with growing attention his blunted footsteps in his narrow shoes. Why did he watch those footsteps with such tension? And why was he standing there, alone on the winter terrace where the light from the party room laid a sickly yellow rectangle on the snow? And the footsteps? At the end of the terrace there was a little fence about waist-high. When he leaned against the fence he knew it was very loose and he felt he *had known that it would be loose* and remained leaning against it. The penthouse was on the fifteenth floor and the lights from the city glowed before him. He was thinking that if he gave the rickety fence one push he would fall, but he remained calm against the sagging fence, his mind somehow sheltered, content.

He felt inexcusably disturbed when a voice called from the terrace. It was Marian and she cried softly: "Aah! Aah!" Then after a moment she added: "Ken, come here. What are you doing out there?" Ken stood up. Then with his balance righted he gave the fence a slight push. It did not break. "This fence is rotten — snow probably. I wonder how many people have ever committed suicide here."

"How many?"

"Sure. It's such an easy thing."

"Come back."

Very carefully he walked on the backward footprints he had made before. "It must be an inch of snow." He stooped down and felt the snow with his middle finger. "No, two inches."

"I'm cold." Marian put her hand on his coat, opened the door and steered him into the party. The room was quieter now and people were going home. In the bright light, after the dark outside, Ken saw that Marian looked tired. Her black eyes were reproachful, harried, and Ken could not bear to look into them.

"Hon, do your sinuses bother you?"

Lightly her forefinger stroked her forehead and the bridge of her nose. "It worries me so when you get in this condition."

"Condition! Me?"

"Let's put on our things and go."

But he could not stand the look in Marian's eyes and he hated her for inferring he was drunk. "I'm going to Jim Johnson's party later."

After the search for overcoats and the ragged good-bys a little group went down in the elevator and stood on the sidewalk, whistling for cabs. They discussed addresses, and Marian, the editor and Ken shared the first taxi going downtown. Ken's shame was lulled a little, and in the taxi he began to talk about Mabel.

"It's so sad about Mabel," he said.

"What do you mean?" Marian asked.

"Everything. She's obviously going apart at the seams. Disintegrating, poor thing."

Marian, who did not like the conversation, said to Howards: "Shall we go through the park? It's nice when it snows, and quicker."

"I'll go on to Fifth and Fourteenth Street," Howards said. He said to the driver: "Go through the park, please."

"The trouble with Mabel is she is a has-been. Ten years ago she used to be an honest painter and set-designer. Maybe it's a failure of imagination or drinking too much. She's lost her honesty and does the same thing over and over — repeats over and over."

"Nonsense," Marian said. "She gets better every year and she's made a lot of money."

They were driving through the park and Ken watched the winter landscape. The snow was heavy on the park trees and occasionally the wind slid the banked snow from the boughs, although the trees did not bow down. In the taxi Ken began to recite the old nursery verse about the wind, and again the words left sinister echoes and his cold palms dampened.

"I haven't thought of that jingle in years," John Howards said.

"Jingle? It's as harrowing as Dostoevski."

"I remember we used to sing it in kindergarten. And when a child had a birthday there would be a blue or pink ribbon on the tiny chair and we would then sing *Happy Birthday*."

John Howards was hunched on the edge of the seat next to Marian. It was hard to imagine this tall, lumbering editor in his huge galoshes singing in a kindergarten years ago.

Ken asked: "Where did you come from?"

"Kalamazoo," Howards said.

"I always wondered if there really was such a place or a — figure of speech."

"It was and is such a place," Howards said. "The family moved to Detroit when I was ten years old." Again Ken felt a sense of strangeness and thought that there are certain people who have preserved so little of childhood that the mention of kindergarten chairs and family moves seems somehow outlandish. He suddenly conceived a story written about such a man — he would call it *The Man in the Tweed Suit* — and he brooded silently as the story evolved in his mind with a brief flash of the old elation that came so seldom now.

"The weatherman says it's going down to zero tonight," Marian said.

"You can drop me here," Howards said to the driver as he opened his wallet and handed some money to Marian. "Thanks for letting me share the cab. And that's my part," he added with a smile. "It's so good to see you again. Let's have lunch one of these days and bring your husband if he would care to come." After he stumbled out of the taxi he called to Ken, "I'm looking forward to your next book, Harris."

"Idiot," Ken said after the cab started again. "I'll drop you home and then stop for a moment at Jim Johnson's."

"Who's he — why do you have to go?"

"He's a painter I know and I was invited."

"You take up with so many people these days. You go around with one crowd and then shift to another."

Ken knew that the observation was true, but he could not help it. In the past few years he would associate with one group — for a long time he and Marian had different circles of friends — until he would get drunk or make a scene so that the whole periphery was unpleasant to him and he felt angry and unwanted. Then he would change to another circle — and every change was to a group less stable than the one before, with shabbier apartments and cheaper drinks. Now he was glad to go wherever he was invited, to strangers where a voice might guide him and the flimsy sheaves of alcohol solace his jagged nerves.

"Ken, why don't you get help? I can't go on with this."

"Why, what's the matter?"

"You know," she said. He could feel her tense and stiff in the taxicab. "Are you really going on to another party? Can't you see you are destroying yourself? Why were you leaning against that terrace fence? Don't you realize you are — sick? Come home."

The words disturbed him, but he could not bear the thought of going home with Marian tonight. He had a presentiment that if they were alone in the apartment something dreadful might come about, and his nerves warned him of this undefined disaster.

In the old days after a cocktail party they would be glad to go home alone, talk over the party with a few quiet drinks, raid the icebox and go to bed, secure against the world outside. Then one evening after a party something had happened — he had a blackout and said or did something he could not remember and did not want to remember; afterward there was only the smashed typewriter and shafts of shameful recollection that he could not face and the memory of her fearful eyes. Marian stopped drinking and tried to talk him into joining AA. He went with her to a meeting and even stayed on the wagon with her for five days — until the horror of the unremembered night was a little distant. Afterward, when he had to drink alone, he resented her milk and her eternal coffee and she resented his drinking liquor. In this tense situation he felt the psychiatrist was somehow responsible and wondered if he had hypnotized Marian. Anyway now the evenings were spoiled and unnatural. Now he could feel her sitting upright in the taxi and he wanted to kiss her as in the old days when they were going home after a party. But her body was stiff in his embrace.

"Hon, let's be like we used to be. Let's go home and get a buzz on peacefully and hash over the evening. You used to love to do that. You used to enjoy a few drinks when we were quiet, alone. Drink with me and cozy like in the old days. I'll skip the other party if you will. Please, Hon. You're not one bit alcoholic. And it makes me feel like a lush your not drinking — I feel unnatural. And you're not a bit alcoholic, no more than I am."

"I'll fix a bowl of soup and you can turn in." But her voice was hopeless and sounded smug to Ken. Then she said: "I've tried so hard to keep our marriage and to help you. But it's like struggling in quicksand. There's so much behind the drinking and I'm so tired."

"I'll be just a minute at the party — go on with me."

"I can't go on."

The cab stopped and Marian paid the fare. She asked as she left the cab, "Do you have enough money to go on? — if you must go on."

"Naturally."

Jim Johnson's apartment was way over on the West Side, in a Puerto Rican neighborhood. Open garbage cans stood out on the curb and wind blew papers on the snowy sidewalk. When the taxi stopped Ken was so inattentive that the driver had to call him. He looked at the meter and opened his billfold — he had not one single dollar bill, only fifty cents, which was not enough. "I've run out of money, except this fifty cents," Ken said, handing the driver the money. "What shall I do?"

The driver looked at him. "Nothing, just get out. There's nothing to be done."

Ken got out. "Fifteen cents over and no tip — sorry —"

"You should have taken the money from the lady."

This party was held on the walk-up top floor of a cold-water flat and layered smells of cooking were at each landing of the stairs. The room was crowded, cold, and the gas jets were burning blue on the stove, the oven open for warmth. Since there was little furniture except a studio couch, most of the guests sat on the floor. There were rows of canvases propped against the wall and on an easel a picture of a purple junk yard and two green suns. Ken sat down on the floor next to a pink-cheeked young man wearing a brown leather jacket.

"It's always somehow soothing to sit in a painter's studio. Painters don't have the problems writers have. Who ever heard of a painter getting stuck? They have something to work with — the canvas to be prepared, the brush and so on. Where is a blank page — painters aren't neurotic as many writers are."

"I don't know," the young man said. "Didn't van Gogh cut off his ear?"

"Still the smell of paint, the colors and the activity is soothing. Not like a blank page and a silent room. Painters can whistle when they work or even talk to people."

"I know a painter once who killed his wife."

When Ken was offered rum punch or sherry, he took sherry and it tasted metallic as though coins had been soaked in it.

"You a painter?"

"No," said the young man. "A writer — that is, I write."

"What is your name?"

"It wouldn't mean anything to you. I haven't published my book yet." After a pause he added: "I had a short story in *Bolder Accent* — it's one of the little magazines — maybe you've heard of it."

"How long have you been writing?"

"Eight — ten years. Of course I have to do part-time jobs on the outside, enough to eat and pay the rent."

"What kind of jobs do you do?"

"All kinds. Once for a year I had a job in a morgue. It was wonderful pay and I could do my own work four or five hours every day. But after about a year I began to feel the job was not good for my work. All those cadavers — so I changed to a job frying hot dogs at Coney Island. Now I'm a night clerk in a real crummy hotel. But I can work at home all afternoon and at night I can think over my book — and there's lots of human interest on the job. Future stories, you know."

"What makes you think you are a writer?"

The eagerness faded from the young man's face and when he pressed his fingers to his flushed cheek they left white marks. "Just because I know. I have worked so hard and I have faith in my talent." He went on after a pause. "Of course one story in a little magazine after ten years is not such a brilliant beginning. But think of the struggles nearly every writer has — even the great geniuses. I have time and determination — and when this last novel finally breaks into print the world will recognize the talent."

The open earnestness of the young man was distasteful to Ken, for he felt in it something that he himself had long since lost. "Talent," he said bitterly. "A small, one-story talent — that is the most treacherous thing that God can give. To work on and on, hoping, believing until youth is wasted — I have seen this sort of thing so much. A small talent is God's greatest curse."

"But how do you know I have a small talent — how do you know it's not great? You don't know — you've never read a word I've written!" he said indignantly.

"I wasn't thinking about you in particular. I was just talking abstractly."

The smell of gas was strong in the room — smoke lay in drafty layers close to the low ceiling. The floor was cold and Ken reached for a pillow nearby and sat on it. "What kind of things do you write?"

"My last book is about a man called Brown — I wanted it to be a common name, as a symbol of general humanity. He loves his wife and he has to kill her because —"

"Don't say anything more. A writer should never tell his work in advance. Besides, I've heard it all before."

"How could you? I never told you, finished telling —"

"It's the same thing in the end," Ken said. "I heard the whole thing seven years — eight years ago in this room."

The flushed face paled suddenly. "Mr. Harris, although you've written two published books, I think you're a mean man." His voice rose. "Don't pick on me!"

The young man stood up, zipped his leather jacket and stood sullenly in a corner of the room.

After some moments Ken began to wonder why he was there. He knew no one at the party except his host and the picture of the garbage dump and the two suns irritated him. In the room of strangers there was no voice to guide him and the sherry was sharp in his dry mouth. Without saying good-by to anyone Ken left the room and went downstairs.

He remembered he had no money and would have to walk home. It was still snowing, and the wind shrilled at the street corners and the temperature was nearing zero. He was many blocks away from home when he saw a drug store at a familiar corner and the thought of hot coffee came to him. If he could just drink some really hot coffee, holding his hands around the cup, then his brain would clear and he would have the strength to hurry home and face his wife and the thing that was going to happen when he was home. Then something occurred that in the beginning seemed ordinary, even natural. A man in a Homburg hat was about to pass him on the deserted street and when they were quite near Ken said: "Hello there, it's about zero, isn't it?"

The man hesitated for a moment.

"Wait," he went on. "I'm in something of a predicament. I've lost my money — never mind how — and I wonder if you would give me change for a cup of coffee."

When the words were spoken Ken realized suddenly that the situation was not ordinary and he and the stranger exchanged that look of mutual shame, distrust, between the beggar and the begged. Ken stood with his hands in his pockets — he had lost his gloves somewhere — and the stranger glanced a final time at him, then hurried away.

"Wait," Ken called. "You think I'm a mugger — I'm not! I'm a writer — I'm not a criminal."

The stranger hurried to the other side of the street, his brief case bouncing against his knees as he moved. Ken reached home after midnight.

Marian was in bed with a glass of milk on the bedside table. He made himself a highball and brought it in the bedroom, although usually these days he gulped liquor in secret and quickly.

"Where is the clock?"

"In the clothes hamper."

He found the clock and put it on the table by the milk. Marian gave him a strange stare.

"How was your party?"

"Awful." After a while he added, "This city is a desolate place. The parties, the people — the suspicious strangers."

"You are the one who always likes parties."

"No, I don't. Not any more." He sat on the twin bed beside Marian and suddenly the tears came to his eyes. "Hon, what happened to the apple farm?"

"Apple farm?"

"*Our* apple farm — don't you remember?"

"It was so many years ago and so much has happened."

But although the dream had long since been forgotten, its freshness was renewed again. He could see the apple blossoms in the spring rain, the gray old farmhouse. He was milking at dawn, then tending the vegetable garden with the green curled lettuce, the dusty summer corn, the eggplant and the purple cabbages iridescent in the dew. The country breakfast would be pancakes and the sausage of home-raised pork. When morning chores and breakfast were done, he would work at his novel for four hours, then in the afternoon there were fences to be mended, wood to be split. He saw the farm in all its weathers — the snowbound spells when he would finish a whole short novel at one stretch; the mild, sweet, luminous days of May; the green summer pond where he fished for their own trout; the blue October and the apples. The dream, unblemished by reality, was vivid, exact.

"And in the evening," he said, seeing the firelight and the rise and fall of shadows on the farmhouse wall, "we would really study Shakespeare, and read the Bible all the way through."

For a moment Marian was caught in the dream. "That was the first year we were married," she said in a tone of injury or surprise. "And after the apple farm was started we were going to start a child."

"I remember," he said vaguely, although this was a part he had quite forgotten. He saw an indefinite little boy of six or so in denim jeans . . . then the child vanished and he saw himself clearly, on the horse — or rather mule — carrying the finished manuscript of a great novel on the way to the nearest village to post it to the publisher.

"We could live on almost nothing — and live well. I would do all the work — manual work is what pays nowadays — raise everything we eat. We'll have our own hogs and a cow and chickens." After a pause he added, "There won't even be a liquor bill. I will make cider and applejack. Have a press and all."

"I'm tired," Marian said, and she touched her fingers to her forehead.

"There will be no more New York parties and in the evening we'll read the Bible all the way through. I've never read the Bible all the way through, have you?"

"No," she said, "but you don't have to have an apple farm to read the Bible."

"Maybe I have to have the apple farm to read the Bible and to write well too."

"Well, tant pis." The French phrase infuriated him; for a year before they were married she had taught French in high school and occasionally when she was peeved or disappointed with him she used a French phrase that often he did not understand.

He felt a gathering tension between them that he wanted at all cost to wear through. He sat on the bed, hunched and miserable, gazing at the prints on the bedroom wall. "You see, something so screwy has happened to my sights. When I was young I was sure I was going to be a great writer. And then the years passed — I settled on being a fine minor writer. Can you feel the dying fall of this?"

"No, I'm exhausted," she said after a while. "I have been thinking of the Bible too, this last year. One of the first commandments is *Thou shalt have no other gods before me!* But you and other people like you have made a god of this — illusion. You disregard all other responsibilities — family, finances and even self-respect. You disregard anything that might interfere with your strange god. The golden calf was nothing to this."

"And after settling to be a minor writer I had to lower my sights still further. I wrote scripts for television and tried to become a competent hack. But I failed even to carry that through. Can you understand the horror? I've even become mean-hearted, jealous — I was never that way before. I was a pretty good person when I was happy. The last and final thing is to give up and get a job writing advertising. Can you understand the horror?"

"I've often thought that might be a solution. Anything, darling, to restore your self-respect."

"Yes," he said. "But I'd rather get a job in a morgue or fry hot dogs."

Her eyes were apprehensive. "It's late. Get to bed."

"At the apple farm I would work so hard — laboring work as well as writing. And it would be peaceful and — safe. Why can't we do it, Baby-love?"

She was cutting a hangnail and did not even look at him.

"Maybe I could borrow from your Aunt Rose — in a strictly legal, banking way. With business mortgages on the farm and the crops. And I would dedicate the first book to her."

"Borrow from — not my Aunt Rose!" Marian put the scissors on the table. "I'm going to sleep."

"Why don't you believe in me — and the apple farm? Why don't you want it? It would be so peaceful and — safe. We would be alone and far away — why don't you want it?"

Her black eyes were wide open and he saw in them an expression he had only seen once before. "Because," she said deliberately, "I wouldn't be alone and far away with you on that crazy apple farm for anything — without doctors, friends and help." The apprehension had quickened to fright and her eyes glowed with fear. Her hands picked at the sheet.

Ken's voice was shocked. "Baby, you're not afraid of me! Why, I wouldn't touch your smallest eyelash. I don't even want the wind to blow on you — I couldn't hurt —"

Marian settled her pillow and, turning her back, lay down. "All right. Good night."

For a while he sat dazed, then he knelt on the floor beside Marian's bed and his hand rested gently on her buttocks. The dull pulse of desire was prompted by the touch. "Come! I'll take off my clothes. Let's cozy." He waited, but she did not move or answer.

"Come, Baby-love."

"No," she said. But his love was rising and he did not notice her words — his hand trembled and the fingernails were dingy against the white blanket. "No more," she said. "Not ever."

"Please, love. Then afterward we can be at peace and can sleep. Darling, darling, you're all I have. You're the gold in my life!"

Marian pushed his hand away and sat up abruptly. The fear was replaced by a flash of anger, and the blue vein was prominent on her temple. "Gold in your life —" Her voice intended irony but somehow failed. "In any case — I'm your bread and butter."

The insult of the words reached him slowly, then anger leaped as sudden as a flame. "I — I —"

"You think you're the only one who has been disappointed. I married a writer who I thought would become a great writer. I was glad to support you — I thought it would pay off. So I worked at an office while you could sit there — lowering your sights. God, what has happened to us?"

"I — I —" But rage would not yet let him speak.

"Maybe you could have been helped. If you had gone to the doctor when that block started. We've both known for a long time you are — sick."

Again he saw the expression he had seen before — it was the look that was the only thing he remembered in that awful blackout — the black eyes brilliant with fear and the prominent temple vein. He caught, reflected the same expression, so that their eyes were fixed for a time, blazing with terror.

Unable to stand this, Ken picked up the scissors from the bedside table and held them above his head, his eyes fixed on her temple vein. "Sick!" he said at last. "You mean — crazy. I'll teach you to be afraid that I am crazy. I'll teach you to talk about bread and butter. I'll teach you to think I'm crazy!"

Marian's eyes sparkled with alarm and she tried weakly to move. The vein writhed in her temple. "Don't you move." Then with a great effort he opened his hand and the scissors fell on the carpeted floor. "Sorry," he said. "Excuse me." After a dazed look around the room he saw the typewriter and went to it quickly.

"I'll take the typewriter in the living room. I didn't finish my quota today — you have to be disciplined about things like that."

He sat at the typewriter in the living room, alternating X and R for the sound. After some lines of this he paused and said in an empty voice: "This story is sitting up on its hind legs at last." Then he began to write: *The lazy brown fox jumped over the cunning dog.* He wrote this a number of times, then leaned back in his chair.

"Dearest Pie," he said urgently. "You know how I love you. You're the only woman I ever thought about. You're my life. Don't you understand, my dearest Pie?"

She didn't answer and the apartment was silent except for the rumble of the radiator pipes.

"Forgive me," he said. "I'm so sorry I picked up the scissors. You know I wouldn't even pinch you too hard. Tell me you forgive me. Please, please tell me."

Still there was no answer.

"I'm going to be a good husband. I'll even get a job in an advertising office. I'll be a Sunday poet — writing only on weekends and holidays. I will, my darling, I will!" he said desperately. "Although I'd much rather fry hot dogs in the morgue."

Was it the snow that made the rooms so silent? He was conscious of his own heart beating and he wrote:

Why am I so afraid

Why am I so afraid

Why am I so afraid???

He got up and in the kitchen opened the icebox door. "Hon, I'm going to fix you something good to eat. What's that dark thing in the saucer in the corner? Why, it's the liver from last Sunday's dinner — you're crazy about chicken liver or would you rather have something piping hot like soup? Which, Hon?"

There was no sound.

"I bet you haven't even eaten a bite of supper. You must be exhausted — with those awful parties and drinking and walking — without a living bite. I have to take care of you. We'll eat and afterward we can cozy."

He stood still, listening. Then, with the grease-jelled chicken liver in his hands, he tiptoed to the bedroom. The room and bath were both empty. Carefully he placed the chicken liver on the white bureau scarf. Then he stood in the doorway, his foot raised to walk and left suspended for some moments. Afterward he opened closets, even the broom closet in the kitchen, looked behind furniture and peered under the bed. Marian was nowhere at all. Finally he realized that the leopard coat and her purse were gone. He was panting when he sat down to telephone.

"Hey, Doctor. Ken Harris speaking. My wife has disappeared. Just walked out while I was writing at the typewriter. Is she with you?

Did she phone?" He made squares and wavy lines on the pad. "Hell yes, we quarreled! I picked up the scissors — no, I did not touch her! I wouldn't hurt her little fingernail. No, she's not hurt — how did you get that idea?" Ken listened. "I just want to tell you this. I know you have hypnotized my wife — poisoned her mind against me. If anything happens between my wife and me I'm going to kill you. I'll go up to your nosy Park Avenue office and kill you dead."

Alone in the empty, silent rooms, he felt an undefinable fear that reminded him of his ghost-haunted babyhood. He sat on the bed, his shoes still on, cradling his knees with both arms. A line of poetry came to him. "My love, my love, my love, why have you left me alone?" He sobbed and bit his trousered knee.

After a while he called the places he thought she might be, accused friends of interfering with their marriage or of hiding Marian... When he called Mabel Goodley he had forgotten the episode of the early evening and he said he wanted to come around to see her. When she said it was three o'clock and she had to get up in the morning he asked what friends were for if not for times like this. And he accused her of hiding Marian, of interfering with their marriage and of being in cahoots with the evil psychiatrist...

At the end of the night it stopped snowing. The early dawn was pearl gray and the day would be fair and very cold. At sunrise Ken put on his overcoat and went downstairs. At that hour there was no one on the street. The sun dappled the fresh snow with gold, and shadows were cold lavender. His senses searched the frozen radiance of the morning and he was thinking he should have written about such a day — that was what he had really meant to write.

A hunched and haggard figure with luminous, lost eyes, Ken plodded slowly toward the subway. He thought of the wheels of the train and the gritty wind, the roar. He wondered if it was true that in the final moment of death the brain blazes with all the images of the past — the apple trees, the loves, the cadence of lost voices — all fused and vivid in the dying brain. He walked very slowly, his eyes fixed on his solitary footsteps and the blank snow ahead.

A mounted policeman was passing along the curb near him. The horse's breath showed in the still, cold air and his eyes were purple, liquid.

"Hey, Officer. I have something to report. My wife picked up the scissors at me — aiming for that little blue vein. Then she left the apartment. My wife is very sick — crazy. She ought to be helped before something awful happens. She didn't eat a bite of supper — not even the little chicken liver."

Ken plodded on laboriously, and the officer watched him as he went away. Ken's destination was as uncontrollable as the unseen wind and Ken thought only of his footsteps and the unmarked way ahead.

The Ballad of the Sad Café

The town itself is dreary; not much is there except the cotton mill, the two-room houses where the workers live, a few peach trees, a church with two colored windows, and a miserable main street only a hundred yards long. On Saturdays the tenants from the nearby farms come in for a day of talk and trade. Otherwise the town is lonesome, sad, and like a place that is far off and estranged from all other places in the world. The nearest train stop is Society City, and the Greyhound and White Bus Lines use the Forks Falls Road which is three miles away. The winters here are short and raw, the summers white with glare and fiery hot.

If you walk along the main street on an August afternoon there is nothing whatsoever to do. The largest building, in the very center of the town, is boarded up completely and leans so far to the right that it seems bound to collapse at any minute. The house is very old. There is about it a curious, cracked look that is very puzzling until you suddenly realize that at one time, and long ago, the right side of the front porch had been painted, and part of the wall — but the painting was left unfinished and one portion of the house is darker and dingier than the other. The building looks completely deserted. Nevertheless, on the second floor there is one window which is not boarded; sometimes in the late afternoon when the heat is at its worst a hand will slowly open the shutter and a face will look down on the town. It is a face like the terrible dim faces known in dreams — sexless and white, with two gray crossed eyes which are turned inward so sharply that they seem to be exchanging with each other one long and secret gaze of grief. The face lingers at the window for an hour or so, then the shutters are closed once more, and as likely as not there will not be another soul to be seen along the main street. These August afternoons — when your shift is finished there is absolutely nothing to do; you might as well walk down to the Forks Falls Road and listen to the chain gang.

However, here in this very town there was once a café. And this old boarded-up house was unlike any other place for many miles around. There were tables with cloths and paper napkins, colored streamers from the electric fans, great gatherings on Saturday nights. The owner of the place was Miss Amelia Evans. But the person most responsible for the success and gaiety of the place was a hunchback called Cousin Lymon. One other person had a part in the story of this café — he was the former husband of Miss Amelia, a terrible character who returned to the town after a long term in the penitentiary, caused ruin, and then went on his way again. The café has long since been closed, but it is still remembered.

The place was not always a café. Miss Amelia inherited the building from her father, and it was a store that carried mostly feed, guano, and staples such as meal and snuff. Miss Amelia was rich. In addition to the store she operated a still three miles back in the swamp, and ran out the best liquor in the county. She was a dark, tall woman with bones and muscles like a man. Her hair was cut short and brushed back from the forehead, and there was about her sunburned face a tense, haggard quality. She might have been a handsome woman if, even then, she was not slightly cross-eyed. There were those who would have courted her, but Miss Amelia cared nothing for the love of men and was a solitary person. Her marriage had been unlike any other marriage ever contracted in this county — it was a strange and dangerous marriage, lasting only for ten days, that left the whole town wondering and shocked. Except for this queer marriage Miss Amelia had lived her life alone. Often she spent whole nights back in her shed in the swamp, dressed in overalls and gum boots, silently guarding the low fire of the still.

With all things which could be made by the hands Miss Amelia prospered. She sold chitterlins and sausage in the town near-by. On fine autumn days she ground sorghum, and the syrup from her vats was dark golden and delicately flavored. She built the brick privy behind her store in only two weeks and was skilled in carpentering.

It was only with people that Miss Amelia was not at ease. People, unless they are nilly-willy or very sick, cannot be taken into the hands and changed overnight to something more worth-while and profitable. So that the only use that Miss Amelia had for other people was to make money out of them. And in this she succeeded. Mortgages on crops and property, a sawmill, money in the bank — she was the richest woman for miles around. She would have been rich as a congressman if it were not for her one great failing, and that was her passion for lawsuits and the courts. She would involve herself in long and bitter litigation over just a trifle. It was said that if Miss Amelia so much as stumbled over a rock in the road she would glance around instinctively as though looking for something to sue about it. Aside from these lawsuits she lived a steady life and every day was very much like the day that had gone before. With the exception of her ten-day marriage, nothing happened to change this until the spring of the year that Miss Amelia was thirty years old.

It was toward midnight on a soft quiet evening in April. The sky was the color of a blue swamp iris, the moon clear and bright. The crops that spring promised well and in the past weeks the mill had run a night shift. Down by the creek the square brick factory was yellow with light, and there was the faint, steady hum of the looms. It was such a night when it is good to hear from faraway, across the dark fields, the slow song of a Negro on his way to make love. Or when it is pleasant to sit quietly and pick up a guitar, or simply to rest alone and think of nothing at all. The street that evening was deserted, but Miss Amelia's store was lighted and on the porch outside there were five people. One of these was Stumpy MacPhail, a foreman with a red face and dainty, purplish hands. On the top step were two boys in overalls, the Rainey twins — both of them lanky and slow, with white hair and sleepy green eyes. The other man was Henry Macy, a shy and timid person with gentle manners and nervous ways, who sat on the edge of the bottom step. Miss Amelia herself stood leaning against the side of the open door, her feet crossed in their big swamp boots, patiently untying knots in a rope she had come across. They had not talked for a long time.

One of the twins, who had been looking down the empty road, was the first to speak. "I see something coming," he said.

"A calf got loose," said his brother.

The approaching figure was still too distant to be clearly seen. The moon made dim, twisted shadows of the blossoming peach trees along the side of the road. In the air the odor of blossoms and sweet spring grass mingled with the warm, sour smell of the near-by lagoon.

"No. It's somebody's youngun," said Stumpy MacPhail.

Miss Amelia watched the road in silence. She had put down her rope and was fingering the straps of her overalls with her brown bony hand. She scowled, and a dark lock of hair fell down on her forehead. While they were waiting there, a dog from one of the houses down the road began a wild, hoarse howl that continued until a voice called out and hushed him. It was not until the figure was quite close, within the range of the yellow light from the porch, that they saw clearly what had come.

The man was a stranger, and it is rare that a stranger enters the town on foot at that hour. Besides, the man was a hunchback. He was scarcely more than four feet tall and he wore a ragged, dusty coat that reached only to his knees. His crooked little legs seemed too thin to carry the weight of his great warped chest and the hump that sat on his shoulders. He had a very large head, with deep-set blue eyes and a sharp little mouth. His face was both soft and sassy — at the moment his pale skin was yellowed by dust and there were lavender shadows beneath his eyes. He carried a lopsided old suitcase which was tied with a rope.

"Evening," said the hunchback, and he was out of breath.

Miss Amelia and the men on the porch neither answered his greeting nor spoke. They only looked at him.

"I am hunting for Miss Amelia Evans."

Miss Amelia pushed back her hair from her forehead and raised her chin. "How come?"

"Because I am kin to her," the hunchback said.

The twins and Stumpy MacPhail looked up at Miss Amelia.

"That's me," she said. "How do you mean 'kin'?"

"Because —" the hunchback began. He looked uneasy, almost as though he was about to cry. He rested the suitcase on the bottom step, but did not take his hand from the handle. "My mother was Fanny Jesup and she come from Cheehaw. She left Cheehaw some thirty years ago when she married her first husband. I remember hearing her tell how she had a half-sister named Martha. And back in Cheehaw today they tell me that was your mother."

Miss Amelia listened with her head turned slightly aside. She ate her Sunday dinners by herself; her place was never crowded with a flock of relatives, and she claimed kin with no one. She had had a great-aunt who owned the livery stable in Cheehaw, but that aunt was now dead. Aside from her there was only one double first cousin who lived in a town twenty miles away, but this cousin and Miss Amelia did not get on so well, and when they chanced to pass each other they spat on the side of the road. Other people had tried very hard, from time to time, to work out some kind of far-fetched connection with Miss Amelia, but with absolutely no success.

The hunchback went into a long rigmarole, mentioning names and places that were unknown to the listeners on the porch and seemed to have nothing to do with the subject. "So Fanny and Martha Jesup were half-sisters. And I am the son of Fanny's third husband. So that would make you and I —" He bent down and began to unfasten his suitcase. His hands were like dirty sparrow claws and they were trembling. The bag was full of all manner of junk — ragged clothes and odd rubbish that looked like parts out of a sewing machine, or something just as worthless. The hunchback scrambled among these belongings and brought out an old photograph. "This is a picture of my mother and her half-sister."

Miss Amelia did not speak. She was moving her jaw slowly from side to side, and you could tell from her face what she was thinking about. Stumpy MacPhail took the photograph and held it out toward the light. It was a picture of two pale, withered-up little children of about two and three years of age. The faces were tiny white blurs, and it might have been an old picture in anyone's album.

Stumpy MacPhail handed it back with no comment. "Where you come from?" he asked.

The hunchback's voice was uncertain. "I was traveling."

Still Miss Amelia did not speak. She just stood leaning against the side of the door, and looked down at the hunchback. Henry Macy winked nervously and rubbed his hands together. Then quietly he left the bottom step and disappeared. He is a good soul, and the hunchback's situation had touched his heart. Therefore he did not want to wait and watch Miss Amelia chase this newcomer off her property and run him out of town. The hunchback stood with his bag open on the bottom step; he sniffled his nose, and his mouth quivered. Perhaps he began to feel his dismal predicament. Maybe he realized what a miserable thing it was to be a stranger in the town with a suitcase full of junk, and claiming kin with Miss Amelia. At any rate he sat down on the steps and suddenly began to cry.

It was not a common thing to have an unknown hunchback walk to the store at midnight and then sit down and cry. Miss Amelia rubbed back her hair from her forehead and the men looked at each other uncomfortably. All around the town was very quiet.

At last one of the twins said: "I'll be damned if he ain't a regular Morris Finestein."

Everyone nodded and agreed, for that is an expression having a certain special meaning. But the hunchback cried louder because he could not know what they were talking about. Morris Finestein was a person who had lived in the town years before. He was only a quick, skipping little Jew who cried if you called him Christkiller, and ate light bread and canned salmon every day. A calamity had come over him and he had moved away to Society City. But since then if a man were prissy in any way, or if a man ever wept, he was known as a Morris Finestein.

"Well, he is afflicted," said Stumpy MacPhail. "There is some cause."

Miss Amelia crossed the porch with two slow, gangling strides. She went down the steps and stood looking thoughtfully at the stranger. Gingerly, with one long brown forefinger, she touched the hump on his back. The hunchback still wept, but he was quieter now. The night was silent and the moon still shone with a soft, clear light—it was getting colder. Then Miss Amelia did a rare thing; she pulled out a bottle from her hip pocket and after polishing off the top with the palm of her hand she handed it to the hunchback to drink. Miss Amelia could seldom be persuaded to sell her liquor on credit, and for her to give so much as a drop away free was almost unknown.

"Drink," she said. "It will liven your gizzard."

The hunchback stopped crying, neatly licked the tears from around his mouth, and did as he was told. When he was finished, Miss Amelia took a slow swallow, warmed and washed her mouth with it, and spat. Then she also drank. The twins and the foreman had their own bottle they had paid for.

"It is smooth liquor," Stumpy MacPhail said. "Miss Amelia, I have never known you to fail."

The whisky they drank that evening (two big bottles of it) is important. Otherwise, it would be hard to account for what followed.

Perhaps without it there would never have been a café. For the liquor of Miss Amelia has a special quality of its own. It is clean and sharp on the tongue, but once down a man it glows inside him for a long time afterward. And that is not all. It is known that if a message is written with lemon juice on a clean sheet of paper there will be no sign of it. But if the paper is held for a moment to the fire then the letters turn brown and the meaning becomes clear. Imagine that the whisky is the fire and that the message is that which is known only in the soul of a man — then the worth of Miss Amelia's liquor can be understood. Things that have gone unnoticed, thoughts that have been harbored far back in the dark mind, are suddenly recognized and comprehended. A spinner who has thought only of the loom, the dinner pail, the bed, and then the loom again — this spinner might drink some on a Sunday and come across a marsh lily. And in his palm he might hold this flower, examining the golden dainty cup, and in him suddenly might come a sweetness keen as pain. A weaver might look up suddenly and see for the first time the cold, weird radiance of midnight January sky, and a deep fright at his own smallness stop his heart. Such things as these, then, happen when a man has drunk Miss Amelia's liquor. He may suffer, or he may be spent with joy — but the experience has shown the truth; he has warmed his soul and seen the message hidden there.

They drank until it was past midnight, and the moon was clouded over so that the night was cold and dark. The hunchback still sat on the bottom steps, bent over miserably with his forehead resting on his knee. Miss Amelia stood with her hands in her pockets, one foot resting on the second step of the stairs. She had been silent for a long time. Her face had the expression often seen in slightly cross-eyed persons who are thinking deeply, a look that appears to be both very wise and very crazy. At last she said: "I don't know your name."

"I'm Lymon Willis," said the hunchback.

"Well, come on in," she said. "Some supper was left in the stove and you can eat."

Only a few times in her life had Miss Amelia invited anyone to eat with her, unless she was planning to trick them in some way, or make money out of them. So the men on the porch felt there was something wrong. Later, they said among themselves that she must have been drinking back in the swamp the better part of the afternoon.

At any rate she left the porch, and Stumpy MacPhail and the twins went on off home. She bolted the front door and looked all around to see that her goods were in order. Then she went to the kitchen, which was at the back of the store. The hunchback followed her, dragging his suitcase, sniffing and wiping his nose on the sleeve of his dirty coat.

"Sit down," said Miss Amelia. "I'll just warm up what's here."

It was a good meal they had together on that night. Miss Amelia was rich and she did not grudge herself food. There was fried chicken (the breast of which the hunchback took on his own plate), mashed rootabeggars, collard greens, and hot, pale golden, sweet potatoes. Miss Amelia ate slowly and with the relish of a farm hand. She sat with both elbows on the table, bent over the plate, her knees spread wide apart and her feet braced on the rungs of the chair. As for the hunchback, he gulped down his supper as though he had not smelled food in months. During the meal one tear crept down his dingy cheek — but it was just a little leftover tear and meant nothing at all. The lamp on the table was well-trimmed, burning blue at the edges of the wick, and casting a cheerful light in the kitchen. When Miss Amelia had eaten her supper she wiped her plate carefully with a slice of light bread, and then poured her own clear, sweet syrup over the bread. The hunchback did likewise — except that he was more finicky and asked for a new plate. Having finished, Miss Amelia tilted back her chair, tightened her fist, and felt the hard, supple muscles of her right arm beneath the clean, blue cloth of her shirt-sleeves — an unconscious habit with her, at the close of a meal. Then she took the lamp from the table and jerked her head toward the staircase as an invitation for the hunchback to follow after her.

Above the store there were the three rooms where Miss Amelia had lived during all of her life — two bedrooms with a large parlor in between. Few people had even seen these rooms, but it was generally known that they were well-furnished and extremely clean. And now Miss Amelia was taking up with her a dirty little hunchbacked stranger, come from God knows where. Miss Amelia walked slowly, two steps at a time, holding the lamp high. The hunchback hovered so close behind her that the swinging light made on the staircase wall one great, twisted shadow of the two of them. Soon the premises above the store were dark as the rest of the town.

* * *

The next morning was serene, with a sunrise of warm purple mixed with rose. In the fields around the town the furrows were newly plowed, and very early the tenants were at work setting out the young, deep green tobacco plants. The wild crows flew down close to the fields, making swift blue shadows on the earth. In town the people set out early with their dinner pails, and the windows of the mill were blinding gold in the sun. The air was fresh and the peach trees light as March clouds with their blossoms.

Miss Amelia came down at about dawn, as usual. She washed her head at the pump and very shortly set about her business. Later in the morning she saddled her mule and went to see about her property, planted with cotton, up near the Forks Falls Road. By noon, of course, everybody had heard about the hunchback who had come to the store in the middle of the night. But no one as yet had seen him. The day soon grew hot and the sky was a rich, midday blue. Still no one had laid an eye on this strange guest. A few people remembered that Miss Amelia's mother had had a half-sister — but there was some difference of opinion as to whether she had died or had run off with a tobacco stringer. As for the hunchback's claim, everyone thought it was a trumped-up business. And the town, knowing Miss Amelia, decided that surely she had put him out of the house after feeding him. But toward evening, when the sky had whitened, and the shift was done, a woman claimed to have seen a crooked face at the window of one of the rooms up over the store. Miss Amelia herself said nothing. She clerked in the store for a while, argued for an hour with a farmer over a plow shaft, mended some chicken wire, locked up near sundown, and went to her rooms. The town was left puzzled and talkative.

The next day Miss Amelia did not open the store, but stayed locked up inside her premises and saw no one. Now this was the day that the rumor started — the rumor so terrible that the town and all the country about were stunned by it. The rumor was started by a weaver called Merlie Ryan. He is a man of not much account — sallow, shambling, and with no teeth in his head. He has the three-day malaria, which means that every third day the fever comes on him. So on two days he is dull and cross, but on the third day he livens up and sometimes has an idea or two, most of which are foolish. It was while Merlie Ryan was in his fever that he turned suddenly and said:

"I know what Miss Amelia done. She murdered that man for something in that suitcase."

He said this in a calm voice, as a statement of fact. And within an hour the news had swept through the town. It was a fierce and sickly tale the town built up that day. In it were all the things which cause the heart to shiver — a hunchback, a midnight burial in the swamp, the dragging of Miss Amelia through the streets of the town on the way to prison, the squabbles over what would happen to her property — all told in hushed voices and repeated with some fresh and weird detail. It rained and women forgot to bring in the washing from the lines. One or two mortals, who were in debt to Miss Amelia, even put on Sunday clothes as though it were a holiday. People clustered together on the main street, talking and watching the store.

It would be untrue to say that all the town took part in this evil festival. There were a few sensible men who reasoned that Miss Amelia, being rich, would not go out of her way to murder a vagabond for a few trifles of junk. In the town there were even three good people, and they did not want this crime, not even for the sake of the interest and the great commotion it would entail; it gave them no pleasure to think of Miss Amelia holding to the bars of the penitentiary and being electrocuted in Atlanta. These good people judged Miss Amelia in a different way from what the others judged her. When a person is as contrary in every single respect as she was and when the sins of a person have amounted to such a point that they can hardly be remembered all at once — then this person plainly requires a special judgment. They remembered that Miss Amelia had been born dark and somewhat queer of face, raised motherless by her father who was a solitary man, that early in youth she had grown to be six feet two inches tall which in itself is not natural for a woman, and that her ways and habits of life were too peculiar ever to reason about. Above all, they remembered her puzzling marriage, which was the most unreasonable scandal ever to happen in this town.

So these good people felt toward her something near to pity. And when she was out on her wild business, such as rushing in a house to drag forth a sewing machine in payment for a debt, or getting herself worked up over some matter concerning the law — they had toward her a feeling which was a mixture of exasperation, a ridiculous little inside tickle, and a deep, unnamable sadness. But enough of the good people, for there were only three of them; the rest of the town was making a holiday of this fancied crime the whole of the afternoon.

Miss Amelia herself, for some strange reason, seemed unaware of all this. She spent most of her day upstairs. When down in the store, she prowled around peacefully, her hands deep in the pockets of her overalls and head bent so low that her chin was tucked inside the collar of her shirt. There was no bloodstain on her anywhere. Often she stopped and just stood somberly looking down at the cracks in the floor, twisting a lock of her short-cropped hair, and whispering something to herself. But most of the day was spent upstairs.

Dark came on. The rain that afternoon had chilled the air, so that the evening was bleak and gloomy as in wintertime. There were no stars in the sky, and a light, icy drizzle had set in. The lamps in the houses made mournful, wavering flickers when watched from the street. A wind had come up, not from the swamp side of the town but from the cold black pinewoods to the north.

The clocks in the town struck eight. Still nothing had happened. The bleak night, after the gruesome talk of the day, put a fear in some people, and they stayed home close to the fire. Others were gathered in groups together. Some eight or ten men had convened on the porch of Miss Amelia's store. They were silent and were indeed just waiting about. They themselves did not know what they were waiting for, but it was this: in times of tension, when some great action is impending, men gather and wait in this way. And after a time there will come a moment when all together they will act in unison, not from thought or from the will of any one man, but as though their instincts had merged together so that the decision belongs to no single one of them, but to the group as a whole. At such a time no individual hesitates. And whether the matter will be settled peaceably, or whether the joint action will result in ransacking, violence, and crime, depends on destiny. So the men waited soberly on the porch of Miss Amelia's store, not one of them realizing what they would do, but knowing inwardly that they must wait, and that the time had almost come.

Now the door to the store was open. Inside it was bright and natural-looking. To the left was the counter where slabs of white meat, rock candy, and tobacco were kept. Behind this were shelves of salted white meat and meal. The right side of the store was mostly filled with farm implements and such. At the back of the store, to the left, was the door leading up the stairs, and it was open. And at the far right of the store there was another door which led to a little room that Miss Amelia called her office. This door was also open. And at eight o'clock that evening Miss Amelia could be seen there sitting before her rolltop desk, figuring with a fountain pen and some pieces of paper.

The office was cheerfully lighted, and Miss Amelia did not seem to notice the delegation on the porch. Everything around her was in great order, as usual. This office was a room well-known, in a dreadful way, throughout the country. It was there Miss Amelia transacted all business. On the desk was a carefully covered typewriter which she knew how to run, but used only for the most important documents. In the drawers were literally thousands of papers, all filed according to the alphabet. This office was also the place where Miss Amelia received sick people, for she enjoyed doctoring and did a great deal of it. Two whole shelves were crowded with bottles and various paraphernalia. Against the wall was a bench where the patients sat. She could sew up a wound with a burnt needle so that it would not turn green. For burns she had a cool, sweet syrup. For unlocated sickness there were any number of different medicines which she had brewed herself from unknown recipes. They wrenched loose the bowels very well, but they could not be given to small children, as they caused bad convulsions; for them she had an entirely separate draught, gentler and sweet-flavored. Yes, all in all, she was considered a good doctor. Her hands, though very large and bony, had a light touch about them. She possessed great imagination and used hundreds of different cures. In the face of the most dangerous and extraordinary treatment she did not hesitate, and no disease was so terrible but what she would undertake to cure it. In this there was one exception. If a patient came with a female complaint she could do nothing. Indeed at the mere mention of the words her face would slowly darken with shame, and she would stand there craning her neck against the collar of her shirt, or rubbing her swamp boots together, for all the world like a great, shamed, dumb-tongued child. But in other matters people trusted her. She charged no fees whatsoever and always had a raft of patients.

On this evening Miss Amelia wrote with her fountain pen a good deal. But even so she could not be forever unaware of the group waiting out there on the dark porch, and watching her. From time to time she looked up and regarded them steadily. But she did not holler out to them to demand why they were loafing around her property like a sorry bunch of gabbies. Her face was proud and stern, as it always was when she sat at the desk of her office. After a time their peering in like that seemed to annoy her. She wiped her cheek with a red handkerchief, got up, and closed the office door.

Now to the group on the porch this gesture acted as a signal. The time had come. They had stood for a long while with the night raw and gloomy in the street behind them. They had waited long and just at that moment the instinct to act came on them. All at once, as though moved by one will, they walked into the store. At that moment the eight men looked very much alike — all wearing blue overalls, most of them with whitish hair, all pale of face, and all with a set, dreaming look in the eye. What they would have done next no one knows. But at that instant there was a noise at the head of the staircase. The men looked up and then stood dumb with shock. It was the hunchback, whom they had already murdered in their minds. Also, the creature was not at all as had been pictured to them — not a pitiful and dirty little chatterer, alone and beggared in this world. Indeed, he was like nothing any man among them had ever beheld until that time. The room was still as death.

The hunchback came down slowly with the proudness of one who owns every plank of the floor beneath his feet. In the past days he had greatly changed. For one thing he was clean beyond words. He still wore his little coat, but it was brushed off and neatly mended. Beneath this was a fresh red and black checkered shirt belonging to Miss Amelia. He did not wear trousers such as ordinary men are meant to wear, but a pair of tight-fitting little knee-length breeches. On his skinny legs he wore black stockings, and his shoes were of a special kind, being queerly shaped, laced up over the ankles, and newly cleaned and polished with wax. Around his neck, so that his large, pale ears were almost completely covered, he wore a shawl of lime-green wool, the fringes of which almost touched the floor.

The hunchback walked down the store with his stiff little strut and then stood in the center of the group that had come inside. They cleared a space about him and stood looking with hands loose at their sides and eyes wide open. The hunchback himself got his bearings in an odd manner. He regarded each person steadily at his own eye-level, which was about belt line for an ordinary man. Then with shrewd deliberation he examined each man's lower regions — from the waist to the sole of the shoe. When he had satisfied himself he closed his eyes for a moment and shook his head, as though in his opinion what he had seen did not amount to much. Then with assurance, only to confirm himself, he tilted back his head and took in the halo of faces around him with one long, circling stare. There was a half-filled sack of guano on the left side of the store, and when he had found his bearings in this way, the hunchback sat down upon it. Cozily settled, with his little legs crossed, he took from his coat pocket a certain object.

Now it took some moments for the men in the store to regain their ease. Merlie Ryan, he of the three-day fever who had started the rumor that day, was the first to speak. He looked at the object which the hunchback was fondling, and said in a hushed voice:

"What is it you have there?"

Each man knew well what it was the hunchback was handling. For it was the snuffbox which had belonged to Miss Amelia's father. The snuffbox was of blue enamel with a dainty embellishment of wrought gold on the lid. The group knew it well and marveled. They glanced warily at the closed office door, and heard the low sound of Miss Amelia whistling to herself.

"Yes, what is it, Peanut?"

The hunchback looked up quickly and sharpened his mouth to speak. "Why, this is a lay-low to catch meddlers."

The hunchback reached in the box with his scrambly little fingers and ate something, but he offered no one around him a taste. It was not even proper snuff which he was taking, but a mixture of sugar and cocoa. This he took, though, as snuff, pocketing a little wad of it beneath his lower lip and licking down neatly into this with a flick of his tongue which made a frequent grimace come over his face.

"The very teeth in my head have always tasted sour to me," he said in explanation. "This is the reason why I take this kind of sweet snuff."

The group still clustered around, feeling somewhat gawky and bewildered. This sensation never quite wore off, but it was soon tempered by another feeling — an air of intimacy in the room and a vague festivity. Now the names of the men of the group there on that evening were as follows: Hasty Malone, Robert Calvert Hale,

Merlie Ryan, Reverend T. M. Willin, Rosser Cline, Rip Wellborn, Henry Ford Crimp, and Horace Wells. Except for Reverend Willin, they are all alike in many ways as has been said — all having taken pleasure from something or other, all having wept and suffered in some way, most of them tractable unless exasperated. Each of them worked in the mill, and lived with others in a two- or three-room house for which the rent was ten dollars or twelve dollars a month. All had been paid that afternoon, for it was Saturday. So, for the present, think of them as a whole.

The hunchback, however, was already sorting them out in his mind. Once comfortably settled he began to chat with everyone, asking questions such as if a man was married, how old he was, how much his wages came to in an average week, et cetera — picking his way along to inquiries which were downright intimate. Soon the group was joined by others in the town, Henry Macy, idlers who had sensed something extraordinary, women come to fetch their men who lingered on, and even one loose, towhead child who tiptoed into the store, stole a box of animal crackers, and made off very quietly. So the premises of Miss Amelia were soon crowded, and she herself had not yet opened her office door.

There is a type of person who has a quality about him that sets him apart from other and more ordinary human beings. Such a person has an instinct which is usually found only in small children, an instinct to establish immediate and vital contact between himself and all things in the world. Certainly the hunchback was of this type. He had only been in the store half an hour before an immediate contact had been established between him and each other individual. It was as though he had lived in the town for years, was a well-known character, and had been sitting and talking there on that guano sack for countless evenings. This, together with the fact that it was Saturday night, could account for the air of freedom and illicit gladness in the store. There was a tension, also, partly because of the oddity of the situation and because Miss Amelia was still closed off in her office and had not yet made her appearance.

She came out that evening at ten o'clock. And those who were expecting some drama at her entrance were disappointed. She opened the door and walked in with her slow, gangling swagger. There was a streak of ink on one side of her nose, and she had knotted the red handkerchief about her neck. She seemed to notice nothing unusual.

Her gray, crossed eyes glanced over to the place where the hunchback was sitting, and for a moment lingered there. The rest of the crowd in her store she regarded with only a peaceable surprise.

"Does anyone want waiting on?" she asked quietly.

There were a number of customers, because it was Saturday night, and they all wanted liquor. Now Miss Amelia had dug up an aged barrel only three days past and had siphoned it into bottles back by the still. This night she took the money from the customers and counted it beneath the bright light. Such was the ordinary procedure. But after this what happened was not ordinary. Always before, it was necessary to go around to the dark back yard, and there she would hand out your bottle through the kitchen door. There was no feeling of joy in the transaction. After getting his liquor the customer walked off into the night. Or, if his wife would not have it in the home, he was allowed to come back around to the front porch of the store and guzzle there or in the street. Now, both the porch and the street before it were the property of Miss Amelia, and no mistake about it — but she did not regard them as premises; the premises began at the front door and took in the entire inside of the building. There she had never allowed liquor to be opened or drunk by anyone but herself. Now for the first time she broke this rule. She went to the kitchen, with the hunchback close at her heels, and she brought back the bottles into the warm, bright store. More than that she furnished some glasses and opened two boxes of crackers so that they were there hospitably in a platter on the counter and anyone who wished could take one free.

She spoke to no one but the hunchback, and she only asked him in a somewhat harsh and husky voice: "Cousin Lymon, will you have yours straight, or warmed in a pan with water on the stove?"

"If you please, Amelia," the hunchback said. (And since what time had anyone presumed to address Miss Amelia by her bare name, without a title of respect? — Certainly not her bridegroom and her husband of ten days. In fact, not since the death of her father, who for some reason had always called her Little, had anyone dared to address her in such a familiar way.) "If you please, I'll have it warmed."

Now, this was the beginning of the café. It was as simple as that. Recall that the night was gloomy as in wintertime, and to have sat around the property outside would have made a sorry celebration. But inside there was company and a genial warmth. Someone had rattled up the stove in the rear, and those who bought bottles shared their liquor with friends. Several women were there and they had twists of licorice, a Nehi, or even a swallow of the whisky. The hunchback was still a novelty and his presence amused everyone. The bench in the office was brought in, together with several extra chairs. Other people leaned against the counter or made themselves comfortable on barrels and sacks. Nor did the opening of liquor on the premises cause any rambunctiousness, indecent giggles, or misbehavior whatsoever. On the contrary the company was polite even to the point of a certain timidness. For people in this town were then unused to gathering together for the sake of pleasure. They met to work in the mill. Or on Sunday there would be an all-day camp meeting — and though that is a pleasure, the intention of the whole affair is to sharpen your view of Hell and put into you a keen fear of the Lord Almighty. But the spirit of a café is altogether different. Even the richest, greediest old rascal will behave himself, insulting no one in a proper café. And poor people look about them gratefully and pinch up the salt in a dainty and modest manner. For the atmosphere of a proper café implies these qualities: fellowship, the satisfactions of the belly, and a certain gaiety and grace of behavior. This had never been told to the gathering in Miss Amelia's store that night. But they knew it of themselves, although never, of course, until that time had there been a café in the town.

Now, the cause of all this, Miss Amelia, stood most of the evening in the doorway leading to the kitchen. Outwardly she did not seem changed at all. But there were many who noticed her face. She watched all that went on, but most of the time her eyes were fastened lonesomely on the hunchback. He strutted about the store, eating from his snuffbox, and being at once sour and agreeable. Where Miss Amelia stood, the light from the chinks of the stove cast a glow, so that her brown, long face was somewhat brightened. She seemed to be looking inward. There was in her expression pain, perplexity, and uncertain joy. Her lips were not so firmly set as usual, and she swallowed often. Her skin had paled and her large empty hands were sweating. Her look that night, then, was the lonesome look of the lover.

This opening of the café came to an end at midnight. Everyone said good-bye to everyone else in a friendly fashion. Miss Amelia shut the front door of her premises, but forgot to bolt it. Soon everything —

the main street with its three stores, the mill, the houses — all the town, in fact — was dark and silent. And so ended three days and nights in which had come an arrival of a stranger, an unholy holiday, and the start of the café.

Now time must pass. For the next four years are much alike. There are great changes, but these changes are brought about bit by bit, in simple steps which in themselves do not appear to be important. The hunchback continued to live with Miss Amelia. The café expanded in a gradual way. Miss Amelia began to sell her liquor by the drink, and some tables were brought into the store. There were customers every evening, and on Saturday a great crowd. Miss Amelia began to serve fried catfish suppers at fifteen cents a plate. The hunchback cajoled her into buying a fine mechanical piano. Within two years the place was a store no longer, but had been converted into a proper café, open every evening from six until twelve o'clock.

Each night the hunchback came down the stairs with the air of one who has a grand opinion of himself. He always smelled slightly of turnip greens, as Miss Amelia rubbed him night and morning with pot liquor to give him strength. She spoiled him to a point beyond reason, but nothing seemed to strengthen him; food only made his hump and his head grow larger while the rest of him remained weakly and deformed. Miss Amelia was the same in appearance. During the week she still wore swamp boots and overalls, but on Sunday she put on a dark red dress that hung on her in a most peculiar fashion. Her manners, however, and her way of life were greatly changed. She still loved a fierce lawsuit, but she was not so quick to cheat her fellow man and to exact cruel payments. Because the hunchback was so extremely sociable she even went about a little — to revivals, to funerals, and so forth. Her doctoring was as successful as ever, her liquor even finer than before, if that were possible. The café itself proved profitable and was the only place of pleasure for many miles around.

So for the moment regard these years from random and disjointed views. See the hunchback marching in Miss Amelia's footsteps when on a red winter morning they set out for the pinewoods to hunt. See them working on her properties — with Cousin Lymon standing by and doing absolutely nothing, but quick to point out any laziness among the hands. On autumn afternoons they sat on the back steps chopping sugar cane. The glaring summer days they spent back in the swamp where the water cypress is a deep black green, where beneath the tangled swamp trees there is a drowsy gloom. When the path leads through a bog or a stretch of blackened water see Miss Amelia bend down to let Cousin Lymon scramble on her back — and see her wading forward with the hunchback settled on her shoulders, clinging to her ears or to her broad forehead. Occasionally Miss Amelia cranked up the Ford which she had bought and treated Cousin Lymon to a picture-show in Cheehaw, or to some distant fair or cockfight; the hunchback took a passionate delight in spectacles. Of course, they were in their café every morning, they would often sit for hours together by the fireplace in the parlor upstairs. For the hunchback was sickly at night and dreaded to lie looking into the dark. He had a deep fear of death. And Miss Amelia would not leave him by himself to suffer with this fright. It may even be reasoned that the growth of the café came about mainly on this account; it was a thing that brought him company and pleasure and that helped him through the night. So compose from such flashes an image of these years as a whole. And for a moment let it rest.

Now some explanation is due for all this behavior. The time has come to speak about love. For Miss Amelia loved Cousin Lymon. So much was clear to everyone. They lived in the same house together and were never seen apart. Therefore, according to Mrs. MacPhail, a warty-nosed old busybody who is continually moving her sticks of furniture from one part of the front room to another; according to her and to certain others, these two were living in sin. If they were related, they were only a cross between first and second cousins, and even that could in no way be proved. Now, of course Miss Amelia was a powerful blunderbuss of a person, more than six feet tall — and Cousin Lymon a weakly little hunchback reaching only to her waist. But so much the better for Mrs. Stumpy MacPhail and her cronies, for they and their kind glory in conjunctions which are ill-matched and pitiful. So let them be. The good people thought that if those two had found some satisfaction of the flesh between themselves, then it was a matter concerning them and God alone. All sensible people agreed in their opinion about this conjecture — and their answer was a plain, flat *no*. What sort of thing, then, was this love?

First of all, love is a joint experience between two persons — but the fact that it is a joint experience does not mean that it is a similar experience to the two people involved. There are the lover and the beloved, but these two come from different countries. Often the beloved is only a stimulus for all the stored-up love which has lain quiet within the lover for a long time hitherto. And somehow every lover knows this. He feels in his soul that his love is a solitary thing. He comes to know a new, strange loneliness and it is this knowledge which makes him suffer. So there is only one thing for the lover to do. He must house his love within himself as best he can; he must create for himself a whole new inward world — a world intense and strange, complete in himself. Let it be added here that this lover about whom we speak need not necessarily be a young man saving for a wedding ring — this lover can be man, woman, child, or indeed any human creature on this earth.

Now, the beloved can also be of any description. The most outlandish people can be the stimulus for love. A man may be a doddering great-grandfather and still love only a strange girl he saw in the streets of Cheehaw one afternoon two decades past. The preacher may love a fallen woman. The beloved may be treacherous, greasy-headed, and given to evil habits. Yes, and the lover may see this as clearly as anyone else — but that does not affect the evolution of his love one whit. A most mediocre person can be the object of a love which is wild, extravagant, and beautiful as the poison lilies of the swamp. A good man may be the stimulus for a love both violent and debased, or a jabbering madman may bring about in the soul of someone a tender and simple idyll. Therefore, the value and quality of any love is determined solely by the lover himself.

It is for this reason that most of us would rather love than be loved. Almost everyone wants to be the lover. And the curt truth is that, in a deep secret way, the state of being beloved is intolerable to many. The beloved fears and hates the lover, and with the best of reasons. For the lover is forever trying to strip bare his beloved. The lover craves any possible relation with the beloved, even if this experience can cause him only pain.

It has been mentioned before that Miss Amelia was once married. And this curious episode might as well be accounted for at this point. Remember that it all happened long ago, and that it was Miss Amelia's only personal contact, before the hunchback came to her, with this phenomenon — love.

The town then was the same as it is now, except there were two stores instead of three and the peach trees along the street were more crooked and smaller than they are now. Miss Amelia was nineteen years old at the time, and her father had been dead many months. There was in the town at that time a loom-fixer named Marvin Macy. He was the brother of Henry Macy, although to know them you would never guess that those two could be kin. For Marvin Macy was the handsomest man in this region — being six feet one inch tall, hard-muscled, and with slow gray eyes and curly hair. He was well off, made good wages, and had a gold watch which opened in the back to a picture of a waterfall. From the outward and worldly point of view Marvin Macy was a fortunate fellow; he needed to bow and scrape to no one and always got just what he wanted. But from a more serious and thoughtful viewpoint Marvin Macy was not a person to be envied, for he was an evil character. His reputation was as bad, if not worse, than that of any young man in the county. For years, when he was a boy, he had carried about with him the dried and salted ear of a man he had killed in a razor fight. He had chopped off the tails of squirrels in the pinewoods just to please his fancy, and in his left hip pocket he carried forbidden marijuana weed to tempt those who were discouraged and drawn toward death. Yet in spite of his well-known reputation he was the beloved of many females in this region — and there were at the time several young girls who were clean-haired and soft-eyed, with tender sweet little buttocks and charming ways. These gentle young girls he degraded and shamed. Then finally, at the age of twenty-two, this Marvin Macy chose Miss Amelia. That solitary, gangling, queer-eyed girl was the one he longed for. Nor did he want her because of her money, but solely out of love.

And love changed Marvin Macy. Before the time when he loved Miss Amelia it could be questioned if such a person had within him a heart and soul. Yet there is some explanation for the ugliness of his character, for Marvin Macy had had a hard beginning in this world. He was one of seven unwanted children whose parents could hardly be called parents at all; these parents were wild younguns who liked to fish and roam around the swamp. Their own children, and there was a new one almost every year, were only a nuisance to them.

At night when they came home from the mill they would look at the children as though they did not know wherever they had come from. If the children cried they were beaten, and the first thing they learned in this world was to seek the darkest corner of the room and try to hide themselves as best they could. They were as thin as little whitehaired ghosts, and they did not speak, not even to each other. Finally, they were abandoned by their parents altogether and left to the mercies of the town. It was a hard winter, with the mill closed down almost three months, and much misery everywhere. But this is not a town to let white orphans perish in the road before your eyes. So here is what came about: the eldest child, who was eight years old, walked into Cheehaw and disappeared — perhaps he took a freight train somewhere and went out into the world, nobody knows. Three other children were boarded out amongst the town, being sent around from one kitchen to another, and as they were delicate they died before Easter time. The last two children were Marvin Macy and Henry Macy, and they were taken into a home. There was a good woman in the town named Mrs. Mary Hale, and she took Marvin Macy and Henry Macy and loved them as her own. They were raised in her household and treated well.

But the hearts of small children are delicate organs. A cruel beginning in this world can twist them into curious shapes. The heart of a hurt child can shrink so that forever afterward it is hard and pitted as the seed of a peach. Or again, the heart of such a child may fester and swell until it is a misery to carry within the body, easily chafed and hurt by the most ordinary things. This last is what happened to Henry Macy, who is so opposite to his brother, is the kindest and gentlest man in town. He lends his wages to those who are unfortunate, and in the old days he used to care for the children whose parents were at the café on Saturday night. But he is a shy man, and he has the look of one who has a swollen heart and suffers. Marvin Macy, however, grew to be bold and fearless and cruel. His heart turned tough as the horns of Satan, and until the time when he loved Miss Amelia he brought to his brother and the good woman who raised him nothing but shame and trouble.

But love reversed the character of Marvin Macy. For two years he loved Miss Amelia, but he did not declare himself. He would stand near the door of her premises, his cap in his hand, his eyes meek and longing and misty gray. He reformed himself completely. He was good to his brother and foster mother, and he saved his wages and learned thrift. Moreover, he reached out toward God. No longer did he lie around on the floor of the front porch all day Sunday, singing and playing his guitar; he attended church services and was present at all religious meetings. He learned good manners: he trained himself to rise and give his chair to a lady, and he quit swearing and fighting and using holy names in vain. So for two years he passed through this transformation and improved his character in every way. Then at the end of the two years he went one evening to Miss Amelia, carrying a bunch of swamp flowers, a sack of chitterlins, and a silver ring — that night Marvin Macy declared himself.

And Miss Amelia married him. Later everyone wondered why. Some said it was because she wanted to get herself some wedding presents. Others believed it came about through the nagging of Miss Amelia's great-aunt in Cheehaw, who was a terrible old woman. Anyway, she strode with great steps down the aisle of the church wearing her dead mother's bridal gown, which was of yellow satin and at least twelve inches too short for her. It was a winter afternoon and the clear sun shone through the ruby windows of the church and put a curious glow on the pair before the altar. As the marriage lines were read Miss Amelia kept making an odd gesture — she would rub the palm of her right hand down the side of her satin wedding gown. She was reaching for the pocket of her overalls, and being unable to find it her face became impatient, bored, and exasperated. At last when the lines were spoken and the marriage prayer was done Miss Amelia hurried out of the church, not taking the arm of her husband, but walking at least two paces ahead of him.

The church is no distance from the store so the bride and groom walked home. It is said that on the way Miss Amelia began to talk about some deal she had worked up with a farmer over a load of kindling wood. In fact, she treated her groom in exactly the same manner she would have used with some customer who had come into the store to buy a pint from her. But so far all had gone decently enough; the town was gratified, as people had seen what this love had done to Marvin Macy and hoped that it might also reform his bride. At least, they counted on the marriage to tone down Miss Amelia's temper, to put a bit of bride-fat on her, and to change her at last into a calculable woman.

They were wrong. The young boys who watched through the

window on that night said that this is what actually happened: The bride and groom ate a grand supper prepared by Jeff, the old Negro who cooked for Miss Amelia. The bride took second servings of everything, but the groom picked with his food. Then the bride went about her ordinary business — reading the newspaper, finishing an inventory of the stock in the store, and so forth. The groom hung about in the doorway with a loose, foolish, blissful face and was not noticed. At eleven o'clock the bride took a lamp and went upstairs. The groom followed close behind her. So far all had gone decently enough, but what followed after was unholy.

Within half an hour Miss Amelia had stomped down the stairs in breeches and a khaki jacket. Her face had darkened so that it looked quite black. She slammed the kitchen door and gave it an ugly kick. Then she controlled herself. She poked up the fire, sat down, and put her feet up on the kitchen stove. She read the Farmer's Almanac, drank coffee, and had a smoke with her father's pipe. Her face was hard, stern, and had now whitened to its natural color. Sometimes she paused to jot down some information from the Almanac on a piece of paper. Toward dawn she went into her office and uncovered her typewriter, which she had recently bought and was only just learning how to run. That was the way in which she spent the whole of her wedding night. At daylight she went out to her yard as though nothing whatsoever had occurred and did some carpentering on a rabbit hutch which she had begun the week before and intended to sell somewhere.

A groom is in a sorry fix when he is unable to bring his well-beloved bride to bed with him, and when the whole town knows it. Marvin Macy came down that day still in his wedding finery, and with a sick face. God knows how he had spent the night. He moped about the yard, watching Miss Amelia, but keeping some distance away from her. Then toward noon an idea came to him and he went off in the direction of Society City. He returned with presents — an opal ring, a pink enamel doreen of the sort which was then in fashion, a silver bracelet with two hearts on it, and a box of candy which had cost two dollars and a half. Miss Amelia looked over these fine gifts and opened the box of candy, for she was hungry. The rest of the presents she judged shrewdly for a moment to sum up their value — then she put them in the counter out for sale. The night was spent in much the same manner as the preceding one — except that Miss

Amelia brought her feather mattress to make a pallet by the kitchen stove, and she slept fairly well.

Things went on like this for three days. Miss Amelia went about her business as usual, and took great interest in some rumor that a bridge was to be built some ten miles down the road. Marvin Macy still followed her about around the premises, and it was plain from his face how he suffered. Then on the fourth day he did an extremely simple-minded thing: he went to Cheehaw and came back with a lawyer. Then in Miss Amelia's office he signed over to her the whole of his worldly goods, which was ten acres of timberland which he had bought with the money he had saved. She studied the paper sternly to make sure there was no possibility of a trick and filed it soberly in the drawer of her desk. That afternoon Marvin Macy took a quart bottle of whisky and went with it alone out in the swamp while the sun was still shining. Toward evening he came in drunk, went up to Miss Amelia with wet wide eyes, and put his hand on her shoulder. He was trying to tell her something, but before he could open his mouth she had swung once with her fist and hit his face so hard that he was thrown back against the wall and one of his front teeth was broken.

The rest of this affair can only be mentioned in bare outline. After this first blow Miss Amelia hit him whenever he came within arm's reach of her, and whenever he was drunk. At last she turned him off the premises altogether, and he was forced to suffer publicly. During the day he hung around just outside the boundary line of Miss Amelia's property and sometimes with a drawn crazy look he would fetch his rifle and sit there cleaning it, peering at Miss Amelia steadily. If she was afraid she did not show it, but her face was sterner than ever, and often she spat on the ground. His last foolish effort was to climb in the window of her store one night and to sit there in the dark, for no purpose whatsoever, until she came down the stairs next morning. For this Miss Amelia set off immediately to the courthouse in Cheehaw with some notion that she could get him locked in the penitentiary for trespassing. Marvin Macy left the town that day, and no one saw him go, or knew just where he went. On leaving he put a long curious letter, partly written in pencil and partly with ink, beneath Miss Amelia's door. It was a wild love letter — but in it were also included threats, and he swore that in his life he would get even with her. His marriage had lasted for ten days. And the town felt the special satisfaction that people feel when someone has been thoroughly done in by some scandalous and terrible means.

Miss Amelia was left with everything that Marvin Macy had ever owned — his timberwood, his gild watch, every one of his possessions. But she seemed to attach little value to them and that spring she cut up his Klansman's robe to cover her tobacco plants. So all that he had ever done was to make her richer and to bring her love. But, strange to say, she never spoke of him but with a terrible and spiteful bitterness. She never once referred to him by name but always mentioned him scornfully as "that loom-fixer I was married to."

And later, when horrifying rumors concerning Marvin Macy reached the town, Miss Amelia was very pleased. For the true character of Marvin Macy finally revealed itself, once he had freed himself of his love. He became a criminal whose picture and whose name were in all the papers in the state. He robbed three filling stations and held up the A&P store of Society City with a sawed-off gun. He was suspected of the murder of Slit-Eye Sam who was a noted highjacker. All these crimes were connected with the name of Marvin Macy, so that his evil became famous through many counties. Then finally the law captured him, drunk, on the floor of a tourist cabin, his guitar by his side, and fifty-seven dollars in his right shoe. He was tried, sentenced, and sent off to the penitentiary near Atlanta. Miss Amelia was deeply gratified.

Well, all this happened a long time ago, and it is the story of Miss Amelia's marriage. The town laughed a long time over this grotesque affair. But though the outward facts of this love are indeed sad and ridiculous, it must be remembered that the real story was that which took place in the soul of the lover himself. So who but God can be the final judge of this or any other love? On the very first night of the café there were several who suddenly thought of this broken bridegroom, locked in the gloomy penitentiary, many miles away. And in the years that followed, Marvin Macy was not altogether forgotten in the town. His name was never mentioned in the presence of Miss Amelia or the hunchback. But the memory of his passion and his crimes, and the thought of him trapped in his cell in the penitentiary, was like a troubling undertone beneath the happy love of Miss Amelia and the gaiety of the café. So do not forget this Marvin Macy, as he is to act a terrible part in the story which is yet to come.

* * *

During the four years in which the store became a café the rooms upstairs were not changed. This part of the premises remained exactly as it had been all of Miss Amelia's life, as it was in the time of her father, and most likely his father before him. The three rooms, it is already known, were immaculately clean. The smallest object had its exact place, and everything was wiped and dusted by Jeff, the servant of Miss Amelia, each morning. The front room belonged to Cousin Lymon — it was the room where Marvin Macy had stayed during the few nights he was allowed on the premises, and before that it was the bedroom of Miss Amelia's father. The room was furnished with a large chifforobe, a bureau covered with a stiff white linen cloth crocheted at the edges, and a marble-topped table. The bed was immense, an old fourposter made of carved, dark rosewood. On it were two feather mattresses, bolsters, and a number of handmade comforts. The bed was so high that beneath it were two wooden steps — no occupant had ever used these steps before, but Cousin Lymon drew them out each night and walked up in state. Beside the steps, but pushed modestly out of view, there was a china chamberpot painted with pink roses. No rug covered the dark, polished floor and the curtains were of some white stuff, also crocheted at the edges.

On the other side of the parlor was Miss Amelia's bedroom, and it was smaller and very simple. The bed was narrow and made of pine. There was a bureau for her breeches, shirts, and Sunday dress, and she had hammered two nails in the closet wall on which to hang her swamp boots. There were no curtains, rugs, or ornaments of any kind.

The large middle room, the parlor, was elaborate. The rosewood sofa, upholstered in threadbare green silk, was before the fireplace. Marble-topped tables, two Singer sewing machines, a big vase of pampas grass — everything was rich and grand. The most important piece of furniture in the parlor was a big, glass-doored cabinet in which was kept a number of treasures and curios. Miss Amelia had added two objects to this collection — one was a large acorn from a water oak, the other a little velvet box holding two small, grayish stones. Sometimes when she had nothing much to do, Miss Amelia would take out this velvet box and stand by the window with the stones in the palm of her hand, looking down at them with a mixture of fascination, dubious respect, and fear. They were the kidney stones of Miss Amelia herself, and had been taken from her by the doctor in Cheehaw some years ago. It had been a terrible experience, from the first minute to the last, and all she had got out of it were those two little stones; she was bound to set great store by them, or else admit to a mighty sorry bargain. So she kept them and in the second year of Cousin Lymon's stay with her she had them set as ornaments in a watch chain which she gave to him. The other object she had added to the collection, the large acorn, was precious to her — but when she looked at it her face was always saddened and perplexed.

"Amelia, what does it signify?" Cousin Lymon asked her.

"Why, it's just an acorn," she answered. "Just an acorn I picked up on the afternoon Big Papa died."

"How do you mean?" Cousin Lymon insisted.

"I mean it's just an acorn I spied on the ground that day. I picked it up and put it in my pocket. But I don't know why."

"What a peculiar reason to keep it," Cousin Lymon said.

The talks of Miss Amelia and Cousin Lymon in the rooms upstairs, usually in the first few hours of the morning when the hunchback could not sleep, were many. As a rule, Miss Amelia was a silent woman, not letting her tongue run wild on any subject that happened to pop into her head. There were certain topics of conversation, however, in which she took pleasure. All these subjects had one point in common — they were interminable. She liked to contemplate problems which could be worked over for decades and still remain insoluble. Cousin Lymon, on the other hand, enjoyed talking on any subject whatsoever, as he was a great chatterer. Their approach to any conversation was altogether different. Miss Amelia always kept to the broad, rambling generalities of the matter, going on endlessly in a low, thoughtful voice and getting nowhere — while Cousin Lymon would interrupt her suddenly to pick up, magpie fashion, some detail which, even if unimportant, was at least concrete and bearing on some practical facet close at hand. Some of the favorite subjects of Miss Amelia were: the stars, the reason why Negroes are black, the best treatment for cancer, and so forth. Her father was also an interminable subject which was dear to her.

"Why, Law," she would say to Lymon. "Those days I slept. I'd go to bed just as the lamp was turned on and sleep — why, I'd sleep like I was drowned in warm axle grease. Then come daybreak Big Papa would walk in and put his hand down on my shoulder. 'Get stirring, Little,' he would say. Then later he would holler up the stairs from the kitchen when the stove was hot. 'Fried grits,' he would holler. 'White meat and gravy. Ham and eggs.' And I'd run down the stairs and dress by the hot stove while he was out washing at the pump. Then off we'd go to the still or maybe—"

"The grits we had this morning was poor," Cousin Lymon said. "Fried too quick so that the inside never heated."

"And when Big Papa would run off the liquor in those days—" The conversation would go on endlessly, with Miss Amelia's long legs stretched out before the hearth; for winter or summer there was always a fire in the grate, as Lymon was cold-natured. He sat in a low chair across from her, his feet not quite touching the floor and his torso usually well-wrapped in a blanket or the green wool shawl. Miss Amelia never mentioned her father to anyone else except Cousin Lymon.

That was one of the ways in which she showed her love for him. He had her confidence in the most delicate and vital matters. He alone knew where she kept the chart that showed where certain barrels of whisky were buried on a piece of property near-by. He alone had access to her bankbook and the key to the cabinet of curios. He took money from the cash register, whole handfuls of it, and appreciated the loud jingle it made inside his pockets. He owned almost everything on the premises, for when he was cross Miss Amelia would prowl about and find him some present—so that now there was hardly anything left close at hand to give him. The only part of her life that she did not want Cousin Lymon to share with her was the memory of her ten-day marriage. Marvin Macy was the one subject that was never, at any time, discussed between the two of them.

So let the slow years pass and come to a Saturday evening six years after the time when Cousin Lymon came first to the town. It was August and the sky had burned above the town like a sheet of flame all day. Now the green twilight was near and there was a feeling of repose. The street was coated an inch deep with dry golden dust and the little children ran about half-naked, sneezed often, sweated, and were fretful. The mill had closed down at noon. People in the houses along the main street sat resting on their steps and the women had palmetto fans. At Miss Amelia's there was a sign at the front of the premises saying CAFÉ. The back porch was cool with latticed shadows and there Cousin Lymon sat turning the ice-cream freezer — often he unpacked the salt and ice and removed the dasher to lick a bit and see how the work was coming on. Jeff cooked in the kitchen. Early that morning Miss Amelia had put a notice on the wall of the front porch reading: Chicken Dinner — Twenty Cents Tonite. The café was already open and Miss Amelia had just finished a period of work in her office. All the eight tables were occupied and from the mechanical piano came a jingling tune.

In a corner, near the door and sitting at a table with a child, was Henry Macy. He was drinking a glass of liquor, which was unusual for him, as liquor went easily to his head and made him cry or sing. His face was very pale and his left eye worked constantly in a nervous tic, as it was apt to do when he was agitated. He had come into the café sidewise and silent, and when he was greeted he did not speak. The child next to him belonged to Horace Wells, and he had been left at Miss Amelia's that morning to be doctored.

Miss Amelia came out from her office in good spirits. She attended to a few details in the kitchen and entered the café with the pope's nose of a hen between her fingers, as that was her favorite piece. She looked about the room, saw that in general all was well, and went over to the corner table by Henry Macy. She turned the chair around and sat straddling the back, as she only wanted to pass the time of day and was not yet ready for her supper. There was a bottle of Kroup Kure in the hip pocket of her overalls — a medicine made from whisky, rock candy, and a secret ingredient. Miss Amelia uncorked the bottle and put it to the mouth of the child. Then she turned to Henry Macy and, seeing the nervous winking of his left eye, she asked:

"What ails you?"

Henry Macy seemed on the point of saying something difficult, but, after a long look into the eyes of Miss Amelia, he swallowed and did not speak.

So Miss Amelia returned to her patient. Only the child's head showed above the table top. His face was very red, with the eyelids half-closed and the mouth partly open. He had a large, hard, swollen boil on his thigh, and had been brought to Miss Amelia so that it could be opened. But Miss Amelia used a special method with children; she did not like to see them hurt, struggling, and terrified. So she had kept the child around the premises all day, giving him licorice and frequent doses of the Kroup Kure, and toward evening she tied a napkin around his neck and let him eat his fill of the dinner. Now as he sat at the table his head wobbled slowly from side to side and sometimes as he breathed there came from him a little worn-out grunt.

There was a stir in the café and Miss Amelia looked around quickly. Cousin Lymon had come in. The hunchback strutted into the café as he did every night, and when he reached the exact center of the room he stopped short and looked shrewdly around him, summing up the people and making a quick pattern of the emotional material at hand that night. The hunchback was a great mischief-maker. He enjoyed any kind of to-do, and without saying a word he could set people at each other in a way that was miraculous. It was due to him that the Rainey twins had quarreled over a jackknife two years past, and had not spoken one word to each other since. He was present at the big fight between Rip Wellborn and Robert Calvert Hale, and every other fight for that matter since he had come into the town. He nosed around everywhere, knew the intimate business of everybody, and trespassed every waking hour. Yet, queerly enough, in spite of this it was the hunchback who was most responsible for the great popularity of the café. Things were never so gay as when he was around. When he walked into the room there was always a quick feeling of tension, because with this busybody about there was never any telling what might descend on you, or what might suddenly be brought to happen in the room. People are never so free with themselves and so recklessly glad as when there is some possibility of commotion or calamity ahead. So when the hunchback marched into the café everyone looked around at him and there was a quick outburst of talking and a drawing of corks.

Lymon waved his hand to Stumpy MacPhail who was sitting with Merlie Ryan and Henry Ford Crimp. "I walked to Rotten Lake today to fish," he said. "And on the way I stepped over what appeared at first to be a fallen tree. But then as I stepped over I felt something stir and I taken this second look and there I was straddling this here alligator long as from the front door to the kitchen and thicker than a hog."

The hunchback chattered on. Everyone looked at him from time to time, and some kept track of his chattering and others did not.

There were times when every word he said was nothing but lying and bragging. Nothing he said tonight was true. He had lain in bed with a summer quinsy all day long, and had only got up in the late afternoon in order to turn the ice-cream freezer. Everybody knew this, yet he stood there in the middle of the café and held forth with such lies and boasting that it was enough to shrivel the ears.

Miss Amelia watched him with her hands in her pockets and her head turned to one side. There was a softness about her gray, queer eyes and she was smiling gently to herself. Occasionally she glanced from the hunchback to the other people in the café — and then her look was proud, and there was in it the hint of a threat, as though daring anyone to try to hold him to account for all his foolery. Jeff was bringing in the suppers, already served on the plates, and the new electric fans in the café made a pleasant stir of coolness in the air.

"The little youngun is asleep," said Henry Macy finally.

Miss Amelia looked down at the patient beside her, and composed her face for the matter in hand. The child's chin was resting on the table edge and a trickle of spit or Kroup Kure had bubbled from the corner of his mouth. His eyes were quite closed, and a little family of gnats had clustered peacefully in the corners. Miss Amelia put her hand on his head and shook it roughly, but the patient did not awake. So Miss Amelia lifted the child from the table, being careful not to touch the sore part of his leg, and went into the office. Henry Macy followed after her and they closed the office door.

Cousin Lymon was bored that evening. There was not much going on, and in spite of the heat the customers in the café were good-humored. Henry Ford Crimp and Horace Wells sat at the middle table with their arms around each other, sniggering over some long joke — but when he approached them he could make nothing of it as he had missed the beginning of the story. The moonlight brightened the dusty road, and the dwarfed peach trees were black and motionless: there was no breeze. The drowsy buzz of swamp mosquitoes was like an echo of the silent night. The town seemed dark, except far down the road to the right there was the flicker of a lamp. Somewhere in the darkness a woman sang in a high wild voice and the tune had no start and no finish and was made up of only three notes which went on and on and on. The hunchback stood leaning against the banister of the porch, looking down the empty road as though hoping that someone would come along.

There were footsteps behind him, then a voice: "Cousin Lymon, your dinner is set out upon the table."

"My appetite is poor tonight," said the hunchback, who had been eating sweet snuff all the day. "There is a sourness in my mouth."

"Just a pick," said Miss Amelia. "The breast, the liver, and the heart."

Together they went back into the bright café, and sat down with Henry Macy. Their table was the largest one in the café, and on it there was a bouquet of swamp lilies in a Coca-Cola bottle. Miss Amelia had finished with her patient and was satisfied with herself. From behind the closed office door there had come only a few sleepy whimpers, and before the patient could wake up and become terrified it was all over. The child was now slung across the shoulder of his father, sleeping deeply, his little arms dangling loose along his father's back and his puffed-up face very red — they were leaving the café to go home.

Henry Macy was still silent. He ate carefully, making no noise when he swallowed, and was not a third as greedy as Cousin Lymon who had claimed to have no appetite and was now putting down helping after helping of the dinner. Occasionally Henry Macy looked across at Miss Amelia and again held his peace.

It was a typical Saturday night. An old couple who had come in from the country hesitated for a moment at the doorway, holding each other's hand, and finally decided to come inside. They had lived together so long, this old country couple, that they looked as similar as twins. They were brown, shriveled, and like two little walking peanuts. They left early, and by midnight most of the other customers were gone. Rosser Cline and Merlie Ryan still played checkers, and Stumpy MacPhail sat with a liquor bottle on his table (his wife would not allow it in the home) and carried on peaceable conversations with himself. Henry Macy had not yet gone away, and this was unusual, as he almost always went to bed soon after nightfall. Miss Amelia yawned sleepily, but Lymon was restless and she did not suggest that they close up for the night.

Finally, at one o'clock, Henry Macy looked up at the corner of the ceiling and said quietly to Miss Amelia: "I got a letter today."

Miss Amelia was not one to be impressed by this, because all sorts of business letters and catalogues came addressed to her.

"I got a letter from my brother," said Henry Macy.

The hunchback, who had been goose-stepping about the café with his hands clasped behind his head, stopped suddenly. He was quick to sense any change in the atmosphere of a gathering. He glanced at each face in the room and waited.

Miss Amelia scowled and hardened her right fist. "You are welcome to it," she said.

"He is on parole. He is out of the penitentiary."

The face of Miss Amelia was very dark, and she shivered although the night was warm. Stumpy MacPhail and Merlie Ryan pushed aside their checker game. The café was very quiet.

"Who?" asked Cousin Lymon. His large, pale ears seemed to grow on his head and stiffen. "What?"

Miss Amelia slapped her hands palm down on the table. "Because Marvin Macy is a —" But her voice hoarsened and after a few moments she only said: "He belongs to be in that penitentiary the balance of his life."

"What did he do?" asked Cousin Lymon.

There was a long pause, as no one knew exactly how to answer this. "He robbed three filling stations," said Stumpy MacPhail. But his words did not sound complete and there was a feeling of sins left unmentioned.

The hunchback was impatient. He could not bear to be left out of anything, even a great misery. The name Marvin Macy was unknown to him, but it tantalized him as did any mention of subjects which others knew about and of which he was ignorant — such as any reference to the old sawmill that had been torn down before he came, or a chance word about poor Morris Finestein, or the recollection of any event that had occurred before his time. Aside from this inborn curiosity, the hunchback took a great interest in robbers and crimes of all varieties. As he strutted around the table he was muttering the words "released on parole" and "penitentiary" to himself. But although he questioned insistently, he was unable to find anything, as nobody would dare to talk about Marvin Macy before Miss Amelia in the café.

"The letter did not say very much," said Henry Macy. "He did not say where he was going."

"Humph!" said Miss Amelia, and her face was still hardened and very dark. "He will never set his split hoof on my premises."

She pushed back her chair from the table, and made ready to close the café. Thinking about Marvin Macy may have set her to brooding, for she hauled the cash register back to the kitchen and put it in a private place. Henry Macy went off down the dark road. But Henry Ford Crimp and Merlie Ryan lingered for a time on the front porch. Later Merlie Ryan was to make certain claims, to swear that on that night he had a vision of what was to come. But the town paid no attention, for that was just the sort of thing that Merlie Ryan would claim. Miss Amelia and Cousin Lymon talked for a time in the parlor. And when at last the hunchback thought that he could sleep she arranged the mosquito netting over his bed and waited until he had finished with his prayers. Then she put on her long nightgown, smoked two pipes, and only after a long time went to sleep.

That autumn was a happy time. The crops around the countryside were good, and over at the Forks Falls market the price of tobacco held firm that year. After the long hot summer the first cool days had a clean bright sweetness. Goldenrod grew along the dusty roads, and the sugar cane was ripe and purple. The bus came each day from Cheehaw to carry off a few of the younger children to the consolidated school to get an education. Boys hunted foxes in the pinewoods, winter quilts were aired out on the wash lines, and sweet potatoes bedded in the ground with straw against the colder months to come. In the evening, delicate shreds of smoke rose from the chimneys, and the moon was round and orange in the autumn sky. There is no stillness like the quiet of the first cold nights in the fall. Sometimes, late in the night when there was no wind, there could be heard in the town the thin wild whistle of the train that goes through Society City on its way far off to the North.

For Miss Amelia Evans this was a time of great activity. She was at work from dawn until sundown. She made a new and bigger condenser for her still, and in one week ran off enough liquor to souse the whole county. Her old mule was dizzy from grinding so much sorghum, and she scalded her Mason jars and put away pear preserves. She was looking forward greatly to the first frost, because she had traded for three tremendous hogs, and intended to make much barbecue, chitterlins, and sausage.

During these weeks there was a quality about Miss Amelia that many people noticed. She laughed often, with a deep ringing laugh, and her whistling had a sassy, tuneful trickery. She was forever trying out her strength, lifting up heavy objects, or poking her tough biceps with her finger. One day she sat down to her typewriter and wrote a story — a story in which there were foreigners, trap doors, and millions of dollars. Cousin Lymon was with her always, traipsing along behind her coat-tails, and when she watched him her face had a bright, soft look, and when she spoke his name there lingered in her voice the undertone of love.

The first cold spell came at last. When Miss Amelia awoke one morning there were frost flowers on the windowpanes, and rime had silvered the patches of grass in the yard. Miss Amelia built a roaring fire in the kitchen stove, then went out of doors to judge the day. The air was cold and sharp, the sky pale green and cloudless. Very shortly people began to come in from the country to find out what Miss Amelia thought of the weather; she decided to kill the biggest hog, and word got round the countryside. The hog was slaughtered and a low oak fire started in the barbecue pit. There was the warm smell of pig blood and smoke in the back yard, the stamp of footsteps, the ring of voices in the winter air. Miss Amelia walked around giving orders and soon most of the work was done.

She had some particular business to do in Cheehaw that day, so after making sure that all was going well, she cranked up her car and got ready to leave. She asked Cousin Lymon to come with her, in fact, she asked him seven times, but he was loath to leave the commotion and wanted to remain. This seemed to trouble Miss Amelia, as she always liked to have him near to her, and was prone to be terribly homesick when she had to go any distance away. But after asking him seven times, she did not urge him any further. Before leaving she found a stick and drew a heavy line all around the barbecue pit, about two feet back from the edge, and told him not to trespass beyond that boundary. She left after dinner and intended to be back before dark.

Now, it is not so rare to have a truck or an automobile pass along the road and through the town on the way from Cheehaw to somewhere else. Every year the tax collector comes to argue with rich people such as Miss Amelia. And if somebody in the town, such as Merlie Ryan, takes a notion that he can connive to get a car on credit, or to pay down three dollars and have a fine electric icebox such as they advertise in the store windows of Cheehaw, then a city man will come out asking meddlesome questions, finding out all his troubles, and ruining his chances of buying anything on the installment plan. Sometimes, especially since they are working on the Forks Falls highway, the cars hauling the chain gang come through the town. And frequently people in automobiles get lost and stop to inquire how they can find the right road again. So, late that afternoon it was nothing unusual to have a truck pass the mill and stop in the middle of the road near the café of Miss Amelia. A man jumped down from the back of the truck, and the truck went on its way.

The man stood in the middle of the road and looked about him. He was a tall man, with brown curly hair, and slow-moving, deep-blue eyes. His lips were red and he smiled the lazy, half-mouthed smile of the braggart. The man wore a red shirt, and a wide belt of tooled leather; he carried a tin suitcase and a guitar. The first person in the town to see this newcomer was Cousin Lymon, who had heard the shifting of gears and come around to investigate. The hunchback stuck his head around the corner of the porch, but did not step out altogether into full view. He and the man stared at each other, and it was not the look of two strangers meeting for the first time and swiftly summing up each other. It was a peculiar stare they exchanged between them, like the look of two criminals who recognize each other. Then the man in the red shirt shrugged his left shoulder and turned away. The face of the hunchback was very pale as he watched the man go down the road, and after a few moments he began to follow along carefully, keeping many paces away.

It was immediately known throughout the town that Marvin Macy had come back again. First, he went to the mill, propped his elbows lazily on a window sill and looked inside. He liked to watch others hard at work, as do all born loafers. The mill was thrown into a sort of numb confusion. The dyers left the hot vats, the spinners and weavers forgot about their machines, and even Stumpy MacPhail, who was foreman, did not know exactly what to do. Marvin Macy still smiled his wet half-mouthed smiles, and when he saw his brother, his bragging expression did not change. After looking over the mill Marvin Macy went down the road to the house where he had been raised, and left his suitcase and guitar on the front porch. Then he walked around the millpond, looked over the church, the three stores, and the rest of the town. The hunchback trudged along quietly at some distance behind him, his hands in his pockets, and his little face still very pale.

It had grown late. The red winter sun was setting, and to the west the sky was deep gold and crimson. Ragged chimney swifts flew to their nests; lamps were lighted. Now and then there was the smell of smoke, and the warm rich odor of the barbecue slowly cooking in the pit behind the café. After making the rounds of the town Marvin Macy stopped before Miss Amelia's premises and read the sign above the porch. Then, not hesitating to trespass, he walked through the side yard. The mill whistle blew a thin, lonesome blast, and the day's shift was done. Soon there were others in Miss Amelia's back yard beside Marvin Macy — Henry Ford Crimp, Merlie Ryan, Stumpy MacPhail, and any number of children and people who stood around the edges of the property and looked on. Very little was said. Marvin Macy stood by himself on one side of the pit, and the rest of the people clustered together on the other side. Cousin Lymon stood somewhat apart from everyone, and he did not take his eyes from the face of Marvin Macy.

"Did you have a good time in the penitentiary?" asked Merlie Ryan, with a silly giggle.

Marvin Macy did not answer. He took from his hip pocket a large knife, opened it slowly, and honed the blade on the seat of his pants. Merlie Ryan grew suddenly very quiet and went to stand directly behind the broad back of Stumpy MacPhail.

Miss Amelia did not come home until almost dark. They heard the rattle of her automobile while she was still a long distance away, then the slam of the door and a bumping noise as though she were hauling something up the front steps of her premises. The sun had already set, and in the air there was the blue smoky glow of early winter evenings. Miss Amelia came down the back steps slowly, and the group in her yard waited very quietly. Few people in this world could stand up to Miss Amelia, and against Marvin Macy she had this special bitter hate. Everyone waited to see her burst into a terrible holler, snatch up some dangerous object, and chase him altogether out of town. At first she did not see Marvin Macy, and her face had the relieved and dreamy expression that was natural to her when she reached home after having gone some distance away.

Miss Amelia must have seen Marvin Macy and Cousin Lymon at the same instant. She looked from one to the other, but it was not the wastrel from the penitentiary on whom she finally fixed her gaze of sick amazement. She, and everyone else, was looking at Cousin Lymon, and he was a sight to see.

The hunchback stood at the end of the pit, his pale face lighted by the soft glow from the smoldering oak fire. Cousin Lymon had a very peculiar accomplishment, which he used whenever he wished to ingratiate himself with someone. He would stand very still, and with just a little concentration, he could wiggle his large pale ears with marvelous quickness and ease. This trick he always used when he wanted to get something special out of Miss Amelia, and to her it was irresistible. Now as he stood there the hunchback's ears were wiggling furiously on his head, but it was not Miss Amelia at whom he was looking this time. The hunchback was smiling at Marvin Macy with an entreaty that was near to desperation. At first Marvin Macy paid no attention to him, and when he did finally glance at the hunchback it was without any appreciation whatsoever.

"What ails this Brokeback?" he asked with a rough jerk of his thumb.

No one answered. And Cousin Lymon, seeing that his accomplishment was getting him nowhere, added new efforts of persuasion. He fluttered his eyelids, so that they were like pale, trapped moths in his sockets. He scraped his feet around on the ground, waved his hands about, and finally began doing a little trotlike dance. In the last gloomy light of the winter he resembled the child of a swamp-haunt.

Marvin Macy, alone of all the people in the yard, was unimpressed.

"Is the runt throwing a fit?" he asked, and when no one answered he stepped forward and gave Cousin Lymon a cuff on the side of his head. The hunchback staggered, then fell back on the ground. He sat where he had fallen, still looking up at Marvin Macy, and with great effort his ears managed one last forlorn little flap.

Now everyone turned to Miss Amelia to see what she would do. In all these years no one had so much as touched a hair of Cousin Lymon's head, although many had had the itch to do so. If anyone even spoke crossly to the hunchback, Miss Amelia would cut off this rash mortal's credit and find ways of making things go hard for him a long time afterward. So now if Miss Amelia had split open Marvin

Macy's head with the ax on the back porch no one would have been surprised. But she did nothing of the kind.

There were times when Miss Amelia seemed to go into a sort of trance. And the cause of these trances was usually known and understood. For Miss Amelia was a fine doctor, and did not grind up swamp roots and other untried ingredients and give them to the first patient who came along; whenever she invented a new medicine she always tried it out first on herself. She would swallow an enormous dose and spend the following day walking thoughtfully back and forth from the café to the brick privy. Often, when there was a sudden keen gripe, she would stand quite still, her queer eyes staring down at the ground and her fists clenched; she was trying to decide which organ was being worked upon, and what misery the new medicine might be most likely to cure. And now as she watched the hunchback and Marvin Macy, her face wore this same expression, tense with reckoning some inward pain, although she had taken no new medicine that day.

"That will learn you, Brokeback," said Marvin Macy.

Henry Macy pushed back his limp whitish hair from his forehead and coughed nervously. Stumpy MacPhail and Merlie Ryan shuffled their feet, and the children and black people on the outskirts of the property made not a sound. Marvin Macy folded the knife he had been honing, and after looking about him fearlessly he swaggered out of the yard. The embers in the pit were turning to gray feathery ashes and it was now quite dark.

That was the way Marvin Macy came back from the penitentiary. Not a living soul in all the town was glad to see him. Even Mrs. Mary Hale, who was a good woman and had raised him with love and care—at the first sight of him even this old foster mother dropped the skillet she was holding and burst into tears. But nothing could faze that Marvin Macy. He sat on the back steps of the Hale house, lazily picking his guitar, and when the supper was ready, he pushed the children of the household out of the way and served himself a big meal, although there had been barely enough hoecakes and white meat to go round. After eating he settled himself in the best and warmest sleeping place in the front room and was untroubled by dreams.

Miss Amelia did not open the café that night. She locked the doors and all the windows very carefully, nothing was seen of her and Cousin Lymon, and a lamp burned in her room all the night long.

Marvin Macy brought with him bad fortune, right from the first, as could be expected. The next day the weather turned suddenly, and it became hot. Even in the early morning there was a sticky sultriness in the atmosphere, the wind carried the rotten smell of the swamp, and delicate shrill mosquitoes webbed the green millpond. It was unseasonable, worse than August, and much damage was done. For nearly everyone in the county who owned a hog had copied Miss Amelia and slaughtered the day before. And what sausage could keep in such weather as this? After a few days there was everywhere the smell of slowly spoiling meat, and an atmosphere of dreary waste. Worse yet, a family reunion near the Forks Falls highway ate pork roast and died, every one of them. It was plain that their hog had been infected — and who could tell whether the rest of the meat was safe or not? People were torn between the longing for the good taste of pork, and the fear of death. It was a time of waste and confusion.

The cause of all this, Marvin Macy, had no shame in him. He was seen everywhere. During work hours he loafed about the mill, looking in at the windows, and on Sundays he dressed in his red shirt and paraded up and down the road with his guitar. He was still handsome — with his brown hair, his red lips, and his broad strong shoulders; but the evil in him was now too famous for his good looks to get him anywhere. And this evil was not measured only by the actual sins he had committed. True, he had robbed those filling stations. And before that he had ruined the tenderest girls in the county and laughed about it. Any number of wicked things could be listed against him, but quite apart from these crimes there was about him a secret meanness that clung to him almost like a smell. Another thing — he never sweated, not even in August, and that surely is a sign worth pondering over.

Now it seemed to the town that he was more dangerous than he had ever been before, as in the penitentiary in Atlanta he must have learned the method of laying charms. Otherwise how could his effect on Cousin Lymon be explained? For since first setting eyes on Marvin Macy the hunchback was possessed by an unnatural spirit. Every minute he wanted to be following along behind this jailbird, and he was full of silly schemes to attract attention to himself. Still Marvin Macy either treated him hatefully or failed to notice him at all.

Sometimes the hunchback would give up, perch himself on the banister of the front porch much as a sick bird huddles on a telephone wire, and grieve publicly.

"But why?" Miss Amelia would ask, staring at him with her crossed, gray eyes, and her fists closed tight.

"Oh, Marvin Macy," groaned the hunchback, and the sound of the name was enough to upset the rhythm of his sobs so that he hiccuped. "He has been to Atlanta."

Miss Amelia would shake her head and her face was dark and hardened. To begin with she had no patience with any traveling; those who had made the trip to Atlanta or traveled fifty miles from home to see the ocean — those restless people she despised. "Going to Atlanta does no credit to him."

"He has been to the penitentiary," said the hunchback, miserable with longing.

How are you going to argue against such envies as these? In her perplexity Miss Amelia did not herself sound any too sure of what she was saying. "Been to the penitentiary, Cousin Lymon? Why, a trip like that is no travel to brag about."

During these weeks Miss Amelia was closely watched by everyone. She went about absent-mindedly, her face remote as though she had lapsed into one of her gripe trances. For some reason, after the day of Marvin Macy's arrival, she put aside her overalls and wore always the red dress she had before this time reserved for Sundays, funerals, and sessions of the court. Then as the weeks passed she began to take some steps to clear up the situation. But her efforts were hard to understand. If it hurt her to see Cousin Lymon follow Marvin Macy about the town, why did she not make the issues clear once and for all, and tell the hunchback that if he had dealings with Marvin Macy she would turn him off the premises? That would have been simple, and Cousin Lymon would have had to submit to her, or else face the sorry business of finding himself loose in the world. But Miss Amelia seemed to have lost her will; for the first time in her life she hesitated as to just what course to pursue. And, like most people in such a position of uncertainty, she did the worst thing possible — she began following several courses at once, all of them contrary to each other.

The café was opened every night as usual, and, strangely enough, when Marvin Macy came swaggering through the door, with the hunchback at his heels, she did not turn him out. She even gave him free drinks and smiled at him in a wild, crooked way. At the same time she set a terrible trap for him out in the swamp that surely would have killed him if he had got caught. She let Cousin Lymon invite him to Sunday dinner, and then tried to trip him up as he went down the steps. She began a great campaign of pleasure for Cousin Lymon — making exhausting trips to various spectacles being held in distant places, driving the automobile thirty miles to a Chautauqua, taking him to Forks Falls to watch a parade. All in all it was a distracting time for Miss Amelia. In the opinion of most people she was well on her way in the climb up fools' hill, and everyone wanted to see how it would all turn out.

The weather turned cold again, the winter was upon the town, and night came before the last shift in the mill was done. Children kept on all their garments when they slept, and women raised the backs of their skirts to toast themselves dreamily at the fire. After it rained, the mud in the road made hard frozen ruts, there were faint flickers of lamplight from the windows of the houses, the peach trees were scrawny and bare. In the dark, silent nights of wintertime the café was the warm center point of the town, the lights shining so brightly that they could be seen a quarter of a mile away. The great iron stove at the back of the room roared, crackled, and turned red. Miss Amelia had made red curtains for the windows, and from a salesman who passed through the town she bought a great bunch of paper roses that looked very real.

But it was not only the warmth, the decorations, and the brightness, that made the café what it was. There is a deeper reason why the café was so precious to this town. And this deeper reason has to do with a certain pride that had not hitherto been known in these parts. To understand this new pride the cheapness of human life must be kept in mind. There were always plenty of people clustered around a mill — but it was seldom that every family had enough meal, garments, and fat back to go the rounds. Life could become one long dim scramble just to get the things needed to keep alive. And the confusing point is this: All useful things have a price, and are bought only with money, as that is the way the world is run. You know without having to reason about it the price of a bale of cotton, or a quart of molasses. But no value has been put on human life; it is given to us free and taken without being paid for. What is it worth? If you look around, at times the value may seem to be little or nothing at all. Often after you have sweated and tried and things are not better for you, there comes a feeling deep down in the soul that you are not worth much.

But the new pride that the café brought to this town had an effect on almost everyone, even the children. For in order to come to the café you did not have to buy the dinner, or a portion of liquor. There were cold bottled drinks for a nickel. And if you could not even afford that, Miss Amelia had a drink called Cherry Juice which sold for a penny a glass, and was pink-colored and very sweet. Almost everyone, with the exception of Reverend T. M. Willin, came to the café at least once during the week. Children love to sleep in houses other than their own, and to eat at a neighbor's table; on such occasions they behave themselves decently and are proud. The people in the town were likewise proud when sitting at the tables in the café. They washed before coming to Miss Amelia's, and scraped their feet very politely on the threshold as they entered the café. There, for a few hours at least, the deep bitter knowing that you are not worth much in this world could be laid low.

The café was a special benefit to bachelors, unfortunate people, and consumptives. And here it may be mentioned that there was some reason to suspect that Cousin Lymon was consumptive. The brightness of his gray eyes, his insistence, his talkativeness, and his cough — these were all signs. Besides, there is generally supposed to be some connection between a hunched spine and consumption. But whenever this subject had been mentioned to Miss Amelia she had become furious; she denied these symptoms with bitter vehemence, but on the sly she treated Cousin Lymon with hot chest plasters, Kroup Kure, and such. Now this winter the hunchback's cough was worse, and sometimes even on cold days he would break out in a heavy sweat. But this did not prevent him from following along after Marvin Macy.

Early every morning he left the premises and went to the back door of Mrs. Hale's house, and waited and waited — as Marvin Macy was a lazy sleeper. He would stand there and call out softly. His voice was just like the voices of children who squat patiently over those tiny little holes in the ground where doodlebugs are thought to live, poking the hole with a broom straw, and calling plaintively: "Doodlebug, Doodlebug — fly away home. Mrs. Doodlebug, Mrs. Doodlebug. Come out, come out. Your house is on fire and all your children are burning up." In just such a voice — at once sad, luring, and resigned — would the hunchback call Marvin Macy's name each morning. Then when Marvin Macy came out for the day, he would trail him about the town, and sometimes they would be gone for hours together out in the swamp.

And Miss Amelia continued to do the worst thing possible: that is, to try to follow several courses at once. When Cousin Lymon left the house she did not call him back, but only stood in the middle of the road and watched lonesomely until he was out of sight. Nearly every day Marvin Macy turned up with Cousin Lymon at dinnertime, and ate at her table. Miss Amelia opened the pear preserves, and the table was well-set with ham or chicken, great bowls of hominy grits, and winter peas. It is true that on one occasion Miss Amelia tried to poison Marvin Macy — but there was a mistake, the plates were confused, and it was she herself who got the poisoned dish. This she quickly realized by the slight bitterness of the food, and that day she ate no dinner. She sat tilted back in her chair, feeling her muscle, and looking at Marvin Macy.

Every night Marvin Macy came to the café and settled himself at the best and largest table, the one in the center of the room. Cousin Lymon brought him liquor, for which he did not pay a cent. Marvin Macy brushed the hunchback aside as if he were a swamp mosquito, and not only did he show no gratitude for these favors, but if the hunchback got in his way he would cuff him with the back of his hand, or say: "Out of my way, Brokeback — I'll snatch you baldheaded." When this happened Miss Amelia would come out from behind her counter and approach Marvin Macy very slowly, her fists clenched, her peculiar red dress hanging awkwardly around her bony knees. Marvin Macy would also clench his fists and they would walk slowly and meaningfully around each other. But, although everyone watched breathlessly, nothing ever came of it. The time for the fight was not yet ready.

There is one particular reason why this winter is remembered and still talked about. A great thing happened. People woke up on the second of January and found the whole world about them altogether changed. Little ignorant children looked out of the windows, and they were so puzzled that they began to cry. Old people harked back and could remember nothing in these parts to equal the phenomenon. For in the night it had snowed. In the dark hours after midnight the dim flakes started falling softly on the town. By dawn the ground was covered, and the strange snow banked the ruby windows of the church, and whitened the roofs of the houses. The snow gave the town a drawn, bleak look. The two-room houses near the mill were dirty, crooked, and seemed about to collapse, and somehow everything was dark and shrunken. But the snow itself — there was a beauty about it few people around here had ever known before. The snow was not white, as Northerners had pictured it to be; in the snow there were soft colors of blue and silver, the sky was a gentle shining gray. And the dreamy quietness of falling snow — when had the town been so silent?

People reacted to the snowfall in various ways. Miss Amelia, on looking out of her window, thoughtfully wiggled the toes of her bare feet, gathered close to her neck the collar of her nightgown. She stood there for some time, then commenced to draw the shutters and lock every window on the premises. She closed the place completely, lighted the lamps, and sat solemnly over her bowl of grits. The reason for this was not that Miss Amelia feared the snowfall. It was simply that she was unable to form an immediate opinion of this new event, and unless she knew exactly and definitely what she thought of a matter (which was nearly always the case) she preferred to ignore it. Snow had never fallen in this county in her lifetime, and she had never thought about it one way or the other. But if she admitted this snowfall she would have to come to some decision, and in those days there was enough distraction in her life as it was already. So she poked about the gloomy, lamp-lighted house and pretended that nothing had happened. Cousin Lymon, on the contrary, chased around in the wildest excitement, and when Miss Amelia turned her back to dish him some breakfast he slipped out of the door.

Marvin Macy laid claim to the snowfall. He said that he knew snow, had seen it in Atlanta, and from the way he walked about the town that day it was as though he owned every flake. He sneered at the little children who crept timidly out of the houses and scooped up handfuls of snow to taste. Reverend Willin hurried down the road with a furious face, as he was thinking deeply and trying to weave the snow into his Sunday sermon. Most people were humble and glad about this marvel; they spoke in hushed voices and said "thank you" and "please" more than was necessary. A few weak characters, of course, were demoralized and got drunk — but they were not numerous. To everyone this was an occasion and many counted their money and planned to go to the café that night.

Cousin Lymon followed Marvin Macy about all day, seconding his claim to the snow. He marveled that snow did not fall as does rain, and stared up at the dreamy, gently falling flakes until he stumbled from dizziness. And the pride he took on himself, basking in the glory of Marvin Macy — it was such that many people could not resist calling out to him: " 'Oho,' said the fly on the chariot wheel. 'What a dust we do raise.' "

Miss Amelia did not intend to serve a dinner. But when, at six o'clock, there was the sound of footsteps on the porch she opened the front door cautiously. It was Henry Ford Crimp, and though there was no food, she let him sit at a table and served him a drink. Others came. The evening was blue, bitter, and though the snow fell no longer there was a wind from the pine trees that swept up delicate flurries from the ground. Cousin Lymon did not come until after dark, with him Marvin Macy, and he carried his tin suitcase and his guitar.

"So you mean to travel?" said Miss Amelia quickly.

Marvin Macy warmed himself at the stove. Then he settled down at his table and carefully sharpened a little stick. He picked his teeth, frequently taking the stick out of his mouth to look at the end and wipe it on the sleeve of his coat. He did not bother to answer.

The hunchback looked at Miss Amelia, who was behind the counter. His face was not in the least beseeching; he seemed quite sure of himself. He folded his hands behind his back and perked up his ears confidently. His cheeks were red, his eyes shining, and his clothes were soggy wet. "Marvin Macy is going to visit a spell with us," he said.

Miss Amelia made no protest. She only came out from behind the counter and hovered over the stove, as though the news had made her suddenly cold. She did not warm her backside modestly, lifting her skirt only an inch or so, as do most women when in public. There was not a grain of modesty about Miss Amelia, and she frequently seemed to forget altogether that there were men in the room. Now as she stood warming herself, her red dress was pulled up quite high in the back so that a piece of her strong, hairy thigh could be seen by anyone who cared to look at it. Her head was turned to one side; and she had begun talking with herself, nodding and wrinkling her forehead, and there was the tone of accusation and reproach in her voice although the words were not plain. Meanwhile, the hunchback and Marvin Macy had gone upstairs — up to the parlor with the pampas grass and the two sewing machines, to the private rooms where Miss Amelia had lived the whole of her life. Down in the café you could hear them bumping around, unpacking Marvin Macy, and getting him settled.

That is the way Marvin Macy crowded into Miss Amelia's home. At first Cousin Lymon, who had given Marvin Macy his own room, slept on the sofa in the parlor. But the snowfall had a bad effect on him; he caught a cold that turned into a winter quinsy, so Miss Amelia gave up her bed to him. The sofa in the parlor was much too short for her, her feet lapped over the edges, and often she rolled off onto the floor. Perhaps it was this lack of sleep that clouded her wits; everything she tried to do against Marvin Macy rebounded on herself. She got caught in her own tricks, and found herself in many pitiful positions. But still she did not put Marvin Macy off the premises, as she was afraid that she would be left alone. Once you have lived with another, it is a great torture to have to live alone. The silence of a firelit room when suddenly the clock stops ticking, the nervous shadows in an empty house — it is better to take in your mortal enemy than face the terror of living alone.

The snow did not last. The sun came out and within two days the town was just as it had always been before. Miss Amelia did not open her house until every flake had melted. Then she had a big house cleaning and aired everything out in the sun. But before that, the very first thing she did on going out again into her yard, was to tie a rope to the largest branch of the chinaberry tree. At the end of the rope she tied a crocus sack tightly stuffed with sand. This was the punching bag she made for herself and from that day on she would box with it out in her yard every morning. Already she was a fine fighter — a little heavy on her feet, but knowing all manner of mean holds and squeezes to make up for this.

Miss Amelia, as has been mentioned, measured six feet two inches in height. Marvin Macy was one inch shorter. In weight they were about even — both of them weighing close to a hundred and sixty pounds. Marvin Macy had the advantage in slyness of movement, and in toughness of chest. In fact from the outward point of view the odds were altogether in his favor. Yet almost everybody in the town was betting on Miss Amelia; scarcely a person would put up money on Marvin Macy. The town remembered the great fight between Miss Amelia and a Forks Falls lawyer who had tried to cheat her. He had been a huge strapping fellow, but he was left three-quarters dead when she had finished with him. And it was not only her talent as a boxer that had impressed everyone — she could demoralize her enemy by making terrifying faces and fierce noises, so that even the spectators were sometimes cowed. She was brave, she practiced faithfully with her punching bag, and in this case she was clearly in the right. So people had confidence in her, and they waited. Of course there was no set date for this fight. There were just the signs that were too plain to be overlooked.

During these times the hunchback strutted around with a pleased little pinched-up face. In many delicate and clever ways he stirred up trouble between them. He was constantly plucking at Marvin Macy's trouser leg to draw attention to himself. Sometimes he followed in Miss Amelia's footsteps — but these days it was only in order to imitate her awkward long-legged walk; he crossed his eyes and aped her gestures in a way that made her appear to be a freak. There was something so terrible about this that even the silliest customers of the café, such as Merlie Ryan, did not laugh. Only Marvin Macy drew up the left corner of his mouth and chuckled. Miss Amelia, when this happened, would be divided between two emotions. She would look at the hunchback with a lost, dismal reproach — then turn toward Marvin Macy with her teeth clamped.

"Bust a gut!" she would say bitterly.

And Marvin Macy, most likely, would pick up the guitar from the floor beside his chair. His voice was wet and slimy, as he always had too much spit in his mouth. And the tunes he sang glided slowly from his throat like eels. His strong fingers picked the strings with dainty skill, and everything he sang both lured and exasperated. This was usually more than Miss Amelia could stand.

"Bust a gut!" she would repeat, in a shout.

But always Marvin Macy had the answer ready for her. He would cover the strings to silence the quivering leftover tones, and reply with slow, sure insolence.

"Everything you holler at me bounces back on yourself. Yah! Yah!"

Miss Amelia would have to stand there helpless, as no one has ever invented a way out of this trap. She could not shout out abuse that would bounce back on herself. He had the best of her, there was nothing she could do.

So things went on like this. What happened between the three of them during the nights in the rooms upstairs nobody knows. But the café became more and more crowded every night. A new table had to be brought in. Even the Hermit, the crazy man named Rainer Smith, who took to the swamp years ago, heard something of the situation and came one night to look in at the window and brood over the gathering in the bright café. And the climax each evening was the time when Miss Amelia and Marvin Macy doubled their fists, squared up, and glared at each other. Usually this did not happen after any especial argument, but it seemed to come about mysteriously, by means of some instinct on the part of both of them. At these times the café would become so quiet that you could hear the bouquet of paper roses rustling in the draft. And each night they held this fighting stance a little longer than the night before.

The fight took place on Ground Hog Day, which is the second of February. The weather was favorable, being neither rainy nor sunny, and with a neutral temperature. There were several signs that this was the appointed day, and by ten o'clock the news spread all over the county. Early in the morning Miss Amelia went out and cut down her punching bag. Marvin Macy sat on the back step with a tin can of hog fat between his knees and carefully greased his arms and his legs. A hawk with a bloody breast flew over the town and circled twice around the property of Miss Amelia. The tables in the café were moved out to the back porch, so that the whole big room was cleared for the fight. There was every sign. Both Miss Amelia and Marvin Macy ate four helpings of half-raw roast for dinner, and then lay down in the afternoon to store up strength. Marvin Macy rested in the big room upstairs, while Miss Amelia stretched herself out on the bench in her office. It was plain from her white stiff face what a torment it was for her to be lying still and doing nothing, but she lay there quiet as a corpse with her eyes closed and her hands crossed on her chest.

Cousin Lymon had a restless day, and his little face was drawn and tightened with excitement. He put himself up a lunch, and set out to find the ground hog — within an hour he returned, the lunch eaten, and said that the ground hog had seen his shadow and there was to be bad weather ahead. Then, as Miss Amelia and Marvin Macy were both resting to gather strength, and he was left to himself, it occurred to him that he might as well paint the front porch. The house had not been painted for years — in fact, God knows if it had ever been painted at all. Cousin Lymon scrambled around, and soon he had painted half the floor of the porch a gay bright green. It was a loblolly job, and he smeared himself all over. Typically enough he did not even finish the floor, but changed over to the walls, painting as high as he could reach and then standing on a crate to get up a foot higher. When the paint ran out, the right side of the floor was bright green and there was a jagged portion of wall that had been painted. Cousin Lymon left it at that.

There was something childish about his satisfaction with his painting. And in this respect a curious fact should be mentioned. No one in the town, not even Miss Amelia, had any idea how old the hunchback was. Some maintained that when he came to town he was about twelve years old, still a child — others were certain that he was well past forty. His eyes were blue and steady as a child's, but there were lavender crepy shadows beneath these blue eyes that hinted of age. It was impossible to guess his age by his hunched queer body. And even his teeth gave no clue — they were all still in his head (two were broken from cracking a pecan), but he had stained them with so much sweet snuff that it was impossible to decide whether they were old teeth or young teeth. When questioned directly about his age the hunchback professed to know absolutely nothing — he had no idea how long he had been on the earth, whether for ten years or a hundred! So his age remained a puzzle.

Cousin Lymon finished his painting at five-thirty o'clock in the afternoon. The day had turned colder and there was a wet taste in the air. The wind came up from the pinewoods, rattling windows, blowing an old newspaper down the road until at last it caught upon a thorn tree. People began to come in from the country; packed automobiles that bristled with the poked-out heads of children, wagons drawn by old mules who seemed to smile in a weary, sour way and plodded along with their tired eyes half-closed. Three young boys came from Society City. All three of them wore yellow rayon shirts and caps put on backward — they were as much alike as triplets, and could always be seen at cockfights and camp meetings. At six o'clock the mill whistle sounded the end of the day's shift and the crowd was complete. Naturally, among the newcomers there were some riffraff, unknown characters, and so forth — but even so the gathering was quiet. A hush was on the town and the faces of people were strange in the fading light. Darkness hovered softly; for a moment the sky was a pale clear yellow against which the gables of the church stood out in dark and bare outline, then the sky died slowly and the darkness gathered into night.

Seven is a popular number, and especially it was a favorite with Miss Amelia. Seven swallows of water for hiccups, seven runs around the millpond for cricks in the neck, seven doses of Amelia Miracle Mover as a worm cure — her treatment nearly always hinged on this number. It is a number of mingled possibilities, and all who love mystery and charms set store by it. So the fight was to take place at seven o'clock. This was known to everyone, not by announcement or words, but understood in the unquestioning way that rain is understood, or an evil odor from the swamp. So before seven o'clock everyone gathered gravely around the property of Miss Amelia. The cleverest got into the café itself and stood lining the walls of the room. Others crowded onto the front porch, or took a stand in the yard.

Miss Amelia and Marvin Macy had not yet shown themselves. Miss Amelia, after resting all afternoon on the office bench, had gone upstairs. On the other hand Cousin Lymon was at your elbow every minute, threading his way through the crowd, snapping his fingers nervously, and batting his eyes. At one minute to seven o'clock he squirmed his way into the café and climbed up on the counter. All was very quiet.

It must have been arranged in some manner beforehand. For just at the stroke of seven Miss Amelia showed herself at the head of the stairs. At the same instant Marvin Macy appeared in front of the café and the crowd made way for him silently. They walked toward each other with no haste, their fists already gripped, and their eyes like the eyes of dreamers. Miss Amelia had changed her red dress for her old overalls, and they were rolled up to the knees. She was barefooted and she had an iron strengthband around her right wrist. Marvin Macy had also rolled his trouser legs — he was naked to the waist and heavily greased; he wore the heavy shoes that had been issued him when he left the penitentiary. Stumpy MacPhail stepped forward from the crowd and slapped their hip pockets with the palm of his right hand to make sure there would be no sudden knives. They were alone in the cleared center of the bright café.

There was no signal, but they both struck out simultaneously. Both blows landed on the chin, so that the heads of Miss Amelia and Marvin Macy bobbed back and they were left a little groggy. For a few seconds after the first blows they merely shuffled their feet around on the bare floor, experimenting with various positions, and making mock fists. Then, like wildcats, they were suddenly on each other. There was the sound of knocks, panting, and thumpings on the floor. They were so fast that it was hard to take in what was going on — but once Miss Amelia was hurled backward so that she staggered and almost fell, and another time Marvin Macy caught a knock on the shoulder that spun him round like a top. So the fight went on in this wild violent way with no sign of weakening on either side.

During a struggle like this, when the enemies are as quick and strong as these two, it is worth-while to turn from the confusion of the fight itself and observe the spectators. The people had flattened back as close as possible against the walls. Stumpy MacPhail was in a corner, crouched over and with his fists tight in sympathy, making strange noises. Poor Merlie Ryan had his mouth so wide open that a fly buzzed into it, and was swallowed before Merlie realized what had happened. And Cousin Lymon — he was worth watching. The hunchback still stood on the counter, so that he was raised above everyone else in the café. He had his hands on his hips, his big head thrust forward, and his little legs bent so that the knees jutted outward. The excitement had made him break out in a rash, and his pale mouth shivered.

Perhaps it was half an hour before the course of the fight shifted. Hundreds of blows had been exchanged, and there was still a deadlock. Then suddenly Marvin Macy managed to catch hold of Miss Amelia's left arm and pinion it behind her back. She struggled and got a grasp around his waist; the real fight was now begun. Wrestling is the natural way of fighting in this county — as boxing is too quick and requires much thinking and concentration. And now that Miss Amelia and Marvin were locked in a hold together the crowd came out of its daze and pressed in closer. For a while the fighters grappled muscle to muscle, their hipbones braced against each other. Backward and forward, from side to side, they swayed in this way. Marvin Macy still had not sweated, but Miss Amelia's overalls were drenched and so much sweat had trickled down her legs that she left wet footprints on the floor. Now the test had come, and in these moments of terrible effort, it was Miss Amelia who was the stronger. Marvin Macy was greased and slippery, tricky to grasp, but she was stronger. Gradually she bent him over backward, and inch by inch she forced him to the floor. It was a terrible thing to watch and their deep hoarse breaths were the only sound in the café. At last she had him down, and straddled; her strong big hands were on his throat.

But at that instant, just as the fight was won, a cry sounded in the café that caused a shrill bright shiver to run down the spine. And what took place has been a mystery ever since. The whole town was there to testify what happened, but there were those who doubted their own eyesight. For the counter on which Cousin Lymon stood was at least twelve feet from the fighters in the center of the café. Yet at the instant Miss Amelia grasped the throat of Marvin Macy the hunchback sprang forward and sailed through the air as though he had grown hawk wings. He landed on the broad strong back of Miss Amelia and clutched at her neck with his clawed little fingers.

The rest is confusion. Miss Amelia was beaten before the crowd could come to their senses. Because of the hunchback the fight was won by Marvin Macy, and at the end Miss Amelia lay sprawled on the floor, her arms flung outward and motionless. Marvin Macy stood over her, his face somewhat popeyed, but smiling his old half-mouthed smile. And the hunchback, he had suddenly disappeared. Perhaps he was frightened about what he had done, or maybe he was so delighted that he wanted to glory with himself alone — at any rate he slipped out of the café and crawled under the back steps. Someone poured water on Miss Amelia, and after a time she got up slowly and dragged herself into her office. Through the open door the crowd could see her sitting at her desk, her head in the crook of her arm, and she was sobbing with the last of her grating, winded breath. Once she gathered her right fist together and knocked it three times on the top of her office desk, then her hand opened feebly and lay palm upward and still. Stumpy MacPhail stepped forward and closed the door.

The crowd was quiet, and one by one the people left the café. Mules were waked up and untied, automobiles cranked, and the three boys from Society City roamed off down the road on foot. This was not a fight to hash over and talk about afterward; people went home and pulled the covers up over their heads. The town was dark, except for the premises of Miss Amelia, but every room was lighted there the whole night long.

Marvin Macy and the hunchback must have left the town an hour or so before daylight. And before they went away this is what they did:

They unlocked the private cabinet of curios and took everything in it.

They broke the mechanical piano.

They carved terrible words on the café tables.

They found the watch that opened in the back to show a picture of a waterfall and took that also.

They poured a gallon of sorghum syrup all over the kitchen floor and smashed the jars of preserves.

They went out in the swamp and completely wrecked the still, ruining the big new condenser and the cooler, and setting fire to the shack itself.

They fixed a dish of Miss Amelia's favorite food, grits with sausage, seasoned it with enough poison to kill off the county, and placed this dish temptingly on the café counter.

They did everything ruinous they could think of without actually breaking into the office where Miss Amelia stayed the night. Then they went off together, the two of them.

That was how Miss Amelia was left alone in the town. The people would have helped her if they had known how, as people in this town will as often as not be kindly if they have a chance. Several housewives nosed around with brooms and offered to clear up the wreck. But Miss Amelia only looked at them with lost crossed eyes and shook her head. Stumpy MacPhail came in on the third day to buy a plug of Queenie tobacco, and Miss Amelia said the price was one dollar. Everything in the café had suddenly risen in price to be worth one dollar. And what sort of a café is that? Also, she changed very queerly as a doctor. In all the years before she had been much more popular than the Cheehaw doctor. She had never monkeyed with a patient's soul, taking away from him such real necessities as liquor, tobacco, and so forth. Once in a great while she might carefully warn a patient never to eat fried watermelon or some such dish it had never occurred to a person to want in the first place. Now all this wise doctoring was over. She told one-half of her patients that they were going to die outright, and to the remaining half she recommended cures so farfetched and agonizing that no one in his right mind would consider them for a moment.

Miss Amelia let her hair grow ragged, and it was turning gray. Her face lengthened, and the great muscles of her body shrank until she was thin as old maids are thin when they go crazy. And those gray eyes — slowly day by day they were more crossed, and it was as though they sought each other to exchange a little glance of grief and lonely recognition. She was not pleasant to listen to; her tongue had sharpened terribly.

When anyone mentioned the hunchback she would say only this: "Ho! If I could lay hand to him I would rip out his gizzard and throw it to the cat!" But it was not so much the words that were terrible, but the voice in which they were said. Her voice had lost its old vigor; there was none of the ring of vengeance it used to have when she would mention "that loom-fixer I was married to," or some other enemy. Her voice was broken, soft, and sad as the wheezy whine of the church pump-organ.

For three years she sat out on the front steps every night, alone and silent, looking down the road and waiting. But the hunchback never returned. There were rumors that Marvin Macy used him to climb into windows and steal, and other rumors that Marvin Macy had sold him into a side show. But both these reports were traced back to Merlie Ryan. Nothing true was ever heard of him. It was in the fourth year that Miss Amelia hired a Cheehaw carpenter and had him board up the premises, and there in those closed rooms she has remained ever since.

Yes, the town is dreary. On August afternoons the road is empty, white with dust, and the sky above is bright as glass. Nothing moves — there are no children's voices, only the hum of the mill. The peach trees seem to grow more crooked every summer, and the leaves are dull gray and of a sickly delicacy. The house of Miss Amelia leans so much to the right that it is now only a question of time when it will collapse completely, and people are careful not to walk around the yard. There is no good liquor to be bought in the town; the nearest still is eight miles away, and the liquor is such that those who drink it grow warts on their livers the size of goobers, and dream themselves into a dangerous inward world. There is absolutely nothing to do in the town. Walk around the millpond, stand kicking at a rotten stump, figure out what you can do with the old wagon wheel by the side of the road near the church. The soul rots with boredom. You might as well go down to the Forks Falls highway and listen to the chain gang.

The Twelve Mortal Men

The Forks Falls highway is three miles from the town, and it is here the chain gang has been working. The road is of macadam, and the county decided to patch up the rough places and widen it at a certain dangerous place. The gang is made up of twelve men, all wearing black and white striped prison suits, and chained at the ankles. There is a guard, with a gun, his eyes drawn to red slits by the glare. The gang works all the day long, arriving huddled in the prison cart soon after daybreak, and being driven off again in the gray August twilight. All day there is the sound of the picks striking into the clay earth, hard sunlight, the smell of sweat. And every day there is music. One dark voice will start a phrase, half-sung, and like a question. And after a moment another voice will join in, soon the whole gang will be singing. The voices are dark in the golden glare, the music intricately blended, both somber and joyful. The music will swell until at last it seems that the sound does not come from the twelve men on the gang, but from the earth itself, or the wide sky. It is music that causes the heart to broaden and the listener to grow cold with ecstasy and fright. Then slowly the music will sink down until at last there remains one lonely voice, then a great hoarse breath, the sun, the sound of the picks in the silence.

And what kind of gang is this that can make such music? Just twelve mortal men, seven of them black and five of them white boys from this county. Just twelve mortal men who are together.

The Member of the Wedding

Part One

It happened that green and crazy summer when Frankie was twelve years old. This was the summer when for a long time she had not been a member. She belonged to no club and was a member of nothing in the world. Frankie had become an unjoined person who hung around in doorways, and she was afraid. In June the trees were bright dizzy green, but later the leaves darkened, and the town turned black and shrunken under the glare of the sun. At first Frankie walked around doing one thing and another. The sidewalks of the town were gray in the early morning and at night, but the noon sun put a glaze on them, so that the cement burned and glittered like glass. The sidewalks finally became too hot for Frankie's feet, and also she got herself in trouble. She was in so much secret trouble that she thought it was better to stay at home — and at home there was only Berenice Sadie Brown and John Henry West. The three of them sat at the kitchen table, saying the same things over and over, so that by August the words began to rhyme with each other and sound strange. The world seemed to die each afternoon and nothing moved any longer. At last the summer was like a green sick dream, or like a silent crazy jungle under glass. And then, on the last Friday of August, all this was changed: it was so sudden that Frankie puzzled the whole blank afternoon, and still she did not understand.

"It is so very queer," she said. "The way it all just happened."

"Happened? Happened?" said Berenice.

John Henry listened and watched them quietly.

"I have never been so puzzled."

"But puzzled about what?"

"The whole thing," Frankie said.

And Berenice remarked: "I believe the sun has fried your brains."

"Me too," John Henry whispered.

Frankie herself almost admitted maybe so. It was four o'clock in the afternoon and the kitchen was square and gray and quiet. Frankie sat at the table with her eyes half closed, and she thought about a wedding. She saw a silent church, a strange snow slanting down against the colored windows. The groom in this wedding was her brother, and there was a brightness where his face should be. The bride was there in a long white train, and the bride also was faceless. There was something about this wedding that gave Frankie a feeling she could not name.

"Look here at me," said Berenice. "You jealous?"

"Jealous?"

"Jealous because your brother going to be married?"

"No," Frankie said. "I just never saw any two people like them. When they walked in the house today it was so queer."

"You jealous," said Berenice. "Go and behold yourself in the mirror. I can see from the color in your eye."

There was a watery kitchen mirror hanging above the sink. Frankie looked, but her eyes were gray as they always were. This summer she was grown so tall that she was almost a big freak, and her shoulders were narrow, her legs too long. She wore a pair of blue track shorts, a B.V.D. undervest, and she was barefooted. Her hair had been cut like a boy's, but it had not been cut for a long time and was now not even parted. The reflection in the glass was warped and crooked, but Frankie knew well what she looked like; she drew up her left shoulder and turned her head aside.

"Oh," she said. "They were the two prettiest people I ever saw. I just can't understand how it happened."

"But what, Foolish?" said Berenice. "Your brother come home with the girl he means to marry and took dinner today with you and your Daddy. They intend to marry at her home in Winter Hill this coming Sunday. You and your Daddy are going to the wedding. And that is the A and the Z of the matter. So whatever ails you?"

"I don't know," said Frankie. "I bet they have a good time every minute of the day."

"Less us have a good time," John Henry said.

"Us have a good time?" Frankie said. "Us?"

The three of them sat at the table again and Berenice dealt the cards for three-handed bridge. Berenice had been the cook since Frankie could remember. She was very black and broad-shouldered and short. She always said that she was thirty-five years old, but she had been saying that at least three years. Her hair was parted, plaited, and greased close to the skull, and she had a flat and quiet face. There was only one thing wrong about Berenice — her left eye was bright blue glass. It stared out fixed and wild from her quiet, colored face, and why she had wanted a blue eye nobody human would ever know. Her right eye was dark and sad. Berenice dealt slowly, licking her thumb when the sweaty cards stuck together. John Henry watched each card as it was being dealt. His chest was white and wet and naked, and he wore around his neck a tiny lead donkey tied by a string. He was blood kin to Frankie, first cousin, and all summer he would eat dinner and spend the day with her, or eat supper and spend the night; and she could not make him go home. He was small to be six years old, but he had the largest knees that Frankie had ever seen, and on one of them there was always a scab or a bandage where he had fallen down and skinned himself. John Henry had a little screwed white face and he wore tiny gold-rimmed glasses. He watched all of the cards very carefully, because he was in debt; he owed Berenice more than five million dollars.

"I bid one heart," said Berenice.

"A spade," said Frankie.

"I want to bid spades," said John Henry. "That's what I was going to bid."

"Well, that's your tough luck. I bid them first."

"Oh, you fool jackass!" he said. "It's not fair!"

"Hush quarreling," said Berenice. "To tell the truth, I don't think either one of you got such a grand hand to fight over the bid about. I bid two hearts."

"I don't give a durn about it," Frankie said. "It is immaterial with me."

As a matter of fact this was so: she played bridge that afternoon like John Henry, just putting down any card that suddenly occurred to her. They sat together in the kitchen, and the kitchen was a sad and ugly room. John Henry had covered the walls with queer, child drawings, as far up as his arm would reach. This gave the kitchen a crazy look, like that of a room in the crazy-house. And now the old kitchen made Frankie sick. The name for what had happened to her Frankie did not know, but she could feel her squeezed heart beating against the table edge.

"The world is certainy a small place," she said.

"What makes you say that?"

"I mean sudden," said Frankie. "The world is certainy a sudden place."

"Well, I don't know," said Berenice. "Sometimes sudden and sometimes slow."

Frankie's eyes were half closed, and to her own ears her voice sounded ragged, far away:

"To me it is sudden."

For only yesterday Frankie had never thought seriously about a wedding. She knew that her only brother, Jarvis, was to be married. He had become engaged to a girl in Winter Hill just before he went to Alaska. Jarvis was a corporal in the army and he had spent almost two years in Alaska. Frankie had not seen her brother for a long, long time, and his face had become masked and changing, like a face seen under water. But Alaska! Frankie had dreamed of it constantly, and especially this summer it was very real. She saw the snow and frozen sea and ice glaciers. Esquimau igloos and polar bears and the beautiful Northern lights. When Jarvis had first gone to Alaska, she had sent him a box of homemade fudge, packing it carefully and wrapping each piece separately in waxed paper. It had thrilled her to think that her fudge would be eaten in Alaska, and she had a vision of her brother passing it around to furry Esquimaux. Three months later, a thank-you letter had come from Jarvis with a five-dollar bill enclosed. For a while she mailed candy almost every week, sometimes divinity instead of fudge, but Jarvis did not send her another bill, except at Christmas time. Sometimes his short letters to her father disturbed her a little. For instance, this summer he mentioned once that he had been in swimming and that the mosquitoes were something fierce. This letter jarred upon her dream, but after a few days of bewilderment, she returned to her frozen seas and snow. When Jarvis had come back from Alaska, he had gone straight to Winter Hill. The bride was named Janice Evans and the plans for the wedding were like this: her brother had wired that he and the bride were coming this Friday to spend the day, then on the following Sunday there was to be the wedding, traveling nearly a hundred miles to Winter Hill, and Frankie had already packed a suitcase. She looked forward to the time her brother and the bride should come, but she did not picture them to herself, and did not think about the wedding. So on the day before the visit she only commented to Berenice:

"I think it's a curious coincidence that Jarvis would get to go to Alaska and that the very bride he picked to marry would come from a place called Winter Hill. Winter Hill," she repeated slowly, her eyes closed, and the name blended with dreams of Alaska and cold snow. "I wish tomorrow was Sunday instead of Friday. I wish I had already left town."

"Sunday will come," said Berenice.

"I doubt it," said Frankie. "I've been ready to leave this town so long. I wish I didn't have to come back here after the wedding. I wish I was going somewhere for good. I wish I had a hundred dollars and could just light out and never see this town again."

"It seems to me you wish for a lot of things," said Berenice.

"I wish I was somebody else except me."

So the afternoon before it happened was like the other August afternoons. Frankie had hung around the kitchen, then toward dark she had gone out into the yard. The scuppernong arbor behind the house was purple and dark in the twilight. She walked slowly. John Henry West was sitting beneath the August arbor in a wicker chair, his legs crossed and his hands in his pockets.

"What are you doing?" she asked.

"I'm thinking."

"About what?"

He did not answer.

Frankie was too tall this summer to walk beneath the arbor as she had always done before. Other twelve-year-old people could still walk around inside, give shows, and have a good time. Even small grown ladies could walk underneath the arbor. And already Frankie was too big; this year she had to hang around and pick from the edges like the grown people. She stared into the tangle of dark vines, and there was the smell of crushed scuppernongs and dust. Standing beside the arbor, with dark coming on, Frankie was afraid. She did not know what caused this fear, but she was afraid.

"I tell you what," she said. "Suppose you eat supper and spend the night with me."

John Henry took his dollar watch from his pocket and looked

at it as though the time would decide whether or not he would come, but it was too dark under the arbor for him to read the numbers.

"Go on home and tell Aunt Pet. I'll meet you in the kitchen."

"All right."

She was afraid. The evening sky was pale and empty and the light from the kitchen window made a yellow square reflection in the darkening yard. She remembered that when she was a little girl she believed that three ghosts were living in the coal house, and one of the ghosts wore a silver ring.

She ran up the back steps and said: "I just now invited John Henry to eat supper and spend the night with me."

Berenice was kneading a lump of biscuit dough, and she dropped it on the flour-dusted table. "I thought you were sick and tired of him."

"I am sick and tired of him," said Frankie. "But it seemed to me he looked scared."

"Scared of what?"

Frankie shook her head. "Maybe I mean lonesome," she said finally.

"Well, I'll save him a scrap of dough."

After the darkening yard the kitchen was hot and bright and queer. The walls of the kitchen bothered Frankie — the queer drawings of Christmas trees, airplanes, freak soldiers, flowers. John Henry had started the first pictures one long afternoon in June, and having already ruined the wall, he went on and drew whenever he wished. Sometimes Frankie had drawn also. At first her father had been furious about the walls, but later he said for them to draw all the pictures out of their systems, and he would have the kitchen painted in the fall. But as the summer lasted, and would not end, the walls had begun to bother Frankie. That evening the kitchen looked strange to her, and she was afraid.

She stood in the doorway and said: "I just thought I might as well invite him."

So at dark John Henry came to the back door with a little weekend bag. He was dressed in his white recital suit and had put on shoes and socks. There was a dagger buckled to his belt. John Henry had seen snow. Although he was only six years old, he had gone to Birmingham last winter, and there he had seen snow. Frankie had never seen snow.

"I'll take the week-end bag," said Frankie. "You can start right in making a biscuit man."

"O.K."

John Henry did not play with the dough; he worked on the biscuit man as though it were a very serious business. Now and then he stopped off, settled his glasses with his little hand, and studied what he had done. He was like a tiny watchmaker, and he drew up a chair and knelt on it so that he could get directly over the work. When Berenice gave him some raisins, he did not stick them all around as any other human child would do; he used only two for the eyes; but immediately he realized they were too large — so he divided one raisin carefully and put in eyes, two specks for the nose, and a little grinning raisin mouth. When he had finished, he wiped his hands on the seat of his shorts, and there was a little biscuit man with separate fingers, a hat on, and even a walking stick. John Henry had worked so hard that the dough was now gray and wet. But it was a perfect little biscuit man, and, as a matter of fact, it reminded Frankie of John Henry himself.

"I better entertain you now," she said.

They ate supper at the kitchen table with Berenice, since her father had telephoned that he was working late at his jewelry store. When Berenice brought the biscuit man from the oven, they saw that it looked exactly like any biscuit man ever made by a child — it had swelled so that all the work of John Henry had been cooked out, the fingers were run together, and the walking stick resembled a sort of tail. But John Henry just looked at it through his glasses, wiped it with his napkin, and buttered the left foot.

It was a dark, hot August night. The radio in the dining room was playing a mixture of many stations: a war voice crossed with the gabble of an advertiser, and underneath there was the sleazy music of a sweet band. The radio had stayed on all the summer long, so finally it was a sound that as a rule they did not notice. Sometimes, when the noise became so loud that they could not hear their own ears, Frankie would turn it down a little. Otherwise, music and voices came and went and crossed and twisted with each other, and by August they did not listen any more.

"What do you want to do?" asked Frankie. "Would you like for me to read to you out of Hans Brinker or would you rather do something else?"

"I rather do something else," he said.

"What?"

"Less play out."

"I don't want to," Frankie said.

"There's a big crowd going to play out tonight."

"You got ears," Frankie said. "You heard me."

John Henry stood with his big knees locked, then finally he said: "I think I better go home."

"Why, you haven't spent the night! You can't eat supper and just go on off like that."

"I know it," he said quietly. Along with the radio they could hear the voices of the children playing in the night. "But less go out, Frankie. They sound like they having a mighty good time."

"No they're not," she said. "Just a lot of ugly silly children. Running and hollering and running and hollering. Nothing to it. We'll go upstairs and unpack your week-end bag."

Frankie's room was an elevated sleeping porch which had been built onto the house, with a stairway leading up from the kitchen. The room was furnished with an iron bed, a bureau, and a desk. Also Frankie had a motor which could be turned on and off; the motor could sharpen knives, and, if they were long enough, it could be used for filing down your fingernails. Against the wall was the suitcase packed and ready for the trip to Winter Hill. On the desk there was a very old typewriter, and Frankie sat down before it, trying to think of any letters she could write: but there was nobody for her to write to, as every possible letter had already been answered, and answered even several times. So she covered the typewriter with a raincoat and pushed it aside.

"Honestly," John Henry said, "don't you think I better go home?"

"No," she answered, without looking around at him. "You sit there in the corner and play with the motor."

Before Frankie there were now two objects — a lavender seashell and a glass globe with snow inside that could be shaken into a snowstorm. When she held the seashell to her ear, she could hear the warm wash of the Gulf of Mexico, and think of a green palm island far away. And she could hold the snow globe to her narrowed eyes and watch the whirling white flakes fall until they blinded her. She dreamed of Alaska. She walked up a cold white hill and looked on a snowy wasteland far below. She watched the sun make colors in the ice, and heard dream voices, saw dream things. And everywhere there was the cold white gentle snow.

"Look," John Henry said, and he was staring out of the window. "I think those big girls are having a party in their clubhouse."

"Hush!" Frankie screamed suddenly. "Don't mention those crooks to me."

There was in the neighborhood a clubhouse, and Frankie was not a member. The members of the club were girls who were thirteen and fourteen and even fifteen years old. They had parties with boys on Saturday night. Frankie knew all of the club members, and until this summer she had been like a younger member of their crowd, but now they had this club and she was not a member. They had said she was too young and mean. On Saturday night she could hear the terrible music and see from far away their light. Sometimes she went around to the alley behind the clubhouse and stood near a honeysuckle fence. She stood in the alley and watched and listened. They were very long, those parties.

"Maybe they will change their mind and invite you," John Henry said.

"The son-of-a-bitches."

Frankie sniffled and wiped her nose in the crook of her arm. She sat down on the edge of the bed, her shoulders slumped and her elbows resting on her knees. "I think they have been spreading it all over town that I smell bad," she said. "When I had those boils and that black bitter smelling ointment, old Helen Fletcher asked what was that funny smell I had. Oh, I could shoot every one of them with a pistol."

She heard John Henry walking up to the bed, and then she felt his hand patting her neck with tiny little pats. "I don't think you smell so bad," he said. "You smell sweet."

"The son-of-a-bitches," she said again. "And there was something else. They were talking nasty lies about married people. When I think of Aunt Pet and Uncle Ustace. And my own father! The nasty lies! I don't know what kind of fool they take me for."

"I can smell you the minute you walk in the house without even looking to see if it is you. Like a hundred flowers."

"I don't care," she said. "I just don't care."

"Like a thousand flowers," said John Henry, and still he was patting his sticky hand on the back of her bent neck.

Frankie sat up, licked the tears from around her mouth, and wiped off her face with her shirttail. She sat still, her nose widened, smelling herself. Then she went to her suitcase and took out a bottle of Sweet Serenade. She rubbed some on the top of her head and poured some more down inside the neck of her shirt.

"Want some on you?"

John Henry was squatting beside the open suitcase and he gave a little shiver when she poured the perfume over him. He wanted to meddle in her traveling suitcase and look carefully at everything she owned. But Frankie only wanted him to get a general impression, and not count and know just what she had and what she did not have. So she strapped the suitcase and pushed it back against the wall.

"Boy!" she said. "I bet I use more perfume than anybody in this town."

The house was quiet except for the low rumble of the radio in the dining room downstairs. Long ago her father had come home and Berenice had closed the back door and gone away. There was no longer the sound of children's voices in the summer night.

"I guess we ought to have a good time," said Frankie.

But there was nothing to do. John Henry stood, his knees locked and his hands clasped behind his back, in the middle of the room. There were moths at the window — pale green moths and yellow moths that fluttered and spread their wings against the screen.

"Those beautiful butterflies," he said. "They are trying to get in."

Frankie watched the soft moths tremble and press against the window screen. The moths came every evening when the lamp on her desk was lighted. They came from out of the August night and fluttered and clung against the screen.

"To me it is the irony of fate," she said. "The way they come here. Those moths could fly anywhere. Yet they keep hanging around the windows of this house."

John Henry touched the gold rim of his glasses to settle them on his nose and Frankie studied his flat little freckled face.

"Take off those glasses," she said suddenly.

John Henry took them off and blew on them. She looked through the glasses and the room was loose and crooked. Then she pushed back her chair and stared at John Henry. There were two damp white circles around his eyes.

"I bet you don't need those glasses," she said. She put her hand down on the typewriter. "What is this?"

"The typewriter," he said.

Frankie picked up the shell. "And this?"

"The shell from the Bay."

"What is that little thing crawling there on the floor?"

"Where?" he asked, looking around him.

"That little thing crawling along near your feet."

"Oh," he said. He squatted down. "Why, it's an ant. I wonder how it got up here."

Frankie tilted back in her chair and crossed her bare feet on her desk. "If I were you I'd just throw those glasses away," she said. "You can see good as anybody."

John Henry did not answer.

"They don't look becoming."

She handed the folded glasses to John Henry and he wiped them with his pink flannel glasses rag. He put them back on and did not answer.

"O.K." she said. "Suit yourself. I was only telling you for your own good."

They went to bed. They undressed with their backs turned to each other and then Frankie switched off the motor and the light. John Henry knelt down to say his prayers and he prayed for a long time, not saying the words aloud. Then he lay down beside her.

"Good night," she said.

"Good night."

Frankie stared up into the dark. "You know it is still hard for me to realize that the world turns around at the rate of about a thousand miles an hour."

"I know it," he said.

"And to understand why it is that when you jump up in the air you don't come down in Fairview or Selma or somewhere fifty miles away."

John Henry turned over and made a sleepy sound.

"Or Winter Hill," she said. "I wish I was starting for Winter Hill right now."

Already John Henry was asleep. She heard him breathe in the darkness, and now she had what she had wanted so many nights that summer; there was somebody sleeping in the bed with her. She lay in the dark and listened to him breathe, then after a while she raised herself on her elbow. He lay freckled and small in the moonlight, his chest white and naked, and one foot hanging from the edge of the bed. Carefully she put her hand on his stomach and moved closer; it felt as though a little clock was ticking inside him and he smelled of sweat and Sweet Serenade. He smelled like a sour little rose. Frankie leaned down and licked him behind the ear. Then she breathed deeply, settled herself with her chin on his sharp damp shoulder, and closed her eyes: for now, with somebody sleeping in the dark with her, she was not so much afraid.

The sun woke them early the next morning, the white August sun. Frankie could not make John Henry go home. He saw the ham Berenice was cooking, and that the special company dinner was going to be good. Frankie's father read the paper in the living room, then went downtown to wind the watches at his jewelry store.

"If that brother of mine don't bring me a present from Alaska, I will be seriously mad," said Frankie.

"Me too," agreed John Henry.

And what were they doing that August morning when her brother and the bride came home? They were sitting in the arbor shade and talking about Christmas. The glare was hard and bright, the sun-drunk bluejays screamed and murmured among themselves. They talked, and their voices tired down into a little tune and they said the same things over and over. They just drowsed in the dark shade of the arbor, and Frankie was a person who had never thought about a wedding. That was the way they were that August morning when her brother and the bride walked in the house.

"Oh, Jesus!" Frankie said. The cards on the table were greasy and the late sun slanted across the yard. "The world is certainy a sudden place."

"Well, stop commenting about it," said Berenice. "You don't have your mind on the game."

Frankie, however, had some of her mind on the game. She played the queen of spades, which were trumps, and John Henry threw off a little two of diamonds. She looked at him. He was staring at the back of her hand as though what he wanted and needed was angled eyesight that could cut around corners and read people's cards.

"You got a spade," said Frankie.

John Henry put his donkey necklace in his mouth and looked away.

"Cheater," she said.

"Go on and play your spade," said Berenice.

Then he argued: "It was hid behind the other card."

"Cheater."

But still he would not play. He sat there sad and holding up the game.

"Make haste," said Berenice.

"I can't," he said finally. "It's a jack. The only spade I got is a jack. I don't want to play my jack down under Frankie's queen. I'm not going to do it either."

Frankie threw her cards down on the table. "See!" she said to Berenice. "He don't even follow the first beginning laws! He is a child! It is hopeless! Hopeless! Hopeless!"

"Maybe so," said Berenice.

"Oh," Frankie said, "I am sick unto death."

She sat with her bare feet on the rungs of the chair, her eyes closed, and her chest against the table edge. The red greasy cards were messed together on the table, and the sight of them made Frankie sick. They had played cards after dinner every single afternoon; if you would eat those old cards, they would taste like a combination of all the dinners of that August, together with a sweaty-handed nasty taste. Frankie swept the cards from the table. The wedding was bright and beautiful as snow and the heart in her was mashed. She got up from the table.

"It is a known truth that gray-eyed people are jealous."

"I told you I wasn't jealous," Frankie said, and she was walking fast around the room. "I couldn't be jealous of one of them without being jealous of them both. I sociate the two of them together."

"Well, I were jealous when my foster brother married," said Berenice. "I admit that when John married Clorina I sent a warning I would tear the ears off her head. But you see I didn't. Clorina got ears like anybody else. And now I love her."

"J A," said Frankie. "Janice and Jarvis. Isn't that the strangest thing?"

"What?"

"J A," she said. "Both their names begin with J A."

"And? What about it?"

Frankie walked round and round the kitchen table. "If only my name was Jane," she said. "Jane or Jasmine."

"I don't follow your frame of mind," said Berenice.

"Jarvis and Janice and Jasmine. See?"

"No," said Berenice. "By the way, I heard this morning on the radio that the French people are chasing the Germans out of Paris."

"Paris," Frankie repeated in a hollow tone. "I wonder if it is against the law to change your name. Or to add to it."

"Naturally. It is against the law."

"Well, I don't care," she said. "F. Jasmine Addams."

On the staircase leading to her room there was a doll, and John Henry brought it to the table and sat rocking it in his arms. "You serious when you gave me this," he said. He pulled up the doll's dress and fingered the real panties and body-waist. "I will name her Belle."

Frankie stared at the doll for a minute. "I don't know what went on in Jarvis's mind when he brought me that doll. Imagine bringing me a doll! And Janice tried to explain that she had pictured me as a little girl. I had counted on Jarvis bringing me something from Alaska."

"Your face when you unwrapped the package was a study," said Berenice.

It was a large doll with red hair and china eyes that opened and closed, and yellow eyelashes. John Henry held her in a lying-down position, so that the eyes were shut, and he was now trying to open them by pulling up the eyelashes.

"Don't do that! It makes me nervous. In fact, take that doll somewhere out of my sight."

John Henry took it to the back porch where he could pick it up when he went home.

"Her name is Lily Belle," he said.

The clock ticked very slowly on the shelf above the stove, and it was only quarter to six. The glare outside the window was still hard and yellow and bright. In the back yard the shade beneath the arbor was black and solid. Nothing moved. From somewhere far away came the sound of whistling, and it was a grieving August song that did not end. The minutes were very long.

Frankie went again to the kitchen mirror and stared at her own face. "The big mistake I made was to get this close crew-cut. For the wedding I ought to have long bright yellow hair. Don't you think so?"

She stood before the mirror and she was afraid. It was the summer of fear, for Frankie, and there was one fear that could be figured in arithmetic with paper and a pencil at the table. This August she was twelve and five-sixths years old. She was five feet five and three quarter inches tall, and she wore a number seven shoe. In the past year she had grown four inches, or at least that was what she judged. Already the hateful little summer children hollered to her: "Is it cold up there?" And the comments of grown people made Frankie shrivel on her heels. If she reached her height on her eighteenth birthday, she had five and one-sixth growing years ahead of her. Therefore, according to mathematics and unless she could somehow stop herself, she would grow to be over nine feet tall. And what would be a lady who is over nine feet high? She would be a Freak.

In the early autumn of every year the Chattahoochee Exposition came to town. For a whole October week the fair went on down at the fair grounds. There was the Ferris Wheel, the Flying Jinney, the Palace of Mirrors — and there, too, was the House of the Freaks. The House of the Freaks was a long pavilion which was lined on the inside with a row of booths. It cost a quarter to go into the general tent, and you could look at each Freak in his booth. Then there were special private exhibitions farther back in the tent which cost a dime apiece. Frankie had seen all of the members of the Freak House last October:

The Giant
The Fat Lady
The Midget
The Wild Nigger
The Pin Head
The Alligator Boy
The Half-Man Half-Woman

The Giant was more than eight feet high, with huge loose hands and a hang-jaw face. The Fat Lady sat in a chair, and the fat on her was like loose-powdered dough which she kept slapping and working with her hands — next was the squeezed Midget who minced around in little trick evening clothes. The Wild Nigger came from a savage island. He squatted in his booth among the dusty bones and palm leaves and he ate raw living rats. The fair gave a free admission to his show to all who brought rats of the right size, and so children carried them down in strong sacks and shoe boxes. The Wild Nigger knocked the rat's head over his squatted knee and ripped off the fur and crunched and gobbled and flashed his greedy Wild Nigger eyes. Some said that he was not a genuine Wild Nigger, but a crazy colored man from Selma. Anyway, Frankie did not like to watch him very long. She pushed through the crowd to the Pin Head booth, where John Henry had stood all afternoon. The little Pin Head skipped and giggled and sassed around, with a shrunken head no larger than an orange, which was shaved except for one lock tied with a pink bow at the top. The last booth was always very crowded, for it was the booth of the Half-Man Half-Woman, a morphidite and a miracle of science. This Freak was divided completely in half — the left side was a man and the right side a woman. The costume on the left was a leopard skin and on the right side a brassiere and a spangled skirt. Half the face was dark-bearded and the other half bright glazed with paint. Both eyes were strange. Frankie had wandered around the tent and looked at every booth. She was afraid of all the Freaks, for it seemed to her that they had looked at her in a secret way and tried to connect their eyes with hers, as though to say: we know you. She was afraid of their long Freak eyes. And all the year she had remembered them, until this day.

"I doubt if they ever get married or go to a wedding," she said. "Those Freaks."

"What freaks you talking about?" asked Berenice.

"At the fair," said Frankie. "The ones we saw there last October."

"Oh, those folks."

"I wonder if they make a big salary," she said.

And Berenice answered: "How would I know?"

John Henry held out an imaginary skirt and, touching his finger to the top of his big head, he skipped and danced like the Pin Head around the kitchen table.

Then he said: "She was the cutest little girl I ever saw. I never saw anything so cute in my whole life. Did you, Frankie?"

"No," she said. "I didn't think she was cute."

"Me and you both," said Berenice.

"Shoo!" John Henry argued. "She was, too."

"If you want my candy opinion," said Berenice, "that whole crowd of folks down yonder at the fair just give me the creeps. Ever last one of them."

Frankie watched Berenice through the mirror, and finally she asked in a slow voice. "Do *I* give you the creeps?"

"You?" asked Berenice.

"Do you think I will grow into a Freak?" Frankie whispered.

"You?" said Berenice again. "Why, certainy not, I trust Jesus."

Frankie felt better. She looked sidewise at herself in the mirror. The clock ticked six slow times, and then she said: "Well, do you think I will be pretty?"

"Maybe. If you file down them horns a inch or two."

Frankie stood with her weight resting on her left leg, and she slowly shuffled the ball of her right foot on the floor. She felt a splinter go beneath the skin. "Seriously," she said.

"I think when you fill out you will do very well. If you behave."

"But by Sunday," Frankie said. "I want to do something to improve myself before the wedding."

"Get clean for a change. Scrub your elbows and fix yourself nice. You will do very well."

Frankie looked for a last time at herself in the mirror, and then she turned away. She thought about her brother and the bride, and there was a tightness in her that would not break.

"I don't know what to do. I just wish I would die."

"Well, die then!" said Berenice.

And: "Die," John Henry echoed in a whisper.

The world stopped.

"Go home," said Frankie to John Henry.

He stood with his big knees locked, his dirty little hand on the edge of the white table, and he did not move.

"You heard me," Frankie said. She made a terrible face at him and grabbed the frying pan that hung above the stove. She chased him three times around the table, then up through the front hall and out of the door. She locked the front door and called again: "Go home."

"Now what makes you act like that?" asked Berenice. "You are too mean to live."

Frankie opened the door to the stairway that led to her room, and sat down on one of the lower steps. The kitchen was silent and crazy and sad.

"I know it," she said. "I intend to sit still by myself and think over everything for a while."

This was the summer when Frankie was sick and tired of being Frankie. She hated herself, and had become a loafer and a big no-good who hung around the summer kitchen: dirty and greedy and mean and sad. Besides being too mean to live, she was a criminal. If the Law knew about her, she could be tried in the courthouse and locked up in the jail. Yet Frankie had not always been a criminal and a big no-good. Until the April of that year, and all the years of her life before, she had been like other people. She belonged to a club and was in the seventh grade at school. She worked for her father on Saturday morning and went to the show every Saturday afternoon. She was not the kind of person ever to think of being afraid. At night she slept in the bed with her father, but not because she was scared of the dark.

Then the spring of that year had been a long queer season. Things began to change and Frankie did not understand this change. After the plain gray winter the March winds banged on the windowpanes, and clouds were shirred and white on the blue sky. April that year came sudden and still, and the green of the trees was a wild bright green. The pale wistarias bloomed all over town, and silently the blossoms shattered. There was something about the green trees and the flowers of April that made Frankie sad. She did not know why she was sad, but because of this peculiar sadness, she began to realize she ought to leave the town. She read the war news and thought about the world and packed her suitcase to go away; but she did not know where she should go.

It was the year when Frankie thought about the world. And she did not see it as a round school globe, with the countries neat and different-colored. She thought of the world as huge and cracked and loose and turning a thousand miles an hour. The geography book at school was out of date; the countries of the world had changed. Frankie read the war news in the paper, but there were so many foreign places, and the war was happening so fast, that sometimes she did not understand. It was the summer when Patton was chasing the Germans across France. And they were fighting, too, in Russia and Saipan. She saw the battles, and the soldiers. But there were too many different battles, and she could not see in her mind the millions and millions of soldiers all at once. She saw one Russian soldier, dark and frozen with a frozen gun, in Russian snow. The single Japs with slanted eyes on a jungle island gliding among green vines. Europe and the people hung in trees and the battleships on the blue oceans. Four-motor planes and burning cities and a soldier in a steel war helmet, laughing. Sometimes these pictures of the war, the world, whirled in her mind and she was dizzy. A long time ago she had predicted that it would take two months to win the whole war, but now she did not know. She wanted to be a boy and go to the war as a Marine. She thought about flying aeroplanes and winning gold medals for bravery. But she could not join the war, and this made her sometimes feel restless and blue. She decided to donate blood to the Red Cross; she wanted to donate a quart a week and her blood would be in the veins of Australians and Fighting French and Chinese, all over the whole world, and it would be as though she were close kin to all of these people. She could hear the army doctors saying that the blood of Frankie Addams was the reddest and the strongest blood that they had ever known. And she could picture ahead, in the years after the war, meeting the soldiers who had her blood, and they would say that they owed their life to her; and they would not call her Frankie — they would call her Addams. But this plan for donating her blood to the war did not come true. The Red Cross would not take her blood. She was too young. Frankie felt mad with the Red Cross, and left out of everything. The war and the world were too fast and big and strange. To think about the world for very long made her afraid. She was not afraid of Germans or bombs or Japanese. She was afraid because in the war they would not include her, and because the world seemed somehow separate from herself.

So she knew she ought to leave the town and go to some place far away. For the late spring, that year, was lazy and too sweet. The long afternoons flowered and lasted and the green sweetness sickened her. The town began to hurt Frankie. Sad and terrible happenings had never made Frankie cry, but this season many things made Frankie suddenly wish to cry. Very early in the morning she would sometimes go out into the yard and stand for a long time looking at the sunrise sky. And it was as though a question came into her heart, and the sky did not answer. Things she had never noticed much before began to hurt her: home lights watched from the evening sidewalks, an unknown voice from an alley. She would stare at the lights and listen to the voice, and something inside her stiffened and waited. But the lights would darken, the voice fall silent, and though she waited, that was all. She was afraid of these things that made her suddenly wonder who she was, and what she was going to be in the world, and why she was standing at that minute, seeing a light, or listening, or staring up into the sky: alone. She was afraid, and there was a queer tightness in her chest.

One night in April, when she and her father were going to bed, he looked at her and said, all of a sudden: "Who is this great big long-legged twelve-year-old blunderbuss who still wants to sleep with her old Papa." And she was too big to sleep with her father any more. She had to sleep in her upstairs room alone. She began to have a grudge against her father and they looked at each other in a slant-eyed way. She did not like to stay at home.

She went around town, and the things she saw and heard seemed to be left somehow unfinished, and there was the tightness in her that would not break. She would hurry to do something, but what she did was always wrong. She would call her best friend, Evelyn Owen, who owned a football suit and a Spanish shawl, and one would dress in the football suit and the other in the Spanish shawl and they would go down to the ten-cent store together. But that was a wrong thing and not what Frankie wanted. Or after the pale spring twilights, with the smell of dust and flowers sweet and bitter in the air, evenings of lighted windows and the long drawn calls at supper time, when the chimney swifts had gathered and whirled above the town and flown off somewhere to their home together, leaving the sky empty and wide; after the long twilights of this season, when Frankie had walked around the sidewalks of the town, a jazz sadness quivered her nerves and her heart stiffened and almost stopped.

Because she could not break this tightness gathering within her, she would hurry to do something. She would go home and put the coal scuttle on her head, like a crazy person's hat, and walk around the kitchen table. She would do anything that suddenly occurred to her — but whatever she did was always wrong, and not at all what she had wanted. Then, having done these wrong and silly things, she would stand, sickened and empty, in the kitchen door and say:

"I just wish I could tear down this whole town."

"Well, tear it down, then. But quit hanging around here with that gloomy face. Do something."

And finally the troubles started.

She did things and she got herself in trouble. She broke the law. And having once become a criminal, she broke the law again, and then again. She took the pistol from her father's bureau drawer and carried it all over town and shot up the cartridges in a vacant lot. She changed into a robber and stole a three-way knife from the Sears and Roebuck Store. One Saturday afternoon in May she committed a secret and unknown sin. In the MacKeans' garage, with Barney MacKean, they committed a queer sin, and how bad it was she did not know. The sin made a shriveling sickness in her stomach, and she dreaded the eyes of everyone. She hated Barney and wanted to kill him. Sometimes alone in the bed at night she planned to shoot him with the pistol or throw a knife between his eyes.

Her best friend, Evelyn Owen, moved away to Florida, and Frankie did not play with anybody any more. The long and flowering spring was over and the summer in the town was ugly and lonesome and very hot. Every day she wanted more and more to leave the town: to light out for South America or Hollywood or New York City. But although she packed her suitcase many times, she could never decide to which of these places she ought to go, or how she would get there by herself.

So she stayed home and hung around the kitchen, and the summer did not end. By dog days she was five feet five and three-quarter inches tall, a great big greedy loafer who was too mean to live. She was afraid, but not as she had been before. There was only the fear of Barney, her father, and the Law. But even these fears were finally gone; after a long time the sin in the MacKeans' garage became far from her and was remembered only in her dreams. And she would not think of her father or the Law. She stuck close in the kitchen with John Henry and Berenice. She did not think about the war, the world. Nothing hurt her any longer; she did not care. She never stood alone in the back yard in order to stare up at the sky. She paid no attention to sounds and summer voices, and did not walk the streets of town at night. She would not let things make her sad and she would not care. She ate and wrote shows and practiced throwing knives against the side of the garage and played bridge at the kitchen table. Each day was like the day before, except that it was longer, and nothing hurt her any more.

So that Friday when it happened, when her brother and the bride came to the house, Frankie knew that everything was changed; but why this was so, and what would happen to her next, she did not know. And though she tried to talk with Berenice, Berenice did not know either.

"It gives me this kind of pain," she said, "to think about them."

"Well, don't," said Berenice. "You done nothing but think and carry on about them all this afternoon."

Frankie sat on the bottom step of the stairs to her room, staring into the kitchen. But although it gave her a kind of a pain, she had to think about the wedding. She remembered the way her brother and the bride had looked when she walked into the living room, that morning at eleven o'clock. There had been in the house a sudden silence, for Jarvis had turned off the radio when they came in; after the long summer, when the radio had gone on day and night, so that no one heard it any more, the curious silence had startled Frankie. She stood in the doorway, coming from the hall, and the first sight of her brother and the bride had shocked her heart. Together they made in her this feeling that she could not name. But it was like the feelings of the spring, only more sudden and more sharp. There was the same tightness and in the same queer way she was afraid. Frankie thought until her mind was dizzy and her foot had gone to sleep.

Then she asked Berenice: "How old were you when you married your first husband?"

While Frankie was thinking, Berenice had changed into her Sunday clothes, and now she sat reading a magazine. She was waiting for the people who were due to meet her at six o'clock, Honey and T. T. Williams; the three of them were going to eat supper at the New Metropolitan Tea Room and sashay together around the town. As Berenice read, she moved her lips to shape each word. Her dark eye looked up as Frankie spoke, but, since Berenice did not raise her head, the blue glass eye seemed to go on reading the magazine. This two-sighted expression bothered Frankie.

"I were thirteen years old," said Berenice.

"What made you get married so young for?"

"Because I wanted to," said Berenice. "I were thirteen years old and I haven't growed a inch since."

Berenice was very short, and Frankie looked hard at her and asked: "Does marrying really stop your growth?"

"It certainy do," said Berenice.

"I didn't know that," Frankie said.

Berenice had been married four different times. Her first husband was Ludie Freeman, a brickmason, and the favorite and best one of the four; he gave Berenice her fox fur, and once they had gone to Cincinnati and seen snow. Berenice and Ludie Freeman had seen a whole winter of Northern snow. They loved each other and were married for nine years, until the November he was sick and died. The other three husbands were all bad, each one worse than the one before, and it made Frankie blue just to hear about them. The first was a sorry old liquor-drinker. The next went crazy on Berenice: he did crazy things, had eating dreams in the night and swallowed a corner of the sheet; and what with one thing and another he distracted Berenice so much that finally she had to quit him. The last husband was terrible. He gouged out Berenice's eye and stole her furniture away from her. She had to call the Law on him.

"Did you marry with a veil every time?" asked Frankie.

"Two times with a veil," said Berenice.

Frankie could not keep still. She walked around the kitchen, although there was a splinter in her right foot and she was limping, her thumbs hooked in the belt of her shorts and her undershirt clinging and wet.

Finally she opened the drawer of the kitchen table and selected a long sharp butcher knife. Then she sat down and rested the ankle of her sore foot on her left knee. The sole of her foot was long and narrow, pitted with ragged whitish scars, as every summer Frankie stepped on many nails; Frankie had the toughest feet in town. She could slice off waxy yellow rinds from the bottoms of her feet, and it did not hurt her very much, although it would hurt other people. But she did not chisel for the splinter immediately — she just sat there, her ankle on her knee and the knife in her right hand, looking across the table at Berenice.

"Tell me," she said. "Tell me exactly how it was."

"You know!" said Berenice. "You seen them."

"But tell me," Frankie said.

"I will discuss it for the last time," said Berenice. "Your brother and the bride come late this morning and you and John Henry hurried in from the back yard to see them. The next thing I realize you busted back through the kitchen and run up to your room. You came down with your organdie dress on and lipstick a inch thick from one ear to the next. Then you all just sat around up in the living room.

It was hot. Jarvis had brought Mr. Addams a bottle of whiskey and they had liquor drinks and you and John Henry had lemonade. Then after dinner your brother and the bride took the three-o'clock train back to Winter Hill. The wedding will be this coming Sunday. And that is all. Now, is you satisfied?"

"I am so disappointed they couldn't stay longer — at least spend the night. After Jarvis being away so long. But I guess they want to be together as long as they can. Jarvis said he had some army papers to fill out at Winter Hill." She took a deep breath. "I wonder where they will go after the wedding."

"On their honeymoon. Your brother will have a few days' leave."

"I wonder where that honeymoon will be."

"Well, I'm sure I don't know."

"Tell me," Frankie said again. "Exactly what did they look like?"

"Look like?" said Berenice. "Why, they looked natural. Your brother is a good-looking blond white boy. And the girl is kind of brunette and small and pretty. They make a nice white couple. You seen them, Foolish."

Frankie closed her eyes, and, though she did not see them as a picture, she could feel them leaving her. She could feel the two of them together on the train, riding and riding away from her. They were them, and leaving her, and she was her, and sitting left all by herself there at the kitchen table. But a part of her was with them, and she could feel this part of her own self going away, and farther away; farther and farther, so that a drawn-out sickness came in her, going away and farther away, so that the kitchen Frankie was an old hull left there at the table.

"It is so queer," she said.

She bent over the sole of her foot, and there was something wet, like tears or sweat drops on her face; she sniffled and began to cut for the splinter.

"Don't that hurt you none?" asked Berenice.

Frankie shook her head and did not answer. Then after a moment she said: "Have you ever seen any people that afterward you remembered more like a feeling than a picture?"

"How you mean?"

"I mean this," said Frankie slowly. "I saw them O.K. Janice had on a green dress and green high-heel dainty shoes. Her hair was done up in a knot. Dark hair and a little piece of it was loose. Jarvis sat by her on the sofa. He had on his brown uniform and he was sunburned and very clean. They were the two prettiest people I ever saw. Yet it was like I couldn't see all of them I wanted to see. My brains couldn't gather together quick enough and take it all in. And then they were gone. You see what I mean?"

"You hurting yourself," said Berenice. "What you need is a needle."

"I don't care anything about my old feet," Frankie said.

It was only half-past six, and the minutes of the afternoon were like bright mirrors. From outside there was no longer the sound of whistling and in the kitchen nothing moved. Frankie sat facing the door that opened onto the back porch. There was a square cat-hole cut in a corner of the back door, and near-by a saucer of lavender sour milk. In the beginning of dog days Frankie's cat had gone away. And the season of dog days is like this: it is the time at the end of the summer when as a rule nothing can happen — but if a change does come about, that change remains until dog days are over. Things that are done are not undone and a mistake once made is not corrected.

That August Berenice scratched a mosquito bite under her right arm and it became a sore: that sore would never heal until dog days were over. Two little families of August gnats picked out the corners of John Henry's eyes to settle down in, and though he often shook himself and blinked, those gnats were there to stay. Then Charles disappeared. Frankie did not see him leave the house and walk away, but on the fourteenth of August, when she called him to his supper, he did not come, and he was gone. She looked for him everywhere and sent John Henry wailing out his name through all the streets of town. But it was the season of dog days and Charles did not come back again. Every afternoon Frankie said exactly the same words to Berenice, and the answers of Berenice were always the same. So that now the words were like an ugly little tune they sang by heart.

"If only I just knew where he has gone."

"Quit worrying yourself about that old alley cat. I done told you he ain't coming back."

"Charles is not alley. He is almost pure Persian."

"Persian as I is," Berenice would say. "You seen the last of that old tomcat. He gone off to hunt a friend."

"To hunt a friend?"

"Why, certainy. He roamed off to find himself a ladyfriend."

"You really think so?"

"Naturally."

"Well, why don't he bring his friend home with him. He ought to know I would be only too glad to have a whole family of cats."

"You seen the last of that old alley cat."

"If only I just knew where he is gone."

And so each gloomy afternoon their voices sawed against each other, saying the same words, which finally reminded Frankie of a raggedy rhyme said by two crazies. She would end by telling Berenice: "It looks to me like everything has just walked off and left me." And she would put her head down on the table and feel afraid.

But this afternoon Frankie suddenly changed all this. An idea came to her, and she put down the knife and got up from the table.

"I know what I ought to do," she suddenly said. "Listen."

"I can hear."

"I ought to notify the police force. They will find Charles."

"I wouldn't do that," said Berenice.

Frankie went to the hall telephone and explained to the Law about her cat. "He is almost pure Persian," she said. "But with short hair. A very lovely color of gray and with a little white spot on his throat. He answers to the name of *Charles,* but if he don't answer to that, he might come if you call *Charlina.* My name is Miss F. Jasmine Addams and the address is 124 Grove Street."

Berenice was giggling when she came back, a soft high giggle. "Whew! They going to send around here and tie you up and drag you off to Milledgeville. Them fat blue police chasing tomcats around alleys and hollering: *Oh Charles, Oh come here, Charlina!* Sweet Jesus!"

"Aw, shut up," Frankie said.

Berenice was sitting at the table; she had stopped giggling and her dark eye roved in a teasing way as she sloshed coffee into a white china saucer to cool.

"At the same time," she said, "I can't see how it is such a wise idea to trifle around with the Law. No matter for what reason."

"I'm not trifling with the Law."

"You just now set there and spelled them out your name and your house number. Where they can lay hold of you if ever they take the notion."

"Well, let them!" said Frankie angrily. "I don't care! I don't care!" And suddenly she did not care if anybody knew she was a criminal or not. "Let them come get me for all I care."

"I was just teasing you," said Berenice. "The trouble with you is that you don't have no sense of humor any more."

"Maybe I'd be better off in jail."

Frankie walked around the table and she could feel them going away. The train was traveling to the North. Mile after mile they went away, farther and farther away from the town, and as they traveled to the North, a coolness came into the air and dark was falling like the evening dark of wintertime. The train was winding up into the hills, the whistle wailing in a winter tone, and mile after mile they went away. They passed among themselves a box of bought store candy, with chocolates set in dainty, pleated shells, and watched the winter miles pass by the window. Now they had gone a long, long way from town and soon would be in Winter Hill.

"Sit down," said Berenice. "You make me nervous."

Suddenly Frankie began to laugh. She wiped her face with the back of her hand and went back to the table. "Did you hear what Jarvis said?"

"What?"

Frankie laughed and laughed.

"They were talking about whether to vote for C. P. MacDonald. And Jarvis said: *Why, I wouldn't vote for that scoundrel if he was running to be the dog-catcher.* I never heard anything so witty in my life."

Berenice did not laugh. Her dark eye glanced down in a corner, quickly saw the joke, and then looked back at Frankie. Berenice wore her pink crepe dress and her hat with the pink plume was on the table. The blue glass eye made the sweat on her dark face look bluish also. Berenice was stroking the hat plume with her hand.

"And you know what Janice remarked?" asked Frankie. "When Papa mentioned about how much I've grown, she said she didn't think I looked so terribly big. She said she got the major portion of her growth before she was thirteen. She did, Berenice!"

"O.K.! All right."

"She said she thought I was a lovely size and would probably not grow any taller. She said all fashion models and movie stars —"

"She did not," said Berenice. "I heard her. She only remarked that you probably had already got your growth. But she didn't go on and on like that. To hear you tell it, anybody would think she took her text on the subject."

"She said —"

"This is a serious fault with you, Frankie. Somebody just makes a loose remark and then you cozen it in your mind until nobody would recognize it. Your Aunt Pet happened to mention to Clorina that you had sweet manners and Clorina passed it on to you. For what it was worth. Then next thing I know you are going all around and bragging how Mrs. West thought you had the finest manners in town and ought to go to Hollywood, and I don't know what all you didn't say. You keep building on to any little compliment you hear about yourself. Or, if it is a bad thing, you do the same. You cozen and change things too much in your own mind. And that is a serious fault."

"Quit preaching at me," Frankie said.

"I ain't preaching. It is the solemn truth."

"I admit it a little," said Frankie finally. She closed her eyes and the kitchen was very quiet. She could feel the beating of her heart, and when she spoke her voice was a whisper. "What I need to know is this. Do you think I made a good impression?"

"Impression? Impression?"

"Yes," said Frankie, her eyes still closed.

"Well, how would I know?" said Berenice.

"I mean how did I act? What did I do?"

"Why, you didn't do anything."

"Nothing?" asked Frankie.

"No. You just watched the pair of them like they was ghosts. Then, when they talked about the wedding, them ears of yours stiffened out the size of cabbage leaves — "

Frankie raised her hand to her left ear. "They didn't," she said bitterly. Then after a while she added, "Some day you going to look down and find that big fat tongue of yours pulled out by the roots and laying there before you on the table. Then how do you think you will feel?"

"Quit talking so rude," said Berenice.

Frankie scowled down at the splinter in her foot. She finished cutting it out with the knife and said, "That would have hurt anybody else but me." Then she was walking round and round the room again. "I am so scared I didn't make a good impression."

"What of it?" said Berenice. "I wish Honey and T.T. would come on. You make me nervous."

Frankie drew up her left shoulder and bit her lower lip. Then suddenly she sat down and banged her forehead on the table.

"Come on," said Berenice. "Don't act like that."

But Frankie sat stiff, her face in the crook of her elbow and her fists clenched tight. Her voice had a ragged and strangled sound. "They were so pretty," she was saying. "They must have such a good time. And they went away and left me."

"Sit up," said Berenice. "Behave yourself."

"They came and went away," she said. "They went away and left me with this feeling."

"Hooee!" said Berenice finally. "I bet I know something."

The kitchen was silent and she tapped four times with her heel: one, two, three — *bang!* Her live eye was dark and teasing and she tapped with her heel, then took up the beating with a dark jazz voice that was like a song.

Frankie got a crush!
Frankie got a crush!
Frankie got a crush!
On the *Wedd*-ing!

"Quit," said Frankie.

Frankie got a crush!
Frankie got a crush!

Berenice went on and on, and her voice was jazzed like the heart that beats in your head when you have fever. Frankie was dizzy, and she picked up the knife from the kitchen table.

"You better quit!"

Berenice stopped very suddenly. The kitchen was suddenly shrunken and quiet.

"You lay down that knife."

"Make me."

She steadied the end of the handle against her palm and bent the blade slowly. The knife was limber, sharp, and long.

"Lay it down, DEVIL!"

But Frankie stood up and took careful aim. Her eyes were narrowed and the feel of the knife made her hands stop trembling.

"Just throw it!" said Berenice. "You just!"

All the house was very quiet. The empty house seemed to be waiting. And then there was the knife whistle in the air and the sound the blade made when it struck. The knife hit the middle of the stairway door and shivered there. She watched the knife until it did not shiver any longer.

"I am the best knife-thrower in this town," she said.

Berenice, who stood behind her, did not speak.

"If they would have a contest I would win."

Frankie pulled the knife from the door and laid it on the kitchen table. Then she spat on her palm and rubbed her hands together.

Berenice said finally: "Frances Addams, you going to do that once too often."

"I never miss outside of a few inches."

"You know what your father said about knife-throwing in this house."

"I warned you to quit picking with me."

"You are not fit to live in a house," said Berenice.

"I won't be living in this one much longer. I'm going to run away from home."

"And a good riddance to a big old bad rubbage," said Berenice.

"You wait and see. I'm leaving town."

"And where you think you are going?"

Frankie looked at all the corners of the room, and then said, ""I don't know."

"I do," said Berenice. "You going crazy. That's where you going."

"No," said Frankie. She stood very still, looking around the queerly pictured wall, and then she closed her eyes. "I'm going to Winter Hill. I'm going to the wedding. And I swear to Jesus by my two eyes I'm never coming back here any more."

She had not been sure that she would throw the knife until it struck and shivered on the stairway door. And she had not known that she would say these words until already they were spoken. The swear was like the sudden knife; she felt it strike in her and tremble. Then when the words were quiet, she said again:

"After the wedding I'm not coming back."

Berenice pushed back the damp bangs of Frankie's hair and finally she asked: "Sugar? You serious?"

"Of course!" said Frankie. "Do you think I would stand here and swear that swear and tell a story? Sometimes, Berenice, I think it takes you longer to realize a fact than it does anybody who ever lived."

"But," said Berenice, "you say you don't know where you're going. You going, but you don't know where. That don't make no sense to me."

Frankie stood looking up and down the four walls of the room. She thought of the world, and it was fast and loose and turning, faster and looser and and bigger than ever it had been before. The pictures of the war sprang out and clashed together in her mind. She saw bright flowered islands and a land by a northern sea with the gray waves on the shore. Bombed eyes and the shuffle of soldiers' feet. Tanks and a plane, wing broken, burning and downward-falling in a desert sky. The world was cracked by the loud battles and turning a thousand miles a minute. The names of places spun in Frankie's mind: China, Peachville, New Zealand, Paris, Cincinnati, Rome. She thought of the huge and turning world until her legs began to tremble and there was sweat on the palms of her hands. But still she did not know where she should go. Finally she stopped looking around the four kitchen walls and said to Berenice:

"I feel just exactly like somebody has peeled all the skin off me. I wish I had some cold good chocolate ice cream."

Berenice had her hands on Frankie's shoulders and was shaking her head and staring with the live eye narrowed into Frankie's face.

"But every word I told you was the solemn truth," she said. "I'm not coming back here after the wedding."

There was a sound, and when they turned they saw that Honey and T. T. Williams were standing in the doorway. Honey, though he was her foster brother, did not resemble Berenice — and it was almost as though he came from some foreign country, like Cuba or Mexico. He was light-skinned, almost lavender in color, with quiet narrow eyes like oil, and a limber body. Behind him stood T. T. Williams, and he was very big and black; he was gray-haired, older even than Berenice, and he wore a church suit with a red badge in the buttonhole. T. T. Williams was a beau of Berenice, a well-off colored man who owned a colored restaurant. Honey was a sick, loose person. The army would not include him, and he had shoveled in a gravel pit until he broke one of his insides and could not do heavy work any more. They stood dark and grouped together in the door.

"What you all creep up like that for?" asked Berenice. "I didn't even hear you."

"You and Frankie too busy discussing something," said T.T.

"I am ready to go," said Berenice. "I been ready. But do you wish a small little quickie before we start?"

T. T. Williams looked at Frankie and shuffled his feet. He was very proper, and he liked to please everybody, and he always wanted to do the right thing.

"Frankie ain't no tattle-tale," said Berenice. "Is you?"

Frankie would not even answer such a question. Honey wore a dark red rayon slack suit and she said: "That sure is a cute suit you got on, Honey. Where did you get it?"

Honey could talk like a white school-teacher; his lavender lips could move as quick and light as butterflies. But he only answered with a colored word, a dark sound from the throat that can mean anything. "Ahhnnh," he said.

The glasses were before them on the table, and the hair-straightening bottle that held gin, but they did not drink. Berenice said something about Paris and Frankie had the extra feeling that they were waiting for her to leave. She stood in the door and looked at them. She did not want to go away.

"You wish water in yours, T.T.?" asked Berenice.

They were together around the table and Frankie stood extra in the door alone. "So long, you all," she said.

" 'Bye Sugar," said Berenice. "You forget all that foolishness we was discussing. And if Mr. Addams don't come home by dark, you go on over to the Wests'. Go play with John Henry."

"Since when have I been scared of the dark?" said Frankie. "So long."

"So long," they said.

She closed the door, but behind her she could hear their voices. With her head against the kitchen door she could hear the murmuring dark sounds that rose and fell in a gentle way. Ayee—ayee. And then Honey spoke above the idle wash of voices and he asked: "What was it between you and Frankie when we come in the house?" She waited, her ear pressed close against the door, to hear what Berenice would say. And finally the words were: "Just foolishness. Frankie was carrying on with foolishness." She listened until at last she heard them go away.

The empty house was darkening. She and her father were alone at night, as Berenice went to her own home directly after supper. Once they had rented the front bedroom. It was the year after her grandmother died, when Frankie was nine. They rented the front bedroom to Mr. and Mrs. Marlowe. The only thing Frankie remembered about them was the remark said at the last, that they were common people. Yet for the season they were there, Frankie was fascinated by Mr. and Mrs. Marlowe and the front room. She loved to go in when they were away and carefully, lightly meddle with their things — with Mrs. Marlowe's atomizer which skeeted perfume, the gray-pink powder puff, the wooden shoe-trees of Mr. Marlowe. They left mysteriously after an afternoon that Frankie did not understand. It was a summer Sunday and the hall door of the Marlowes' room was open. She could see only a portion of the room, part of the dresser and only the footpiece of the bed with Mrs. Marlowe's corset on it. But there was a sound in the quiet room she could not place, and when she stepped over the threshold she was startled by a sight that, after a single glance, sent her running to the kitchen, crying: Mr. Marlowe is having a fit! Berenice had hurried through the hall, but when she looked into the front room, she merely bunched her lips and banged the door. And evidently told her father, for that evening he said the Marlowes would have to leave. Frankie had tried to question Berenice and find out what was the matter. But Berenice had only said that they were common people and added that with a certain party in the house they ought at least to know enough to shut a door. Though Frankie knew she was the certain party, still she did not understand. What kind of a fit was it? she asked. But Berenice would only answer: Baby, just a common fit. And Frankie knew from the voice's tones that there was more to it than she was told. Later she only remembered the Marlowes as common people, and being common they owned common things — so that long after she had ceased to think about the Marlowes or fits, remembering merely the name and the fact that once they had rented the front bedroom, she associated common people with gray-pink powder puffs and perfume atomizers. The front bedroom had not been rented since.

Frankie went to the hall hatrack and put on one of her father's hats. She looked at her dark ugly mug in the mirror. The conversation about the wedding had somehow been wrong. The questions she had asked that afternoon had all been the wrong questions, and Berenice had answered her with jokes. She could not name the feeling in her, and she stood there until dark shadows made her think of ghosts.

Frankie went out to the street before the house and looked up into the sky. She stood staring with her fist on her hip and her mouth open. The sky was lavender and slowly darkening. She heard in the neighborhood the sound of evening voices and noticed the light fresh smell of watered grass. This was the time of the early evening when, since the kitchen was too hot, she would go for a little while outdoors. She practiced knife-throwing, or sat before the cold-drink store in the front yard. Or she would go around to the back yard, and there the arbor was cool and dark. She wrote shows, although she had outgrown all of her costumes, and was too big to act in them beneath the arbor; this summer she had written very cold shows — shows about Esquimaux and frozen explorers. Then when night had come she would go again back in the house.

But this evening Frankie did not have her mind on knives or cold-drink stores or shows. Nor did she want to stand there staring up into the sky; for her heart asked the old questions, and in the old way of the spring she was afraid.

She felt she needed to think about something ugly and plain, so she turned from the evening sky and stared at her own house. Frankie lived in the ugliest house in town, but now she knew that she would not be living there much longer. The house was empty, dark. Frankie turned and walked to the end of the block, and around the corner, and down the sidewalk to the Wests'. John Henry was leaning against the banisters of his front porch, with a lighted window behind him, so that he looked like a little black paper doll on a piece of yellow paper.

"Hey," she said. "I wonder when that Papa of mine is coming home from town."

John Henry did not answer.

"I don't want to go back in that dark old ugly house all by myself."

She stood on the sidewalk, looking at John Henry, and the smart political remark came back to her. She hooked her thumb in the pocket of her pants and asked: "If you were going to vote in an election, who would you vote for?"

John Henry's voice was bright and high in the summer night. "I don't know," he said.

"For instance, would you cast your vote for C. P. MacDonald to be mayor of this town?"

John Henry did not answer.

"Would you?"

But she could not get him to talk. There were times when John Henry would not answer anything you said to him. So she had to remark without an argument behind her, and all by herself like that it did not sound so very smart: "Why, I wouldn't vote for him if he was running to be dog-catcher."

The darkening town was very quiet. For a long time now her brother and the bride had been at Winter Hill. They had left the town a hundred miles behind them, and now were in a city far away. They were them and in Winter Hill, together, while she was her and in the same old town all by herself. The long hundred miles did not make her sadder and make her feel more far away than the knowing that they were them and both together and she was only her and parted from them, by herself. And as she sickened with this feeling a thought and explanation suddenly came to her, so that she knew and almost said aloud: *They are the we of me.* Yesterday, and all the twelve years of her life, she had only been Frankie. She was an *I* person who had to walk around and do things by herself. All other people had a *we* to claim, all others except her. When Berenice said *we,* she meant Honey and Big Mama, her lodge, or her church. The *we* of her father was the store. All members of clubs have a *we* to belong to and to talk about. The soldiers in the army can say *we*, and even the criminals on chain-gangs. But the old Frankie had had no *we* to claim, unless it would be the terrible summer *we* of her and John Henry and Berenice — and that was the last *we* in the world she wanted. Now all this was suddenly over with and changed. There was her brother and the bride, and it was as though when first she saw them something she had known inside of her: *They are the we of me.* And that was why it made her feel so queer, for them to be away in Winter Hill while she was left all by herself; the hull of the old Frankie left there in the town alone.

"Why are you all bent over like that?" John Henry said.

"I think I have a kind of pain," said Frankie. "I must have ate something."

John Henry was still standing on the banisters, holding to the post.

"Listen," she said finally. "Suppose you come on over and eat supper and spend the night with me."

"I can't," he answered.

"Why?"

John Henry walked across the banisters, holding out his arms for balance, so that he was like a little blackbird against the yellow window light. He did not answer until he safely reached the other post.

"Just because."

"Because why?"

He did not say anything, and so she added: "I thought maybe me and you could put up my Indian tepee and sleep out in the back yard. And have a good time."

Still John Henry did not speak.

"We're blood first cousins. I entertain you all the time. I've given you so many presents."

Quietly, lightly, John Henry walked back across the banisters and then stood looking out at her with his arm around the post again.

"Sure enough," she called. "Why can't you come?"

At last he said, "Because, Frankie, I don't want to."

"Fool jackass!" she screamed. "I only asked you because I thought you looked so ugly and so lonesome."

Lightly John Henry jumped down from the banisters. And his voice as he called back to her was a clear child's voice.

"Why, I'm not a bit lonesome."

Frankie rubbed the wet palms of her hands along the sides of her shorts and said in her mind: Now turn around and take yourself on home. But in spite of this order, she was somehow unable to turn around and go. It was not yet night. Houses along the street were dark, lights showed in windows. Darkness had gathered in the thick-leaved trees and shapes in the distance were ragged and gray. But the night was not yet in the sky.

"I think something is wrong," she said. "It is too quiet. I have a peculiar warning in my bones. I bet you a hundred dollars it's going to storm."

John Henry watched her from behind the banister.

"A terrible terrible dog-day storm. Or maybe even a cyclone."

Frankie stood waiting for the night. And just at that moment a horn began to play. Somewhere in the town, not far away, a horn began a blues tune. The tune was grieving and low. It was the sad horn of some colored boy, but who he was she did not know. Frankie stood stiff, her head bent and her eyes closed, listening. There was something about the tune that brought back to her all of the spring: flowers, the eyes of strangers, rain.

The tune was low and dark and sad. Then all at once, as Frankie listened, the horn danced into a wild jazz spangle that zigzagged upward with sassy nigger trickiness. At the end of the jazz spangle the music rattled thin and far away. Then the tune returned to the first blues song, and it was like the telling of that long season of trouble. She stood there on the dark sidewalk and the drawn tightness of her heart made her knees lock and her throat feel stiffened. Then, without warning, the thing happened that at first Frankie could not believe. Just at the time when the tune should be laid, the music finished, the horn broke off. All of a sudden the horn stopped playing. For a moment Frankie could not take it in, she felt so lost.

She whispered finally to John Henry West: "He has stopped to bang the spit out of his horn. In a second he will finish."

But the music did not come again. The tune was left broken, unfinished. And the drawn tightness she could no longer stand. She felt she must do something wild and sudden that never had been done before. She hit herself on the head with her fist, but that did not help any at all. And she began to talk aloud, although at first she paid no attention to her own words and did not know in advance what she would say.

"I told Berenice that I was leaving town for good and she did not believe me. Sometimes I honestly think she is the biggest fool that ever drew breath." She complained aloud, and her voice was fringed and sharp like the edge of a saw. She talked and did not know from one word to the next what she would say. She listened to her own voice, but the words she heard did not make much sense. "You try to impress something on a big fool like that and it's just like talking to a block of cement. I kept on telling and telling and telling her. I told her I had to leave this town for good because it is inevitable."

She was not talking to John Henry. She did not see him any more. He had moved from the lighted window; but he was still listening from the porch, and after a little while he asked her:

"Where?"

Frankie did not answer. She was suddenly very still and quiet. For a new feeling had come to her. The sudden feeling was that she knew deep in her where she would go. She knew, and in another minute the name of the place would come to her. Frankie bit the knuckles of her fist and waited: but she did not hunt for the name of the place and did not think about the turning world. She saw in her mind her brother and the bride, and the heart in her was squeezed so hard that Frankie almost felt it break.

John Henry was asking in his high child voice: "You want me to eat supper and sleep in the tepee with you?"

She answered: "No."

"You just a little while ago invited me!"

But she could not argue with John Henry West or answer anything he said. For it was just at that moment that Frankie understood. She knew who she was and how she was going into the world. Her squeezed heart suddenly opened and divided. Her heart divided like two wings. And when she spoke her voice was sure.

"I know where I'm going," she said.

He asked her: "Where?"

"I'm going to Winter Hill," she said. "I'm going to the wedding."

She waited, to give him a chance to say: "I already knew that, anyhow." Then finally she spoke the sudden truth aloud.

"I'm going with them. After the wedding at Winter Hill, I'm going off with the two of them to whatever place that they will ever go. I'm going with them."

He did not answer.

"I love the two of them so much. We'll go to every place together. It's like I've known it all my life, that I belong to be with them. I love the two of them so much."

And having said this, she did not need to wonder and puzzle any more. She opened her eyes, and it was night. The lavender sky had at last grown dark and there was slanted starlight and twisted shade. Her heart had divided like two wings and she had never seen a night so beautiful.

Frankie stood looking into the sky. For when the old question came to her — the one who she was and what she would be in the world, and why she was standing there that minute — when the old question came to her, she did not feel hurt and unanswered. At last she knew just who she was and understood where she was going. She loved her brother and the bride and she was a member of the wedding. The three of them would go into the world and they would always be together. And finally, after the scared spring and the crazy summer, she was no more afraid.

Part Two

I

The day before the wedding was not like any day that F. Jasmine had ever known. It was the Saturday she went into the town, and suddenly, after the closed blank summer, the town opened before her and in a new way she belonged. Because of the wedding, F. Jasmine felt connected with all she saw, and it was as a sudden member that on this Saturday she went around the town. She walked the streets entitled as a queen and mingled everywhere. It was the day when, from the beginning, the world seemed no longer separate from herself and when all at once she felt included. Therefore, many things began to happen — nothing that came about surprised F. Jasmine and, until the last at least, all was natural in a magic way.

At the country house of an uncle of John Henry, Uncle Charles, she had seen old blindered mules going round and round in the same circle, grinding juice from the sugar cane for syrup. In the sameness of her tracks that summer, the old Frankie had somehow resembled that country mule; in town she browsed around the counters of the ten-cent store, or sat on the front row of the Palace show, or hung around her father's store, or stood on street corners watching soldiers. Now this morning was altogether different. She went into places she had never dreamed of entering until that day. For one thing, F. Jasmine went to a hotel — it was not the finest hotel in the town, or even the next to the finest, but nevertheless it was a hotel and F.

Jasmine was there. Furthermore, she was there with a soldier, and that, too, was an unforeseen event, as she had never in her life laid eyes on him until that day. Only yesterday, if the old Frankie had glimpsed a box-like vision of this scene, as a view seen through a wizard's periscope, she would have bunched her mouth with unbelief. But it was a morning when many things occurred, and a curious fact about this day was a twisted sense of the astonishing; the unexpected did not make her wonder, and only the long known, the familiar, struck her with a strange surprise.

The day began when she waked up at dawn, and it was as though her brother and the bride had, in the night, slept on the bottom of her heart, so that the first instant she recognized the wedding. Next, and immediately, she thought about the town. Now that she was leaving home she felt in a curious way as though on this last day the town called to her and was now waiting. The windows of her room were cool dawn-blue. The old cock at the MacKeans' was crowing. Quickly she got up and turned on the bed-lamp and the motor.

It was the old Frankie of yesterday who had been puzzled, but F. Jasmine did not wonder any more; already she felt familiar with the wedding for a long, long time. The black dividing night had something to do with this. In the twelve years before, whenever a sudden change had come about there was a certain doubt during the time when it was happening; but after sleeping through a night, and on the very next day, the change did not seem so sudden after all. Two summers past, when she had traveled with the Wests to Port Saint Peter on the bay, the first sea evening with the scalloped gray ocean and empty sand was to her like a foreign place, and she had gone around with slanted eyes and put her hands on things in doubt. But after the first night, as soon as she awoke next day, it was as though she had known Port Saint Peter all her life. Now it was likewise with the wedding. No longer questioning, she turned to other things.

She sat at her desk wearing only the blue-and-white striped trousers of her pajamas which were rolled up above the knees, vibrating her right foot on the ball of her bare foot, and considering all that she must do on this last day. Some of these things she could name to herself, but there were other things that could not be counted on her fingers or made into a list with words. To start with, she decided to make herself some visiting cards with *Miss F. Jasmine Addams, Esq.,* engraved with squinted letters on a tiny card. So she put on her green visor eyeshade, cut up some cardboard, and fitted ink pens behind both ears. But her mind was restless and zigzagged to other things, and soon she began to get ready for town. She dressed carefully that morning in her most grown and best, the pink organdie, and put on lipstick and Sweet Serenade. Her father, a very early riser, was stirring in the kitchen when she went downstairs.

"Good morning, Papa."

Her father was Royal Quincy Addams and he owned a jewelry store just off the main street of the town. He answered her with a kind of grunt, for he was a grown person who liked to drink three cups of coffee before he started conversation for the day; he deserved a little peace and quiet before he put his nose down to the grindstone. F. Jasmine had heard him bungling about his room when once she waked up to drink water in the night, and his face was pale as cheese this morning, his eyes had a pink and ragged look. It was a morning when he despised a saucer because his cup would rattle against it and not fit, so he put his cup down on the table or stove top until brown circles were left all over everywhere and flies settled in quiet rings. There was some sugar spilt on the floor, and each time his step made a gritty sound his face shivered. This morning he wore a pair of saggy-kneed gray trousers and a blue shirt unfastened at the collar and with the tie loose. Since June she had had this secret grudge against him that almost she did not admit — since the night he had asked her who was the great big blunderbuss who still wanted to sleep with her old Papa — but now she had this grudge no longer. All of a sudden it seemed to F. Jasmine that she saw her father for the first time, and she did not see him only as he was at that one minute, but pictures of the old days swirled in her mind and crossed each other. Remembrance, changing and fast, made F. Jasmine stop very still and stand with her head cocked, watching him both in the actual room and from somewhere inside her. But there were things that must be said, and when she spoke her voice was not unnatural.

"Papa, I think I ought to tell you now. I'm not coming back here after the wedding."

He had ears to hear with, loose large ears with lavender rims, but he did not listen. He was a widowman, for her mother had died the very day that she was born — and, as a widowman, set in his ways. Sometimes, especially in the early morning, he did not listen to things she said or new suggestions. So she sharpened her voice and chiseled the words into his head.

"I have to buy a wedding dress and some wedding shoes and a pair of pink, sheer stockings."

He heard and, after a consideration, gave her a permission nod. The grits boiled slowly with blue gluey bubbles, and as she set the table, she watched him and remembered. There were the winter mornings with frost flowers on the windowpanes and the roaring stove and the look of his brown crusty hand as he leaned over her shoulder to help with a hard part of the last-minute arithmetic that she was working at the table, his voice explaining. Blue long spring evenings, she saw also, and her father on the dark front porch with his feet propped on the banisters, drinking the frosted bottles of beer he had sent her to bring home from Finny's Place. She saw him bent over the workbench down at the store, dipping a tiny spring in gasoline, or whistling and peering with his round jeweler's glass into a watch. Remembrances came suddenly and swirled, each colored with its own season, and for the first time she looked back on all the twelve years of her life and thought of them from a distance as a whole.

"Papa," she said, "I will write you letters."

Now he walked the dawn-stale kitchen like a person who has lost something, but has forgotten what it is that he has lost. Watching him, the old grudge was forgotten, and she felt sorry. He would miss her in the house all by himself when she was gone. He would be lonesome. She wanted to speak some sorry words and love her father, but just at that moment he cleared his throat in the special way he used when he was going to lay down the law to her and said:

"Will you please tell me what has become of the monkey-wrench and screw-driver that were in my tool chest on the back porch?"

"The monkey-wrench and screw-driver —" F. Jasmine stood with her shoulders hunched, her left foot drawn up to the calf of the right leg. "I borrowed them, Papa."

"Where are they now?"

F. Jasmine considered. "Over at the Wests'."

"Now pay attention and listen to me," her father said, holding the spoon that had been stirring the grits, and shaking it to mark the words. "If you don't have the sense and judgment to leave things alone —" He stared at her in a long and threatening way, and finished: "You'll have to be taught. From now on you walk the chalkline. Or you'll have to be taught." He sniffed suddenly. "Is that toast burning?"

It was still early in the morning when F. Jasmine left the house that day. The soft gray of the dawn had lightened and the sky was the wet pale blue of a watercolor sky just painted and not yet dried. There was a freshness in the bright air and cool dew on the burnt brown grass. From a back yard down the street, F. Jasmine could hear children's voices. She heard the calling voices of the neighborhood children who were trying to dig a swimming pool. They were all sizes and ages, members of nothing, and in the summers before, the old Frankie had been like leader or president of the swimming-pool diggers in that part of town — but now that she was twelve years old, she knew in advance that, though they would work and dig in various yards, not doubting to the very last the cool clear swimming pool of water, it would all end in a big wide ditch of shallow mud.

Now, as F. Jasmine crossed her yard, she saw in her mind's eye the swarming children and heard from down the street their chanting cries — and this morning, for the first time in her life, she heard a sweetness in these sounds, and she was touched. And, strange to say, her own home yard which she had hated touched her a little too; she felt she had not seen it for a long time. There, under the elm tree was her old cold-drink store, a light packing case that could be dragged around according to the shade, with a sign reading, DEW DROP INN. It was the time of morning when, the lemonade in a bucket underneath the store, she used to settle herself with her bare feet on the counter and the Mexican hat tilted down over her face — her eyes closed, smelling the strong smell of sun-warmed straw, waiting. And sometimes there would be customers, and she would send John Henry to the A&P to buy some candy, but other times the Tempter Satan got the best of her and she drank up all the stock instead. But now this morning the store looked very small and staggered, and she knew that she would never run it any more. F. Jasmine thought of the whole idea as something over and done with that had happened long ago. A sudden plan came to her: after tomorrow, when she was with Janice and Jarvis, in the far place where they would be, she would look back on the old days and — But this was a plan F. Jasmine did not finish, for, as the names lingered in her mind, the gladness of the wedding rose up inside her and, although the day was an August day, she shivered.

The main street, too, seemed to F. Jasmine like a street returned to after many years, although she had walked up and down it only Wednesday. There were the same brick stores, about four blocks of them, the big white bank, and in the distance the many-windowed cotton mill. The wide street was divided by a narrow aisle of grass on either side of which the cars drove slowly in a browsing way. The glittering gray sidewalks and passing people, the striped awning over the stores, all was the same — yet, as she walked the street that morning, she felt free as a traveler who had never seen the town before.

And that was not all; she had no sooner walked down the left side of the main street and up again on the right sidewalk, when she realized a further happening. It had to do with various people, some known to her and others strangers, she met and passed along the street. An old colored man, stiff and proud on his rattling wagon seat, drove a sad blindered mule down toward the Saturday market. F. Jasmine looked at him, he looked at her, and to the outward appearance that was all. But in that glance, F. Jasmine felt between his eyes and her own eyes a new unnamable connection, as though they were known to each other — and there even came an instant vision of his home field and country roads and quiet dark pine trees as the wagon rattled past her on the paved town street. And she wanted him to know her, too — about the wedding.

Now the same thing happened again and again on those four blocks: with a lady going into MacDougal's store, with a small man waiting for the bus before the big First National Bank, with a friend of her father's called Tut Ryan. It was a feeling impossible to explain in words — and later when she tried to tell of it at home Berenice raised up her eyebrows and dragged the word in a mocking way: Connection? Connection? But nevertheless it was there, this feeling — a connection close as answers to calls. Furthermore, on the sidewalk before the First National Bank she found a dime and any other day that would have been a grand surprise, but now this morning she only paused to shine the dime on her dress front and put it in her pink pocketbook. Under the fresh blue early sky the feeling as she walked along was one of newly risen lightness, power, entitlement.

It was in a place called the Blue Moon that she first told about the wedding, and she came to the Blue Moon in a roundabout way, as it was not on the main street, but on the street called Front Avenue which bordered the river. She was in this neighborhood because she had heard the organ of the monkey and the monkey-man and had set out immediately to find them. She had not seen the monkey and the monkey-man through the whole summer and it seemed a sign to her that she should run across them on this last day in town. She had not seen them for so long that sometimes she thought the pair of them might even be dead. They did not go around the streets in wintertime, for the cold wind made them sick; they went South in October to Florida and came back to the town in warm late spring.

They, the monkey and the monkey-man, wandered to other towns also — but the old Frankie would come across them on various shaded streets through all the summers she could remember, except this one. He was a darling little monkey, and the monkey-man was nice also; the old Frankie had always loved them, and now she was dying to tell her plans and let them know about the wedding. So, when she first heard the broken-sounding, faint organ, she went at once in search of it, and the music seemed to come from near the river on Front Avenue. So she turned from the main street and hurried down the side street, but just before she reached Front Avenue the organ stopped, and when she gazed up and down the avenue she could not see the monkey or the monkey-man and all was silent and they were nowhere in sight. They had stopped, maybe, in a doorway or a shop — so F. Jasmine walked slowly with a watchful air.

Front Avenue was a street that had always drawn her, although it had the sorriest, smallest stores in town. On the left side of the street there were warehouses, and in between were glimpses of brown river and green trees. On the right side there was a place with a sign reading Prophylactic Military, the business of which had often puzzled her, then other various places: a smelly fish shop with the shocked eyes of a single fish staring from some crushed ice in the window, a pawnshop, a second-hand clothing store with out-of-style garments hanging from the narrow entrance and a row of broken shoes lined up on the sidewalk outside. Then finally there was the place called the Blue Moon. The street itself was cobbled with brick and angry-looking in the glare, and along the gutter she passed some eggshells and rotten lemon peels. It was not a fine street, but nevertheless the old Frankie had liked to come here now and then at certain times.

The street was quiet in the mornings and on the week-day afternoons. But toward evening, or on holidays, the street would fill with the soldiers who came from the camp nine miles away. They seemed to prefer Front Avenue to almost any other street, and sometimes the pavement resembled a flowing river of brown soldiers. They came to town on holidays and went around in glad, loud gangs together, or walked the sidewalks with grown girls. And the old Frankie had always watched them with a jealous heart; they came from all over the whole country and were soon going all over the world. They went around in gangs together, those lasting twilights of the summertime — while the old Frankie dressed in her khaki shorts and Mexican hat, watched from a distance by herself. Noises and weathers of distant places seemed to hover about them in the air. She imagined the many cities that these soldiers came from, and thought of the countries where they would go — while she was stuck there in the town forever. And stealing jealousy sickened her heart. But now this morning her heart was occupied with one intention: to tell of the wedding and her plans. So, after walking down the burning pavement, hunting for the monkey and the monkey-man, she came to the Blue Moon and it occurred to her that maybe they were there.

The Blue Moon was a place at the end of Front Avenue, and often the old Frankie had stood out on the sidewalk with her palms and nose pressed flat against the screen door, watching all that went on there. Customers, most of them soldiers, sat at the boothed tables, or stood at the counter having drinks, or crowded around the jukebox. Here sometimes there were sudden commotions. Late one afternoon when she passed the Blue Moon, she heard wild angry voices and a sound like a bottle being thrown, and as she stood there a policeman came out on the sidewalk pushing and jerking a torn-looking man with wobbly legs. The man was crying, shouting; there was blood on his ripped shirt and dirty tears dripped down his face. It was an April afternoon of rainbow showers, and by and by the Black Maria screamed down the street, and the poor, arrested criminal was thrown into the prisoners' cage and carried off down to the jail. The old Frankie knew the Blue Moon well, although she had never been inside. There was no written law to keep her out, no lock and chain on the screen door. But she had known in an unworded way that it was a forbidden place to children. The Blue Moon was a place for holiday soldiers and the grown and free. The old Frankie had known she had no valid right to enter there, so she had only hung around the edges and never once had she gone inside. But now this morning before the wedding all of this was changed. The old laws she had known before meant nothing to F. Jasmine, and without a second thought she left the street and went inside.

There in the Blue Moon was the red-headed soldier who was to weave in such an unexpected way through all that day before the wedding. F. Jasmine, however, did not notice him at first; she looked for the monkey-man, but he was not there. Aside from the soldier the only other person in the room was the Blue Moon owner, a Portuguese, who stood behind the counter. This was the person F. Jasmine picked to be the first to hear about the wedding, and he was chosen simply because he was the one most likely and near.

After the fresh brightness of the street, the Blue Moon seemed dark. Blue neon lights burned over the dim mirror behind the counter, tinting the faces in the place pale green, and an electric fan turned slowly so that the room was scalloped with warm stale waves of breeze. At that early morning hour the place was very quiet. There were booth tables across the room, all empty. At the back of the Blue Moon a lighted wooden stairway led up to the second floor. The place smelled of dead beer and morning coffee. F. Jasmine ordered coffee from the owner behind the counter, and after he had brought it to her, he sat down on a stool across from her. He was a sad, pale man with a very flat face. He wore a long white apron and, hunched on the stool with his feet on the rungs, he was reading a romance magazine. The telling of the wedding gathered inside her, and when it was so ready she could no longer resist, she hunted in her mind a good opening remark — something grown and off-hand, to start between them the conversation. She said in a voice that trembled a little: "It certainly has been an unseasonable summer, hasn't it?"

The Portuguese at first did not seem to hear her and went on reading the romance magazine. So she repeated her remark, and when his eyes were turned to hers and his attention caught, she went on in a higher voice: "Tomorrow this brother of mine and his bride are marrying at Winter Hill." She went straight to the story, as a circus dog breaks through the paper hoop, and as she talked, her voice became clearer; more definite, and sure. She told her plans in a way that made them sound completely settled, and not in the least open to question. The Portuguese listened with his head cocked to one side, his dark eyes ringed with ash-gray circles, and now and then he wiped his damp veined dead-white hands on his stained apron. She told about the wedding and her plans and he did not dispute with her or doubt.

It is far easier, it came to her as she remembered Berenice, to convince strangers of the coming to pass of dearest wants than those in your own home kitchen. The thrill of speaking certain words — Jarvis and Janice, wedding and Winter Hill — was such that F. Jasmine, when she had finished, wanted to start all over again. The Portuguese took from behind his ear a cigarette which he tapped on the counter but did not light. In the unnatural neon glow his face looked startled, and when she had finished he did not speak. With the telling of the wedding still sounding inside her, as the last chord of a guitar murmurs a long time after the strings are struck, F. Jasmine turned toward the entrance and the framed blazing street beyond the door: dark people passed along the sidewalk and footsteps echoed in the Blue Moon.

"It gives me a funny feeling," she said. "After living in this town all my whole life, to know that after tomorrow I'll never be back here any more."

It was then she noticed him for the first time, the soldier who at the very end would twist so strangely that last, long day. Later, on thinking back, she tried to recall some warning hint of future craziness — but at the time he looked to her like any other soldier standing at a counter drinking beer. He was not tall, nor short, nor fat, nor thin — except for the red hair there was nothing at all unusual about him. He was one of the thousands of soldiers who came to the town from the camp near-by. But as she looked into this soldier's eyes, in the dim light of the Blue Moon, she realized that she gazed at him in a new way.

That morning, for the first time, F. Jasmine was not jealous. He might have come from New York or California — but she did not envy him. He might be on his way to England or India — she was not jealous. In the restless spring and crazy summer, she had watched the soldiers with a sickened heart, for they were the ones who came and went, while she was stuck there in the town forever. But now, on this day before the wedding, all this was changed; her eyes as she looked into the soldier's eyes were clear of jealousy and want. Not only did she feel that unexplainable connection she was to feel between herself and other total strangers of that day, there was another sense of recognition: it seemed to F. Jasmine they exchanged the special look of friendly, free travelers who meet for a moment at some stop along the way. The look was long. And with the lifting of the jealous weight, F. Jasmine felt at peace. It was quiet in the Blue Moon, and the telling of the wedding seemed still to murmur in the room. After this long gaze of fellow travelers, it was the soldier who finally turned his face away.

"Yes," said F. Jasmine, after a moment and to no one in particular, "it gives me a mighty funny feeling. In a way it's like I ought to do all the things I would have done if I was staying in the town forever. Instead of this one day. So I guess I better get a move on. Adios." She spoke the last word to the Portuguese, and at the same time her hand reached automatically to lift the Mexican hat she had worn all summer until that day, but, finding nothing, the gesture withered and her hand felt shamed. Quickly she scratched her head, and with a last glance at the soldier, left the Blue Moon.

It was the morning different from all other mornings she had ever known because of several reasons. First, of course, there was the telling of the wedding. Once, and a long time ago, the old Frankie had liked to go around the town playing a game. She had walked all around — through the north side of town with the grass-lawned houses and the sad mills section and colored Sugarville — wearing her Mexican hat and the high-laced boots and a cowboy rope tied round her waist, she had gone around pretending to be Mexican. Me no speak English — Adios Buenos Noches — abla pokie peekie poo, she had jabbered in mock Mexican. Sometimes a little crowd of children gathered and the old Frankie would swell up with pride and trickery — but when the game was over, and she was home, there would come over her a cheated discontent. Now this morning reminded her of those old days of the Mexican game. She went to the same places, and the people, mostly strangers to her, were the same. But this morning she was not trying to trick people and pretend; far from it, she wanted only to be recognized for her true self. It was a need so strong, this want to be known and recognized, that F. Jasmine forgot the wild hard glare and choking dust and miles (it must have been at least five miles) of wandering all over town.

A second fact about that day was the forgotten music that sprang suddenly into her mind — snatches of orchestra minuets, march tunes and waltzes, and the jazz horn of Honey Brown — so that her feet in the patent-leather shoes stepped always according to a tune. A last difference about that morning was the way her world seemed layered in three different parts, all the twelve years of the old Frankie, the present day itself, and the future ahead when the J A three of them would be together in all the many distant places.

As she walked along, it seemed as though the ghost of the old Frankie, dirty and hungry-eyed, trudged silently along not far from her, and the thought of the future, after the wedding, was constant as the very sky. That day alone seemed equally important as both the long past and the bright future — as a hinge is important to a swinging door. And since it was the day when past and future mingled, F. Jasmine did not wonder that it was strange and long. So these were the main reasons why F. Jasmine felt, in an unworded way, that this was a morning different from all mornings she had ever known. And of all these facts and feelings the strongest of all was the need to be known for her true self and recognized.

Along the shaded sidewalks on the north side of the town, near the main street, she passed a row of lace-curtained boarding houses with empty chairs behind the banisters until she came upon a lady sweeping her front porch. To this lady, after the opening remark about the weather, F. Jasmine told her plans and, as with the Portuguese in the Blue Moon café and all the other people she was to meet that day, the telling of the wedding had an end and a beginning, a shape like a song.

First, just at the moment she commenced, a sudden hush came in her heart; then, as the names were named and the plan unfolded, there was a wild rising lightness and at the end content. The lady meanwhile leaned on the broom, listening. Behind her there was a dark open hall, with a bare stairway, and to the left a table for letters, and from this dark hall came the strong hot smell of cooking turnip greens. The strong waves of smell and the dark hall seemed to mingle with F. Jasmine's joy, and when she looked into the lady's eyes, she loved her, though she did not even know her name.

The lady neither argued nor accused. She did not say anything. Until at the very end, just as F. Jasmine turned to go, she said: "Well, I declare." But already F. Jasmine, a quick gay band tune marching her feet, was hurrying on her way again.

In a neighborhood of shaded summer lawns she turned down a

side street and met some men mending the road. The sharp smell of melted tar and hot gravel and the loud tractor filled the air with noisy excitement. It was the tractor-man F. Jasmine chose to hear her plans — running beside him, her head thrown back to watch his sunburned face, she had to cup her hands around her mouth to make her voice heard. Even so it was uncertain if he understood, for when she stopped, he laughed and yelled back to her something she could not quite catch. Here, among the racket and excitement, was the place F. Jasmine saw the ghost of the old Frankie plainest of all — hovering close to the commotion, chewing a great big lump of tar, hanging around at noon to watch the lunch-pails being opened. There was a fine big motorcycle parked near the street menders, and before going on F. Jasmine looked at it admiringly, then spat on the broad leather seat and shined it carefully with her fist. She was in a very nice neighborhood near the edge of town, a place of new brick houses with flower-bordered sidewalks and cars parked in paved driveways; but the finer the neighborhood, the fewer people are about, so F. Jasmine turned back toward the center of the town. The sun burned like an iron lid on her head and her slip was stuck wet to her chest, and even the organdie dress was wet and clinging in spots also. The march tune had softened to a dreaming song on a violin that slowed her footsteps to a wander. To this kind of music she crossed to the opposite side of the town, beyond the main street and the mill, to the gray crooked streets of the mill section, where, among the choking dust and sad gray rotten shacks, there were more listeners to tell about the wedding.

(From time to time, as she went around, a little conversation buzzed on the bottom of her mind. It was the voice of Berenice when later she would know about this morning. And you just roamed around, the voice said, taking up with total strangers! I never heard of such a thing in all my life! So the Berenice voice sounded, heard but unnoticed like the buzzing of a fly.)

From the sad alleys and crooked streets of the mill section she crossed the unseen line dividing Sugarville from the white people's town. Here were the same two-room shacks and rotted privies, as in the mill section, but round thick chinaberry trees cast solid shade and often cool ferns grew in pots upon the porches. This was a part of town well known to her, and as she walked along she found herself remembering these familiar lanes in long-past times and other weathers — the ice-pale mornings in the wintertime when even the orange fires under the black iron pots of wash-women seemed to be shivering, the windy autumn nights.

Meanwhile, the glare was dizzy bright and she met and talked to many people, some known to her by sight and name, some strangers. The plans about the wedding stiffened and fixed with each new telling and finally came unchangeable. By eleven-thirty she was very tired, and even the tunes dragged with exhaustion; the need to be recognized for her true self was for the time being satisfied. So she went back to the place from which she started — to the main street where the glittering sidewalks were baked and half-deserted in the white glare.

Always she went by her father's store whenever she came to town. Her father's store was on the same block as the Blue Moon, but two doors from the main street and in a much better location. It was a narrow store with precious jewels in velvet boxes placed in the window. Beyond the window was her father's workbench, and when you walked along the sidewalk you could see her father working there, his head bent over the tiny watches, and his big brown hands hovered as carefully as butterflies. You could see her father like a public person in the town, well known to all by sight and name. But her father was not proud and did not even look up at those who stopped and gazed at him. This morning, however, he was not at his bench, but behind the counter rolling down his shirt-sleeves as though making ready to put on his coat and go outside.

The long glass showcase was bright with jewels and watches and silverware and the store smelled of watch-fixing kerosene. Her father wiped the sweat from his long upper lip with his forefinger and rubbed his nose in a troubled way.

"Where in the world have you been all morning? Berenice has called here twice trying to locate you."

"I've been all over the whole town," she said.

But he did not listen. "I'm going around to your Aunt Pet's," he said. "She's had a sad piece of news today."

"What sad piece of news?" F. Jasmine asked.

"Uncle Charles is dead."

Uncle Charles was the great-uncle of John Henry West, but though she and John Henry were first cousins, Uncle Charles was not blood kin to her. He lived twenty-one miles out on the Renfroe Road in a shaded wooden country house surrounded by red cotton fields. An old, old man, he had been sick a long time; it was said he had one foot in the grave—and he always wore bedroom slippers. Now he was dead. But that had nothing to do with the wedding, and so F. Jasmine only said: "Poor Uncle Charles. That certainy is a pity."

Her father went back behind the gray sour velvet curtain that divided the store into two parts, the larger public part in front and behind a small dusty private part. Behind the curtain was the water cooler, some shelves of boxes, and the big iron safe where diamond rings were locked away from robbers in the night. F. Jasmine heard her Papa moving around back there, and she settled herself carefully at the workbench before the front window. A watch, already taken apart, was laid out on the green blotter.

There was a strong streak of watchmaker's blood in her and always the old Frankie had loved to sit at her father's bench. She would put on her father's glasses with the jeweler's loupe attached and, scowling busily, dip them in gasoline. She worked with the lathe, too. Sometimes a little crowd of sidewalk lazies would collect to watch her from the street and she would imagine how they said: "Frankie Addams works for her father and makes fifteen dollars a week. She fixes the hardest watches in the store and goes to the Woodmen of the World Club with her father. Look at her. She is a credit to the family and a big credit to the whole town." So she would imagine these conversations, as she scowled with a busy expression at a watch. But now today she looked down at the watch spread out on the blotter, and did not put on the jeweler's loupe. There was something more she ought to say about the death of Uncle Charles.

When her father returned to the front of the store, she said: "At one time Uncle Charles was one of the leading citizens. It will be a loss to the whole county."

The words did not seem to impress her father. "You had better go on home. Berenice has been phoning to locate you."

"Well, remember you said I could get a wedding dress. And stockings and shoes."

"Charge them at MacDougal's."

"I don't see why we always have to trade at MacDougal's just because it's a local store," she grumbled as she went out of the door. "Where I am going there will be stores a hundred times bigger than MacDougal's."

The clock in the tower of the First Baptist Church clanged twelve, the mill whistle wailed. There was a drowsing quietness about the street, and even the very cars, parked slantwise with their noses toward the center aisle of grass, were like exhausted cars that have all gone to sleep. The few people out at the noon hour kept close beneath the blunt shade of the awnings. The sun took the color from the sky and the brick stores seemed shrunken, dark, beneath the glare — one building had an overhanging cornice at the top which, from a distance, gave it the queer look of a brick building that has begun to melt. In this noon quietness, she heard again the organ of the monkey-man, the sound that always magnetized her footsteps so that she automatically went toward it. This time she would find them and tell them good-bye.

As F. Jasmine hurried down the street, she saw the two of them in her mind's eye — and wondered if they would remember her. The old Frankie had always loved the monkey and the monkey-man. They resembled each other — they both had an anxious, questioning expression, as though they wondered every minute if what they did was wrong. The monkey, in fact, was nearly always wrong; after he danced to the organ tune, he was supposed to take off his darling little cap and pass it around to the audience, but likely as not he would get mixed up and bow and reach out his cap to the monkey-man, and not the audience. And the monkey-man would plead with him, and finally begin to chatter and fuss. When he would make as if to slap the monkey, the monkey would cringe down and chatter also — and they would look at each other with the same scared exasperation, their wrinkled faces very sad. After watching them a long time, the old Frankie, fascinated, began to take on the same expression as she followed them around. And now F. Jasmine was eager to see them.

She could hear the broken-sounding organ plainly, although they were not on the main street, but up farther and probably just around the corner of the next block. So F. Jasmine hurried toward them. As she neared the corner, she heard other sounds that puzzled her curiosity so that she listened and stopped. Above the music of the organ there was the sound of a man's voice quarreling and the excited higher fussing of the monkey-man. She could hear the monkey chattering also. Then suddenly the organ stopped and the two different voices were loud and mad. F. Jasmine had reached the corner, and it was the corner by the Sears and Roebuck store; she passed the store slowly, then turned and faced a curious sight.

It was a narrow street that went downhill toward Front Avenue, blinding bright in the wild glare. There on the sidewalk was the monkey, the monkey-man, and a soldier holding out a whole fistful of dollar bills — it looked at the first glance like a hundred dollars. The soldier looked angry, and the monkey-man was pale and excited also. Their voices were quarreling and F. Jasmine gathered that the soldier was trying to buy the monkey. The monkey himself was crouched and shivering down on the sidewalk close to the brick wall of the Sears and Roebuck store. In spite of the hot day, he had on his little red coat with silver buttons and his little face, scared and desperate, had the look of someone who is just about to sneeze. Shivering and pitiful, he kept bowing at nobody and offering his cap into the air. He knew the furious voices were about him and he felt blamed.

F. Jasmine was standing near-by, trying to take in the commotion, listening and still. Then suddenly the soldier grabbed at the monkey's chain, but the monkey screamed, and before she knew what it was all about, the monkey had skittered up her leg and body and was huddled on her shoulder with his little monkey hands around her head. It happened in a flash, and she was so shocked she could not move. The voices stopped and, except for the monkey's jibbered scream, the street was silent. The soldier stood slack-jawed, surprised, still holding out the handful of dollar bills.

The monkey-man was the first to recover; he spoke to the monkey in a gentle voice, and in another second the monkey sprang from off her shoulder and landed on the organ which the monkey-man was carrying on his back. The two of them went away. They quickly hurried around the corner and at the last second, just as they turned, they both looked back with the same expression — reproaching and sly. F. Jasmine leaned against the brick wall, and she still felt the monkey on her shoulder and smelt his dusty, sour smell; she shivered. The soldier muttered until the pair of them were out of sight, and F. Jasmine noticed then that he was red-haired and the same soldier who had been in the Blue Moon. He stuffed the bills in his side pocket.

"He certainy is a darling monkey," F. Jasmine said. "But it gave me a mighty funny feeling to have him run up me like that."

The soldier seemed to realize her for the first time. The look on his face changed slowly, and the angry expression went away. He was looking at F. Jasmine from the top of her head, down the organdie best dress, and to the black pumps she was wearing.

"I guess you must have wanted the monkey a whole lot," she said. "I've always wanted a monkey, too."

"What?" he asked. Then he remarked in a muffled voice, as if his tongue were made of felt or a very thick piece of blotting paper. "Which way are we going?" the soldier said. "Are you going my way or am I going yours?"

F. Jasmine had not expected this. The soldier was joining with her like a traveler who meets another traveler in a tourist town. For a second, it occurred to her that she had heard this remark before, perhaps in a picture show — that furthermore it was a set remark requiring a set answer. Not knowing the ready-made reply, she answered carefully.

"Which way are you going?"

"Hook on," he said, sticking out his elbow.

They walked down the side street, on their shrunken noontime shadows. The soldier was the only person during that day who spoke first to F. Jasmine and invited her to join with him. But, when she began to tell about the wedding, something seemed lacking. Perhaps it was because she had already told her plans to so many people all over town that now she could rest satisfied. Or perhaps it was because she felt the soldier was not really listening. He looked at the pink organdie dress from the corner of his eye, and there was a half-smile on his mouth. F. Jasmine could not match her steps to his, although she tried, for his legs seemed loosely fastened to his body so that he walked in a rambling way.

"What state do you come from, if I may ask?" she said politely.

In that second that passed before his answer there was time for her skimming mind to picture Hollywood, New York, and Maine. The soldier answered: "Arkansas."

Now of all the forty-eight states in the Union, Arkansas was one of the very few that had never especially appealed to her — but her imagination, balked, immediately turned the opposite way so that she asked:

"Do you have any idea where you will be going?"

"Just banging around," the soldier said. "I'm out loose on a three-day pass."

He had mistaken the meaning of her question, for she had asked it to him as a soldier liable to be sent to any foreign country in the world, but, before she could explain what she had meant, he said:

"There's a kind of hotel around the corner I'm staying at." Then, still looking at the pleated collar of her dress, he added: "It seems like I've seen you somewhere before. Do you ever go dancing at the Idle Hour?"

They walked down Front Avenue, and now the street was beginning to have the air of Saturday afternoon. A lady was drying her yellow hair in the window of the second floor above the fish store, and she called down to two soldiers who passed along the street. A street preacher, a known town character, was preaching on a corner to a group of warehouse colored boys and scraggly children. But F. Jasmine did not have her mind on what was going on around her. The soldier's mention of dancing and the Idle Hour touched like a story-tale wand upon her mind. She realized for the first time that she was walking with a soldier, with one of the groups of loud, glad gangs that roamed around the streets together or walked with the grown girls. They danced at the Idle Hour and had a good time, while the old Frankie was asleep. And she had never danced with anybody, excepting Evelyn Owen, and had never put foot in the Idle Hour.

And now F. Jasmine walked with a soldier who in his mind included her in such unknown pleasures. But she was not altogether proud. There was an uneasy doubt that she could not quite place or name. The noon air was thick and sticky as hot syrup, and there was the stifling smell of the dye-rooms from the cotton mill. She heard the organ-grinder sounding faintly from the main street.

The soldier stopped: "This is the hotel," he said.

They were before the Blue Moon and F. Jasmine was surprised to hear it spoken of as a hotel, as she had thought it was only a café. When the soldier held the screen door open for her, she noticed that he swayed a little. Her eyes saw blinding red, then black, after the glare, and it took them a minute to get used to the blue light. She followed the soldier to one of the booths on the right.

"Care for a beer," he said, not in an asking voice, but as though he took her reply for granted.

F. Jasmine did not enjoy the taste of beer; once or twice she had sneaked swallows from her father's glass and it was sour. But the soldier had not left her any choice. "I would be delighted," she said. "Thank you."

Never had she been in a hotel, although she had often thought about them and written about them in her shows. Her father had stayed in hotels several times, and once, from Montgomery, he had brought her two little tiny cakes of hotel soap which she had saved. She looked around the Blue Moon with new curiosity. All of a sudden she felt very proper. On seating herself at the booth table, she carefully smoothed down her dress, as she did when at a party or in church, so as not to sit the pleats out of the skirt. She sat up straight and on her face there was a proper expression. But the Blue Moon still seemed to her more like a kind of café than a real hotel. She did not see the sad, pale Portuguese, and a laughing fat lady with a golden tooth poured beer for the soldier at the counter. The stairway at the back led probably to the hotel rooms upstairs, and the steps were lighted by a blue neon bulb and covered wth a runner of linoleum. A sassy chorus on the radio was singing an advertisement: Denteen Chewing Gum! Denteen Chewing Gum! Denteen! The beery air reminded her of a room where a rat has died behind a wall. The soldier walked back to the booth, carrying two glasses of the beer; he licked some foam that had spilled over his hand and wiped the hand on his trousers seat. When he was settled in the booth, F. Jasmine said, in a voice that was absolutely new to her — a high voice spoken through the nose, dainty and dignified:

"Don't you think it is mighty exciting? Here we are sitting here at this table and in a month from now there's no telling where on earth we'll be. Maybe tomorrow the army will send you to Alaska like they sent my brother. Or to France or Africa or Burma. And I don't have any idea where I will be. I'd like for us to go to Alaska for a while, and then go somewhere else. They say that Paris has been liberated. In my opinion the war will be over next month."

The soldier raised his glass, and threw back his head to gulp the beer. F. Jasmine took a few swallows also, although it tasted nasty to her. Today she did not see the world as loose and cracked and turning a thousand miles an hour, so that the spinning views of war and distant lands made her mind dizzy. The world had never been so close to her. Sitting across from the soldier at that booth in the

Blue Moon, she suddenly saw the three of them — herself, her brother, and the bride — walking beneath a cold Alaskan sky, along the sea where green ice waves lay frozen and folded on the shore; they climbed a sunny glacier shot through with pale cold colors and a rope tied the three of them together, and friends from another glacier called in Alaskan their J A names. She saw them next in Africa, where, with a crowd of sheeted Arabs, they galloped on camels in the sandy wind. Burma was jungle-dark, and she had seen pictures in *Life* magazine. Because of the wedding, these distant lands, the world, seemed altogether possible and near: as close to Winter Hill as Winter Hill was to the town. It was the actual present, in fact, that seemed to F. Jasmine a little bit unreal.

"Yes, it's mighty exciting," she said again.

The soldier, his beer finished, wiped his wet mouth with the back of his freckled hand. His face, although not fat, seemed swollen, and it was glossy in the neon light. He had a thousand little freckles, and the only thing that seemed to her pretty was his bright, red curly hair. His eyes were blue, set close together, and the whites were raw. He was staring at her with a peculiar expression, not as one traveler gazes at another, but as a person who shares a secret scheme. For several minutes he did not talk. Then, when at last he spoke, the words did not make sense to her and she did not understand. It seemed to her the soldier said:

"Who is a cute dish?"

There were no dishes on the table and she had the uneasy feeling he had begun to talk a kind of double-talk. She tried to turn the conversation.

"I told you my brother is a Member of the Armed Forces."

But the soldier did not seem to listen. "I could of sworn I'd run into you some place before."

The doubt in F. Jasmine deepened. She realized now that the soldier thought she was much older than she was, but her pleasure in this was somehow uncertain. To make conversation she remarked:

"Some people are not partial to red hair. But to me it's my favorite color." She added, remembering her brother and the bride, "Except dark brown and yellow. I always think it's a pity for the Lord to waste curly hair on boys. When so many girls are going around with hair as straight as pokers."

The soldier leaned over the booth table and, still staring at her, he began to walk his fingers, the second and third fingers of both hands, across the table toward her. The fingers were dirty, with rinds of black beneath the nails. F. Jasmine had the sense that something strange was going to happen, when just at that moment there was a sudden racket and commotion and three or four soldiers shoved each other into the hotel. There was a babble of voices and the screen door banged. The soldier's fingers stopped walking across the table and, when he glanced at the other soldiers, the peculiar expression was scattered from his eyes.

"That certainy is a darling little monkey," she said.

"What monkey?"

The doubt deepened to the feeling that something was wrong. "Why, the monkey you tried to buy a few minutes ago. What's the matter with you?"

Something was wrong and the soldier put his fists up to his head. His body limpened and he leaned back in the seat of the booth, as though collapsed. "Oh, that monkey!" he said in his slurred voice. "The walk in the sun after all those beers. I was slamming around all night." He sighed, and his hands were open loose upon the table. "I guess maybe I'm just about beat."

For the first time F. Jasmine began to wonder what she was doing there and if she ought not to take herself on home. The other soldiers had crowded around a table near the stairway, and the lady with the golden tooth was busy behind the counter. F. Jasmine had finished her beer and a lace of creamy foam lined the inside of the empty glass. The hot, close smell in the hotel suddenly made her feel a little queer.

"I have to go home now. Thank you for treating me."

She got up from the booth, but the soldier reached out toward her and caught a piece of her dress. "Hey!" he said. "Don't just walk off like that. Let's fix up something for this evening. How bout a date for nine o'clock?"

"A date?" F. Jasmine felt as though her head was big and loose. The beer made her legs feel peculiar, too, almost as though she had four legs to manage instead of two. On any other day than this it would have seemed almost impossible that anyone, much less a soldier, would have invited her to a date. The very word, *date,* was a grown word used by older girls. But here again there was a blight upon her pleasure. If he knew she was not yet thirteen, he would never have invited her, or probably never joined with her at all. There was a troubled sense, a light uneasiness. "I don't know —"

"Sure," he urged. "Suppose we link up here at nine o'clock. We can go to the Idle Hour or something. That suit you all right? Here at nine o'clock."

"O.K." she said finally. "I will be delighted."

Again she was on the burning sidewalks, where passing walkers looked dark and shrunken in the angry glare. It took her a little while to come back to the wedding feeling of that morning, for the half-hour in the hotel had slightly distracted her frame of mind. But it did not take her very long, and by the time she reached the main street, the wedding feeling was recovered. She met a little girl, two grades below her at the school, and stopped her on the street to tell her her plans. She told her also that a soldier had invited her to have a date, and now she told it in a bragging tone. The girl went with her to buy the wedding clothes, which took an hour and meant the trying-on of more than a dozen beautiful dresses.

But the main thing that brought back the wedding frame of mind was an accident that occurred on the way home. It was a mysterious trick of sight and the imagination. She was walking home when all at once there was a shock in her as though a thrown knife struck and shivered in her chest. F. Jasmine stopped dead in her tracks, one foot still raised, and at first she could not take it in just what had happened. There was something sideways and behind her that had flashed across the very corner edge of her left eye; she had half-seen something, a dark double shape, in the alley she had just that moment passed. And because of this half-seen object, the quick flash in the corner of her eye, there had sprung up in her the sudden picture of her brother and the bride. Ragged and bright as lightning she saw the two of them as they had been when, for a moment, they stood together before the living-room mantelpiece, his arm around her shoulders. So strong was this picture that F. Jasmine felt suddenly that Jarvis and Janice were there behind her in the alley, and she had caught a glimpse of them — although she knew, and well enough, that they were in Winter Hill, almost a hundred miles away.

F. Jasmine lowered her raised foot to the pavement and slowly turned to look around. The alley lay between two grocery stores: a narrow alley, dark in the glare. She did not look at it directly, for somehow it was as though she was almost afraid. Her eyes stole slowly down the brick wall and she glimpsed again the dark double shapes. And what was there? F. Jasmine was stunned. There in the alley were only two colored boys, one taller than the other and with his arm resting on the shorter boy's shoulder. That was all — but something about the angle or the way they stood, or the pose of their shapes, had reflected the sudden picture of her brother and the bride that had so shocked her. And with this vision of them plain and exact the morning ended, and she was home by two o'clock.

2

The afternoon was like the center of the cake that Berenice had baked last Monday, a cake which failed. The old Frankie had been glad the cake had failed, not out of spite, but because she loved these fallen cakes the best. She enjoyed the damp, gummy richness near the center, and did not understand why grown people thought such cakes a failure. It was a loaf cake, that last Monday, with the edges risen light and high and the middle moist and altogether fallen — after the bright, high morning the afternoon was dense and solid as the center of that cake. And because it was the last of all the afternoons, F. Jasmine found an unfamiliar sweetness in the known old kitchen ways and tones. At two o'clock, when she came in, Berenice was pressing clothes. John Henry sat at the table blowing soapbubbles with a spool, and he gave her a long, green, secret look.

"Where in the world have you been?" asked Berenice.

"We know something you don't know," John Henry said. "Do you know what?"

"What?"

"Berenice and me are going to the wedding."

F. Jasmine was taking off her organdie dress, and his words startled her.

"Uncle Charles is dead."

"I heard that, but —"

"Yes," said Berenice. "The poor old soul passed on this morning. They're taking the body to the family graveyard in Opelika. And John Henry is to stay with us for several days."

Now that she knew the death of Uncle Charles would in a sense affect the wedding, she made room for it in her thoughts. While

Berenice finished pressing clothes, F. Jasmine sat in her petticoat on the stairs leading up to her room; she closed her eyes. Uncle Charles lived in a shady wooden house out in the country, and he was too old to eat corn on the cob. In June of this summer he took sick, and ever since he had been critical. He lay in the bed, shrunken and brown and very old. He complained that the pictures were hung crooked on the wall, and they took down all the framed pictures — it was not that. He complained that his bed was placed in a wrong corner, and so they moved the bed — it was not that. Then his voice failed, and when he tried to talk, it was as though his throat had filled with glue, and they could not understand the words. One Sunday the Wests had gone out to see him and taken Frankie with them; she had tiptoed to the open door of the back bedroom. He looked like an old man carved in brown wood and covered with a sheet. Only his eyes had moved, and they were like blue jelly, and she had felt they might come out from the sockets and roll like blue wet jelly down his stiff face. She had stood in the doorway staring at him — then tiptoed away, afraid. They finally made out that he complained the sun shone the wrong way through the window, but that was not the thing that hurt him so. And it was death.

F. Jasmine opened her eyes and stretched herself.

"It is a terrible thing to be dead!" she said.

"Well," said Berenice. "The old man suffered a lot and he had lived up his span. The Lord appointed the time for him."

"I know. But at the same time it seems mighty queer that he would have to die the very day before the wedding. And why on earth do you and John Henry have to go tagging to the wedding? Seems to me like you would just stay home."

"Frankie Addams," said Berenice, and she suddenly put her arms akimbo, "you are the most selfish human being that ever breathed. We all been cooped up in this kitchen and —"

"Don't call me Frankie!" she said. "I don't wish to have to remind you any more."

It was the time of early afternoon when in the old days a sweet band would be playing. Now with the radio turned off, the kitchen was solemn and silent and there were sounds from far away. A colored voice called from the sidewalk, calling the names of vegetables in a dark slurred tone, a long unwinding hollering in which there were no words. Somewhere, near in the neighborhood, there was the sound of a hammer and each stroke left a round echo.

"You would be mighty surprised if you knew whereall I've been today. I was all over this whole town. I saw the monkey and the monkey-man. There was this soldier who was trying to buy the monkey and holding a hundred dollars in his hand. Have you ever seen anybody try to buy a monkey on the street?"

"No. Was he drunk?"

"Drunk?" F. Jasmine said.

"Oh," said John Henry. "The monkey and the monkey-man!"

Berenice's question had disturbed F. Jasmine, and she took a minute to consider. "I don't think he was drunk. People don't get drunk in broad daylight." She had meant to tell Berenice about the soldier, but now she hesitated. "All the same there was something —" Her voice trailed at the end, and she watched a rainbow soapbubble floating in silence across the room. Here in the kitchen, barefooted and wearing only her petticoat, it was hard to realize and judge the soldier. About the promise for that evening she felt double-minded. The indecision bothered her, and so she changed the subject. "I hope you washed and ironed everything good of mine today. I have to take them to Winter Hill."

"What for?" said Berenice. "You only going to be there just one day."

"You heard me," F. Jasmine said. "I told you I wasn't coming back here after the wedding."

"Fool's hill. You have a whole lot less of sense than I was giving you credit for. What makes you think they want to take you along with them? Two is company and three is a crowd. And that is the main thing about a wedding. Two is company and three is a crowd."

F. Jasmine always found it hard to argue with a known saying. She loved to use them in her shows and in her conversation, but they were very hard to argue with, and so she said:

"You wait and see."

"Remember back to the time of the flood? Remember Noah and the ark?"

"And what has that got to do with it?" she asked.

"Remember the way he admitted them creatures."

"Oh, hush up your big old mouth," she said.

"Two by two," said Berenice. "He admitted them creatures two by two."

The argument that afternoon was, from the beginning to the end, about the wedding. Berenice refused to follow F. Jasmine's frame of mind. From the first it was as though she tried to catch F. Jasmine by the collar, like the Law catches a no-good in the wrong, and jerk her back where she had started — back to the sad and crazy summer that now seemed to F. Jasmine like a time remembered from long ago. But F. Jasmine was stubborn and not to be caught. Berenice had flaws to find in all of her ideas, and from the first word to the last she did her terrible, level best to try and deny the wedding. But F. Jasmine would not let it be denied.

"Look," F. Jasmine said, and she picked up the pink organdie dress that she had just taken off. "Remember when I bought this dress the collar had teeny little pleats. But you have been ironing the collar like it was supposed to be ruffled. Now we got to set those little pleats like they ought to be."

"And who is going to do it?" said Berenice. She picked up the dress and judged the collar. "I got more to do with my time and trouble."

"Well, it's got to be done," F. Jasmine argued. "It's the way the collar is supposed to be. And besides, I might be wearing it out somewhere this evening."

"And where, pray tell me?" said Berenice. "Answer the question I asked when you came in. Where in the world have you been all morning?"

It was exactly as F. Jasmine had known it would be — the way Berenice refused to understand. And, since it was more a matter of feelings than of words or facts, she found it difficult to explain. When she spoke of connections, Berenice gave her a long, uncomprehending stare — and, when she went on to the Blue Moon and the many people, the broad, flat nose of Berenice widened and she shook her head. F. Jasmine did not mention the soldier; although she was on the verge of speaking of him several times, something warned her not to.

When she had finished, Berenice said:

"Frankie, I honestly believe you have turned crazy on us. Walking around all over town and telling total strangers this big tale. You know in your soul this mania of yours is pure foolishness."

"You wait and see," F. Jasmine said. "They will take me."

"And if they don't?"

F. Jasmine picked up the shoe box with the silver slippers and the wrapped box with the wedding dress. "These are my wedding clothes. I'll show them to you later."

"And if they don't?"

F. Jasmine had already started up the stairs, but she stopped and turned back toward the kitchen. The room was silent.

"If they don't, I will kill myself," she said. "But they will."

"Kill yourself how?" asked Berenice.

"I will shoot myself in the side of the head with a pistol."

"Which pistol?"

"The pistol that Papa keeps under his handkerchiefs along with Mother's picture in the right-hand bureau drawer."

Berenice did not answer for a minute and her face was a puzzle. "You heard what Mr. Addams told you about playing with that pistol. Go on upstairs now. Dinner will be ready in a little while."

It was a late dinner, this last meal that the three of them would ever eat together at the kitchen table. On Saturdays they were not regular about the times of meals, and they began the dinner at four o'clock, when already the August sun was slanting long and stale across the yard. It was the time of afternoon when the bars of sunlight crossed the back yard like the bars of a bright strange jail. The two fig trees were green and flat, the arbor sun-crossed and casting solid shade. The sun in the afternoon did not slant through the back windows of the house, so that the kitchen was gray. The three of them began their dinner at four o'clock, and the dinner lasted until twilight. There was hopping-john cooked with the ham bone, and as they ate they began to talk of love. It was a subject F. Jasmine had never talked about in all her life. In the first place, she had never believed in love and had never put any of it in her shows. But this afternoon when Berenice began this conversation, F. Jasmine did not stop up both her ears, but as she quietly ate the peas and rice and pot-liquor she listened.

"I have heard of many a queer thing," said Berenice. "I have knew mens to fall in love with girls so ugly that you wonder if their eyes is straight. I have seen some of the most peculiar weddings anybody could conjecture. Once I knew a boy with his whole face burned off so that —"

"Who?" asked John Henry.

Berenice swallowed a piece of cornbread and wiped her mouth with the back of her hand. "I have knew womens to love veritable Satans and thank Jesus when they put their split hooves over the threshold. I have knew boys to take it into their heads to fall in love with other boys. You know Lily Mae Jenkins?"

F. Jasmine thought a minute, and then answered: "I'm not sure."

"Well, you either know him or you don't know him. He prisses around with a pink satin blouse and one arm akimbo. Now this Lily Mae fell in love with a man name Juney Jones. A man, mind you. And Lily Mae turned into a girl. He changed his nature and his sex and turned into a girl."

"Honest?" F. Jasmine asked. "Did he really?"

"He did," said Berenice. "To all intents and purposes."

F. Jasmine scratched behind her ear and said: "It's funny I can't think who you are talking about. I used to think I knew so many people."

"Well, you don't need to know Lily Mae Jenkins. You can live without knowing him."

"Anyway, I don't believe you," F. Jasmine said.

"Well, I ain't arguring with you," said Berenice. "What was it we was speaking about?"

"About peculiar things."

"Oh, yes."

They stopped off a few minutes to get on with the dinner. F. Jasmine ate with her elbows on the table and her bare heels hooked on the rungs of the chair. She and Berenice sat opposite each other, and John Henry faced the window. Now hopping-john was F. Jasmine's very favorite food. She had always warned them to wave a plate of rice and peas before her nose when she was in her coffin, to make certain there was no mistake; for if a breath of life was left in her, she would sit up and eat, but if she smelled the hopping-john, and did not stir, then they could just nail down the coffin and be certain she was truly dead. Now Berenice had chosen for her death-test a piece of fried fresh-water trout, and for John Henry it was divinity fudge. But though F. Jasmine loved the hopping-john the very best, the others also liked it well enough, and all three of them enjoyed the dinner that day: the ham knuckle, the hopping-john, cornbread, hot baked sweet potatoes, and the buttermilk. And as they ate, they carried on the conversation.

"Yes, as I was just now telling you," said Berenice. "I have seen many a peculiar thing in my day. But one thing I never knew and never heard tell about. No siree, I never did."

Berenice stopped talking and sat there shaking her head, waiting for them to question her. But F. Jasmine would not speak. And it was John Henry who raised his curious face from his plate and asked: "What, Berenice?"

"No," said Berenice. "I never before in all my days heard of anybody falling in love with a wedding. I have knew many peculiar things, but I never heard of that before."

F. Jasmine grumbled something.

"So I have been thinking it over and have come to a conclusion."

"How?" John Henry suddenly asked. "How did that boy change into a girl?"

Berenice glanced at him and straightened the napkin tied around his neck. "It was just one of them things, Candy Lamb. I don't know."

"Don't listen at her," F. Jasmine said.

"So I have been thinking it over in my mind and come to this conclusion. What you ought to begin thinking about is a beau."

"What?" F. Jasmine asked.

"You heard me," said Berenice. "A beau. A nice little white boy beau."

F. Jasmine put down her fork and sat with her head turned to one side. "I don't want any beau. What would I do with one?"

"Do, Foolish?" asked Berenice. "Why, make him treat you to the picture show. For one thing."

F. Jasmine pulled the bangs of her hair down over her forehead and slid her feet across the rung of the chair.

"Now you belong to change from being so rough and greedy and big," said Berenice. "You ought to fix yourself up nice in your dresses. And speak sweetly and act sly."

F. Jasmine said in a low voice: "I'm not rough and greedy any more. I already changed that way."

"Well, excellent," said Berenice. "Now catch you a beau."

F. Jasmine wanted to tell Berenice about the soldier, the hotel, and the invitation for the evening date. But something checked her, and she hinted around the edges of the subject: "What kind of a beau? Do you mean something like — " F. Jasmine paused, for at home in the kitchen that last afternoon, the soldier seemed unreal.

"Now that I cannot advise," said Berenice. "You got to decide for yourself."

"Something like a soldier who would maybe take me dancing at the Idle Hour?" She did not look at Berenice.

"Who is talking about soldiers and dancing? I'm talking about a nice little white boy beau your own age. How about that little old Barney?"

"Barney MacKean?"

"Why, certainy. He would do very well to begin with. You could make out with him until somebody else comes along. He would do."

"That mean nasty Barney!" The garage had been dark, with thin needling sunlight coming through the cracks of the closed door, and with the smell of dust. But she did not let herself remember the unknown sin that he had showed her, that later made her want to throw a knife between his eyes. Instead, she shook herself hard and began mashing peas and rice together on her plate. "You are the biggest crazy in this town."

"The crazy calls the sane the crazy."

So they began to eat again, all except John Henry. F. Jasmine was busy slicing open cornbread and spreading it with butter and mashing her hopping-john and drinking milk. Berenice ate more slowly, peeling off bits of ham from the knuckle in a dainty way. John Henry looked from one of them to the other, and after listening to their talk he had stopped eating to think for a little while. Then after a minute he asked:

"How many of them did you catch? Them beaus."

"How many?" said Berenice. "Lamb, how many hairs is in these plaits? You talking to Berenice Sadie Brown."

So Berenice was started, and her voice went on and on. And when she had begun this way, on a long and serious subject, the words flowed one into the other and her voice began to sing. In the gray of the kitchen on summer afternoons the tone of her voice was golden and quiet, and you could listen to the color and the singing of her voice and not follow the words. F. Jasmine let the long tones linger and spin inside her ears, but her mind did not stamp the voice with sense or sentences. She sat there listening at the table, and now and then she thought of a fact that all her life had seemed to her most curious: Berenice always spoke of herself as though she was somebody very beautiful. Almost on this one subject, Berenice was really not in her right mind. F. Jasmine listened to the voice and stared at Berenice across the table: the dark face with the wild blue eye, the eleven greased plaits that fitted her head like a skull-cap, the wide flat nose that quivered as she spoke. And whatever else Berenice might be, she was not beautiful. It seemed to her she ought to give Berenice advice. So she said at the next pause:

"I think you ought to quit worrying about beaus and be content with T.T. I bet you are forty years old. It is time for you to settle down."

Berenice bunched up her lips and stared at F. Jasmine with the dark live eye. "Wisemouth," she said. "How do you know so much? I got as much right as anybody else to continue to have a good time so long as I can. And as far as that goes, I'm not so old as some peoples would try and make out. I can still ministrate. And I got many a long year ahead of me before I resign myself to a corner."

"Well, I didn't mean go into a corner," F. Jasmine said.

"I heard what you meant," said Berenice.

John Henry had been watching and listening, and there was a little crust of pot-liquor around his mouth. A big blue lazy fly was hovering around him and trying to light on his sticky face, so that from time to time John Henry waved his hand to shoo the fly away.

"Did they all treat you to the picture show?" he asked. "All those beaus."

"To the show, or to one thing or another," she answered.

"You mean you never pay your own way?" John Henry asked.

"That's what I'm telling you," said Berenice. "Not when I go out with a beau. Now if I was to go somewhere with a crowd of womens, I would have to pay my way. But I'm not the kind of person to go around with crowds of womens."

"When you all took the trip to Fairview — " F. Jasmine said — for one Sunday that last spring there had been a colored pilot who took up colored people in his aeroplane. "Who paid the way?"

"Now let me see," said Berenice. "Honey and Clorina took care of their expense, except I loaned Honey one dollar and forty cents. Cape Clyde paid his own way. And T.T. paid for himself and for me."

"Then T.T. treated you to the aeroplane ride?"

"That's what I'm telling you. He paid the bus tickets to and from Fairview and the aeroplane ride and the refreshments. The complete trip. Why, naturally he paid the way. How else do you think I could afford to fly around in an aeroplane? Me making six dollars a week."

"I didn't realize that," F. Jasmine admitted finally. "I wonder where T.T. got all of his money."

"Earned it," said Berenice. "John Henry, wipe off your mouth."

So they rested at the table, for the way they ate their meals, this summer, was in rounds: they would eat awhile and then let the food have a chance to spread out and settle inside their stomachs, and a little later they would start in again. F. Jasmine crossed her knife and fork on her empty plate, and began to question Berenice about a matter that had bothered her.

"Tell me. Is it just us who call this hopping-john? Or is it known by that name through all the country? It seems a strange name somehow."

"Well, I have heard it called various things," said Berenice.

"What?"

"Well, I have heard it called peas and rice. Or rice and peas and pot-liquor. Or hopping-john. You can vary and take your pick."

"But I'm not talking about this town," F. Jasmine said. "I mean in other places. I mean through all the world. I wonder what the French call it."

"Oh," said Berenice. "Well, you ask me a question I cannot answer."

"Merci a la parlez," F. Jasmine said.

They sat at the table and did not speak. F. Jasmine was tilted back in her chair, her head turned toward the window and the sun-crossed empty yard. The town was silent and the kitchen was silent except for the clock. F. Jasmine could not feel the world go round, and nothing moved.

"Now a funny thing has happened to me," F. Jasmine began. "I don't hardly know how to tell just what I mean. It was one of those strange things you can't exactly explain."

"What, Frankie?" John Henry asked.

F. Jasmine turned from the window, but before she could speak again there was the sound. In the silence of the kitchen they heard the tone shaft quietly across the room, then again the same note was repeated. A piano scale slanted across the August afternoon. A chord was struck. Then in a dreaming way a chain of chords climbed slowly upward like a flight of castle stairs: but just at the end, when the eighth chord should have sounded and the scale made complete, there was a stop. This next to the last chord was repeated. The seventh chord, which seems to echo all of the unfinished scale, struck and insisted again and again. And finally there was a silence. F. Jasmine and John Henry and Berenice looked at each other. Somewhere in the neighborhood an August piano was being tuned.

"Jesus!" said Berenice. "I seriously believe this will be the last straw."

John Henry shivered. "Me too," he said.

F. Jasmine sat perfectly still before the table crowded with plates and dinner dishes. The gray of the kitchen was a stale gray and the room was too flat and too square. After the silence another note was sounded, and then repeated an octave higher. F. Jasmine raised her eyes each time the tone climbed higher, as though she watched the note move from one part of the kitchen to another; at the highest point her eyes had reached a ceiling corner, then, when a long scale slid downward, her head turned slowly as her eyes crossed from the ceiling corner to the floor corner at the opposite side of the room. The bottom bass note was struck six times, and F. Jasmine was left staring at an old pair of bedroom slippers and an empty beer bottle which were in that corner of the room. Finally she shut her eyes, and shook herself, and got up from the table.

"It makes me sad," F. Jasmine said. "And jittery too." She began to walk around the room. "They tell me that when they want to punish them over in Milledgeville, they tie them up and make them listen to piano-tuning." She walked three times around the table. "There's something I want to ask you. Suppose you ran into somebody who seemed to you terribly peculiar, but you didn't know the reason why."

"In what ways peculiar?"

F. Jasmine thought of the soldier, but she could not further explain. "Say you might meet somebody you think he almost might be a *drunk,* but you're not sure about anything. And he wanted you to join with him and go to a big party or dance. What would you do?"

"Well, on the face of it, I don't know. It would depend on how I feel. I might go with him to the big party and meet up with somebody that suited me better." The live eye of Berenice suddenly narrowed, and she looked hard at F. Jasmine. "But why do you ask that?"

The quietness in the room stretched out until F. Jasmine could hear the drip-drop from the faucet of the sink. She was trying to frame a way to tell Berenice about the soldier. Then all at once the telephone rang. F. Jasmine jumped up and, turning over her empty milk glass, dashed to the hall — but John Henry, who was nearer, reached the telephone first. He knelt on the telephone chair and smiled into the mouthpiece before he said hello. Then he kept on saying hello until F. Jasmine took the receiver from him and repeated the hellos at least two dozen times before she finally hung up.

"Anything like that makes me so mad," she said when they had gone back to the kitchen. "Or when the express truck stops before the door and the man peers at our number and then takes the box somewhere else. I look on those things as a kind of sign." She raked her fingers through her crew-cut blond hair. "You know I'm really going to get my fortune told before I leave home in the morning. It's something I've been meaning to do for a long time."

Berenice said: "Changing the subject, when are you going to show me the new dress? I'm anxious to see what you selected."

So F. Jasmine went up to get the dress. Her room was what was known as a hotbox; the heat from the rest of the house rose up to her room and stayed there. In the afternoon the air seemed to make a buzzing sound, so it was a good idea to keep the motor running. F. Jasmine turned on the motor and opened the closet door. Until this day before the wedding she had always kept her six costumes hung in a row on coat-hangers, and she just threw her ordinary clothes up on the shelf or kicked them into a corner. But when she had come home this afternoon, she had changed this: the costumes were thrown up on the shelf and the wedding dress hung alone in the closet on a coat-hanger. The silver slippers were placed carefully on the floor beneath the dress with the toes pointed north, toward Winter Hill. For some reason F. Jasmine tiptoed around the room as she began to dress.

"Shut your eyes!" she called. "Don't watch me coming down the stairs. Don't open your eyes until I tell you."

It was as though the four walls of the kitchen watched her, and the skillet hanging on the wall was a watching round black eye. The piano-tuning was for a minute silent. Berenice sat with her head bowed, as though she was in church. And John Henry had his head bowed also, but he was peeking. F. Jasmine stood at the foot of the stairs and placed her left hand on her hip.

"Oh, how pretty!" John Henry said.

Berenice raised her head, and when she saw F. Jasmine her face was a study. The dark eye looked from the silver hair ribbon to the soles of the silver slippers. She said nothing.

"Now tell me your honest opinion," F. Jasmine said.

But Berenice looked at the orange satin evening dress and shook her head and did not comment. At first she shook her head with short little turns, but the longer she stared, the longer these shakes became, until at the last shake F. Jasmine heard her neck crack.

"What's the matter?" F. Jasmine asked.

"I thought you was going to get a pink dress."

"But when I got in the store I changed my mind. What is wrong with this dress? Don't you like it, Berenice?"

"No," said Berenice. "It don't do."

"What do you mean? It don't do."

"Exactly that. It just don't do."

F. Jasmine turned to look in the mirror, and she still thought the dress was beautiful. But Berenice had a sour and stubborn look on her face, an expression like that of an old long-eared mule, and F. Jasmine could not understand.

"But I don't see what you mean," she complained. "What is wrong?"

Berenice folded her arms over her chest and said: "Well, if you don't see it I can't explain it to you. Look there at your head, to begin with."

F. Jasmine looked at her head in the mirror.

"You had all your hair shaved off like a convict, and now you tie a silver ribbon around this head without any hair. It just looks peculiar."

"Oh, but I'm washing my hair tonight and going to try to curl it," F. Jasmine said.

"And look at them elbows," Berenice continued. "Here you got on this grown woman's evening dress. Orange satin. And that brown crust on your elbows. The two things just don't mix."

F. Jasmine hunched her shoulders and covered her rusty elbows with her hands.

Berenice gave her head another quick wide shake, then bunched her lips in judgment. "Take it back down to the store."

"But I can't!" said F. Jasmine. "It's bargain basement. They don't take back."

Berenice always had two mottoes. One was the known saying that you can't make a silk purse out of a sow's ear. And the other was the motto that you have to cut your suit according to the cloth, and make the best of what you have. So F. Jasmine was not certain if it was the last of these mottoes that made Berenice change her mind, or if she really began to improve her feelings about the dress. Anyway, Berenice stared for several seconds with her head to one side, and finally said:

"Come here. We'll make it fit better at the waist and see what we can do."

"I think you're just not accustomed to seeing anybody dressed up," F. Jasmine said.

"I'm not accustomed to human Christmas trees in August."

So Berenice took off the sash and patted and pulled the dress in various places. F. Jasmine stood stiff like a hatrack and let her work with the dress. John Henry had got up from his chair and was watching, with the napkin still tied around his neck.

"Frankie's dress looks like a Christmas tree," he said.

"Two-faced Judas!" F. Jasmine said. "You just now said it was pretty. Old double-faced Judas!"

The piano tuned. Whose piano it was F. Jasmine did not know, but the sound of the tuning was solemn and insistent in the kitchen, and it came from somewhere not so far away. The piano-tuner would sometimes fling out a rattling little tune, and then he would go back to one note. And repeat. And bang the same note in a solemn and crazy way. And repeat. And bang. The name of the piano-tuner in the town was Mr. Schwarzenbaum. The sound was enough to shiver the gizzards of musicians and make all listeners feel queer.

"It almost makes me wonder if he does that just to torment us," F. Jasmine said.

But Berenice said no: "They tune pianos the same way in Cincinnati and the world over. It is just the way they do it. Less turn on the radio in the dining room and drown him out."

F. Jasmine shook her head. "No," she said. "I can't explain why.

But I don't want to have that radio turned on again. It reminds me too much of this summer."

"Step back a little now," said Berenice.

She had pinned the waist higher and done one thing and another to the dress. F. Jasmine looked in the mirror over the sink. She could only see herself from the chest up, so after admiring this top part of herself, she stood on a chair and looked at the middle section. Then she began to clear away a corner of the table so she could climb up and see in the mirror the silver shoes, but Berenice prevented her.

"Don't you honestly think it is pretty?" F. Jasmine said. "I think so. Seriously, Berenice. Give me your candy opinion."

But Berenice rared up and spoke in an accusing voice: "I never knew somebody so unreasonable! You ask me my candy opinion, and I give it to you. Then you ask me again, and I give it to you. But what you want is not my honest opinion, but my good opinion on something I know is wrong. Now what kind of way is that to act?"

"All right," F. Jasmine said. "I only want to look good."

"Well, you look very well," said Berenice. "Pretty is as pretty does. You look well enough for anybody's wedding. Excepting your own. And then, pray Jesus, we will be in a position to do better. What I have to do now is get John Henry a fresh suit and figure about the outfit I'm going to wear myself."

"Uncle Charles is dead," John Henry said. "And we are going to the wedding."

"Yes, Baby," said Berenice. And from the sudden dreaming quietness of her, F. Jasmine felt that Berenice was carried back to all the other dead people she knew. The dead were walking in her heart, and she was remembering back to Ludie Freeman and the long-gone time of Cincinnati and the snow.

F. Jasmine thought back to the other seven dead people she knew. Her mother had died the very day that she was born, so she could not count her. There was a picture of her mother in the right-hand drawer of her father's bureau: and the face looked timid and sorry, shut up with the cold folded handkerchiefs in the drawer. Then there was her grandmother who had died when Frankie was nine years old, and F. Jasmine remembered her very well — but with crooked little pictures that were sunken far back in her mind. A soldier from that town called William Boyd had been killed that year in Italy, and she had known him both by sight and name. Mrs. Selway, two blocks away, had died; and F. Jasmine had watched the funeral from the sidewalk, but she was not invited. The solemn grown men stood around out on the front porch and it had rained, there was a gray silk ribbon on the door. She knew Lon Baker, and he was dead also. Lon Baker was a colored boy and he was murdered in the alley out behind her father's store. On an April afternoon his throat was slashed with a razor blade, and all the alley people disappeared in back doorways, and later it was said his cut throat opened like a crazy shivering mouth that spoke ghost words into the April sun. Lon Baker was dead and Frankie knew him. She knew, but only in a chancing kind of way, Mr. Pitkin at Brawer's Shoe Shop, Miss Birdie Grimes, and a man who had climbed poles for the telephone company: all dead.

"Do you think very frequently about Ludie?" F. Jasmine asked.

"You know I do," said Berenice. "I think about the years when me and Ludie was together, and about all the bad times I seen since. Ludie would never have let me be lonesome so that I took up with all kinds of no-good men. Me and Ludie," she said. "Ludie and me."

F. Jasmine sat vibrating her leg and thinking of Ludie and Cincinnati. Of all the dead people out of the world, Ludie Freeman was the one F. Jasmine knew the best, although she had never laid eyes on him, and was not even born when he had died. She knew Ludie and the city of Cincinnati, and the winter when Ludie and Berenice had gone together to the North and seen the snow. A thousand times they had talked of all these things, and it was a conversation that Berenice talked slowly, making each sentence like a song. And the old Frankie used to ask and question about Cincinnati. What exactly they would eat in Cincinnati and how wide would be the Cincinnati streets? And in a chanting kind of voice they talked about the Cincinnati fish, the parlor in the Cincinnati house on Myrtle Street, the Cincinnati picture shows. And Ludie Freeman was a brickmason, making a grand and a regular salary, and he was the man of all her husbands that Berenice had loved.

"Sometimes I almost wish I had never knew Ludie at all," said Berenice. "It spoils you too much. It leaves you too lonesome afterward. When you walk home in the evening on the way from work, it makes a little lonesome quinch come in you. And you take up with too many sorry men to try to get over the feeling."

squeezed her feet so that the toes felt swollen and mashed like ten big sore cauliflowers.

"But I advise you to keep the radio on when you come back," F. Jasmine said suddenly. "Some day very likely you will hear us speaking over the radio."

"What's that?"

"I say very likely we might be asked to speak over the radio some day."

"Speak about what, pray tell me," said Berenice.

"I don't know exactly what about," F. Jasmine said. "But probably some eye-witness account about something. We will be asked to speak."

"I don't follow you," said Berenice. "What are we going to eye-witness? And who will ask us to speak?"

F. Jasmine whirled around and, putting both fists on her hips, she set herself in a staring position. "Did you think I meant you and John Henry and me? Why, I have never heard of anything so funny in my whole life."

John Henry's voice was high and excited. "What, Frankie? Who is speaking on the radio?"

"When I said *we,* you thought I meant you and me and John Henry West. To speak over the world radio. I have never heard of anything so funny since I was born."

John Henry had climbed up to kneel on the seat of his chair and the blue veins showed in his forehead and you could see the strained cords of his neck. "Who?" he hollered. "What?"

"Ha ha ha!" she said, and then she burst out laughing; she went banging around the room and hitting things with her fist. "Ho ho ho!"

And John Henry wailed and F. Jasmine banged around the kitchen in the wedding dress and Berenice got up from the table and raised her right hand for peace. Then suddenly they all stopped at once. F. Jasmine stood absolutely still before the window, and John Henry hurried to the window also and watched on tiptoe with his hands to the sill. Berenice turned her head to see what had happened. And at that moment the piano was quiet.

"Oh!" F. Jasmine whispered.

Four girls were crossing the back yard. They were girls of fourteen and fifteen years old, and they were the club members. First came

"I know it," F. Jasmine said. "But T. T. Williams is not sorry.'

"I wasn't referring to T.T. He and me is just good friends."

"Don't you think you will marry him?" F. Jasmine asked.

"Well, T.T. is a fine upstanding colored gentleman," said Bereni "You never hear tell of T.T. raring around like a lot of other me If I was to marry T.T., I could get out of this kitchen and sta behind the cash register at the restaurant and pat my foot. Furth more, I respect T.T. sincerely. He has walked in a state of grace of his life."

"Well, when are you going to marry him?" she asked. "He is cra about you."

Berenice said: "I ain't going to marry him."

"But you just now was saying —" said F. Jasmine.

"I was saying how sincerely I respect T.T. and sincerely rega him."

"Well, then —?" F. Jasmine said.

"I respect and regard him highly," said Berenice. Her dark e was quiet and sober and her flat nose widened as she spoke. "But don't make me shiver none."

After a moment F. Jasmine said: "To think about the weddi makes me shiver."

"Well, it's a pity," said Berenice.

"It makes me shiver, too, to think about how many dead people already know. Seven in all," she said. "And now Uncle Charles."

F. Jasmine put her fingers in her ears and closed her eyes, but was not death. She could feel the heat from the stove and smell t dinner. She could feel a rumble in her stomach and the beating her heart. And the dead feel nothing, hear nothing, see nothing: on black.

"It would be terrible to be dead," she said, and in the weddin dress she began to walk around the room.

There was a rubber ball on the shelf, and she threw it against th hall door and caught it on the rebound.

"Put that down," said Berenice. "Go take off the dress before yo dirty it. Go do something. Go turn on the radio."

"I told you I don't want that radio on."

And she was walking around the room, and Berenice had said t go do something, but she did not know what to do. She walked i the wedding dress, with her hand on her hip. The silver slippers ha

Helen Fletcher, and then the others walking slowly in single file. They had cut across from the O'Neils' back yard and were passing slowly before the arbor. The long gold sun slanted down on them and made their skin look golden also, and they were dressed in clean, fresh dresses. When they had passed the arbor, their single shadows stretched out long and gangling across the yard. Soon they would be gone. F. Jasmine stood motionless. In the old days that summer she would have waited in the hope that they might call her and tell her she had been elected to the club — and only at the very last, when it was plain that they were only passing, she would have shouted in angry loudness that they were not to cut across her yard. But now she watched them quietly, without jealousy. At the last there came an urge to call out to them about the wedding, but before the words could be formed and spoken, the club of girls was gone. There was only the arbor and the spinning sun.

"Now I wonder —" F. Jasmine said finally. But Berenice cut her short:

"Nothing, Curiosity," she said. "Curiosity, nothing."

When they began the second round of that last dinner, it was past five o'clock, and nearing twilight. It was the time of afternoon when in the old days, sitting with the red cards at the table, they would sometimes begin to criticize the Creator. They would judge the work of God, and mention the ways how they would improve the world. And Holy Lord God John Henry's voice would rise up happy and high and strange, and his world was a mixture of delicious and freak, and he did not think in global terms: the sudden long arm that could stretch from here to California, chocolate dirt and rains of lemonade, the extra eye seeing a thousand miles, a hinged tail that could be let down as a kind of prop to sit on when you wished to rest, the candy flowers.

But the world of the Holy Lord God Berenice Sadie Brown was a different world, and it was round and just and reasonable. First, there would be no separate colored people in the world, but all human beings would be light brown color with blue eyes and black hair. There would be no colored people and no white people to make the colored people feel cheap and sorry all through their lives. No colored people, but all human men and ladies and children as one loving family on the earth. And when Berenice spoke of this first principle her voice was a strong deep song that soared and sang in beautiful dark tones leaving an echo in the corners of the room that trembled for a long time until silence.

No war, said Berenice. No stiff corpses hanging from the Europe trees and no Jews murdered anywhere. No war, and the young boys leaving home in army suits, and no wild cruel Germans and Japanese. No war in the whole world, but peace in all countries everywhere. Also, no starving. To begin with, the real Lord God had made free air and free rain and free dirt for the benefit of all. There would be free food for every human mouth, free meals and two pounds of fatback a week, and after that each able-bodied person would work for whatever else he wished to eat or own. No killed Jews and no hurt colored people. No war and no hunger in the world. And, finally, Ludie Freeman would be alive.

The world of Berenice was a round world, and the old Frankie would listen to the strong deep singing voice, and she would agree with Berenice. But the old Frankie's world was the best of the three worlds. She agreed with Berenice about the main laws of her creation, but she added many things: an aeroplane and a motorcycle to each person, a world club with certificates and badges, and a better law of gravity. She did not completely agree with Berenice about the war; and sometimes she said she would have one War Island in the world where those who wanted to could go, and fight or donate blood, and she might go for a while as a WAC in the Air Corps. She also changed the seasons, leaving out summer altogether, and adding much snow. She planned it so that people could instantly change back and forth from boys to girls, whichever way they felt like and wanted. But Berenice would argue with her about this, insisting that the law of human sex was exactly right just as it was and could in no way be improved. And then John Henry West would very likely add his two cents' worth about this time, and think that people ought to be half boy and half girl, and when the old Frankie threatened to take him to the Fair and sell him to the Freak Pavilion, he would only close his eyes and smile.

So the three of them would sit there at the kitchen table and criticize the Creator and the work of God. Sometimes their voices crossed and the three worlds twisted. The Holy Lord God John Henry West. The Holy Lord God Berenice Sadie Brown. The Holy Lord God Frankie Addams. The Worlds at the end of the long stale afternoons.

But this was a different day. They were not loafing or playing cards, but still eating dinner. F. Jasmine had taken off the wedding dress and was barefooted and comfortable in her petticoat once more. The brown gravy of the peas had stiffened, the food was neither hot nor cold, and the butter had melted. They started in on second helpings, passing the dishes back and forth among themselves, and they did not talk of the ordinary subjects that usually they thought about this time of the afternoon. Instead, there began a strange conversation, and it came about in this way:

"Frankie," said Berenice, "awhile back you started to say something. And we veered off from the subject. It was about something unnatural, I think."

"Oh, yes," F. Jasmine said. "I was going to tell you about something peculiar that happened to me today that I don't hardly realize. Now I don't exactly know how to explain just what I mean."

F. Jasmine broke open a sweet potato and tilted back in her chair. She began to try to tell Berenice what had happened when she had been walking home and suddenly seen something from the tail of her eye, and when she turned to look, it was the two colored boys back at the end of the alley. As she talked, F. Jasmine stopped now and then to pull her lower lip and study just for the right words to tell of a feeling that she had never heard named before. Occasionally she glanced at Berenice, to see if she was following her, and a remarkable look was breaking on Berenice's face: the glass blue eye was bright and astonished, as always, and at first her dark eye was astonished also; then a queer and conniving look changed her expression, and from time to time she turned her head with short little jerks, as though to listen from different earpoints and make sure that what she heard was true.

Before F. Jasmine finished, Berenice had pushed back her plate and reached into her bosom for her cigarettes. She smoked home-rolled cigarettes, but she carried them in a Chesterfield package, so that from the outward appearance she was smoking store Chesterfields. She twisted off a ragged fringe of loose tobacco and raised back her head when she held the match, so that the flame would not go up her nose. A blue layer of smoke hung over the three of them at the table. Berenice held the cigarette between her thumb and forefinger; her hand had been drawn and stiffened by a winter rheumatism so that the last two fingers could not be straightened out. She sat listening and smoking, and when F. Jasmine had finished, there was a long pause, then Berenice leaned forward and asked suddenly:

"Listen at me! Can you see through them bones in my forehead? Have you, Frankie Addams, been reading my mind?"

F. Jasmine did not know what to answer.

"This is one of the queerest things I ever heard of," Berenice went on. "I cannot get over it."

"What I mean —" F. Jasmine started again.

"I know what you mean," said Berenice. "Right here in this very corner of the eye." She pointed to the red-webbed outside corner of the dark eye. "You suddenly catch something there. And this cold shiver run all the way down you. And you whirl around. And then you stand facing Jesus knows what. But not Ludie and not who you want. And for a minute you feel like you been dropped down a well."

"Yes," F. Jasmine said. "That is it."

"Well, this is mighty remarkable," said Berenice. "This is a thing been happening to me all my life. Yet just now is the first time I ever heard it put into words."

F. Jasmine covered her nose and her mouth with her hand, so that it would not be noticed that she was pleased about being so remarkable, and her eyes were closed in a modest way.

"Yes, that is the way when you are in love," said Berenice. "Invariably. A thing known and not spoken."

So that was how the queer conversation began at quarter to six on the last afternoon. It was the first time ever they had talked about love, with F. Jasmine included in the conversation as a person who understood and had worth-while opinions. The old Frankie had laughed at love, maintained it was a big fake, and did not believe in it. She never put any of it in her shows, and never went to love shows at the Palace. The old Frankie had always gone to the Saturday matinee, when the shows were crook shows, war shows, or cowboy shows. And who was it who had caused the confusion at the Palace that last May, when the movie had run an old show on Saturday called *Camille*? The old Frankie. She had been in her seat on the second row and she stamped and put two fingers in her mouth and began to whistle. And the other half-fare people in the first three rows began to whistle and stamp also, and the longer the love picture lasted, the louder they became. So that finally the manager came down with a flashlight and rooted the whole crowd of them out of their seats and marched them up the aisle and left them standing on the sidewalk: done out of their dimes, and disgusted.

The old Frankie had never admitted love. Yet here F. Jasmine was sitting at the table with her knees crossed, and now and then she patted her bare foot on the floor in an accustomed way, and nodded at what Berenice was saying. Furthermore, when she reached out quietly toward the Chesterfield package beside the saucer of melted butter, Berenice did not slap her hand away, and F. Jasmine took herself a cigarette. She and Berenice were two grown people smoking at the dinner table. And John Henry West had his big child head hunched close to his shoulder, watching and listening to all that went on.

"Now I will tell you a story," said Berenice. "And it is to be a warning to you. You hear me, John Henry? You hear me, Frankie?"

"Yes," John Henry whispered. He pointed with his gray little forefinger. "Frankie is smoking."

Berenice sat up straight, her shoulders square, and her dark twisted hands folded before her on the table. She raised her chin and drew in her breath in the way of a singer who is beginning a song. The piano tuned and insisted, but when Berenice began to speak, her dark gold voice rang in the kitchen and they did not listen to the piano notes. But to start this warning Berenice began with the old same story that they had heard many times before. The story of her and Ludie Freeman. A long time ago.

"Now I am here to tell you I was happy. There was no human woman in all the world more happy than I was in them days," she said. "And that includes everybody. You listening to me, John Henry? It includes all queens and millionaires and first ladies of the land. And I mean it includes people of all color. You hear me, Frankie? No human woman in all the world was happier than Berenice Sadie Brown."

She had started with the old story of Ludie. And it began an afternoon in late October almost twenty years ago. The story started at the place where first they met each other, in front of Camp Campbell's Filling Station outside of the city limits of the town. It was the time of the year when the leaves were turning and the countryside was smoky and autumn gray and gold. And the story went on from that first meeting to the wedding at the Welcome Ascension Church in Sugarville. And then on through the years with the two of them together. The house with the brick front steps and the glass windows on the corner of Barrow Street. The Christmas of the fox fur, and the June of the fish fry thrown for twenty-eight invited relatives and guests. The years with Berenice cooking dinner and sewing Ludie's suits and shirts on the machine and the two of them always having a good time. And the nine months they lived up North, in the city of Cincinnati, where there was snow. Then Sugarville again, and days merging one into another, and the weeks, the months, the years together. And the pair of them always had a good time, yet it was not so much the happenings she mentioned as the way she told about these happenings that made F. Jasmine understand.

Berenice spoke in an unwinding kind of voice, and she had said that she was happier than a queen. As she told the story, it seemed to F. Jasmine that Berenice resembled a strange queen, if a queen can be colored and sitting at a kitchen table. She unwound the story of her and Ludie like a colored queen unwinding a bolt of cloth of gold — and at the end, when the story was over, her expression was always the same: the dark eye staring straight ahead, her flat nose widened and trembling, her mouth finished and sad and quiet. As a rule, when the story was over, they would sit for a moment and then suddenly get busy doing something in a hurry: start a hand of cards, or make milkshakes, or just stir around the kitchen with no particular purpose. But this afternoon they did not move or speak for a long time after Berenice had finished, until finally F. Jasmine asked:

"What exactly did Ludie die of?"

"It was something similar to pneumonia," said Berenice. "November the year 1931."

"The very year and the very month I was born," F. Jasmine said.

"The coldest November I ever seen. Every morning there was frost and puddles were crusted with ice. The sunshine was pale yellow like it is in wintertime. Sounds carried far away, and I remember a hound dog that used to howl toward sundown. I kept a fire in the hearth going day and night, and in the evening when I walk around the room there was this shaking shadow following alongside of me on the wall. And everything I seen come to me as a kind of sign."

"I think it is a kind of sign I was born the same year and the same month he died," F. Jasmine said. "Only the dates are different."

"And then it was a Thursday toward six o'clock in the afternoon. About this time of day. Only November. I remember I went to the passage and opened the front door. We were living that year at 233 Prince Street. Dark was coming on, the old hound was howling far away. And I go back in the room and lay down on Ludie's bed. I lay myself down over Ludie with my arms spread out and my face on his face. And I pray that the Lord would contage my strenth to him. And I ask the Lord let it be anybody, but not let it be Ludie. And I lay there and pray for a long time. Until night."

"How?" John Henry asked. It was a question that did not mean anything, but he repeated it in a higher, wailing voice: "How, Berenice?"

"That night he died," she said. She spoke in a sharp tone, as though they had disputed with her. "I tell you he died. Ludie! Ludie Freeman! Ludie Maxwell Freeman died!"

She was finished, and they sat there at the table. Nobody moved. John Henry stared at Berenice, and the fly that had been hovering above him lighted on the left rim of his glasses; the fly walked slowly across the left lens, and over the nosepiece, and across the right lens. It was only when the fly had flown away that John Henry blinked and waved his hand.

"One thing," F. Jasmine said finally. "There is Uncle Charles laying there dead right now. Yet somehow I can't cry. I know I ought to feel sad. Yet I feel sadder about Ludie than I do about Uncle Charles. Although I never laid eyes on Ludie. And I knew Uncle Charles all my life and he was blood kin to blood kin of mine. Maybe it's because I was born so soon after Ludie died."

"Maybe so," said Berenice.

It seemed to F. Jasmine that they might just sit there the rest of the afternoon, without moving or speaking, when suddenly she remembered something.

"You were starting out to tell a different story," she said. "It was some kind of warning."

Berenice looked puzzled for a moment, then she jerked her head up and said: "Oh, yes! I was going to tell you how this thing we was talking about applies to me. And what happened with them other husbands. Now you perk your ears."

But the story of the other three husbands was an old story also. As Berenice began to talk, F. Jasmine went to the refrigerator and brought back to the table some sweetened condensed milk to pour on crackers as a dessert. At first she did not listen very carefully.

"It was the April of the following year that I went one Sunday to the Forks Falls Church. And you ask what I was doing out there and I tell you. I was visiting that Jackson branch of my foster cousins who live out there and we had gone to their church. So there I was praying in this church where the congregation was strangers to me. I had my forehead down on the top of the pew in front of me, and my eyes were open — not gazing around in secret, mind you, but just open. When suddenly this shiver run all the way through me. I had caught sight of something from the corner of my eye. And I looked slowly to the left. And guess what I seen there? There on the pew, just six inches from my eye, was this *thumb*."

"What thumb?" F. Jasmine asked.

"Now I'm telling you," said Berenice. "To understand this, you have to know that there was only one little portion of Ludie Freeman which was not pretty. Every other part about him was handsome and pretty as anyone would ever wish. All except his right thumb, which had been mashed in a hinge. This one thumb had a mashed chewed appearance that was not pretty. You understand?"

"You mean you suddenly saw Ludie's thumb when you were praying?"

"I mean I seen *this* thumb. And as I kneel there a shiver run from my head to my heels. I just kneel there staring at this thumb, and before I looked any further, to find out whose thumb it might be, I begun to pray in earnest. I prayed out loud: Lord, manifest! Lord, manifest!"

"And did He?" F. Jasmine asked. "Manifest?"

Berenice turned aside and made a sound like spitting. "Manifest, my foot!" she said. "You know who that thumb belonged to?"

"Who?"

"Why, Jamie Beale," said Berenice. "That big old no-good Jamie Beale. It was the first time I ever laid eyes on him."

"Is that why you married him?" F. Jasmine asked, for Jamie Beale was the name of the sorry old liquor-drinker, who was the second husband. "Because he had a mashed thumb like Ludie's?"

"Jesus knows," said Berenice. "I don't. I felt drawn to him on account of the thumb. And then one thing led to another. First thing I knew I had married him."

"Well, I think that was silly," F. Jasmine said. "To marry him just because of that thumb."

"Me too," said Berenice. "I'm not trying to dispute with you. I'm just telling you what happened. And the very same thing occurred in the case of Henry Johnson."

Henry Johnson was the third husband, the one who had gone crazy on Berenice. He was all right for three weeks after they had married, but then he went crazy, and he behaved in such a crazy way that finally she had to quit him.

"You mean to sit there and tell me Henry Johnson had one of those mashed thumbs too?"

"No," said Berenice. "It was not the thumb that time. It was the coat."

F. Jasmine and John Henry looked at each other, for what she was saying did not seem to make much sense. But Berenice's dark eye was sober and certain, and she nodded to them in a definite way.

"To understand this, you have to know what happened after Ludie died. He had a policy due to pay off two hundred and fifty dollars. I won't go into the whole business, but what happened was that I was cheated by them policy people out of fifty dollars. And in two days I had to scour around and raise the fifty dollars to make out for the funeral. Because I couldn't let Ludie be put away cheap. I pawned everything I could lay hands on. And I sold my coat and Ludie's coat. To that second-hand clothing store on Front Avenue."

"Oh!" F. Jasmine said. "Then you mean Henry Johnson bought Ludie's coat and you married him because of it."

"Not exactly," said Berenice. "I was walking down that street alongside of the City Hall one evening when I suddenly seen this shape before me. Now the shape of this boy ahead of me was so similar to Ludie through the shoulders and the back of the head that I almost dropped dead there on the sidewalk. I followed and run behind him. It was Henry Johnson, and that was the first time I ever saw him also, since he lived in the country and didn't come much into town. But he had chanced to buy Ludie's coat and he was built on the same shape as Ludie. And from the back view it looked like he was Ludie's ghost or Ludie's twin. But how I married him I don't exactly know, for to begin with it was clear that he did not have his share of sense. But you let a boy hang around and you get fond of him. Anyway, that's how I married Henry Johnson."

"People certainy do curious things."

"You telling me," said Berenice. She glanced at F. Jasmine, who was pouring a slow ribbon of condensed milk over a soda cracker, to finish her dinner with a sweet sandwich.

"I swear, Frankie! I believe you got a tape worm. I am perfectly serious. Your father looks over them big grocery bills and he naturally suspicions that I carry things off."

"You do," F. Jasmine said. "Sometimes."

"He reads over them grocery bills and he complains to me, Berenice, what in the name of holy creation did we do with six cans of condensed milk and forty-leven dozen eggs and eight boxes of marshmallows in one week. And I have to admit to him: Frankie eat them. I have to say to him: Mr. Addams, you think you feeding something human back here in your kitchen. That's what you think. I have to say to him: Yes, you imagine it is something human."

"After today I'm not going to be greedy any more," F. Jasmine said. "But I don't understand the point of what you was telling. I don't see how that about Jamie Beale and Henry Johnson applies to me."

"It applies to everybody and it is a warning."

"But how?"

"Why, don't you see what I was doing?" asked Berenice. "I loved Ludie and he was the first man I loved. Therefore, I had to go and copy myself forever afterward. What I did was to marry off little pieces of Ludie whenever I come across them. It was just my misfortune they all turned out to be the wrong pieces. My intention was to repeat me and Ludie. Now don't you see?"

"I see what you're driving at," F. Jasmine said. "But I don't see how it is a warning applied to me."

"Then do I have to tell you?" asked Berenice.

F. Jasmine did not nod or answer, for she felt that Berenice had laid a trap for her, and was going to make remarks she did not want to hear. Berenice stopped to light herself another cigarette and two blue slow scrolls of smoke came from her nostrils and lazed above the dirty dishes on the table. Mr. Schwarzenbaum was playing an arpeggio. F. Jasmine waited and it seemed a long time.

"You and that wedding at Winter Hill," Berenice said finally. "That is what I am warning about. I can see right through them two gray eyes of yours like they was glass. And what I see is the saddest piece of foolishness I ever knew."

"Gray eyes is glass," John Henry whispered.

But F. Jasmine would not let herself be seen through and outstared; she hardened and tensed her eyes and did not look away from Berenice.

"I see what you have in your mind. Don't think I don't. You see something unheard of at Winter Hill tomorrow, and you right in the center. You think you going to march down the center of the aisle right in between your brother and the bride. You think you going to break into that wedding, and Jesus knows what else."

"No," F. Jasmine said. "I don't see myself walking down the center of the aisle between them."

"I see through them eyes," said Berenice. "Don't argue with me."

John Henry said again, but softer: "Gray eyes is glass."

"But what I'm warning is this," said Berenice. "If you start out falling in love with some unheard-of thing like that, what is going to happen to you? If you take a mania like this, it won't be the last time and of that you can be sure. So what will become of you? Will you be trying to break into weddings the rest of your days? And what kind of life would that be?"

"It makes me sick to listen at people who don't have any sense," F. Jasmine said, and she put her two fingers in her ears, but she did not push in the fingers very tight and she could still hear Berenice.

"You just laying yourself this fancy trap to catch yourself in trouble," Berenice went on. "And you know it. You been through the B section of the seventh grade and you are already twelve years old."

F. Jasmine did not speak of the wedding, but her argument passed over it, and she said: "They will take me. You wait and see."

"And when they don't?"

"I told you," F. Jasmine said. "I will shoot myself with Papa's pistol. But they will take me. And we're never coming back to this part of the country again."

"Well, I been trying to reason seriously," said Berenice. "But I see it is no use. You determined to suffer."

"Who said I was going to suffer?" F. Jasmine said.

"I know you," said Berenice. "You will suffer."

"You are just jealous," F. Jasmine said. "You are just trying to deprive me of all the pleasure of leaving town. And kill the joy of it."

"I am just trying to head this off," said Berenice. "But I see it is no use."

John Henry whispered for the last time: "Gray eyes is glass."

It was past six o'clock, and the slow old afternoon began slowly to die. F. Jasmine took her fingers from her ears and breathed a long tired sigh. When she had sighed, John Henry sighed also, and Berenice concluded with the longest sigh of all. Mr. Schwarzenbaum had played a ragged little waltz; but the piano was not yet tuned to suit him, and he began to harp and insist on another note. Again he played the scale up until the seventh note, and again he stuck there and did not finish. F. Jasmine was no longer watching the music with her eyes; but John Henry was watching, and when the piano stuck on the last note F. Jasmine could see him harden his behind and sit there stiff in the chair, his eyes raised, waiting.

"It is that last note," F. Jasmine said. "If you start with A and go on up to G, there is a curious thing that seems to make the difference between G and A all the difference in the world. Twice as much difference as between any other two notes in the scale. Yet they are side by side there on the piano just as close together as the other notes. Do ray mee fa sol la tee. Tee. Tee. Tee. It could drive you wild."

John Henry was grinning with his snaggle teeth and giggling softly. "Tee-tee," he said, and he pulled at Berenice's sleeve. "Did you hear what Frankie said? Tee-tee."

"Shut your trap," F. Jasmine said. "Quit always being so evil-minded." She got up from the table, but she did not know where to go. "You didn't say anything about Willis Rhodes. Did he have a mashed thumb or a coat or something?"

"Lord!" said Berenice, and her voice was so sudden and shocked that F. Jasmine turned and went back to the table. "Now that is a story would make the hair rise on your head. You mean to say I never told you about what happened with me and Willis Rhodes?"

"No," F. Jasmine said. Willis Rhodes was the last and the worst of the four husbands, and he was so terrible that Berenice had had to call the Law on him. "What?"

"Well, imagine this!" said Berenice. "Imagine a cold bitter January night. And me laying all by myself in the big parlor bed. Alone in the house, because everybody else had gone for the Saturday night to Forks Falls. Me, mind you, who hates to sleep in a empty old bed all by myself and is nervous in a house alone. Past twelve o'clock on this cold bitter January night. Can you remember wintertime, John Henry?"

John Henry nodded.

"Now imagine this!" said Berenice again. She had begun stacking the dishes so that three dirty plates were piled before her on the table. Her dark eye circled around the table, roping in F. Jasmine and John Henry as her audience. F. Jasmine leaned forward, her mouth open and her hands holding the table edge. John Henry shivered down in his chair and he watched Berenice through his glasses without batting his eyes. Berenice had started in a low and creepy voice, then suddenly she stopped and sat there looking at the two of them.

"So what?" F. Jasmine urged, leaning closer across the table. "What happened?"

But Berenice did not speak. She looked from one of them to the other, and shook her head slowly. Then when she spoke again her voice was completely changed, and she said: "Why, I wish you would look yonder. I wish you would look."

F. Jasmine glanced quickly behind her, but there was only the stove, the wall, the empty stair.

"What?" she asked. "What happened?"

"I wish you would look," Berenice repeated. "Them two little pitchers and them four big ears." She got up suddenly from the table. "Come on, less wash the dishes. Then we going to make some cup cakes to take tomorrow on the trip."

There was nothing F. Jasmine could do to show Berenice how she felt. After a long time, when the table before her was already cleared and Berenice stood washing dishes at the sink, she only said:

"If it's anything I mortally despise it's a person who starts out to tell something and works up people's interest and then stops."

"I admit it," said Berenice. "And I am sorry. But it was just one of them things I suddenly realize I couldn't tell you and John Henry."

John Henry was skipping and scuttling back and forth across the kitchen, from the stairway to the back porch door. "Cup cakes!" he sang. "Cup cakes! Cup cakes!"

"You could have sent him out of the room," F. Jasmine said. "And told me. But don't think I care. I don't care a particle what happened. I just wish Willis Rhodes had come in about that time and slit your throat."

"That is a ugly way to talk," said Berenice. "Especially since I got a surprise for you. Go out on the back porch and look in the wicker basket covered with a newspaper."

F. Jasmine got up, but grudgingly, and she walked in a crippled way to the back porch. Then she stood in the doorway holding the pink organdie dress. Contrary to all that Berenice had maintained, the collar was pleated with tiny little pleats, as it was meant to be. She must have done it before dinner when F. Jasmine was upstairs.

"Well, this is mighty nice of you," she said. "I appreciate it."

She would have liked for her expression to be split into two parts, so that one eye stared at Berenice in an accusing way, and the other eye thanked her with a grateful look. But the human face does not divide like this, and the two expressions canceled out each other.

"Cheer up," said Berenice. "Who can tell what will happen? You might dress up in that fresh pink dress tomorrow and meet the cutest little white boy in Winter Hill you ever seen. It's just on such trips as these that you run into beaus."

"But that's not what I'm talking about," F. Jasmine said. Then, after a while, still leaning against the doorway, she added: "Somehow we got off on the wrong kind of conversation."

The twilight was white, and it lasted for a long while. Time in August could be divided into four parts: morning, afternoon, twilight, and dark. At twilight the sky became a curious blue-green which soon faded to white. The air was soft gray, and the arbor and trees were slowly darkening. It was the hour when sparrows gathered and whirled above the rooftops of the town, and when in the darkened elms along the street there was the August sound of the cicadas. Noises at twilight had a blurred sound, and they lingered: the slam of a screen door down the street, voices of children, the whir of a lawnmower from a yard somewhere. F. Jasmine brought in the evening newspaper, and dark was coming in the kitchen. The corners in the room at first were dark, then the drawings on the wall faded. The three of them watched the dark come on in silence.

"The army is now in Paris."

"That's good."

They were quiet awhile and then F. Jasmine said: "I have a lot of things to do. I ought to start out now."

But although she stood ready in the doorway, she did not go. On this last evening, the last time with the three of them together in the kitchen, she felt there was some final thing she ought to say or do before she went away. For many months she had been ready to leave this kitchen, never to return again; but now that the time had come, she stood there with her head and shoulder leaning against the door jamb, somehow unready. It was the darkening hour when the remarks they made had a sad and beautiful sound, although there would be nothing sad or beautiful about the meanings of the words.

F. Jasmine said quietly: "I intend to take two baths tonight. One long soaking bath and scrub with a brush. I'm going to try to scrape this brown crust off my elbows. Then let out the dirty water and take a second bath."

"That's a good idea," said Berenice. "I will be glad to see you clean."

"I will take another bath," John Henry said. His voice was thin and sad; she could not see him in the darkening room, since he stood in the corner by the stove. At seven Berenice had bathed him and dressed him in his shorts again. She heard him shuffle carefully across the room, for after the bath he had put on Berenice's hat and was trying to walk in Berenice's high-heeled shoes. Again he asked a question which by itself meant nothing. "Why?" he asked.

"Why what, Baby?" said Berenice.

He did not answer, and it was F. Jasmine who finally said: "Why is it against the law to change your name?"

Berenice sat in a chair against the pale white light of the window. She held the newspaper open before her, and her head was twisted down and to one side as she strained to see what was printed there. When F. Jasmine spoke, she folded the paper and put it away on the table.

"You can figure that out," she said. "Just because. Think of the confusion."

"I don't see why," F. Jasmine said.

"What is that on your neck?" said Berenice. "I thought it was a head you carried on that neck. Just think. Suppose I would suddenly up and call myself Mrs. Eleanor Roosevelt. And you would begin naming yourself Joe Louis. And John Henry would try to pass off as Henry Ford. Now what kind of confusion do you think that would cause?"

"Don't talk childish," F. Jasmine said. "That is not the kind of changing I mean. I mean from a name that doesn't suit you to a name you prefer. Like I changed from Frankie to F. Jasmine."

"But still it would be a confusion," Berenice insisted. "Suppose we all suddenly change to entirely different names. Nobody would ever know who anybody was talking about. The whole world would go crazy."

"I don't see —"

"Because things accumulate around your name," said Berenice. "You have a name and one thing after another happens to you, and you behave in various ways and do things, so that soon the name begins to have a meaning. Things have accumulated around the name. If it is bad and you have a bad reputation, then you just can't jump out of your name and escape like that. And if it is good and you have a good reputation, then you should be content and satisfied."

"But what had accumulated around my old name?" F. Jasmine asked. Then, when Berenice did not reply at once, F. Jasmine answered her own question. "Nothing! See? My name just didn't mean anything."

"Well, that's not exactly so," said Berenice. "People think of Frankie Addams and it brings to the mind that Frankie is finished with the B section of the seventh grade. And Frankie found the golden egg at the Baptist Easter Hunt. And Frankie lives on Grove Street and —"

"But those things are nothing," F. Jasmine said. "See? They're not worth while. Nothing ever happened to me."

"But it will," said Berenice. "Things will happen."

"What?" F. Jasmine asked.

Berenice sighed and reached for the Chesterfield package inside her bosom. "You pin me down like that and I can't tell you truthfully. If I could I would be a wizard. I wouldn't be sitting here in this kitchen right now, but making a fine living on Wall Street as a wizard. All I can say is that things will happen. Just what, I don't know."

"By the way," F. Jasmine said after a while. "I thought I would go around to your house and see Big Mama. I don't believe in those fortunes, or anything like that, but I thought I might as well."

"Suit yourself. However, I don't think it is necessary."

"I suppose I ought to leave now," F. Jasmine said.

But still she waited in the darkening door and did not go away.

The sounds of the summer twilight crossed within the silence of the kitchen. Mr. Schwarzenbaum had finished tuning the piano, and for the past quarter of an hour he had been playing little pieces. He played music memorized by note, and he was a nervous spry old man who reminded F. Jasmine of a silver spider. His music was spry and stiff also, and he played faint jerking waltzes and nervous lullabies. Farther down the block a solemn radio announced something they could not hear. In the O'Neils' back yard, next door, children were calling and swatting a ball. The sounds of evening canceled out each other, and they were faded in the darkening twilight air. The kitchen itself was very quiet.

"Listen," F. Jasmine said. "What I've been trying to say is this. Doesn't it strike you as strange that I am I, and you are you? I am F. Jasmine Addams. And you are Berenice Sadie Brown. And we can look at each other, and touch each other, and stay together year in and year out in the same room. Yet always I am I, and you are you. And I can't ever be anything else but me, and you can't ever be anything else but you. Have you ever thought of that? And does it seem to you strange?"

Berenice had been rocking slightly in the chair. She was not sitting in a rocking chair, but she had been tilting back in the straight chair, then letting the front legs hit the floor with little taps, her dark stiff hand held to the table edge for balance. She stopped rocking herself when F. Jasmine spoke. And finally she said: "I have thought of it occasionally."

It was the hour when the shapes in the kitchen darkened and voices bloomed. They spoke softly and their voices bloomed like flowers — if sounds can be like flowers and voices bloom. F. Jasmine stood with her hands clasped behind her head, facing the darkening room. She had the feeling that unknown words were in her throat, and she was ready to speak them. Strange words were flowering in her throat and now was the time for her to name them.

"This," she said. "I see a green tree. And to me it is green. And you would call the tree green also. And we would agree on this. But is the color you see as green the same color I see as green? Or say we both call a color black. But how do we know that what you see as black is the same color I see as black?"

Berenice said after a moment: "Those things we just cannot prove."

F. Jasmine scraped her head against the door, and put her hand up to her throat. Her voice shattered and died. "That's not what I meant to say, anyway."

The smoke of Berenice's cigarette lay bitter and warm and stagnant in the room. John Henry shuffled in the high-heeled shoes from the stove to the table and back again. A rat rattled behind the wall.

"This is what I mean," F. Jasmine said. "You are walking down a street and you meet somebody. Anybody. And you look at each other. And you are you. And he is him. Yet when you look at each other, the eyes make a connection. Then you go off one way. And he goes off another way. You go off into different parts of town, and maybe you never see each other again. Not in your whole life. Do you see what I mean?"

"Not exactly," said Berenice.

"I'm talking about this town," F. Jasmine said in a higher voice. "There are all these people here I don't even know by sight or name. And we pass alongside each other and don't have any connection. And they don't know me and I don't know them. And now I'm leaving town and there are all these people I will never know."

"But who do you want to know?" asked Berenice.

F. Jasmine answered: "Everybody. In the world. Everybody in the world."

"Why, I wish you would listen to that," said Berenice. "How about people like Willis Rhodes? How about them Germans? Them Japanese?"

F. Jasmine knocked her head against the door jamb and looked up at the dark ceiling. Her voice broke, and again she said: "That's not what I mean. That's not what I'm talking about."

"Well, what *is* you talking about?" asked Berenice.

F. Jasmine shook her head, almost as though she did not know. Her heart was dark and silent, and from her heart the unknown words flowered and bloomed and she waited to name them. From next door there was the evening sound of children's baseball and the long call: Batteruup! Batteruup! Then the hollow pock of a ball and the clatter of a thrown bat and running footsteps and wild voices. The window was a rectangle of pale clear light and a child ran across the yard and under the dark arbor after the ball. The child was quick as a shadow and F. Jasmine did not see his face — his white shirttails flapped loose behind him like queer wings. Beyond the window the twilight was lasting and pale and still.

"Less play out, Frankie," John Henry whispered. "They sound like they having a mighty good time."

"No," F. Jasmine said. "You do."

Berenice stirred in her chair and said: "I suppose we could turn on the light."

But they did not turn on the light. F. Jasmine felt the unsaid words stick in her throat and a choked sickness made her groan and knock her head against the door jamb. Finally she said again in a high ragged voice:

"This:"

Berenice waited, and when she did not speak again, she asked: "What on earth is wrong with you?"

F. Jasmine could not speak the unknown words, so after a minute she knocked her head a last time on the door and then began to walk around the kitchen table. She walked in a stiff-legged delicate way, as she felt sick, and did not wish to joggle the different foods that she had eaten and mix them up inside her stomach. She began to talk in a high fast voice, but they were the wrong words, and not what she had meant to say.

"Boyoman! Manoboy!" she said. "When we leave Winter Hill we're going to more places than you ever thought about or even knew existed. Just where we will go first I don't know, and it don't matter. Because after we go to that place we're going on to another. We mean to keep moving, the three of us. Here today and gone tomorrow. Alaska, China, Iceland, South America. Traveling on trains. Letting her rip on motorcycles. Flying around all over the world in aeroplanes. Here today and gone tomorrow. All over the world. It's the damn truth. Boyoman!"

F. Jasmine jerked open the drawer of the table and fumbled inside for the butcher knife. She did not need the butcher knife, but she wanted something to grasp in her hand and wave about as she hurried around the table.

"And talking of things happening," she said. "Things will happen so fast we won't hardly have time to realize them. Captain Jarvis Addams sinks twelve Jap battleships and decorated by the President. Miss F. Jasmine Addams breaks all records. Mrs. Janice Addams elected Miss United Nations in beauty contest. One thing after another happening so fast we don't hardly notice them."

"Hold still, Fool," said Berenice. "And lay down that knife."

"And we will meet them. Everybody. We will just walk up to people and know them right away. We will be walking down a dark road and see a lighted house and knock on the door and strangers will rush to meet us and say: Come in! Come in! We will know decorated aviators and New York people and movie stars. We will have thousands of friends, thousands and thousands and thousands of friends. We will belong to so many clubs that we can't even keep track of all of them. We will be members of the whole world. Boyoman! Manoboy!"

Berenice had a very strong long right arm, and when F. Jasmine passed her the next time as she was running around the table, this arm reached out and snatched her by the petticoat so quickly that she was caught up with a jerk that made her bones crack and her teeth rattle.

"*Is* you gone raving wild?" she asked. The long arm pulled F. Jasmine closer and wrapped around her waist. "You sweating like a mule. Lean down and let me feel your forehead. Is you got a fever?"

F. Jasmine pulled one of Berenice's plaits and pretended she was going to saw it off with the knife.

"You trembling," said Berenice. "I truly believe you took a fever walking around in that sun today. Baby, you sure you ain't sick?"

"Sick?" asked F. Jasmine. "Who, me?"

"Set here in my lap," said Berenice. "And rest a minute."

F. Jasmine put the knife on the table and settled down on Berenice's lap. She leaned back and put her face against Berenice's neck; her face was sweaty and Berenice's neck was sweaty also, and they both smelled salty and sour and sharp. Her right leg was flung across Berenice's knee, and it was trembling — but when she steadied her toes on the floor, her leg did not tremble any more. John Henry shuffled toward them in the high-heeled shoes and crowded up jealous and close to Berenice. He put his arm around Berenice's head and held on to her ear. Then after a moment he tried to push F. Jasmine out of her lap, and he pinched F. Jasmine with a mean and tiny little pinch.

"Leave Frankie alone," said Berenice. "She ain't bothered you."

He made a fretting sound: "I'm sick."

"Now no, you ain't. Be quiet and don't grudge your cousin a little bit of love."

"Old mean bossy Frankie," he complained in a high sad voice.

"What she doing so mean right now? She just laying here wore out."

F. Jasmine rolled her head and rested her face against Berenice's shoulder. She could feel Berenice's soft big ninnas against her back, and her soft wide stomach, her warm solid legs. She had been breathing very fast, but after a minute her breath slowed down so that she breathed in time with Berenice; the two of them were close together as one body, and Berenice's stiffened hands were clasped around F. Jasmine's chest. Their backs were to the window, and before them the kitchen was now almost dark. It was Berenice who finally sighed and started the conclusion of that last queer conversation.

"I think I have a vague idea what you were driving at," she said. "We all of us somehow caught. We born this way or that way and we don't know why. But we caught anyhow. I born Berenice. You born Frankie. John Henry born John Henry. And maybe we wants to widen and bust free. But no matter what we do we still caught. Me is me and you is you and he is he. We each one of us somehow caught all by ourself. Is that what you was trying to say?"

"I don't know," F. Jasmine said. "But I don't want to be caught."

"Me neither," said Berenice. "Don't none of us. I'm caught worse than you is."

F. Jasmine understood why she had said this, and it was John Henry who asked in his child voice: "Why?"

"Because I am black," said Berenice. "Because I am colored. Everybody is caught one way or another. But they done drawn completely extra bounds around all colored people. They done squeezed us off in one corner by ourself. So we caught that firstway I was telling you, as all human beings is caught. And we caught as colored people also. Sometimes a boy like Honey feel like he just can't breathe no more. He feel like he got to break something or break himself. Sometimes it just about more than we can stand."

"I know it," F. Jasmine said. "I wish Honey could do something."

"He just feels desperate like."

"Yes," F. Jasmine said. "Sometimes I feel like I want to break something, too. I feel like I wish I could just tear down the whole town."

"So I have heard you mention," said Berenice. "But that won't help none. The point is that we all caught. And we try in one way or another to widen ourself free. For instance, me and Ludie. When I was with Ludie, I didn't feel so caught. But then Ludie died. We go around trying one thing or another, but we caught anyhow."

The conversation made F. Jasmine almost afraid. She lay there close to Berenice and they were breathing very slowly. She could not see John Henry, but she could feel him; he had climbed up on the back rungs of the chair and was hugging Berenice's head. He was holding her ears, for in a moment Berenice said: "Candy, don't wrench my ears like that. Me and Frankie ain't going to float up through the ceiling and leave you."

Water dropped slowly in the kitchen sink and the rat was knocking behind the wall.

"I believe I realize what you were saying," F. Jasmine said. "Yet at the same time you almost might use the word loose instead of caught. Although they are two opposite words. I mean you walk around and you see all the people. And to me they look loose."

"Wild, you mean?"

"Oh, no!" she said. "I mean you don't see what joins them up together. You don't know where they all came from, or where they're going to. For instance, what made anybody ever come to this town in the first place? Where did all these people come from and what are they going to do? Think of all those soldiers."

"They were born," said Berenice. "And they going to die."

F. Jasmine's voice was thin and high. "I know," she said. "But what is it all about? People loose and at the same time caught. Caught and loose. All these people and you don't know what joins them up. There's bound to be some sort of reason and connection. Yet somehow I can't seem to name it. I don't know."

"If you did you would be God," said Berenice. "Didn't you know that?"

"Maybe so."

"We just know so much. Then beyond that we don't know no more."

"But I wish I did." Her back was cramped and she stirred and stretched herself on Berenice's lap, her long legs sprawling out beneath the kitchen table. "Anyway, after we leave Winter Hill I won't have to worry about things any more."

"You don't have to now. Nobody requires you to solve the riddles of the world." Berenice took a deep meaning breath and said: "Frankie, you got the sharpest set of human bones I ever felt."

This was a strong hint for F. Jasmine to stand up. She would turn on the light, then take one of the cup cakes from the stove, and go out to finish her business in the town. But for a moment longer she lay there with her face pressed close to Berenice's shoulder. The sounds of the summer evening were mingled and long-drawn.

"I never did say just what I was talking about," she said finally. "But there's this. I wonder if you have ever thought about this. Here we are — right now. This very minute. Now. But while we're talking right now, this minute is passing. And it will never come again. Never in all the world. When it is gone it is gone. No power on earth could bring it back again. It is gone. Have you ever thought about that?"

Berenice did not answer, and the kitchen was now dark. The three of them sat silent, close together, and they could feel and hear each other's breaths. Then suddenly it started, though why and how they did not know; the three of them began to cry. They started at exactly the same moment, in the way that often on these summer evenings they would suddenly start a song. Often in the dark, that August, they would all at once begin to sing a Christmas carol, or a song like the Slitbelly Blues. Sometimes they knew in advance that they would sing, and they would agree on the tune among themselves.

Or again, they would disagree and start off on three different songs at once, until at last the tunes began to merge and they sang a special music that the three of them made up together. John Henry sang in a high wailing voice, and no matter what he named his tune, it sounded always just the same: one high trembling note that hung like a musical ceiling over the rest of the song. Berenice's voice was dark and definite and deep, and she rapped the offbeats with her heel. The old Frankie sang up and down the middle space between John Henry and Berenice, so that their three voices were joined, and the parts of the song were woven together.

Often they would sing like this and their tunes were sweet and queer in the August kitchen after it was dark. But never before had they suddenly begun to cry; and though their reasons were three different reasons, yet they started at the same instant as though they had agreed together. John Henry was crying because he was jealous, though later he tried to say he cried because of the rat behind the wall. Berenice was crying because of their talk about colored people, or because of Ludie, or perhaps because F. Jasmine's bones were really sharp. F. Jasmine did not know why she cried, but the reason she named was the crew-cut and the fact that her elbows were so rusty. They cried in the dark for about a minute. Then they stopped as suddenly as they had begun. The unaccustomed sound had quieted the rat behind the wall.

"Get up from there," said Berenice. They stood around the kitchen table and F. Jasmine turned on the light. Berenice scratched her head and sniffled a little. "We certainy is a gloomy crowd. Now I wonder what started that."

The light was sudden and sharp after the darkness. F. Jasmine ran the faucet of the sink and put her head beneath the stream of water. And Berenice wiped off her face with a dishrag and patted her plaits before the mirror. John Henry stood like a little old woman dwarf, wearing the pink hat with the plume, and the high-heel shoes. The walls of the kitchen were crazy drawn and very bright. The three of them blinked at each other in the light as though they were three strangers or three ghosts. Then the front door opened and F. Jasmine heard her father trudging slowly down the hall. Already the moths were at the window, flattening their wings against the screen, and the final kitchen afternoon was over at last.

3

Early that evening F. Jasmine passed before the jail; she was on her way to Sugarville to have her fortune told and, though the jail was not directly on the way, she had wanted to have one final look at it before she left the town forever. For the jail had scared and haunted her that spring and summer. It was an old brick jail, three stories high, and surrounded by a cyclone fence topped with barbed wire. Inside were thieves, robbers, and murderers. The criminals were caged in stone cells with iron bars before the windows, and though they might beat on the stone walls or wrench at the iron bars, they could never get out. They wore striped jail clothes and ate cold peas with cockroaches cooked in them and cold cornbread.

F. Jasmine knew some people who had been locked up in jail, all of them colored — a boy called Cape, and a friend of Berenice who was accused by the white lady she worked for of stealing a sweater and a pair of shoes. When you were arrested, the Black Maria screamed to your house and a crowd of policemen burst in the door to haul you off down to the jail. After she took the three-bladed knife from the Sears and Roebuck Store, the jail had drawn the old Frankie — and sometimes on those late spring afternoons she would come to the street across from the jail, a place known as Jail-Widow's Walk, and stare for a long time. Often some criminals would be hanging to the bars; it seemed to her that their eyes, like the long eyes of the Freaks at the fair, had called to her as though to say: We know you. Occasionally, on Saturday afternoon, there would be wild yells and singing and hollering from the big cell known as the Bull Pen. But now this evening the jail was quiet — but from a lighted cell there was one criminal, or rather the outline of his head and his two fists around the bars. The brick jail was gloomy dark, although the yard and some cells were lighted.

"What are you locked up for?" John Henry called. He stood at a little distance from F. Jasmine and he was wearing the jonquil dress, as F. Jasmine had given him all the costumes. She had not wished to take him with her; but he had pleased and pleaded, and finally followed at a distance, anyway. When the criminal did not answer, he called again in a thin, high voice. "Are you going to be hung?"

"Hush up!" F. Jasmine said. The jail did not frighten her this evening, for this time tomorrow she would be far away. She gave the jail a last glance and then walked on. "How would you like for somebody to holler something like that to you if you were in jail?"

It was past eight o'clock when she reached Sugarville. The evening was dusty and lavender. Doors of the crowded houses on either side were open, and from some parlors there was the quavered flutter of oil lamps, lighting up the front-room beds and decorated mantelpieces. Voices sounded slurred and from a distance came the jazz of a piano and horn. Children played in alleyways, leaving whorled footsteps in the dust. The people were dressed for Saturday night, and on a corner she passed a group of jesting colored boys and girls in shining evening dresses. There was a party air about the street that reminded her that she, also, could go that very evening to a date at the Blue Moon. She spoke to people on the street and felt again the unexplainable connection between her eyes and other eyes. Mixed with the bitter dust, and smells of privies and suppertime, the smell of a clematis vine threaded the evening air. The house where Berenice lived was on the corner of Chinaberry Street — a two-room house with a tiny front yard bordered by shards and bottle-caps. A bench on the front porch held pots of cool, dark ferns. The door was only partly open and F. Jasmine could see the gold-gray flutters of the lamplight inside.

"You stay out here," she said to John Henry.

There was the murmuring of a strong, cracked voice behind the door, and when F. Jasmine knocked, the voice was quiet a second and then asked:

"Who that? Who is it?"

"Me," she said, for if she answered her true name, Big Mama would not recognize it. "Frankie."

The room was close, although the wooden shutter stood open, and there was the smell of sickness and fish. The crowded parlor was neat. One bed stood against the right wall, and on the opposite side of the room were a sewing machine and a pump organ. Over the hearth hung a photograph of Ludie Freeman; the mantelpiece was decorated with fancy calendars, fair prizes, souvenirs. Big Mama lay in the bed against the wall next to the door, so that in the daytime she could look out through the front window onto the ferny porch and street outside. She was an old colored woman, shriveled and with bones like broomsticks; on the left side of her face and neck the skin was the color of tallow, so that part of her face was almost white and the rest copper-colored. The old Frankie used to think that Big Mama was slowly turning to a white person, but Berenice had said it was a skin disease that sometimes happened to colored people. Big Mama had done fancy washing and fluted curtains until the year the misery had stiffened her back so that she took to bed. But she had not lost any faculties; instead, she suddenly found second-sight. The old Frankie had always thought she was uncanny, and when she was a little girl Big Mama was connected in her mind with the three ghosts who lived inside the coalhouse. And even now, a child no longer, she still had an eerie feeling about Big Mama. She was lying on three feather pillows, the covers of which were bordered with crochet, and over her bony legs there was a many-colored quilt. The parlor table with the lamp was pulled up close beside the bed so that she could reach the objects on it: a dream-book, a white saucer, a workbasket, a jellyglass of water, a Bible, and other things. Big Mama had been talking to herself before F. Jasmine came in, as she had the constant habit of telling herself just who she was and what she was doing and what she intended to do as she lay there in the bed. There were three mirrors on the walls which reflected the wavelike light from the lamp that fluttered gold-gray in the room and cast giant shadows; the lampwick needed trimming. Someone was walking in the back room.

"I came to get my fortune told," F. Jasmine said.

While Big Mama talked to herself when alone, she could be very silent at other times. She stared at F. Jasmine for several seconds before she answered: "Very well. Draw up that stool before the organ."

F. Jasmine brought the stool close to the bed, and leaning forward, stretched out her palm. But Big Mama did not take her palm. She examined F. Jasmine's face, then spat the wad of snuff into a chamberpot which she pulled from underneath the bed, and finally put on her glasses. She waited so long that it occurred to F. Jasmine that she was trying to read her mind, and this made her uneasy. The walking in the back room stopped and there was no sound in the house.

"Cast back your mind and remember," she said finally. "Tell me the revelation of your last dream."

F. Jasmine tried to cast back her mind, but she did not dream often. Then finally she remembered a dream she had had that summer: "I dreamed there was a door," she said. "I was just looking at it and while I watched, it began slowly to open. And it made me feel funny and I woke up."

"Was there a hand in the dream?"

F. Jasmine thought. "I don't think so."

"Was there a cockroach on that door?"

"Why — I don't think so."

"It signifies as follows." Big Mama slowly closed and opened her eyes. "There going be a change in your life."

Next she took F. Jasmine's palm and studied it for quite a while. "I see here where you going to marry a boy with blue eyes and light hair. You will live to be your threescore and ten, but you must act careful about water. I see here a red-clay ditch and a bale of cotton."

F. Jasmine thought to herself that there was nothing to it, only a pure waste of money and time. "What does that signify?"

But suddenly the old woman raised her head and the cords of her neck stiffened as she called: "You, Satan!"

She was looking at the wall between the parlor and the kitchen, and F. Jasmine turned to look over her shoulder also.

"Yessum," a voice replied from the back room, and it sounded like Honey.

"How many times is I got to tell you to take them big feets off the kitchen table!"

"Yessum," Honey said again. His voice was meek as Moses, and F. Jasmine could hear him put his feet down on the floor.

"Your nose is going to grow into that book, Honey Brown. Put it down and finish up your supper."

F. Jasmine shivered. Had Big Mama looked clear through the wall and seen Honey reading with his feet up on the table? Could those eyes pierce through a pure plank wall? It seemed as though it would behoove her to listen carefully to every word.

"I see here a sum of money. A sum of money. And I see a wedding."

F. Jasmine's outstretched hand trembled a little. "That!" she said. "Tell me about that!"

"The wedding or the money?"

"The wedding."

The lamplight made an enormous shadow of them on the bare boards of the wall. "It's the wedding of a near relation. And I foresee a trip ahead."

"A trip?" she asked. "What kind of a trip? A long trip?"

Big Mama's hands were crooked, spotted with freckly pale blots, and the palms were like melted pink birthday candles. "A short trip," she said.

"But how—?" F. Jasmine began.

"I see a going and a coming back. A departure and a return."

There was nothing to it, for surely Berenice had told her about the trip to Winter Hill and the wedding. But if she could see straight through a wall—"Are you sure?"

"Well—" This time the old cracked voice was not so certain. "I see a departure and a return, but it may not be for *now.* I can't guarantee. For at the same time I see roads, trains, and a sum of money."

"Oh!" F. Jasmine said.

There was the sound of footsteps, and Honey Camden Brown stood on the threshold between the kitchen and the parlor. He wore tonight a yellow shirt with a bow tie, for he was usually a natty dresser—but his dark eyes were sad, and his long face still as stone. F. Jasmine knew what Big Mama had said about Honey Brown. She said he was a boy God had not finished. The Creator had withdrawn His hand from him too soon. God had not finished him, and so he had to go around doing one thing and then another to finish himself up. When she had first heard this remark, the old Frankie did not understand the hidden meaning. Such a remark put her in mind of a peculiar half-boy — one arm, one leg, half a face — a half-person hopping in the gloomy summer sun around the corners of the town. But later she understood it a little better. Honey played the horn, and had been first in his studies at the colored high school. He ordered a French book from Atlanta and learned himself some French. At the same time he would suddenly run hog-wild all over Sugarville and tear around for several days, until his friends would bring him home more dead than living. His lips could move as light as butterflies and he could talk as well as any human she had ever heard — but other times he would answer with a colored jumble that even his own family could not follow. The Creator, Big Mama said, had withdrawn His hand from him too soon, so that he was left eternally unsatisfied. Now he stood there leaning against the door jamb, bony and limp, and although the sweat showed on his face he somehow looked cold.

"Do you wish anything before I go?" he asked.

There was something about Honey that evening that struck F. Jasmine; it was as though, on looking into his sad, still eyes, she felt she had something to say to him. His skin in the lamplight was the color of dark wistaria and the lips were quiet and blue.

"Did Berenice tell you about the wedding?" F. Jasmine asked. But, for once, it was not about the wedding that she felt she had to speak.

"Aaannh," he answered.

"There's nothing I wish now. T.T. is due here in a minute to visit with me for a while and meet up with Berenice. Where you off to, boy?"

"I'm going over to Forks Falls."

"Well, Mr. Up and Sudden, when you done decide that?"

Honey stood leaning against the door jamb, stubborn and quiet.

"Why can't you act like everybody else?" Big Mama said.

"I'll just stay over through Sunday and come back Monday morning."

The feeling that she had something to say to Honey Brown still troubled F. Jasmine. She said to Big Mama: "You were telling me about the wedding."

"Yes." She was not looking at F. Jasmine's palm, but at the organdie dress and the silk hose and the new silver slippers. "I told you you would marry a light-haired boy with blue eyes. Later on."

"But that's not what I'm talking about. I mean the other wedding. And the trip and what you saw about the roads and trains."

"Exactly," said Big Mama, but F. Jasmine had the feeling she was no longer paying much mind to her, although she looked again at her palm. "I foresee a trip with a departure and a return and later a sum of money, roads and trains. Your lucky number is six, although thirteen is sometimes lucky for you too."

F. Jasmine wanted to protest and argue, but how could you argue with a fortune-teller? She wanted at least to understand the fortune better, for the trip with the return did not fit in with the foreseeing of roads and trains.

But as she was about to question further, there were footsteps on the front porch, a door knock, and T.T. came into the parlor. He was very proper, scraping his feet, and bringing Big Mama a carton of ice cream. Berenice had said he did not make her shiver, and it was true he was nobody's pretty man; his stomach was like a watermelon underneath his vest and there were rolls of fat on the back of his neck. He brought in with him the stir of company that she had always loved and envied about this two-room house. Always it had seemed to the old Frankie, when she could come here hunting Berenice, that there would be many people in the room — the family, various cousins, friends. In the wintertime they would sit by the hearth around the draughty, shivering fire and talk with woven voices. On clear autumn nights they were always the first to have sugar cane and Berenice would hack the joints of the slick, purple cane and they would throw the chewed, twisted pieces, marked with their teeth-prints, on a newspaper spread upon the floor. The lamplight gave the room a special look, a special smell.

Now, with the coming of T.T., there was the old sense of company and commotion. The fortune was evidently over, and F. Jasmine put a dime in the white china saucer on the parlor table — for, although there was no fixed price, the future-anxious folks who came to Big Mama usually paid what they felt due.

"I declare I never did see anybody grow like you do, Frankie," Big Mama remarked. "What you ought to do is tie a brickbat to your head." F. Jasmine shriveled on her heels, her knees bent slightly, and her shoulders hunched. "That's a sweet dress you got on. And them silver shoes! And silk stockings! You look like a regular grown girl."

F. Jasmine and Honey left the house at the same time, and she was still fretted by the feeling that she had something to say to him. John Henry, who had been waiting in the lane, rushed toward them, but Honey did not pick him up and swing him around as he sometimes did. There was a cold sadness about Honey this evening. The moonlight was white.

"What are you going to do in Forks Falls?"

"Just mess around."

"Do you put any faith in those fortunes?" When Honey did not answer, she went on: "You remember when she hollered back to you to take your feet off the table. Gave me a shock. How did she know your feet were on the table?"

"The mirror," Honey said. "She has a mirror by the door so she can see what goes on in the kitchen."

"Oh," she said. "I never have believed in fortunes."

John Henry was holding Honey's hand and looking up into his face. "What are horsepowers?"

F. Jasmine felt the power of the wedding; it was as though, on this last evening, she ought to order and advise. There was something she ought to tell Honey, a warning or some wise advice. And as she fumbled in her mind, an idea came to her. It was so new, so unexpected, that she stopped walking and stood absolutely still.

"I know what you ought to do. You ought to go to Cuba or Mexico."

Honey had walked on a few steps farther, but when she spoke he stopped also. John Henry was midway between them, and as he looked from one to the other, his face in the white moonlight had a mysterious expression.

"Sure enough. I'm perfectly serious. It don't do you any good to mess around between Forks Falls and this town. I've seen a whole lot of pictures of Cubans and Mexicans. They have a good time." She paused. "This is what I'm trying to discuss. I don't think you will ever be happy in this town. I think you ought to go to Cuba. You are so light-skinned and you even have a kind of Cuban expression. You could go there and change into a Cuban. You could learn to speak the foreign language and none of those Cubans would ever know you are a colored boy. Don't you see what I mean?"

Honey was still as a dark statue, and as silent.

"What?" John Henry asked again. "What do they look like — them horsepowers?"

With a jerk Honey turned and went on down the lane. "It is fantastic."

"No, it is not!" Pleased that Honey had used the word fantastic to her, she said it quietly to herself before she went on to insist. "It's not a particle fantastic. You mark my words. It's the best thing you can do."

But Honey only laughed and turned off at the next alley. "So long."

The streets in the middle of the town reminded F. Jasmine of a carnival fair. There was the same air of holiday freedom; and, as in the early morning, she felt herself a part of everything, included and gay. On a Main Street corner a man was selling mechanical mice, and an armless beggar, with a tin cup in his lap, sat cross-legged on the sidewalk, watching. She had never seen Front Avenue at night before, for in the evening she was supposed to play in the neighborhood close to home. The warehouses across the street were black, but the square mill at the far end of the avenue was lighted in all its many windows and there was a faint mill humming and the smell of dyeing vats. Most of the businesses were open, and the neon signs made a mingling of varied lights that gave to the avenue a watery look. There were soldiers on corners, and other soldiers strolling along with grown date girls. The sounds were slurred late-summer sounds — footsteps, laughter, and above the shuffled noises, the voice of someone calling from an upper story down into the summer street. The buildings smelled of sunbaked brick and the sidewalk was warm beneath the soles of her new silver shoes. F. Jasmine stopped on the corner across from the Blue Moon. It seemed a long time since that morning when she had joined up with the soldier; the long kitchen afternoon had come between, and the soldier had somehow faded. The date, that afternoon, had seemed so very far away. And now that it was almost nine o'clock, she hesitated. She had the unexplainable feeling that there was a mistake.

"Where are we going?" John Henry asked. "I think it's high time we went home."

His voice startled her, as she had almost forgotten him. He stood there with his knees locked, big-eyed and drabbled in the old tarletan costume. "I have business in town. You go home." He stared up at her and took the bubble gum he had been chewing from his mouth — he tried to park the gum behind his ear, but sweat had made his ear too slippery, so finally he put the gum back in his mouth again. "You know the way home as well as I do. So do what I tell you." For a wonder, John Henry minded her; but, as she watched him going away from her down the crowded street, she felt a hollow sorriness — he looked so babyish and pitiful in the costume.

The change from the street to the inside of the Blue Moon was like the change that comes on leaving the open fairway and entering a booth. Blue lights and moving faces, noise. The counter and tables were crowded with soldiers, and men, and bright-faced ladies. The soldier she had promised to meet was playing the slot machine in a far corner, putting in nickel after nickel, but winning none.

"Oh, it's you," he said when he noticed her standing at his elbow. For a second his eyes had the blank look of eyes that are peering back into the brain to recollect — but only for a second. "I was scared you had stood me up." After putting in a final nickel, he banged the slot machine with his fist. "Let's find a place."

They sat at a table between the counter and the slot machine, and, although by the clock the time was not long, it seemed to F. Jasmine endless. Not that the soldier was not nice to her. He was nice, but their two conversations would not join together, and underneath there was a layer of queerness she could not place and understand. The soldier had washed, and his swollen face, his ears and hands, were clean; his red hair was darkened from wetting and ridged with a comb. He said he had slept that afternoon. He was gay and his talk was sassy. But although she liked gay people and sassy talk, she could not think of any answers. It was again as though the soldier talked a kind of double-talk that, try as she would, she could not follow — yet it was not so much the actual remarks as the tone underneath she failed to understand.

The soldier brought two drinks to the table; after a swallow F. Jasmine suspected there was liquor in them and, although a child no longer, she was shocked. It was a sin and against the law for people under eighteen to drink real liquor, and she pushed the glass away. The soldier was both nice and gay, but after he had had two other drinks she wondered if he could be drunk. To make conversation she remarked that her brother had been swimming in Alaska, but this did not seem to impress him very much. Nor would he talk about the war, nor foreign countries and the world. To his joking remarks she could never find replies that fitted, although she tried. Like a nightmare pupil in a recital who has to play a duet to a piece she does not know, F. Jasmine did her best to catch the tune and follow. But soon she broke down and grinned until her mouth felt wooden. The blue lights in the crowded room, the smoke and noisy commotion, confused her also.

"You're a funny kind of girl," the soldier said finally.

"Patton," she said. "I bet he will win the war in two weeks."

The soldier was quiet now and his face had a heavy look. His eyes gazed at her with the same strange expression she had noticed that day at noon, a look she had never seen on anyone before and could not place. After a while he said, and his voice was softened, blurred: "What did you say your name is, Beautiful?"

F. Jasmine did not know whether or not to like the way he called her, and she spoke her name in a proper voice.

"Well, Jasmine, how bout going on upstairs?" His tone was asking, but when she did not answer at once, he stood up from the table. "I've got a room here."

"Why, I thought we were going to the Idle Hour. Or dancing or something."

"What's the rush?" he said. "The band don't hardly tune up until eleven o'clock."

F. Jasmine did not want to go upstairs, but she did not know how to refuse. It was like going into a fair booth, or fair ride, that once having entered you cannot leave until the exhibition or the ride is finished. Now it was the same with this soldier, this date. She could not leave until it ended. The soldier was waiting at the foot of the stairs and, unable to refuse, she followed after him. They went up two flights, and then along a narrow hall that smelled of wee-wee and linoleum. But every footstep F. Jasmine took, she felt somehow was wrong.

"This sure is a funny hotel," she said.

It was the silence in the hotel room that warned and frightened her, a silence she noticed as soon as the door was closed. In the light of the bare electric bulb that hung down from the ceiling, the room looked hard and very ugly. The flaked iron bed had been slept in and a suitcase of jumbled soldier's clothes lay open in the middle of the floor. On the light oak bureau there was a glass pitcher full of water and a half-eaten package of cinnamon rolls covered with blue-white icing and fat flies. The screenless window was open and the sleazy voile curtains had been tied at the top in a knot together to let in air. There was a lavatory in the corner and, cupping his hands, the soldier dashed cold water to his face — the soap was only a bar of ordinary soap, already used, and over the lavatory a sign read: STRICTLY WASHING. Although the soldier's footsteps sounded, and the water made a trickling noise, the sense of silence somehow remained.

F. Jasmine went to the window which overlooked a narrow alley and a brick wall; a rickety fire-escape led to the ground and light shafted from the two lower stories. Outside there were the August evening sounds of voices and a radio, and in the room there were sounds also — so how could the silence be explained? The soldier sat on the bed, and now she was seeing him altogether as a single person, not as a member of the loud free gangs who for a season roamed the streets of town and then went out into the world together. In the silent room he seemed to her unjoined and ugly. She could not see him any more in Burma, Africa, or Iceland, or even for that matter in Arkansas. She saw him only as he sat there in the room. His light blue eyes, set close together, were staring at her with the peculiar look — with a filmed softness, like eyes that have been washed with milk.

The silence in the room was like that silence in the kitchen when, on a drowsy afternoon, the ticking of the clock would stop — and there would steal over her a mysterious uneasiness that lasted until she realized what was wrong. A few times before she had known such silence — once in the Sears and Roebuck Store the moment before she suddenly became a thief, and again that April afternoon in the MacKeans' garage. It was the forewarning hush that comes before an unknown trouble, a silence caused, not by lack of sounds, but by a waiting, a suspense. The soldier did not take those strange eyes from her and she was scared.

"Come on, Jasmine," he said, in an unnatural voice, broken and low, as he reached out his hand, palm upward, toward her. "Let's quit this stalling."

The next minute was like a minute in the fair Crazy-House, or real Milledgeville. Already F. Jasmine had started for the door, for she could no longer stand the silence. But as she passed the soldier, he grasped her skirt and, limpened by fright, she was pulled down beside him on the bed. The next minute happened, but it was too crazy to be realized. She felt his arms around her and smelled his sweaty shirt. He was not rough, but it was crazier than if he had been rough — and in a second she was paralyzed by horror. She could not push away, but she bit down with all her might upon what must have been the crazy soldier's tongue — so that he screamed out and she was free. Then he was coming toward her with an amazed pained face, and her hand reached the glass pitcher and brought it down upon his head. He swayed a second, then slowly his legs began to crumple, and slowly he sank sprawling to the floor. The sound was hollow like the hammer on a coconut, and with it the silence was broken at last. He lay there still, with the amazed expression on his freckled face that was now pale, and a froth of blood showed on his mouth. But his head was not broken, or even cracked, and whether he was dead or not she did not know.

The silence was over, and it was like those kitchen times when, after the first uncanny moments, she realized the reason for her uneasiness and knew that the ticking of the clock had stopped — but now there was no clock to shake and hold for a minute to her ear before she wound it, feeling relieved. There slanted across her mind twisted remembrances of a common fit in the front room, basement remarks, and nasty Barney; but she did not let these separate glimpses fall together, and the word she repeated was "crazy." There was water on the walls which had been slung out from the pitcher and the soldier had a broken look in the strewn room. F. Jasmine told herself: Get out! And after first starting toward the door, she turned and climbed out on the fire-escape and quickly reached the alley ground.

She ran like a chased person fleeing from the crazy-house at Milledgeville, looking neither to the right nor left, and when she reached the corner of her own home block, she was glad to see John Henry West. He was out looking for bats around the street light, and the familiar sight of him calmed her a little.

"Uncle Royal has been calling you," he said. "What makes you shake like that for, Frankie?"

"I just now brained a crazy man," she told him when she could get her breath. "I brained him and I don't know if he is dead. He was a crazy man."

John Henry stared without surprise. "How did he act like?" And when she did not answer all at once, he went on: "Did he crawl on the ground and moan and slobber?" For that was what the old Frankie had done one day to try to fool Berenice and create some excitement. Berenice had not been fooled. "Did he?"

"No," F. Jasmine said. "He —" But as she looked into those cold, child eyes she knew that she could not explain. John Henry would not understand, and his green eyes gave her a funny feeling. Sometimes his mind was like the pictures he drew with crayons on tablet paper. The other day he had drawn such a one and showed it to her. It was a picture of a telephone man on a telephone pole. The telephone man was leaning against his safety belt, and the picture was complete down to his climbing shoes. It was a careful picture, but after she had looked at it uneasiness had lingered in her mind. She looked at the picture again until she realized what was wrong. The telephone man was drawn in side-view profile, yet this profile had two eyes — one eye just above the nose bridge and another drawn just below. And it was no hurried mistake; both eyes had careful lashes, pupils, and lids. Those two eyes drawn in a side-view face gave her a funny feeling. But reason with John Henry, argue with him? You might as well argue with cement. What did he do it for? Why? Because it was a telephone man. What? Because he was climbing the pole. It was impossible to understand his point of view. And he did not understand her either.

"Forget what I just now told you," she said. But after saying it, she realized that was the worst remark she could have said, for he would be sure not to forget. So she took him by the shoulders and shook him slightly. "Swear you won't tell. Swear this: If I tell I hope God will sew up my mouth and sew down my eyes and cut off my ears with the scissors."

But John Henry would not swear; he only hunched his big head down near his shoulders and answered, very quietly: "Shoo."

She tried again. "If you tell anybody I might be put in jail and we couldn't go to the wedding."

"I ain't going to tell," John Henry said. Sometimes he could be trusted, and other times not. "I'm not a tattle-tale."

Once inside the house, F. Jasmine locked the front door before she went into the living room. Her father was reading the evening paper, in his sock feet, on the sofa. F. Jasmine was glad to have her father between her and the front door. She was afraid of the Black Maria and listened anxiously.

"I wish we were going to the wedding right this minute," she said. "I think that would be the best thing to do."

She went back to the icebox and ate six tablespoons of sweetened condensed milk, and the disgust in her mouth began to go away. The waiting made her feel restless. She gathered up the library books, and stacked them on the living-room table. On one of them, a book from the grown sections which she had not read, she wrote in the front with pencil: *If you want to read something that will shock you, turn to page 66.* On page 66 she wrote: *Electricity. Ha! Ha!* By and by her anxiousness was eased; close to her father she felt less afraid.

"These books belong to go back to the library."

Her father, who was forty-one, looked at the clock: "It's time for everybody under forty-one to get to bed. Quick, march, and without any argument. We have to be up at five o'clock."

F. Jasmine stood in the doorway, unable to leave. "Papa," she said, after a minute, "if somebody hits somebody with a glass pitcher and he falls out cold, do you think he is dead?"

She had to repeat the question, feeling a bitter grudge against him because he did not take her seriously, so that her questions must be asked twice.

"Why, come to think about it, I never hit anybody with a pitcher," he said. "Did you?"

F. Jasmine knew he asked this as a joke, so she only said as she went away: "I'll never be so glad to get to any place in all my life as Winter Hill tomorrow. I will be so thankful when the wedding is over and we have gone away. I will be so thankful."

Upstairs she and John Henry undressed, and after the motor and the light were off, they lay down on the bed together — although she said she could not sleep a wink. But nevertheless she closed her eyes, and when she opened them again a voice was calling and the room was early gray.

Part Three

She said: "Farewell, old ugly house," as, wearing a dotted Swiss dress and carrying the suitcase, she passed through the hall at quarter to six. The wedding dress was in the suitcase, ready to be put on when she reached Winter Hill. At that still hour the sky was the dim silver of a mirror, and beneath it the gray town looked, not like a real town, but like an exact reflection of itself, and to this unreal town she also said farewell. The bus left the station at ten past six — and she sat proud, like an accustomed traveler, apart from her father, John Henry, and Berenice. But after a while a serious doubt came in her, which even the answers of the bus-driver could not quite satisfy. They were supposed to be traveling north, but it seemed to her rather that the bus was going south instead. The sky turned burning pale and the day blazed. They passed the fields of windless corn that had a blue look in the glare, red-furrowed cotton land, stretches of black pine woods. And mile by mile the countryside became more southern. The towns they passed — New City, Leeville, Cheehaw — each town seemed smaller than the one before, until at nine o'clock they reached the ugliest place of all, where they changed busses, called Flowering Branch. Despite its name there were no flowers and no branch — only a solitary country store, with a sad old shredded circus poster on the clapboard wall and a chinaberry tree beneath which stood an empty wagon and a sleeping mule. There they waited for the bus to Sweet Well, and, still doubting anxiously, Frances did not despise the box of lunch that had so shamed her at the first, because it made them look like family people who do not travel very much. The bus left at ten o'clock, and they were in Sweet Well by eleven. The next hours were unexplainable. The wedding was like a dream, for all that came about occurred in a world beyond her power; from the moment when, sedate and proper, she shook hands with the grown people until the time, the wrecked wedding over, when she watched the car with the two of them driving away from her, and, flinging herself down in the sizzling dust, she cried out for the last time: "Take me! Take me!" — from the beginning to the end the wedding was unmanaged as a nightmare. By mid-afternoon it was all finished and the return bus left at four o'clock.

"The show is over and the monkey's dead," John Henry quoted, as he settled himself in the next to the last bus seat beside her father. "Now we go home and go to bed."

Frances wanted the whole world to die. She sat on the back seat, between the window and Berenice, and, though she was no longer sobbing, the tears were like two little brooks, and also her nose ran water. Her shoulders were hunched over her swollen heart and she no longer wore the wedding dress. She was sitting next to Berenice, back with the colored people, and when she thought of it she used the mean word she had never used before, nigger — for now she hated everyone and wanted only to spite and shame. For John Henry West the wedding had only been a great big show, and he had enjoyed her misery at the end as he had enjoyed the angel cake. She mortally despised him, dressed in his best white suit, now stained with strawberry ice cream. Berenice she hated also, for to her it had only meant a pleasure trip to Winter Hill. Her father, who had said that he would attend to her when they got home, she would like to kill. She was against every single person, even strangers in the crowded bus, though she only saw them blurred by tears — and she wished the bus would fall in a river or run into a train. Herself she hated the worst of all, and she wanted the whole world to die.

"Cheer up," said Berenice. "Wipe your face and blow your nose and things will look better by and by."

Berenice had a blue party handkerchief, to match her blue best dress and blue kid shoes — and this she offered to Frances, although it was made of fine georgette and not, of course, due to be blown on. She would not notice it. In the seat between them there were three wet handkerchiefs of her father's, and Berenice began to dry the tears with one, but Frances did not move or budge.

"They put old Frankie out of the wedding." John Henry's big head bobbed over the back of his seat, smiling and snaggled-toothed. Her father cleared his throat and said: "That's sufficient, John Henry. Leave Frankie alone." And Berenice added: "Sit down in that seat now and behave."

The bus rode for a long time, and now direction made no difference to her; she did not care. From the beginning the wedding had been queer like the card games in the kitchen the first week last June. In those bridge games they played and played for many days, but nobody ever drew a good hand, the cards were all sorry, and no high bids made — until finally Berenice suspicioned, saying: "Less us get busy and count these old cards." And they got busy and counted the old cards, and it turned out the jacks and the queens were missing. John Henry at last admitted that he had cut out the jacks and then the queens to keep them company and, after hiding the clipped scraps in the stove, had secretly taken the pictures home. So the fault of the card game was discovered. But how could the failure of the wedding be explained?

The wedding was all wrong, although she could not point out single faults. The house was a neat brick house out near the limits of the small, baked town, and when she first put foot inside, it was as though her eyeballs had been slightly stirred; there were mixed impressions of pink roses, the smell of floor wax, mints and nuts in silver trays. Everybody was lovely to her. Mrs. Williams wore a lace dress, and she asked F. Jasmine two times what grade she was in at school. But she asked, also, if she would like to play out on the swing before the wedding, in the tone grown people use when speaking to a child. Mr. Williams was nice to her, too. He was a sallow man with folds in his cheeks and the skin beneath his eyes was the grain and color of an old apple core. Mr. Williams also asked her what grade she was in at school; in fact, that was the main question asked her at the wedding.

She wanted to speak to her brother and the bride, to talk to them and tell them of her plans, the three of them alone together. But they were never once alone; Jarvis was out checking the car someone was lending for the honeymoon, while Janice dressed in the front bedroom among a crowd of beautiful grown girls. She wandered from one to the other of them, unable to explain. And once Janice put her arms around her, and said she was so glad to have a little sister — and when Janice kissed her, F. Jasmine felt an aching in her throat and could not speak. Jarvis, when she went to find him in the yard, lifted her up in a rough-house way and said: Frankie the lankie the alaga fankie, the tee-legged toe-legged bow-legged Frankie. And he gave her a dollar.

She stood in the corner of the bride's room, wanting to say: I love the two of you so much and you are the we of me. Please take me with you from the wedding, for we belong to be together. Or even if she could have said: May I trouble you to step into the next room, as I have something to reveal to you and Jarvis? And get the three of them in a room alone together and somehow manage to explain. If only she had written it down on the typewriter in advance, so that she could hand it to them and they would read! But this she had not thought to do, and her tongue was heavy in her mouth and dumb. She could only speak in a voice that shook a little — to ask where was the veil?

"I can feel in the atmosphere a storm is brewing," said Berenice. "These two crooked joints can always tell."

There was no veil except a little veil that came down from the wedding hat, and nobody was wearing fancy clothes. The bride was wearing a daytime suit. The only mercy of it was that she had not worn her wedding dress on the bus, as she had first intended, and found it out in time. She stood in a corner of the bride's room until the piano played the first notes of the wedding march. They were all lovely to her at Winter Hill, except that they called her Frankie and treated her too young. It was so unlike what she had expected, and, as in those June card games, there was, from first to last, the sense of something terribly gone wrong.

"Perk up," said Berenice. "I'm planning a big surprise for you. I'm just sitting here planning. Don't you want to know what it is?"

Frances did not answer even by a glance. The wedding was like a dream outside her power, or like a show unmanaged by her in which she was supposed to have no part. The living room was crowded with Winter Hill company, and the bride and her brother stood before the mantelpiece at the end of the room. And seeing them again together was more like singing feeling than a picture that her dizzied eyes could truly see. She watched them with her heart, but all the time she was only thinking: I have not told them and they don't know. And knowing this was heavy as a swallowed stone. And afterward, during the kissing of the bride, refreshments served in the dining room, the stir and party bustle — she hovered close to the two of them, but words would not come. They are not going to take me, she was thinking, and this was the one thought she could not bear.

When Mr. Williams brought their bags, she hastened after with her own suitcase. The rest was like some nightmare show in which a wild girl in the audience breaks onto the stage to take upon herself an unplanned part that was never written or meant to be. You are the we of me, her heart was saying, but she could only say aloud: "Take me!" And they pleaded and begged with her, but she was already in the car. At the last she clung to the steering wheel until her father and somebody else had hauled and dragged her from the car, and even then she could only cry in the dust of the empty road: "Take me! Take me!" But there was only the wedding company to hear, for the bride and her brother had driven away.

Berenice said: "School will begin now in only three more weeks. And you'll go into the A section of the seventh grade and meet a lot of nice new children and make another bosom friend like that Evelyn Owen you were so wild about."

The kind tone Frances could not stand. "I never meant to go with them!" she said. "It was all just a joke. They said they were going to invite me to a visit when they get settled, but I wouldn't go. Not for a million dollars."

"We know all about that," said Berenice. "Now listen to my surprise I've planned. Soon as you get settled in school and have a chance to make these friends, I think it would be a good idea to have a party. A lovely bridge party in the living room, with potato salad and those little olive sandwiches your Aunt Pet had for a club meeting you were so carried away about — the round-shaped kind with the tiny round hole in the middle and the olive showing. A lovely bridge party with delicious refreshments. How would you like that?"

The baby promises rasped her nerves. Her cheap heart hurt, and she pressed her crossed arms over it and rocked a little. "It was a framed game. The cards were stacked. It was a frame-up all around."

"We can have that bridge party going on in the living room. And out in the back yard we can have another party at the same time. A costume party with hot dogs. One party dainty and the other one rough. With prizes for the highest bridge score and the funniest costume. How does that strike you?"

Frances refused to look at Berenice or answer.

"You could call up the society editor of the *Evening Journal* and have the party written up in the paper. And that would make the fourth time your name has been published in the paper."

It would, but a thing like that no longer mattered to her. Once, when her bike ran into an automobile, the paper had called her Fankie Addams. *Fankie!* But now she did not care.

"Don't be so blue," said Berenice. "This is not doomsday."

"Frankie, don't cry," John Henry said. "We will go home and put up the tepee and have a good time."

She could not stop crying and the sobbing had a strangled sound. "Oh, hush up your mouth!"

"Listen to me. Tell me what you would like and I'll try to do it if it's in my power."

"All I would like," said Frances, after a minute, "all I wish in the world, is for no human being ever to speak to me so long as I live."

And Berenice said, finally: "Well. Then bawl, then, Misery."

They did not talk the rest of the way back to the town. Her father slept with a handkerchief over his nose and eyes, snoring a little. John Henry West lay in her father's lap and slept also. The other passengers were drowsy quiet and the bus rocked like a cradle and made a softly roaring sound. Outside the afternoon shimmered and now and then there was a buzzard lazily balanced against the blazing pale sky. They passed red empty crossroads with deep red gulches on either side, and rotten gray shacks set in the lonesome cotton fields. Only the dark pine trees looked cool — and the low blue hills when seen from miles away. Frances watched from the window with a stiff sick face and for four hours did not say a word. They were entering the town, and a change came. The sky lowered and turned a purple-gray against which the trees were a poison green. There was a jellied stillness in the air and then the mutter of the first thunder. A wind came through the treetops with a sound like rushing water, fore-warning storm.

"I told you so," said Berenice, and she was not speaking of the wedding. "I could feel the misery in these joints. After a good storm we will all feel much better."

The rain did not come, and there was only a feeling of expectation in the air. The wind was hot. Frances smiled a little at Berenice's words, but it was a scorning smile that hurt.

"You think it's all over," she said, "but that only shows how little you know."

They thought it was finished, but she would show them. The wedding had not included her, but she would still go into the world. Where she was going she did not know; however, she was leaving town that night. If she could not go in the way she had planned, safe with her brother and the bride, she would go, anyway. Even if she had to commit every crime. For the first time since the night before she thought about the soldier — but only in a glancing way, for her mind was busy with hasty plans. There was a train that passed through the town at two o'clock, and she would take it; the train went north in a general way, probably to Chicago or New York. If the train went to Chicago, she would go on to Hollywood and write shows or get a job as a movie starlet — or, if worse came to worst, even act in comedies. If the train went to New York, she would dress like a boy and give a false name and a false age and join the Marines. Meanwhile, she had to wait until her father was asleep, and she could still hear him moving in the kitchen. She sat at the typewriter and wrote a letter.

Dear Father:

This is a farewell letter until I write you from a different place. I told you I was going to leave town because it is inevitable. I cannot stand this existance any longer because my life has become a burden. I am taking the pistol because who can tell when it might come in handy and I will send back the money to you at the very first opportunaty. Tell Berenice not to worry. The whole thing is a irony of fate and it is inevitable. Later I will write. Please Papa do not try to capture me.

Sincerely Yours,
Frances Addams

The green-and-white moths were nervous at the window screen and the night outside was queer. The hot wind had stopped and the air was so still that it seemed solid and there was a weight against you when you moved. The thunder grumbled low occasionally. Frances sat motionless before the typewriter, wearing the dotted Swiss dress, and the strapped suitcase was beside the door. After a while the light in the kitchen was turned off and her father called from the foot of the stairs: "Good night, Picklepriss. Good night, John Henry."

Frances waited a long time. John Henry was sleeping across the foot of the bed, still dressed and with his shoes on, and his mouth was open and one ear of his glasses frame had come loose. After waiting as long as she could stand it, she took the suitcase and tiptoed very quietly down the stairs. It was dark down there, dark in her father's room, dark through the house. She stood on the threshold of her father's room and he was snoring softly. The hardest time was the few minutes she stood there, listening.

The rest was easy. Her father was a widow-man, set in his ways, and at night he folded his pants over a straight chair and left his wallet, watch, and glasses on the right-hand side of the bureau. She moved very quietly in the darkness and laid hand on the wallet almost immediately. She was careful opening the bureau drawer, stopping to listen each time there was a scraping sound. The pistol felt heavy and cool in her hot hand. It was easy except for the loudness of beating heart and for an accident that happened just as she crept from the room. She stumbled over a wastepaper basket and the snoring stopped. Her father stirred, muttered. She held her breath — then finally, after a minute, the snoring went on again.

She put the letter on the table and tiptoed to the back porch. But there was one thing she had not counted on — John Henry began to call.

"Frankie!" The high child voice seemed to carry through all the rooms of the night house. "Where are you?"

"Hush," she whispered. "Go back to sleep."

She had left the light on in her room, and he stood in the stairway door and looked down into the dark kitchen. "What are you doing down there in the dark?"

"Hush!" she said again in a loud whisper. "I'll be there by the time you get to sleep."

She waited a few minutes after John Henry had gone, then groped to the back door, unlocked it, and stepped outside. But, though she was very quiet, he must have heard her. "Wait, Frankie!" he wailed. "I'm coming."

The child wailing had waked her father, and she knew it before she reached the corner of the house. The night was dark and heavy, and as she ran, she heard her father calling her. Behind the corner of the house she looked and saw the kitchen light go on; the bulb swung back and forth, making a swinging gold reflection on the arbor and the dark yard. He will read the letter now, she thought, and chase and try to capture me. But after she had run a few blocks, the suitcase bumping against her legs and sometimes nearly tripping her, she remembered that her father would have to put on pants and a shirt — for he would not chase her through the streets dressed only in pajama bottoms. She stopped for a second to look behind. No one was there. At the first street light she put down the suitcase and, taking the wallet from the front pocket of her dress, opened it with shaking hands. Inside there was three dollars and fifteen cents. She would have to hop a box car, or something.

All at once, alone there in the night-empty street, she realized she did not know how. It is easy to talk about hopping a freight train, but how did bums and people really do it? She was three blocks from the station and she walked toward it slowly. The station was closed and she went round it and stared at the platform, long and empty under the pale lights, with the Chiclet machines against the station wall and scraps of chewing-gum paper and candy wrappings on the platform. The train tracks gleamed silver and exact and some freight cars were off on a siding in the distance, but they were not hooked to any engine. The train would not come until two o'clock, and would she be able to hop a car, as she had read about, and get away? There was a red lantern a little way down the tracks, and against this colored light she saw a railroad man come walking slowly. She could not hang around like that until two o'clock — but as she left the station, one shoulder dragged down by the weight of the bag, she did not know where she should go.

The streets were lonesome and idle with Sunday night. The red-and-green neon lights in the signboards mixed with the streetlights to make a pale hot haze above the town, but the sky was starless, black. A man in a tilted hat took out his cigarette and turned to stare at her as she passed by. She could not wander around the town like this, for by this time her father would be chasing her. In the alley behind Finny's Place she sat down on the suitcase, and only then she realized that the pistol was still in her left hand. She had been going around with the pistol held right in her hand, and she felt that she had lost her mind. She had said that she would shoot herself if the bride and her brother would not take her. She pointed the pistol at the side of her head and held it there a minute or two. If she squeezed the trigger she would be dead — and deadness was blackness, nothing but pure terrible blackness that went on and on and never ended until the end of all the world. When she lowered the pistol, she told herself that at the last minute she had changed her mind. The pistol she put in her suitcase.

The alley was black and smelled of garbage cans, and it was in this alley where Lon Baker had his throat slashed that spring afternoon so that his neck was like a bloody mouth that gibbered in the sun. It was here Lon Baker had been killed. And had she killed the soldier, when she brained his head with the water pitcher? She was scared in the dark alley and her mind felt splintered. If only there was someone with her! If only she could hunt down Honey Brown and they could go away together! But Honey had gone to Forks Falls and would not be back until tomorrow. Or if she could find the monkey and the monkey-man and join with them to run away! There was a scuttling noise, and she jerked with terror. A cat had leaped up on a garbage can, and in the darkness she could see its outline against the light at the end of the alley. She whispered: "Charles!" and then, "Charlina." But it was not her Persian cat, and when she stumbled toward the can it sprang away.

She could stand the black sour alley no longer and, carrying the suitcase toward the light at the end, she stood close to the sidewalk, but still inside the shadow of a wall. If there was only somebody to tell her what to do and where to go and how to get there! The fortune of Big Mama had turned out true — about the sort of trip and a departure and a return, and even the cotton bales, for the bus had passed a truck of them on the way back from Winter Hill. And there was the sum of money in her father's wallet, so that already she had lived up all the fortune Big Mama had foreseen. Should she go down to the house in Sugarville and say that she had used up the whole future, and what was she now to do?

Beyond the shadow of the alley the gloomy street was like a street that waited, with the winking neon Coca-Cola sign on the next corner, and a lady walking back and forth beneath a street light as though expecting someone. A car, a long closed car that maybe was a Packard, came slowly down the street, and the way it cruised close to the curb reminded her of a gangster's car, so that she shrank back closer to the wall. Then, on the opposite sidewalk, two people passed, and a feeling like a sudden flame sprang up inside her, and for less than a second it seemed that her brother and the bride had come for her and were now *there.* But the feeling blew out instantly and she was just watching a stranger couple passing down the street. There was a hollow in her chest, but at the bottom of this emptiness a heavy weight pressed down and bruised her stomach, so that she felt sick. She told herself she ought to get busy and pick up her feet and go away. But she still stood there, her eyes closed, and her head against the warm brick wall.

When she left the alley, it was a long time after midnight and she had reached the point where any sudden idea seemed a good idea. She had seized on first one notion and then another. To hitch-hike to Forks Falls and track down Honey, or to wire Evelyn Owen to meet her in Atlanta, or even to go back to the house and get John Henry, so that at least there would be somebody with her and she would not have to go into the world alone. But there was some objection to each of these ideas.

Then, all at once, from the tangle of turning impossibilities, she thought of the soldier; and this time the thought was not a glancing one — it lingered, stuck, and did not go away. She wondered if she ought to go to the Blue Moon and find if she had killed the soldier, before she left the town forever. The idea, once seized on, seemed to her good, and she started for Front Avenue. If she had not killed the soldier, then when she found him what could she say? How the next thought occurred to her she did not know, but suddenly it seemed she might as well ask the soldier to marry with her, and then the two of them could go away. Before he had gone crazy, he had been a little nice. And because it was a new and sudden idea, it also seemed reasonable. She remembered a part of the fortune she had forgotten, that she would marry a light-haired person with blue eyes, and the fact that the soldier had light red hair and blue eyes was like a proof that this was the right thing to do.

She hurried faster. The night before was like a time that had happened so long ago that the soldier was unraveled in her memory. But she recalled the silence in the hotel room; and all at once a fit in a front room, the silence, the nasty talk behind the garage — these separate recollections fell together in the darkness of her mind, as shafting searchlights meet in the night sky upon an aeroplane, so that in a flash there came in her an understanding. There was a feeling of cold surprise; she stopped a minute, then went on toward the Blue Moon. The stores were dark and closed, the pawnshop window locked with criss-crossed steel against night robbers, and the only lights were those from the open wooden stairs of buildings and the greenish splash of brightness from the Blue Moon. There was a sound of quarreling voices from an upper story, and the footsteps of two men, far down the street, walking away. She was no longer thinking of the soldier; the discovery of the moment before had scattered him from her mind. There was only knowing that she must find somebody, and anybody, that she could join with to go away. For now she admitted she was too scared to go into the world alone.

She did not leave the town that night, for the Law caught her in the Blue Moon. Officer Wylie was there when she walked in, although she did not see him until she was settled at the window table with the suitcase on the floor beside her. The juke-box sounded a sleazy blues and the Portuguese owner stood with his eyes closed, playing up and down the wooden counter in time to the sad juke tune. There were only a few people in a corner booth and the blue light gave the place a look of being underseas. She did not see the Law until he was standing beside the table, and when she looked up at him, her startled heart quivered a little and then stopped still.

"You're Royal Addams's daughter," the Law said, and her head admitted with a nod. "I'll phone in to headquarters to say you're found. Just stay right here."

The Law went back to the telephone booth. He was calling the Black Maria to haul her off down to the jail, but she did not care. Very likely she had killed that soldier, and they had been following clues and hunting her all over town. Or the Law maybe had found out about the three-way knife she had stolen from the Sears and Roebuck Store. It was not plain just what she was captured for, and the crimes of the long spring and summer merged together as one guilt which she had lost the power to understand. It was as though the things that she had done, the sins committed, had all been done by someone else — a stranger a long time ago. She sat very still, her legs wrapped tight around each other, and her hands clasped in her lap. The Law was a long time at the telephone, and, staring straight ahead of her, she watched two people leave a booth and, leaning close against each other, start to dance. A soldier banged the screen door and walked through the café, and only the distant stranger in her recognized him; when he had climbed up the stairs, she only thought slowly and with no feeling that a curly red head such as that one was like cement. Then her mind went back to thoughts of jail and cold peas and cold cornbread and iron-barred cells. The Law came back from the telephone and sat down across from her and said:

"How did you happen to come in here?"

The Law was big in his blue policeman's suit and, once arrested, it was a bad policy to lie or trifle. He had a heavy face, with a squatty forehead and unmatched ears — one ear was larger than the other one, and had a torn look. When he questioned her, he did not look into her face, but at some point just above her head.

"What am I doing in here?" she repeated. For all at once she had forgotten, and she told the truth when she said finally, "I don't know."

The voice of the Law seemed to come from a distance like a question asked through a long corridor. "Where were you headed for?"

The world was now so far away that Frances could no longer think of it. She did not see the earth as in the old days, cracked and loose and turning a thousand miles an hour; the earth was enormous and still and flat. Between herself and all the places there was a space like an enormous canyon she could not hope to bridge or cross. The plans for the movies or the Marines were only child plans that would never work, and she was careful when she answered. She named the littlest, ugliest place she knew, for to run away there could not be considered so very wrong.

"Flowering Branch."

"Your father phoned headquarters you had left a letter that you were running away. We located him at the bus station and he'll be here in a minute to take you home."

It was her father who had sicked the Law on her, and she would not be carried to the jail. In a way she was sorry. It was better to be in a jail where you could bang the walls than in a jail you could not see. The world was too far away, and there was no way any more that she could be included. She was back to the fear of the summertime, the old feelings that the world was separate from herself — and the failed wedding had quickened the fear to terror. There had been a time, only yesterday, when she felt that every person that she saw was somehow connected with herself and there was between the two of them an instant recognition. Frances watched the Portuguese who still played a mock piano on the counter to the juke-box tune.

He swayed as he played and his fingers skittered up and down the counter, so that a man at the far end protected his glass with his hand. When the tune was over, the Portuguese folded his arms upon his chest; Frances narrowed and tensed her eyes to will him to look at her. He had been the first person she had told the day before about the wedding, but as he gave an owner's look around the place, his glance passed by her in a casual way and there was in those eyes no feeling of connection. She turned to the others in the room, and it was the same with all of them and they were strangers. In the blue light she felt queer as a person drowning. At last she was staring at the Law and finally he looked into her eyes. He looked at her with eyes as china as a doll's, and in them there was only the reflection of her own lost face.

The screen door slammed and the Law said: "Here's your Daddy come to take you home."

Frances was never once to speak about the wedding. Weathers had turned and it was in another season. There were the changes and Frances was now thirteen. She was in the kitchen with Berenice on the day before they moved, the last afternoon that Berenice would be with them; for when it had been decided that she and her father would share with Aunt Pet and Uncle Ustace a house out in the new suburb of town, Berenice had given quit notice and said that she might as well marry T.T. It was the end of an afternoon in late November, and in the east the sky was the color of a winter geranium.

Frances had come back to the kitchen, for the other rooms were hollow since the van had taken the furniture away. There were only the two beds in the downstairs bedrooms and the kitchen furniture, and they were to be moved tomorrow. It was the first time in a long while that Frances had spent an afternoon back in the kitchen, alone with Berenice. It was not the same kitchen of the summer that now seemed so long ago. The pencil pictures had disappeared beneath a coat of calcimine, and new linoleum covered the splintery floor. Even the table had been moved, pushed back against the wall, since now there was nobody to take meals with Berenice.

The kitchen, done over and almost modern, had nothing that would bring to mind John Henry West. But nevertheless there were times when Frances felt his presence there, solemn and hovering and ghost-gray. And at those times there would come a hush — a hush quivered by voiceless words. A similar hush would come, also, when Honey was mentioned or brought to mind, for Honey was out on the road now with a sentence of eight years. Now the hush came that late November afternoon as Frances was making the sandwiches, cutting them into fancy shapes and taking great pains — for Mary Littlejohn was coming at five o'clock. Frances glanced at Berenice, who was sitting idle in a chair, wearing an old raveled sweater, her limp arms hanging at her sides. In her lap there was the thin little pinched fox fur that Ludie had given her many years ago. The fur was sticky and the sharp little face foxwise and sad. The fire from the red stove brushed the room with flickers of light and changing shadows.

"I am just mad about Michelangelo," she said.

Mary was coming at five o'clock to take dinner, spend the night, and ride in the van to the new house tomorrow. Mary collected pictures of great masters and pasted them in an art book. They read poets like Tennyson together; and Mary was going to be a great painter and Frances a great poet — or else the foremost authority on radar. Mr. Littlejohn had been connected with a tractor company and before the war the Littlejohns had lived abroad. When Frances was sixteen and Mary eighteen, they were going around the world together. Frances placed the sandwiches on a plate, along with eight chocolates and some salted nuts; this was to be a midnight feast, to be eaten in the bed at twelve o'clock.

"I told you we're going to travel around the world together."

"Mary Littlejohn," said Berenice, in a tinged voice. "Mary Littlejohn."

Berenice could not appreciate Michelangelo or poetry, let alone Mary Littlejohn. There had at first been words between them on the subject. Berenice had spoken of Mary as being lumpy and marshmallow-white, and Frances had defended fiercely. Mary had long braids that she could very nearly sit on, braids of a woven mixture of corn-yellow and brown, fastened at the ends with rubber bands and, on occasions, ribbons. She had brown eyes with yellow eyelashes, and her dimpled hands tapered at the fingers to little pink blobs of flesh, as Mary bit her nails. The Littlejohns were Catholics, and even on this point Berenice was all of a sudden narrowminded, saying that Roman Catholics worshiped Graven Images and wanted the Pope to rule the world. But for Frances this difference was a final touch of strangeness, silent terror, that completed the wonder of her love.

"There's no use our discussing a certain party. You could not possibly ever understand her. It's just not in you." She had said that once before to Berenice, and from the sudden faded stillness in her eye she knew that the words had hurt. And now she repeated them, angered because of the tinged way Berenice had said the name, but once the words were spoken she was sorry. "Anyhow, I consider it the greatest honor of my existence that Mary has picked me out to be her one most intimate friend. Me! Of all people!"

"Have I ever said anything against her?" said Berenice. "All I said was it makes me nervous to watch her just sitting there sucking them pigtails."

"Braids!"

A flock of strong-winged arrowed geese flew over the yard, and Frances went to the window. There had been frost that morning, silvering the brown grass and the roofs of neighbors' houses, and even the thinned leaves of the rusty arbor. When she turned back to the kitchen, the hush was in the room again. Berenice sat hunched with her elbow on her knee, and her forehead resting in her hand, staring with one mottled eye at the coal scuttle.

The changes had come about at the same time, during the middle of October. Frances had met Mary at a raffle two weeks before. It was the time when countless white and yellow butterflies danced among the last fall flowers; the time, too, of the Fair. First, it was Honey. Made crazy one night by a marihuana cigarette, by something called smoke or snow, he broke into the drugstore of the white man who had been selling them to him, desperate for more. He was locked in the jail, awaiting trial, and Berenice rushed back and forth, canvassing money, seeing a lawyer, and trying to get admission to the jail. She came in on the third day, worn out, and with the red curdled glare already in the eye. A headache, she said she had, and John Henry West put his head down on the table and said he had a headache, also. But nobody paid any mind to him, thinking he copied Berenice. "Run along," she said, "for I don't have the patience to fool with you." Those were the last words spoken to him in the kitchen, and later Berenice recalled them as judgment on her from the Lord. John Henry had meningitis and after ten days he was dead. Until it was all over, Frances had never believed for a serious minute that he could die. It was the time of golden weather and Shasta daisies and the butterflies. The air was chilled, and day after day the sky was a clear green-blue, but filled with light, the color of a shallow wave.

Frances was never allowed to visit John Henry, but Berenice helped the trained nurse every day. She would come in toward dark, and the things that she said in her cracked voice seemed to make John Henry West unreal. "I don't see why he has to suffer so," Berenice would say: and the word *suffer* was one she could not associate with John Henry, a word she shrank from as before an unknown hollow darkness of the heart.

It was the time of the Fair and a big banner arched the main street and for six days and nights the Fair went on down at the fairground. Frances went twice, both times with Mary, and they rode on nearly everything, but did not enter the Freak Pavilion, as Mrs. Littlejohn said it was morbid to gaze at Freaks. Frances bought John Henry a walking stick and sent him the rug she had won at Lotto. But Berenice remarked that he was beyond all this, and the words were eerie and unreal. As the bright days followed one upon the other, the words of Berenice became so terrible that she would listen in a spell of horror, but a part of her could not believe. John Henry had been screaming for three days and his eyeballs were walled up in a corner, stuck and blind. He lay there finally with his head drawn back in a buckled way, and he had lost the strength to scream. He died the Tuesday after the Fair was gone, a golden morning of the most beautiful butterflies, the clearest sky.

Meanwhile Berenice had got a lawyer and had seen Honey at the jail. "I don't know what I've done," she kept saying. "Honey in this fix and now John Henry." Still, there was some part of Frances that did not even yet believe. But on the day he was to be taken to the family graveyard in Opelika, the same place where they had buried Uncle Charles, she saw the coffin, and then she knew. He came to her once or twice in nightmare dreams, like an escaped child dummy from the window of a department store, the wax legs moving stiffly only at joints, and the wax face wizened and faintly painted, coming toward her until terror snatched her awake. But the dreams came only once or twice, and the daytime now was filled with radar, school, and Mary Littlejohn. She remembered John Henry more as he used to be, and it was seldom now that she felt his presence — solemn, hovering, and ghost-gray. Only occasionally at twilight time or when the special hush would come into the room.

"I was by the store about school and Papa had a letter from Jarvis.

He is in Luxembourg," said Frances. "Luxembourg. Don't you think that's a lovely name?"

Berenice roused herself. "Well, Baby — it brings to my mind soapy water. But it's a kind of pretty name."

"There is a basement in the new house. And a laundry room." She added, after a minute, "We will most likely pass through Luxembourg when we go around the world together."

Frances turned back to the window. It was almost five o'clock and the geranium glow had faded from the sky. The last pale colors were crushed and cold on the horizon. Dark, when it came, would come on quickly, as it does in wintertime. "I am simply mad about —" But the sentence was left unfinished for the hush was shattered when, with an instant shock of happiness, she heard the ringing of the bell.

Bibliography

In 1951, Houghton Mifflin Company published an omnibus edition of Carson McCullers's fiction, *The Ballad of the Sad Café and Other Works*. The book reprinted her novels *The Heart Is a Lonely Hunter, Reflections in a Golden Eye*, and *The Member of the Wedding*; it also gathered for the first time her work in shorter forms, the novella *The Ballad of the Sad Café* and six short stories, including the previously unpublished "A Domestic Dilemma." In 1952, Houghton Mifflin brought out the novella and stories under the title *The Ballad of the Sad Café and Collected Short Stories;* in 1955 the book was reissued to include a seventh story, "The Haunted Boy."

Carson McCullers died in 1967. In 1971 her sister, Margarita G. Smith, published *The Mortgaged Heart,* a selection from McCullers's previously uncollected writings. Many of the earliest stories, as well as a few of the latest, were published here in book form for the first time.

The contents of *Collected Stories* are listed below in the order in which they were written. The order of the first ten items is speculative and follows that given by Margarita Smith in *The Mortgaged Heart*.

"Sucker." Written c. 1934. First published, with an author's note, in *The Saturday Evening Post,* September 28, 1963; reprinted in *The Mortgaged Heart,* 1971.

"Court in the West Eighties." Written c. 1934. First published in *The Mortgaged Heart*, 1971.

"Poldi." Written c. 1934–36. First published in *The Mortgaged Heart,* 1971.

"Breath from the Sky." Written c. 1935–36. First published in *The Mortgaged Heart,* 1971.

"The Orphanage." Written c. 1935–36. First published in *The Mortgaged Heart,* 1971.

"Instant of the Hour After." Written c. 1935–36. First published in *The Mortgaged Heart,* 1971.

"Like That." Written c. 1935–36. Purchased by *Story* magazine in 1936 but never published. First published in *The Mortgaged Heart,* 1971.

"Wunderkind." First published in *Story,* December 1936; reprinted in *The Ballad of the Sad Café,* 1951, and *The Mortgaged Heart,* 1971.

"The Aliens." Written c. 1935–36. First published in *The Mortgaged Heart,* 1971.

"Untitled Piece." Written c. 1935–36. First published in *The Mortgaged Heart,* 1971.

"The Jockey." First published in *The New Yorker*, August 23, 1941; reprinted in *The Ballad of the Sad Café,* 1951.

"Madame Zilensky and the King of Finland." First published in *The New Yorker,* December 20, 1941; reprinted in *The Ballad of the Sad Café,* 1951.

"Correspondence." First published in *The New Yorker,* February 7, 1942; reprinted in *The Mortgaged Heart,* 1971.

"A Tree • A Rock • A Cloud." First published in *Harper's Bazaar,* November 1942; reprinted in *The Ballad of the Sad Café,* 1951.

The Ballad of the Sad Café. First published in *Harper's Bazaar,* August 1943; reprinted in *The Best American Short Stories 1944,* edited by Martha Foley, and *The Ballad of the Sad Café,* 1951.

The Member of the Wedding. Part One first published in *Harper's Bazaar,* January 1946; first published in its entirety by Houghton Mifflin Company, 1946.

"Art and Mr. Mahoney." First published in *Mademoiselle,* February 1949; reprinted in *The Mortgaged Heart,* 1971.

"The Sojourner." First published in *Mademoiselle,* May 1950; reprinted in *The Ballad of the Sad Café,* 1951.

"A Domestic Dilemma." First published in *The Ballad of the Sad Café,* 1951.

"The Haunted Boy." Published simultaneously in *Mademoiselle,* November 1955, *Botteghe Oscure,* Fall 1955, and *The Ballad of the Sad Café,* 1955; reprinted in *The Mortgaged Heart,* 1971.

"Who Has Seen the Wind?" First published in *Mademoiselle,* September 1956; reprinted in *The Mortgaged Heart,* 1971.